The Zero Curse

THE ZERO CURSE

(The Zero Enigma, Book II)

Christopher G. Nuttall

The characters and events portrayed in this book are fictitious. Any similarity to real persons, living or dead, is coincidental and not intended by the author.

Text copyright © 2017 Christopher G. Nuttall

All rights reserved.
Printed in the United States of America.

No part of this book may be reproduced, or stored in a retrieval system, or transmitted in any form or by any means, electronic, mechanical, photocopying, recording, or otherwise, without express written permission of the publisher.

ISBN: 1976443849
ISBN 13: 9781976443848

http://www.chrishanger.net
http://chrishanger.wordpress.com/
http://www.facebook.com/ChristopherGNuttall
Cover by Brad Fraunfelter
www.BFillustration.com

All Comments and Reviews Welcome!

DEDICATION

To Larry Niven, who was kind enough to let me borrow one of his concepts, and Jerry Pournelle, who passed away as I was editing this manuscript.

Rest in Peace.

AUTHOR'S NOTE

Reviews are important these days - the more reviews, the more promotion. If you liked this book, please review it on Amazon Kindle or Goodreads.
Thank you.
CGN

PROLOGUE

It was a hot summer day when I realised - for the first time - just how vulnerable I truly was.

I was ten at the time and, despite everything, I hadn't given up hope that I might have a spark of magic. It wasn't *uncommon* for magicians not to show much - if any - signs of magical talent before turning twelve, when they would be schooled in magic. Or so my parents kept telling me, as they tried to teach me more and more arcane disciplines in the hopes of shaking something loose. My sisters were streaking ahead and I…

…I hadn't even managed to cast a single spell.

If I hadn't been able to pick up the Family Sword - which could only be handled by my bloodline - I would have wondered if I was truly my father's daughter. I could sense my father's disappointment and my mother's concern, even though they tried to hide it. They had to wonder if I, Caitlyn Aguirre, would bring down the whole family. Our bloodline was strong in magic. A child born without the ability to use it would shame us.

It *was* a hot month, the hottest on record. My sisters and I would have loved to spend it in the swimming pool or paddling near the beach. Our friends - Alana and Bella's friends, more accurately - had already decamped, leaving Shallot for their country estates where it was cooler. We wanted to go with them too, but we hadn't been allowed to leave. Great Aunt Stregheria had come to stay.

I still find it hard to believe that Great Aunt Stregheria was my *father's* aunt. She was a tall dark woman, the tallest I've ever seen, her hair hanging down loosely in a manner that signified she was an unmarried woman. It was easy to understand *why*. I couldn't help thinking that she looked rather like a vulture, with an angular face and dark eyes that seemed to glitter with malice as she peered down at us from her lofty height. She was one of those unpleasant adults who firmly believed that children should neither be seen nor heard and she hadn't been shy about making her opinions known. She'd been scathing about my failings in magic. *And* she'd drilled my sisters in basic manners until even *Alana* was sick of her.

I didn't know why she bothered to visit us. I still don't. She complained about everything, from the food to the heat. We were in trouble if we didn't curtsey just right when she saw us *and* when we deliberately stayed out of her way. She expected us to wear our formal clothes at all times, even though it was far too hot; she expected us to wait on her at table, as if we were common maids. She'd get up late, have a long breakfast and then spend an hour or two with Dad before…well, we didn't know *what* she was doing. We didn't really care either. We just wanted her gone.

One day, the hottest day of the summer, we managed to slip away early. Mum didn't say anything to us, let alone drag us back into the house. By then, I think she was sick and tired of Great Aunt Stregheria making herself at home. She had a home of her own. I rather hoped it was a cave somewhere high up a mountainside, but I doubted it. Why couldn't she go back home and stop bothering us? Great Aunt Stregheria was the sort of person who gave magic-users a bad name.

There was a little marshy pond down by the grove, one we'd paddled in when we were younger. We thought it was *just* far enough from the house - while still being part of the grounds - to escape detection, at least for a while. Dad hadn't given Great Aunt Stregheria any access to the wards, we thought. She'd have been summoning us all the time if she'd had control. We took off our expensive shoes and splashed through the water, enjoying the cool liquid against our feet. For once, even Alana was too relieved to be away from the witch to indulge in a little malice. We were, just for an hour or two, a normal trio of sisters.

It didn't last, of course.

Great Aunt Stregheria came striding through the grove in high dudgeon, her face twisted with rage. I don't think she was mad at *us*, specifically, but she was *mad*. We froze, fear holding us in place as solidly as any spell, as she stamped towards us. I had no idea where she'd been, or what she'd been doing, but…

"You little brats," she snapped. In hindsight, I suspect she wanted to take her anger out on *someone*. "Get out of there!"

Normally, we would have obeyed instantly. But we were hot and sweaty and very - very - tired of her. We didn't move.

Great Aunt Stregheria lifted her hand and cast a spell. I saw a flash of brilliant greenish light, an instant before the spell stuck me - struck *us*. Alana screamed - I might have screamed too, I'm not sure - as magic flared around her. My skin tingled unpleasantly, as if I was caught in a thunderstorm. I had an instant to see my black hand turning green and warty before the world grew larger. I squeezed my eyes tightly shut as I splashed into the water, then jerked them open as my legs started to move automatically. The tiny pool - so shallow that it barely reached our knees - was suddenly huge.

I broke the water, just in time to see Alana and Bella become frogs. My head swam as I grappled with the sudden change. It wasn't the first time I'd been transfigured, but…but…this was far worse. There were no safeties worked into the spell. I could *feel* the frog's mind gnawing away at mine, threatening to erode my thoughts. The water was practically hypnotic, pulling at me. If I hadn't been panicking, if I hadn't managed to hop *out* of the water, I might have been lost.

The spell on me wore off in an hour, although it wasn't until two years later that I understood *why*. By then, Dad had literally thrown Great Aunt Stregheria out of the hall and ordered her never to return. The spell on my sisters lasted nearly a week before it finally collapsed. Dad was delighted, utterly over the moon. He insisted I had a *definite* magical talent. I had to have *something*, he reasoned, to escape such a complex spell. Our parents had been unable to unravel it for themselves.

I knew better. Alana and Bella had been trapped, but neither of them had been in any danger of losing themselves in an animal's mind. Their magic had even fought the spell when it was first cast. But I had no magic to defend myself. The protective spells Mum and Dad had laid on me had never been anchored properly because there was nothing for them to anchor *to*. It was sheer luck that I'd survived long enough for the spell to unravel. I was defenceless. *Anyone* could cast a spell on me.

It was a lesson I should never have forgotten.

I was a *zero*. And being powerless was my curse.

CHAPTER ONE

The workbench was ugly.
It had been made of dark brown almond-tree wood, once upon a time. It would have gleamed under the light, when it was new; now, it was covered in burn marks and scratches and pieces of mismatched wood where its previous owner had replaced broken drawers and covering with newer material. Half the drawers were tight, so tight that opening them was a struggle; the remainder were so loose that I felt I'd have to replace them sooner rather than later. And I'd found five secret compartments, concealed by careful design rather than magic, one of which had been crammed with gold coins from a bygone era.

Yes, it was ugly. But it was mine and I loved it.

The workbench had been in the family for centuries, according to my father. It had belonged to Anna the Artificer, once upon a time, before it had gone into storage after her death. Her children hadn't had the heart to use it for themselves, apparently. None of them had come close to matching their mother when it came to forging talent. If there hadn't been stories of her fighting a duel with a prospective suitor, I'd have wondered if she'd been a Zero. There were no stories about her forging Objects of Power - at least, none that had been passed down through the ages - but some of her Devices of Power had lasted nearly a decade without maintenance and repair. Very few forgers could make *that* claim.

Dad had given me the workbench, along with a workroom and suite of my very own. He'd said that I was the first person in centuries to live up to Anna's legacy, the first person to deserve to sit at her workbench and forge. Personally, I thought he felt a little guilty. My sisters - Alana and Belladonna - had long since had their rooms decorated, to mark their progress in magic, but I'd never managed to cast even the simplest of spells. Until recently, everyone had assumed that I was either a very slow learner or a freak. And I *was* a freak.

Just a very valuable freak, I thought.

The thought made me smile. It was good to be appreciated, to be something more than my family's private shame. I still didn't understand why I could forge Objects of Power - where everyone else was limited to Devices of Power - but it gave me a talent none of my sisters could match. Alana had never been a good forger - Bella had been too lazy to learn more than the basics and only then because Dad had pushed her nose to the grindstone - yet it wouldn't have mattered if she spent every waking hour at the workbench. I was the only person who could forge Objects of Power.

"I can still turn you into a toad," Alana had said, last night. She'd come home from school, along with Bella. "And you can't do that to me without help, can you?"

"No," I'd said. My sister was a spiteful person, now more than ever. I was careful to wear protective trinkets every time I saw her. "But *anyone* can turn me into a toad."

I leaned back and surveyed my new domain. Dad hadn't skimped on outfitting the chamber, either. Two walls were lined with bookcases, sagging under the weight of reference textbooks and a small collection of reprinted volumes from the Thousand-Year Empire. I wasn't the only one who could read them - I'd had Old Script drilled into my head before I'd reached my first decade - but I was the only one who could make *use* of them. The instructions for making Objects of Power were easy to find, if one had access to a decent library, yet something had been left unsaid. It had been sheer luck that I'd realised that the missing ingredient, something so obvious the ancient magicians had never bothered to write down, had been someone like me.

Maybe I couldn't use magic personally. It didn't make me useless.

A second workbench, covered with handmade tools, sat near the door, next to a furnace, a kiln, a set of cupboards and a giant translucent cauldron. Dad had crammed one of the cupboards with everything a budding forger would want, while Mum had filled the other with potion ingredients. I hated to think how much it must have cost, even though I knew my family was rich *and* that my sisters had earned rewards for themselves, over the years. Being best friends with a commoner had taught me more than anyone had realised. I was almost embarrassed at the thought of bringing Rose into my workroom. A single gemstone - like the ones hidden in one of my drawers - would be more than enough to buy and sell her entire family.

I put the thought aside as I carefully pulled on a set of protective robes, tied my hair into a tight bun and inspected myself in the mirror. My dark face was marred by a nasty burn from when I'd managed to splash hot potion on myself, although it was healing nicely. I had a nasty feeling that I'd have forger's hands - hands covered in burn marks - by the time I was twenty, even though my tutors had drummed safety precautions into me from the very beginning. It wasn't something that bothered me, although Alana had made snide remarks about me not having ladylike hands. It was proof that I was more than just another aristocratic brat entering High Society.

Not that High Society ever really cared about me, I thought.

It was a grim thought. I'd gone to birthday parties, of course, doing the social whirl that ensured that everyone who was anyone in Shallot knew everyone else. But birthday parties for young magicians had been hazardous for me, all the more so as rumours about my magic - or lack of it - had started to spread. Very few people had grasped that I had *no* magic whatsoever, but it *was* clear that I was a very late bloomer. No one had wanted to be associated with me, for fear that whatever had laid me low might be catching. I'd had no true friends until I'd gone to Jude's. Now...

I swallowed, hard. I wasn't looking forward to going back to school, even though I'd declined when Dad had offered to let me stay home. *Rose* was there, after all. I couldn't leave her alone, not after everything she'd done for me. And maybe things would be better, now I'd beaten Isabella.

The school's honour code was strict. Isabella had been beaten fairly and that was all that mattered.

Unless she reasoned she hadn't been beaten fairly, after all. It wasn't an unarguable case.

One by one, I removed the protective amulets and earrings I'd forged over the last couple of weeks, placing them on the small table by the mirror. I felt as if I was naked, utterly unprotected, when I was done, even though the workroom was locked. I'd spent the last six years trying - and often failing - to avoid increasingly nasty pranks from my sisters, pranks that I'd never been able to see coming. Even something as simple as sitting down to dinner could turn into a trial if Alana had had time to hex or jinx the chair. Now…I was protected, as long as I wore the earrings. But I didn't know if I could wear them while forging without ruining my work.

Buttoning up my robe, I strode across to the workbench and looked down at the longsword, resting in a web of silver netting. It was big, easily too big for me to carry, even using both hands. I wasn't exactly a weakling - forging requires physical strength as well as dexterity - but it was still too big for me. Sir Griffons, the man who'd commissioned the sword, was easily twice my size. He had muscles on his muscles…and yet, normally, even *he* would have trouble carrying the sword. I couldn't help thinking that a Kingsman - a servant of His Most Regal Majesty, King Rufus - wouldn't consider the longsword a practical weapon. But it did have its advantages.

I smiled as I studied the blade, carefully planning out the next step. Casting the blade itself had been simple, a task that anyone could do. Dad had even offered to have one of his apprentices do it for me, pointing out that I didn't have to waste *my* time on it. And yet, I'd declined. There was too great a chance that someone else's involvement would taint the metal, making it impossible to turn the long sword into an Object of Power. I intended to experiment, once I returned to school, to see just how much preliminary work I could pass to someone else without ruining the final effect.

And besides, I *wanted* to impress Sir Griffons.

The swordsmen of the Thousand-Year Empire had had swords that could cut through anything, according to legend. Their blades had been as light as feathers, in the hands of their true owners; their scabbards had had magic of their own, healing wounds and boosting strength when swordsmen met in combat. And there had been some truth in the legends. I'd seen blades, passed down through the years, that *had* been magic, when wielded by the descendents of the original owners. My Family Sword, buried in the Family Hearthstone, had powers of its own. You simply couldn't buy a weapon like that for love or money. Even if a family sold off a priceless heirloom - which would have forced them to put a price on 'priceless' - the magic wouldn't work for anyone outside the direct line. Whatever rites and rituals had been used to transfer a blade to a new owner had been lost hundreds of years ago.

Sir Griffons had been obsessed with owning such a sword for as long as I'd been alive. He'd been pushing my father to either crack the secret behind the blades or come up with something new, something that would allow a Device of Power to survive against counterspells. Every year, Dad had tried something new; every year, the blade had either snapped in combat or lost its magic at terrifying speed. Dad and his apprentices had gone through the books hundreds of times, trying dozens of variations in a desperate bid to crack the secret. They'd known the reward would be massive, if they succeeded. The Kingsmen *needed* such blades to do their work. But they'd failed. The problem had seemed insurmountable.

I reached for my notebook and opened it, checking my work one final time. The calculations hadn't been *that* difficult, although I'd had to adapt some of the runes to adjust for modern-day materials. Whoever had come up with the original swords had been a genius, as well as a Zero. The network of runes that channelled magic into the blade had to be precise or the spell would simply refuse to work. Thankfully, I'd learnt the value of precision long ago. My sisters had enough power to compensate for deviations - often very *big* deviations - from perfect spellforms, but lesser magicians needed to be precise. Not that it mattered to me, in any case. I could speak a spell perfectly, with all the accent on the *right* syllables, and nothing would happen.

And yet, I can forge Objects of Power, I reminded myself, as I picked up the etching tool and held it over the sword. *I am unique.*

I'd forged the etching tool myself, as tradition demanded. I wasn't too sure if it mattered - the harmony most magicians experienced when they used tools they'd crafted themselves was alien to me - but it wasn't a tradition I wanted to abandon. Forging had given me a sense of purpose, of achievement, a long time before I'd realised what I could do. And besides, it kept my mind off uncomfortable truths. There were things I didn't want to think about, even now.

Bending over the sword, I carefully pressed the etching tool against the metal and carved out the first rune. The metal was softer than it should have been - the silver cradle made it easier to carve, although I didn't pretend to understand why - but I still moved with immense care. I didn't have *time* to start again from scratch, not when I was due back at school in a couple of days. Besides, I wasn't sure what would happen if I melted down the sword to reuse the metal. In theory, it shouldn't make any difference; in practice, I wasn't so sure. I'd seen forging go horribly wrong because the metal had already been tainted by magic.

The first rune fell into place, neatly. I took a moment to catch my breath - sweat was already trickling down my back - and then started on the second. My calculations insisted that the magic wouldn't take effect until the last rune was in place, but I kept a wary eye on the blade anyway, just in case. A surge of magic that seemingly came out of nowhere would be dangerous, not least because I couldn't sense the surge and take cover until it was too late. As far as magic was concerned, I was the blind girl in the kingdom of the sighted.

My hands were aching by the time I'd worked my way through a dozen runes. I stepped backwards, taking a deep breath. Magicians who forged Devices of Power claimed that the work couldn't be paused, once it was underway, but I'd never had a problem when I'd forged Objects of Power. I rather suspected that my lack of magic actually kept the runes from activating early, too early to let the spellforms take shape properly. It was something else I intended to test, when I had a moment. Rose and I would have a lot of fun testing the limits of my abilities.

And then the lanterns dimmed, just slightly.

I tensed. Someone was outside the main door…no, someone was trying to use magic to *open* the main door. It couldn't be my parents. Mum was in the garden, picking herbs for a potion she wanted to try; Dad was playing host to our very unwelcome guest. And besides, they would have knocked - loudly - if they'd wanted to come in. Very few people would enter a magician's workroom without permission. The servants certainly wouldn't dare. My list of suspects was very short indeed.

Alana, I thought. *She's been quiet - too quiet - since Dad yanked all three of us out of school.*

I slipped back to the mirror, moving as quietly as I could. I'd had far too much practice in sneaking around over the years, although it wasn't as much use as I'd hoped. Even a relatively young magician like my sister could cast wards to protect her belongings. Picking up one of the earrings, I cupped it in my hand and walked to the other workbench as I heard the sound of someone opening the door. It was very quiet, so quiet that I *knew* the intruder meant trouble. There's nothing quite so alarming as the sound of someone doing everything in their power not to be heard. Alana must have assumed that her silencing spell had actually worked. It had, but the runes I'd carved into the door had drawn on the magic to dim the lanterns, then cancelled the spell.

Good thing she didn't cast the spell on herself, I thought, as I kept the earring pressed against my skin. It shouldn't make a difference, according to the books, as long as it was touching me. *She might have noticed that the spell had failed if she'd intended to ensure that she couldn't hear either.*

I kept my back to the door as stealthy footsteps echoed down the tiny corridor, even though I wanted to turn - or run. I had too many bad memories of being hexed to feel *calm* when my sister was behind me. Alana *had* to be annoyed about *something*. Our parents had told her, in no uncertain terms, not to use magic anywhere near my workroom. Even *Alana* would have hesitated, normally, to defy Dad. He wasn't the sort of person anyone defied twice.

"Freeze," Alana said.

I felt the earring grow warm in my hand, tingling just for a second. Alana made a sound that cut off so sharply that it made me jump. I turned, slowly. Alana was standing there, utterly unmoving. A surprised expression dominated her frozen face. I walked towards her slowly, wondering just how long she'd intended to freeze me. She knew - now - that spells simply didn't cling to me for long. It was very possible that she'd never bothered to calculate just how long her spell should have left me frozen.

And spells do cling to her, I thought, feeling a flash of vindictive glee. Alana was a powerful and skilled magician, for her age, but I didn't think she could unfreeze herself without being able to move her hands. Even an upperclassman would have problems. *She might have trapped herself until midnight.*

"That was stupid," I said, doing my best to imitate the tone my mother used when she was reprimanding us for being foolish. "Using magic in here? You could have triggered an explosion."

That wasn't true, I thought. But as long as she believed it was true...

I walked around behind her, wrapped my arms around her chest and picked her up. It wasn't easy. Alana was lighter than me, I thought - she was certainly skinny - but she was as stiff and unmoving as a board. I half-carried, half-dragged her out of the workroom door, down the corridor and through the door into the main house. It was quiet, too quiet. I glanced in either direction, then manhandled Alana into the nearest closet and closed the door. She'd be stuck there until someone found her or the spell wore off.

Or if she manages to free herself, I thought. My sister had always been an overachiever when it came to magic. *She might just make it.*

I shrugged as I turned and walked back to the workroom. It was much more likely that she'd be discovered by one of the maids. They'd been working overtime, the last few days. I rather suspected that whoever found Alana would be tempted to leave her, but the maids would be reluctant to risk being fired. Alana was a vindictive person at the best of times.

And she left me in a cupboard too, hundreds of times, I thought. Perhaps I should have felt guilty. But I didn't. *She did far worse to me.*

I sighed as I stepped through the door. I had work to finish before dinnertime. My parents would let me work until the wee small hours, if I wanted, but I knew I wouldn't be in the mood. I knew it. Our family has the best chef in Shallot, but I wasn't looking forward to dinner.

Great Aunt Stregheria was coming to tea.

CHAPTER TWO

I was tempted, very tempted, to pretend I hadn't heard the dinner gong, when it echoed through the house. But I knew my mother would not be fooled. She'd spelled the gong to ensure that anyone within the grounds could hear it, even if they were in the library or a sealed workroom. I finished the last of the runes, put my protective charms back into place and then hurried to my bedroom. The maids had already laid my clothes on the bed.

At least they don't have to worry about me warding my room, I thought sourly, as I closed the door behind me. My sisters could use magic to keep their possessions safe - and unhexed - but I wasn't so lucky. *They just have to worry about keeping Great Aunt Stregheria happy instead.*

I couldn't help feeling a flicker of sympathy. This time, thankfully, my parents had not insisted that we wait hand and foot on the old crone, but that meant that the duty was shifted to the younger maids. I didn't think there was *any* crime that deserved such a horrific punishment. If Great Aunt Stregheria was rude and thoroughly unpleasant to *us*, her nieces, I dreaded to think how horrible she must be to minor family. I wouldn't have been surprised if I'd been told the maids had quit on the spot rather than work for us any longer.

I quickly discovered that the dress was as frilly and absurd as I feared. Mum didn't normally bother making us dress for dinner, but with Great Aunt Stregheria at the table we had to look our best. I glanced wistfully at the shower, then at the grandfather clock my parents had given me after I returned home. There wasn't time to do more than wash my hands and splash water on my face before I got dressed. Being late for a formal dinner - even a dinner that only featured one guest - was the sort of thing that would lead to a frank exchange of views with my mother. She detested Great Aunt Stregheria, but she detested rudeness still more.

I pulled on the wretched dress, then inspected myself in the mirror. The long white gown looked faintly absurd on my lanky form, even though it contrasted nicely with the colour of my skin. I was lucky that mum hadn't joined other High Society ladies when it came to the latest fashions for growing girls. I'd seen dresses that were so absurdly complex that the wearer needed two maids to help them get the dresses on and off. I couldn't help feeling as though the girls were forced to wear them, which made me wonder why the *adults* wore similar dresses. But then, the dictates of fashion had always been a mystery to me.

Mum would have to use magic to force me into such a dress, I thought.

I smiled at the thought, even though it wasn't really amusing. Thankfully, my mother had given me something relatively comfortable. Alana might enjoy wearing ballroom gowns that were really scaled-down adult dresses, but I never had. I was *not* going to walk around wearing a fanned-out dress so large that sitting down at the dinner table would prove impossible. I'd long since come to believe that the *reason* society ladies stayed so thin was because they couldn't sit down to dinner, while eating on one's feet was regarded as bad manners. But perhaps it had something more to do with the formal dancing afterwards.

Pulling my hair down, I braided it into a long ponytail and inspected it in the mirror. Great Aunt Stregheria would *sniff*, I was sure, if there was even a single hair out of place. She'd probably be looking for some reason to complain, if I knew her. It was a mystery to me why *anyone* asked her back for a second time. I was fairly sure that my father *hadn't* invited her, not after what had happened two years ago. But that *did* raise the question of why she'd come.

And why Dad let her through the gate, I thought, as I clipped on my earrings and concealed a bracelet high up my sleeve. *Mum banned her from the estate after she used her magic on us.*

The second gong rang, the sound echoing through the house. I swallowed hard - the prospect of facing Great Aunt Stregheria again was enough to make me want to run away - and headed for the door. June, the youngest of the maids, stood outside, looking as if she was nerving herself up to knock. I don't know why *she* was so worried. It wasn't as if she was dancing attendance on Great Aunt Stregheria. In her place, I would have been thrilled to be well away from the guest wing.

"You look lovely, My Lady," she said.

"Thank you," I said, tartly. The dress might not have been uncomfortable, but it wasn't what I liked to wear. "Leave the room alone. I'll clean it up later."

June curtseyed, a flicker of...*something*...crossing her face. I felt a stab of guilt, which blurred into the butterflies in my stomach. It was probably too late to commit some hideous crime that would get me sent to bed without supper. And even if I did, my mother would probably insist that having to go to dinner was a worse punishment than going without. An evening with Great Aunt Stregheria would feel like an eternity.

I touched the bracelet on my arm as I walked down the corridor, passing a long row of portraits that glowered down at me disapprovingly. I'd often wondered just how I fitted into the family, even though I could draw and wield the Family Sword. The Aguirre Family dates all the way back to the Thousand-Year Empire, if you believe our historians. We have always been powerful magicians, counsellors to kings...sometimes even kingmakers in our own right. My lack of magic had shamed the entire line. Alana had told me, more than once, that I'd be disowned - or worse - the moment she took over the family. There had been times when I feared my parents would disown me well before they died.

And now they know what I can do, I thought. *They don't want to disown me now.*

A cold shiver ran down my spine as I reached the formal dining room. It was immense, easily large enough to accommodate a couple of hundred people. The large table in the centre of the chamber looked tiny, faintly absurd compared to the immensity of the room. I would have preferred the family dining room, which was smaller and more comfortable, but my mother clearly had other ideas. Perhaps she was hinting that Great Aunt

Stregheria was far from welcome. I rather doubted Great Aunt Stregheria had gotten the message.

My father sat at one end of the table, his face utterly expressionless; my mother sat at the other, her lips so thin with disapproval that they'd practically vanished. Great Aunt Stregheria sat next to my father, her dark eyes cold and hard. Belladonna, my other sister, sat on the far side, as far from our unwelcome guest as she could without being unbearably rude. The tension in the air was so thick that you could cut it with a knife.

"Caitlyn," Dad said. He rose, indicating the seat next to Great Aunt Stregheria. "Please, take a seat."

I nodded, not trusting myself to speak. My mouth was dry. Sitting next to Great Aunt Stregheria...I would sooner have sat next to a basilisk. Or a dragon. At least it would have been over quickly. I walked around the table, pausing long enough to curtsey to my mother, then took the seat. Courtesy forbade me from inching the chair away from the vindictive old crone.

Great Aunt Stregheria turned to look at me. I looked back, fighting down the urge to cringe back in my chair. It was hard to believe that she was related to my father, even though I'd seen her wield the Family Sword too. My father was a tall, powerfully-built man; Great Aunt Stregheria was slight, but with an attitude of power and menace that made her look like a vulture eying wounded prey. Her skin was still flawless, her hair as black as night...I couldn't help wondering if she used magic to keep it that way. My father was twenty or so years younger than her and *he* was already showing signs of going grey.

Perhaps it's having us kids, I thought, as I turned my attention to the table. The maids had covered the table with a white cloth, then laid out a dozen sets of cutlery. *Great Aunt Stregheria never married, let alone had children.*

I should have felt sorry for her, I knew. Even now, Great Aunt Stregheria wore her hair down, signifying an unmarried woman of marriageable age. And yet, she had never married, never had children. It was one of the reasons her brother - my grandfather - had decided to pass the family headship to my father, rather than someone close to them in age. But the nasty part of my mind had no trouble understanding why Great

Aunt Stregheria was still unmarried, despite her family ties. There wasn't enough wealth and power in the world to make someone *willingly* spend the rest of their life with her.

Mum cleared her throat. "Where is Alana?"

Bella looked up. "I haven't seen her all day, Mum…"

I froze as the realisation crashed into my head. I'd left Alana frozen… and she was *still* frozen. It was the only explanation of why she hadn't made it to dinner. Alana admired Great Aunt Stregheria, even though she feared the old crone too. And besides, she knew better than to be late. Alana had always taken the social niceties more seriously than either Bella or me.

Dad eyed me, suspiciously. He practically had a sixth sense for when one of us had done something Not Allowed.

"Caitlyn?"

I wanted to lie. But I knew better. "I…I reflected her spell onto her and left her frozen in the cupboard, near my workroom," I said. "She must still be trapped."

My father gave me a look that promised trouble later, then rang the bell for the maid. When Lucy appeared, he told her where to find Alana and escort her to the dining room as quickly as possible. I groaned inwardly, kicking myself for forgetting. Alana wouldn't have time to change, let alone do anything else. She'd have to come to the table in her afternoon dress. My parents might not object - much - to us casting spells on each other, but they'd be annoyed if we made them look bad in front of outsiders. And Great Aunt Stregheria would rub it in as much as possible.

We sat in uncomfortable silence until Alana arrived, her face a mask that concealed pure rage. I would have to watch my back for the next few days. Alana would slam a hex into me as soon as she got a chance. And while I could protect myself - now - to some extent, she knew I wasn't invulnerable. She was certainly smart enough to think of a way to get around my protections.

"Be seated," Dad said. His dark eyes swept the table. "Let us give thanks to our ancestors for our lineage."

I cupped my hands over the table and muttered the prayer, under my breath. I'd been told that my ancestors looked down on us from the Realm of the Dead, but I didn't really believe it. My ancestors had probably turned their backs on me a long time ago. And I wasn't sure my father believed it either, although he was careful to keep the family shrine in good repair. But Great Aunt Stregheria would have called him out for dishonouring our ancestors, if he'd missed the prayer.

My father rang the bell, again. "Let us eat."

I did my best to ignore the looming presence of Great Aunt Stregheria - and the nasty looks Alana sent me from time to time - as we ate our way through a five-course meal. Henry had outdone himself, as always. I would have enjoyed the carrot soup and roast lamb if I hadn't been uneasily aware that the *real* business would be concluded over dessert. Great Aunt Stregheria had to have a *reason* to visit, after all. Something had to have changed, recently, to make her visit us - and make my parents let her in the house. And I could only think of *one* thing that had changed.

"The trade dispute with Salonika has been resolved, in our favour," Great Aunt Stregheria said. She spent much of her time in Tintagel, the capital of the *Kingdom* of Tintagel. I couldn't help wondering why King Rufus hadn't banished her to some distant estate years ago. "You should be seeing more trading ships over the next few years."

"That is good," my father said. "And the...disagreement...with Valona?"

"It remains unresolved," Great Aunt Stregheria informed him. "Valona is unwilling to make border concessions until we resolve the issue of access to what remains of the Eternal City."

Alana leaned forward. "I thought they could just sail around to the inner sea and travel directly to the Eternal City."

Great Aunt Stregheria sneered at her. "Everyone knows that the waters around the Eternal City are infested with monsters," she said, in the tone one would use to address a very stupid child. "Sailing ships cannot reach the city with any guarantee of return."

Alana looked crushed. I was torn between feeling sorry for her and an odd guilty pleasure in her humiliation. She'd treated me poorly for years. I'd spent more time than I cared to think about as a frog, or a toad, or something inanimate, purely because Alana had wanted to practice her hexes. And yet, she didn't deserve to be verbally shredded by a woman old enough to be her grandmother. Great Aunt Stregheria didn't look remotely ashamed. I was *very* glad she'd never had children.

"We are currently haggling over access rights through the Blyton Pass," Great Aunt Stregheria continued, ignoring my mother's sharp look with practised ease. "But His Majesty is reluctant to allow complete access unless we have the right to inspect caravans leaving the cursed lands."

"One would consider it pointless," Alana muttered. She shot me a sharp look. "There's only one secret to be found, isn't there?"

"Correct," Great Aunt Stregheria said. She turned to look at me. "And now that secret is out."

I tried to look back evenly, although she was sizing me up like a piece of meat on the market stall. There was only *one* secret from the Eternal City that everyone wanted, the secret of how to make Objects of Power. Objects of Power had been what turned a relatively small city in a poorly-populated region into the master of much of the known world, but the secret of how they'd been made had been lost when the city fell. And I'd cracked that secret weeks ago.

And word is spreading, I thought. Dad had taken me from the school immediately after my duel with Isabella, but the rumours had already started. By now, they would be halfway around the world. *No wonder Great Aunt Stregheria came to visit.*

Great Aunt Stregheria turned her attention back to my father. "It has become common for an aristocratic child to be fostered in the home of a distant relative," she said. "Such practices are meant to teach the child social graces and introduce the young one to society without the distracting presence of a pair of doting parents. Many of my friends are playing host to children from across the kingdom and even outside it. The youngsters are gaining much from being fostered."

From being in the capital, I finished. *And meeting people who will grow up to be the next generation of rulers and generals and everything else a society needs to work.*

I understood how it worked, even though I'd never liked it. I'd grown up in Shallot, where there were hundreds of aristocratic children; I knew everyone who was powerful or likely to become so, when their parents died. And yet, my lack of magic ensured that they had never really *been* my peers. I had been an outcast. But someone who grew up on a distant country estate might be the only aristocratic child for miles around. Socialising with children far below their lofty birth just was not done. Sending them to be fostered was the only logical solution.

Unless you decide to spend time with the commoners instead, I thought. Rose was a common-born girl and she was my best friend. *And* she was a powerful magician. She might have been more powerful than either of my sisters, if she'd been trained from birth. *But hardly anyone would do that outside school.*

Great Aunt Stregheria was still speaking. "Such an arrangement has many advantages for the parents as well," she added. She sounded faintly amused. "Quite apart from being free of their little darlings for several years, save for the occasional home visit, they gain access to a network of society patrons and clients who are willing to promote them to the king."

"We are aware of the tradition," my mother said, flatly. Her voice was toneless, but I knew from bitter experience that that meant she was angry. "Is there a *point* to this discussion?"

I blinked. Mum was rarely so rude. She must be *really* upset.

Great Aunt Stregheria looked back at her, then at me.

"Isn't it obvious?" Her eyes bored into mine. I looked away. "I would like to foster Caitlyn in Tintagel."

CHAPTER THREE

My mouth dropped open in shock.

I had never considered, not even in my wildest dreams, that I would be fostered. There was no real benefit to fostering a city-born child, although I knew that some children from Shallot had been fostered in Tintagel. And my lack of magic ensured that I would only shame *more* of my relatives if I had been sent to the capital. There had been times when I'd expected to be banished to the country, but that would have been different. People wouldn't have asked *too* many questions if I'd been sent to a distant estate and told to stay there.

My heart started to pound in terror. I didn't *want* to be sent away. I didn't *want* to be fostered. And I certainly *didn't* want to live with Great Aunt Stregheria. My parents had been strict at times - and too lenient at others - but I had never really doubted that they loved me. Great Aunt Stregheria *didn't* love me - or anyone else, as far as I could tell. None of us, not even Alana, came up to her standards. The thought of spending my days trapped with the old crone was nightmarish.

"I know everyone in the capital," Great Aunt Stregheria said, turning her attention back to my father. "Caitlyn would be introduced to everyone, her talents put to work for the good of the kingdom and the family. She would move in the highest circles, wanting for nothing. I would see to it that her name is on everyone's lips."

Alana made a strangled sound. My mother shot her a look that silenced her as effectively as any freeze spell.

I barely noticed. My body was frozen, held in place by fear. I was painfully aware that my mouth was still open, yet I couldn't close it. My parents wouldn't send me to the capital, would they? Not with Great Aunt Stregheria? And yet, I knew that the old woman was right about the possible advantages. A strong family presence in Tintagel would be very useful to us in the future…

Except this isn't about me or the family, I thought, numbly. *It's about her.*

"She would have a suite - a whole *wing* - of her own," Great Aunt Stregheria assured my parents. "There would be servants and tutors, all trained to prepare her for entry at the very highest level of society; she would be surrounded by friends who would ease her into the social scene. She would be presented to the king and…"

"I wouldn't make that decision without consulting my daughter," Dad said. He sounded oddly amused, although there was a hard edge to his voice. I'd always had the feeling that he disliked his aunt, even though he was very polite to her. But then, he'd often told us that we sometimes needed to be polite to people we didn't like. "And she is quite young."

"Youngsters have been fostered from five before," Great Aunt Stregheria pointed out. She spoke as though it was a done deal, as though my agreement and theirs was little more than a formality. "It would be shameful indeed if she waited until she was nineteen before being presented to the king."

I shivered. Traditionally, young aristocratic girls *were* presented at court when they came of age to marry, although I'd assumed I would never make my debut. My lack of magic shamed my family. Who would want to marry a girl who couldn't cast a single spell? And besides, I rather doubted my father would take a few weeks off to travel to the capital, just to present his daughters to the court. He was important enough that he didn't need to bother.

"We had always intended to allow our daughters to make their debut when they came of age," my mother said. The warning in her voice was clear, if Great Aunt Stregheria cared to hear. "They do not *have* to be presented at court or introduced to His Majesty before then."

"No," Great Aunt Stregheria agreed. "But the sooner Caitlyn is presented, the sooner she can take her place in society."

Alana shifted, but said nothing. Her face wasn't as immobile as she thought. I knew she was fuming, perhaps even planning something stupid. *She* had looked forward to the day *she* was presented at court, even if there were two other sisters to steal some of the limelight. Hearing Great Aunt Stregheria planning to present me *ahead* of time had to sting. It was rare - very rare - for *anyone* to be granted such an honour. And the only time I recalled it happening in my lifetime had been when the heir challenged his guardian for early emancipation, after his guardian had abused his position.

"Caitlyn is a child," my mother said, flatly. "And *she* has no reason to enter society ahead of time. We are still alive. Even if we died tomorrow, my family would assume guardianship until Caitlyn and her sisters came of age."

"Her talents make her important indeed," Great Aunt Stregheria countered. "She *must* be properly prepared for her future role."

Dad's scowl deepened. "And you feel *you* can prepare her?"

"She will have the very best of tutors," Great Aunt Stregheria said. "I will even take her with me, when I negotiate on behalf of the family. She will learn how to use her talents for us."

For you, I thought.

"Cat cannot be unique," Alana pointed out. "Even if there *is* something about her that cannot be duplicated by a *magician*, there will be others like her."

Great Aunt Stregheria smiled, humourlessly. "Can *you* make Objects of Power?"

Alana lowered her eyes. "No."

I looked down at my empty plate. Alana was right. I *couldn't* be unique. The stories of the Thousand-Year Empire had included more Objects of Power than I could make in a thousand years. There *had* to be other Zeroes out there, somewhere. But finding them might be difficult. It would be easy, all too easy, to find people who had never cast a single spell, but still had a talent for magic. Rose hadn't been found until she'd turned twelve.

I'd been lucky, I realised dully. I'd been raised in a family where my lack of magic had been noticeable, but also where I'd been trained to do everything from calculate magical runic diagrams to brewing potions and forging artefacts. My family might just have hit the jackpot at million-to-one odds against. If I'd grown up on a farm, like Rose, my lack of magic might never have been noticed. No one would have cared if I couldn't start a fire with a single word.

"Caitlyn," Dad said. "Do you *want* to go with her?"

I hesitated. Did I dare say no?

Great Aunt Stregheria took my hesitation for indecision. "You will find that you have many more opportunities for using your talents in the capital," she said. "And it will make you a very influential girl."

"And help you too," I muttered.

"Quite," Great Aunt Stregheria said. Was that a glimmer of actual *approval* in her eye? It didn't seem likely. I was probably imagining it. "High Society is *about* trading favours, young lady. You help me and I will help you."

You'll use me as a puppet, I thought.

It made a distressing amount of sense. I was the only Zero - the only *known* Zero. Great Aunt Stregheria would praise me, use me...and then discard me, when I had outlived my usefulness. I knew too much about High Society to feel comfortable in the capital. Shallot was a *little* more dignified, but there was still far too much back-biting and not-so-covert infighting as the various magical families fought for supremacy. And Great Aunt Stregheria was a mistress of it. She'd practically tie me to the forge and *force* me to churn out Objects of Power, using them as bargaining chips to raise her status.

She would have a monopoly, I told myself. I would be too far from my parents for them to intervene. *And the sky would be the limit.*

"There is much I could do for you," Great Aunt Stregheria added. "I have connections to many of the greatest families. It would be easy to arrange a match between you and a suitable young man of noble blood, when you come of age."

Alana made a choking noise. Beside her, Bella had an unconvincing coughing fit. Alana had told me - they'd *both* told me - that I would never get married. Who would want to marry a girl without magic? The lack of magic might be catching. And yet...

"I am too young to get married," I mumbled. I had four years until I came of age. Even then, there was no guarantee I'd get married at once. My parents had been in their twenties when *they'd* married. My sisters - and I - were aristocrats. Any prospective match would have to be carefully scrutinised by both sets of parents before they gave their approval. Marriage in haste, we'd been told, inevitably led to repenting at leisure. "I can't even..."

"We could discuss betrothals," Great Aunt Stregheria said. "I believe..."

"No," Mum said, flatly.

I shot her a grateful look. I knew there were girls and boys who were betrothed from birth, but the custom had been slowly going out of fashion. My parents had discussed such issues with us, during their endless and boring etiquette lessons, yet they'd made it clear that we would have a say in who we married. And a betrothal could cause legal problems, if a grown child decided they didn't want to go through with it. There were families in the city that were still feuding over broken betrothals that had taken place hundreds of years ago.

"As you wish," Great Aunt Stregheria said. She looked displeased, just for a second. "But there are many other benefits I could offer. You would have friends..."

"I have a friend here," I protested. It was true. Rose was the first *real* friend I'd had, perhaps my only one. I'd managed to get on well with Akin Rubén, but I was all too aware that his family and mine were long-term enemies. *And* I'd humiliated his sister too. I didn't know how he'd react to *that*. "I don't want to leave her."

"A common-born girl," Great Aunt Stregheria said. Her lips twisted into a cold sneer. "A decent magician, perhaps, but hardly the right sort of companion for a girl of the very highest blood. You should be surrounded by girls from your circle, girls who can educate you in the social graces..."

I winced. *Like Isabella? Or like Alana?*

"Your...*friend*...can come along as your maid, perhaps," Great Aunt Stregheria said. She looked, just for a moment, if she'd sniffed something disgusting. "It is all a person like her is suited for..."

"*Rose* is my friend," I snapped. The hot flash of anger surprised me. Rose had stood by me even when it would have ruined her time at school. I wouldn't have blamed her if she'd attached herself to Isabella or one of the other well-born students, the girls who could have taught her how to use her magic through example. What did *I* have to offer her? "She isn't a servant!"

"She is a common-born girl with no prospects," Great Aunt Stregheria said, bluntly. "What will happen to her when she graduates? She will not find a decent position, let alone a decent match, because she is lowly-born. She has no dowry, nothing to entice a suitor; she has no patron, no one who will shepherd her career. She is alone in the world."

"She has me." I fought to control my anger. It wasn't easy. Insults directed at me were meaningless - I'd been called so many awful things that I was used to it - but Rose? Rose was my friend. "And you think that I will be important."

Great Aunt Stregheria lifted her eyebrows. "Do you think you will be doing her a favour by patronising her?"

I glared. "Yes."

"You will not," Great Aunt Stregheria said. "And you will certainly not be doing *yourself* a favour. One must choose one's clients carefully."

"I have," I said. It wasn't really true - I'd never thought I'd have a patronage network of my own - but it didn't matter. Besides, Rose would be a worthy investment even if I'd hated the ground she walked on. Untrained and unskilled didn't mean *weak*. "She's a good friend."

"You had no other friends," Great Aunt Stregheria informed me. "If she comes with you, you will soon abandon her. She has nothing to offer you."

My temper snapped. "And you have *everything* to offer and you're still not married!"

Silence fell, like a hammer. I couldn't *believe* what I'd said. Nor could anyone else. Great Aunt Stregheria looked stunned, utterly uncomprehending. I wondered, as my thoughts started to gibber in panic, if I could pretend that nothing had actually happened. Perhaps, if I played dumb, she'd think she imagined it...

She snapped out a word I knew I wasn't supposed to know, let alone *say*, then jabbed her finger at me. Dad started to say something sharp, but it was too late. A flash of brilliant green light darted from her finger and flashed towards me, blazing brightly...and then rebounded. I gasped in pain as my earrings overheated - it was all I could do to keep from tearing them off - and then stared as the spell struck the crone. Great Aunt Stregheria's black skin turned green and warty, just for a second, as she cast a pair of very hasty counterspells. Green light flared around her body, then faded away into nothingness as her skin returned to normal. She'd countered her own spell just in time.

I stared, feeling...*triumph*? I knew to be wary around Alana - and Bella could be unpleasant, whenever she bestirred herself to do something nasty - but Great Aunt Stregheria *terrified* me. Even knowing her spells wouldn't last long, not on me, I was still unwilling to face her. And yet, now...she'd nearly fallen victim to her own spell. Her attempt to turn me into a frog - again - had failed utterly.

My mother's voice was icy cold. "I believe I warned you about using magic on my children," she said. She rose, her hands falling into a casting pose. "You will leave this house."

"The wards will turn on you," Dad added. He didn't rise, but he didn't have to. The house saw *him* as its lord and master. It wouldn't *kill* Great Aunt Stregheria - she was of the blood, after all - but it would evict her on his command. "You will leave."

I heard Bella make a stifled sound. Beside her, Alana looked as if she wanted to be somewhere - anywhere - else. Her hair was trying to stand on end. For once, I was glad I couldn't feel ambient magic. The house wards had to be concentrating on Great Aunt Stregheria, threatening to crush her protections and remove her from the estate. Very few magicians could hope to stand up to an old house, protecting its bloodline. And my sisters could feel the pressure building around the crone, as if a thunderstorm was about to begin...

Great Aunt Stregheria gave me a furious look that - five minutes ago - would have had me cowering, if not begging for mercy. "Did you raise your daughter to be so impossibly rude?"

"Please rest assured that Caitlyn will be punished," Dad said. "But that does not excuse *your* actions. I granted you access to the house on the understanding that you would *not* try to hex my children."

"Children should mind their manners," Great Aunt Stregheria snarled. I felt a flicker of guilt, despite the triumph. I'd touched on a very sore spot indeed. Great Aunt Stregheria's failure to marry and have children might well have cost her the chance to lead the family. "I demand satisfaction!"

"*I* will deal with my daughter," Dad said. He stood, clasping his hands behind his back. I knew better than to think that was a placid pose. Dad didn't need to move his hands to cast spells. "You will go straight to the gatehouse and leave. Your trunks will be forwarded to you."

Great Aunt Stregheria stared at me for a long moment, then pushed her chair back and rose.

"I could have offered you the world," she said, shortly. I wasn't sure just who she was talking to. My father…or me? Perhaps she'd believed that she was doing me a favour. "And instead you chose to reject it."

She stalked out of the room, not looking back. I watched her go, unsure just how I should feel. Unholy glee at beating Great Aunt Stregheria was mingled with fear and guilt and…I told myself, time and time again, that she was a horrible person. But I'd been horrible to her too.

Great Aunt Stregheria wanted to use me, I told myself. It made me feel a little better. *She wouldn't have lowered herself to fostering me - to fostering anyone - if there wasn't anything in it for her.*

Alana giggled, a high-pitched noise that grated on my ears. "Cat…"

"Silence," Dad said, sharply. Alana shut up, at once. I would have been impressed if I hadn't known that Dad's tone promised trouble. "Caitlyn, go straight to my study and wait for me there. I will be up shortly."

I sighed. I'd stepped over a line and now I would have to pay. And yet, I had been provoked. It wasn't fair…

But there was no point in whining about it. "Yes, Dad."

CHAPTER FOUR

The door to my father's study opened the moment I touched it. I couldn't help feeling a flicker of excitement as I stepped inside, even though I knew I was in trouble. Dad's private workplace had always been off limits to us. The room was so heavily warded that even *Mum* couldn't enter without permission. I looked around as I walked towards one of the comfortable armchairs and sat down. I might as well try to stay comfortable while waiting for Dad to arrive.

It *was* a remarkable room, in many ways. Two walls were lined with bookshelves, groaning under the weight of family spellbooks and grimoires; a third was decorated in a detailed family tree leading all the way back to the Thousand-Year Empire. I had no idea how much of it was truly accurate - the family records started to get a little vague a few hundred years back in time - but it looked impressive. My family had given birth to hundreds of movers and shakers over the years. It was hard to shake the impression that neither I nor my sisters would ever live up to them.

I closed my eyes for a long moment, trying to concentrate. Dad was going to be furious, of course. He might well dislike his aunt, but he couldn't condone me being so horribly rude to her. Mum wasn't going to be pleased either. Perhaps I should be glad I was going back to school soon. But I knew, all too well, that my parents had long memories. They'd be happy to put the punishment on hold until the summer holidays.

The door rattled, then opened. I sat upright, bracing myself as Dad stepped into the room and closed the door behind him. He didn't look happy, although there was a distant expression on his face that suggested he was communing with the wards. I couldn't help feeling a stab of bitter guilt as I recalled the implications. My talents might have - finally - revealed themselves, but I could never be the mistress of Aguirre Hall. The blood magics woven into the very walls barely even recognised my presence.

"Stand up," Dad ordered, curtly. "Stand in front of the desk."

I rose, clasping my hands behind my back to keep them from shaking. Dad gave me a sharp look, then walked around the desk to sit behind it. I moved forward until I was in position and forced myself to wait. Dad didn't normally play petty power games by forcing us to wait for him to speak. He had to be more rattled than he cared to admit.

"Tell me something," he said, finally. "What - exactly - were you thinking?"

"She was insulting my friend," I said. I told my hands to stop shaking. They refused to listen. "Dad, I…"

"And you decided to jab a knife in her heart," Dad said. His voice was toneless. "You could have jabbed her with a *real* knife and it would have done less damage."

I swallowed. "Yes, Dad."

"I'm really very displeased with you," Dad told me, flatly. "You will finish the sword tomorrow, correct? After that, you will spend the next two days assisting your mother with the herbal garden. I believe she has a great deal of work which will go quicker with a pair of willing hands."

I had to fight to keep my face expressionless. My sisters hated gardening and spent far too long thinking of ways to get out of assisting with the herbal garden, but I loved it. Plants didn't care about your magic, or lack of it. Two days doing nothing, but gardening would leave me stiff and sore, yet it wasn't a *real* punishment. I'd been uneasily anticipating something far worse. Alana had had to spend a week helping the maids after she tried to play a prank on an important visitor.

"Yes, Dad," I said, when I was sure I could keep the relief out of my voice. Dad *knew* I liked gardening. It wouldn't be pleasant, but it wouldn't be a nightmare either. "I'll start as soon as the sword is finished."

"Very good," my father said. "Now tell me...why did you leave Alana in a cupboard for hours?"

"Dad, she trapped herself," I said, briefly outlining what had happened. "I didn't know the spell would last so long."

"I imagine she didn't either," Dad said. He met my eyes. "Should I be punishing you for that too?"

"She did it to me," I pointed out. My parents hadn't done more than mildly rebuke her, believing that such torments would encourage me to develop my powers. "She did it to me a *lot*."

"True," Dad said. He looked displeased. "Don't do it again, *particularly* when we have guests. Your conduct reflects on us, your parents. And while Aunt Stregheria is unlikely to tell High Society *precisely* what you said to her, the next person you mouth off to may tell the entire world."

I sighed. "Do we *have* to bother with etiquette?"

"Politeness makes the world go 'round," Dad said. He smiled, rather humourlessly. "Being polite can defuse someone's anger, even when there is no common ground between you."

He shrugged. "But here is a more important question. What was happening this evening?"

I took a breath. Dad had asked me to analyse dinner meetings and social engagements before, although I'd never been very good at it. Alana had been better, to the point where she'd tried to encourage Dad to take her to more society engagements. Thankfully, Dad had rarely taken her anywhere he hadn't taken the rest of us. It would have done her ego no good.

"She wanted to make use of me," I said, carefully. "Her offer to foster me in Tintagel was an attempt to put me in her power."

"Indeed," Dad said. "Go on."

I hesitated. "She didn't think of me as a *person*," I added. "She was more interested in talking you into allowing me to go than convincing *me* I wanted to go. She talked in terms of benefits to you and the family, rather than me. Even when she started talking to me, it never seemed to occur to her that I might not *want* the benefits she was offering."

"Very good," my father said. "And why would she do that?"

"Because she thinks she can make use of me," I said, slowly. "By promoting me to the king, by presenting me at court, she presents *herself* as my guardian."

"More or less," Dad said. He leaned forward. "Do you understand the implications?"

I hesitated, then shook my head. It wasn't entirely true - I thought I understood *some* of them - but I needed to hear it from Dad. He had far more experience than I did in manoeuvring through tricky political waters. I tried not to think about the fact that Great Aunt Stregheria had more experience than both of us put together.

"A year ago, it was impossible to forge Objects of Power," Dad said. "You know that as well as I do. Now, someone *has* discovered how to do it. You."

I nodded, shortly.

"Normally, there are very few spells that cannot be analysed and duplicated by other magicians," Dad added. "You know that too."

"Yes," I said. I might not be able to cast spells, but my understanding of theoretical magic was better than either of my sisters. There *were* spells - hundreds of spells - that were tied to specific bloodlines or could only be cast by specific people, yet a skilled theoretical magician could take them apart and rewrite the spells so that anyone could cast them. "But that isn't true of me, is it?"

"No," Dad said. "I imagine that quite a few forgers are trying to find ways to forge without actually *touching* the artefact, which will be quite limited even if they do manage to get it to work. But even if they succeed, the only current source of *true* Objects of Power is you. Word has already leaked out, Cat. The duel you fought has started tongues wagging right across the kingdom."

"I know," I said.

"And you really *had* to pick a fight with Isabella *Rubén*," Dad added. "Some magicians don't believe the stories, but *her* family? Oh yes, *they* believe them."

I tried not to wince. There were spells that could destroy Devices of Power, spells that Isabella had tried to use on me. But I'd forged *Objects of Power* and her spells had been worse than useless. Some adult magicians probably thought that Isabella had miscast her spells - she was only *twelve*, like me - but *her* family wouldn't make that mistake. They knew what I'd done, all right.

"Great Aunt Stregheria is not the only one who wants to make use of you," Dad told me. He pointed a finger towards a pile of letters, perched precariously on his desk. "I have over fifty letters, ranging from requests for private commissions to demands that you be *barred* from any further forging. Your talents have the potential for upsetting the balance of power..."

I stared. "They want to *stop* me from forging?"

Dad's lips twitched. "Right now, we have a monopoly on Objects of Power. That gives us an unbeatable edge. The other families won't like it."

"They could look for their own Zeroes," I said. I remembered, suddenly, all the stories about disappointing children who'd vanished from High Society. Had they been Zeroes too? "I can't be unique."

"Perhaps not," Dad agreed. Alana had said the same thing, back at table. "But tell me...how do you *find* another Zero?"

I considered it for a long moment. The answer *was* fairly simple, at least in theory. Cast spells on potential candidates and see how long the spells lasted. My experiments had proved that spells cast on me simply didn't last very long, no matter how much power the caster pumped into the magic. But doing that on people outside the city would be a logistical nightmare. There would be thousands of potential candidates, far too many to sort through in a hurry.

And some of them will be common-born, I thought. *What will High Society make of that?*

"We have to work on the assumption that you are effectively unique, at least for the moment," Dad said. "And that means that *you* are both a very important person and a very *weak* one."

I fought down a flash of anger. People - my sisters, in particular - had been calling me weak for years. I'd grown to hate the word. And now I'd found a way to compensate for my weakness. Maybe I couldn't cast spells. It didn't make me useless.

"I am unsure if you should be allowed to return to Jude's or not," Dad added. "What do you think?"

"Rose is there," I said, sullenly.

"Yes," Dad agreed. "But how many of the classes can you actually *pass*?"

I glowered at him. "You sent me there when it looked like I couldn't pass *any* of the classes," I pointed out. "I *can* find ways to get through the exams."

"It would be meaningless," Dad said. "Would it not?"

I felt another flash of anger. "I may not be able to use magic to brew a potion," I said, carefully. "But I can forge a stirrer that will let me infuse *precisely* the right amount of magic to make the potion work."

"Your mother wishes to talk about some of the older recipes, the ones that no one has been able to brew for a thousand years," Dad said. "But would using a stirrer of your own design count in the exams?"

"I thought we were graded on how well we'd brewed the potion," I said. "I don't think anyone would complain if we used different tools."

Dad cocked his head. "You didn't want to go to Jude's," he said. "And now you don't want me to pull you *out*?"

"Rose is there," I said. I hesitated, then asked a different question. "Was she right about Rose? Great Aunt Stregheria, I mean. Was she right when she said Rose had no prospects?"

"She would probably not rise to the very highest levels," my father said. He took a moment to gather his thoughts. "Turning her into a reputable name in society would be a very long-term project, although quite a few of the older families have a *lot* of commoner blood. But a skilled magician can always find work. I would be quite happy to offer her patronage if she lives up to her promise."

I relaxed, slightly. "I'm not asking for her to marry the Crown Prince!"

"Glad to hear it," Dad said, sardonically. "The Crown Prince is already married."

"I know," I said. The Royal Wedding had been ten years ago. I had gone, of course, along with just about everyone in High Society, but I'd been so young that I honestly didn't remember any of the details. "It was a joke."

Dad snorted, then leaned forward. "If you want to go back to school, I will reluctantly allow it," he said. "Jude's should be relatively safe…as long as you don't brew forbidden potions without permission. Very few families would risk taking hostile action within the school's grounds."

My fingers touched my dark cheek, delicately. The regrown skin had stopped itching weeks ago, as it blended into my skin, but there were still times when it didn't feel like *me*. I'd been lucky - very lucky - that I hadn't accidentally killed both Rose and myself. As it was, we'd come far too close to being expelled. And yet, if I hadn't been brewing the potion, I wouldn't have discovered how my talents actually worked.

"I will be careful," I said. A thought struck me and I smiled. "If I'm the only one who can make Objects of Power, does it matter if I don't get good grades?"

Dad smiled back. "If you don't get a *passing* grade, you won't be allowed to move up a level," he said. "Imagine being the only nineteen-year-old in first-year classes."

"Ouch," I said. The older students - the upperclassmen - might be responsible for policing the junior students, but they certainly didn't socialise with us. There was an invisible barrier between the years that might as well be made of reinforced iron and stone, for all that it was impassable. An older student in a lower grade would be isolated from her age group as well as her peers. "That would be bad."

"It would be," Dad agreed. He met my eyes. "Rose could come here, you know. I could hire tutors, if she wanted to continue with her studies."

I shook my head. Rose would hate it. She'd feel out of place, in a way that I could understand all too well. And it would cut her off from her family…young girls went into service all the time, but this was different. She would neither be family nor servant, trapped in an ill-defined position that would never resolve itself…

"No," I said. Maybe I'd ask him to take Rose on later, if I had to leave the school, but only then. I had no doubt Rose *would* pass her exams. She might be ignorant, but she was far from stupid. I never had to tell her anything twice. "We'll stay at the school together."

"As you wish," Dad said. He looked down at the desk. "Be careful, Caitlyn."

I nodded. I was always careful. Having a sister who thought that hexing my chair or bed was a laugh had taught me to be *very* careful.

"The family name can protect you from a great many things," Dad added. "But it can't protect you from *everything*. Like it or not, the world changed the moment you crafted your first Object of Power. We may not see many visible changes - yet - but everything turned upside down. Aunt Stregheria is not the only person who will seek to use you."

"Yes, Dad."

My father looked up at me. "Your mother and I believed that you would inherit magic of your own," he said, sombrely. "You were one of three triplets. Everything we knew about magic told us that you'd have it too, that the three of you would form a triad greater than the sum of its parts. We made the choice - and it pained us greatly - to allow your siblings to…*encourage*…you to develop your powers. And there were enough signs that you *did* have some form of magic to convince us to continue. We simply didn't realise what you were."

I couldn't speak. My mouth was dry.

"That was a mistake," he admitted. "We allowed your sisters to bully you relentlessly, for nothing. In doing so, we damaged all three of you. Alana and Bella have bad habits of their own, habits we have failed to curb. In some ways, Aunt Stregheria is right about sending children to out to fostering. A distant relative would be less inclined to put up with unpleasant behaviour."

I looked down. I didn't want to hear it. I didn't want to believe that my parents - who I loved and respected - could make a mistake. And yet, I knew they *had* made a mistake. Everything they'd done in a bid to bring out my magic had been both cruel and pointless. I had no magic. There wasn't even a spark that could be fanned into a flame.

"We will do what we can to make up for it," my father told me. "But that will not be easy."

"I know," I said. I couldn't meet his eyes. I almost wished he was shouting at me instead. "I…it wasn't your fault."

"We knew no better," Dad agreed. "But that doesn't make it *right*."

He rose. "Go back to your bedroom and sleep," he ordered. "Sir Griffons will be here tomorrow afternoon. I believe he's looking forward to inspecting your work."

"Yes, Dad," I said.

Dad sighed. "And that sword will start an avalanche," he added. "I wish you'd come to me, when you figured out what you could do. We could have planned out how to tell the world before it was too late."

I nodded as I turned to leave. He was right. In hindsight, I shouldn't have let Isabella goad me. But, if there was one thing I had learnt in six years of study, it was that there was no way to call back a spell once it was cast.

And we would just have to live with the consequences.

CHAPTER
FIVE

The workroom felt uncomfortably hot as I bent over the sword, carefully carving the last set of runes into the metal. Sweat trickled down my back, reminding me just how much was at stake. A mistake now - even a single rune marginally out of place - would render all of my time and effort utterly wasted. Dad would not be pleased.

I finished drawing out the second-to-last rune, then took a step back. The sword seemed to glow, although I was fairly sure I was imagining it. My calculations insisted that the spellform wouldn't take shape until the very last rune was in place. And yet, I wasn't entirely sure. There were too many hints, clues and misleading statements in the ancient books for me to be completely confident in my own abilities. The writers might well have left out more than one crucial detail.

Wiping the sweat from my brow, I put the etching tool down on the workbench and reached for my spectacles. I'd designed them myself, after discovering the limitations of the original designs. It was surprisingly comforting to know that, in some respects, we were more advanced than the ancient sorcerers. We'd had to come up with too many innovative workarounds for our Devices of Power to be anything else.

I perched the spectacles on my nose and peered around the room. The walls glowed faintly, reflecting the magic embedded into the mansion, but the sword was dead and cold. There was no magic flowing through the blade, not yet. I took a step forward and examined the runes, making very sure that I hadn't made a mistake. Magister Tallyman had insisted, when

I'd been working as a TA, that it was *possible* to correct an error if one caught it in time, but I had never succeeded. The ancient sorcerers hadn't thought it was possible either.

"It's done," I muttered. I'd gone as far as I could without Sir Griffons. "And now..."

I stepped into the antechamber and rang the bell. Lucy entered the room a moment later, curtseying hastily to me. It felt weird to have her show so much respect. The maids had never been particularly impressed with me, even though I was their master's daughter, until I'd insulted Great Aunt Stregheria to her face. Dad might have pronounced a horrific punishment - or at least something most people would *consider* a punishment - but the maids thought I was wonderful. If Great Aunt Stregheria had been horrible to *us*, her great-nieces, how had she treated the maids?

"Please find Sir Griffons and bring him here," I ordered. Family friend or not, Sir Griffons wasn't supposed to wander our halls without an escort. "It's time for him to receive his sword."

Lucy curtseyed again and hurried off. I turned to the table in the antechamber and picked up the latest copy of *Forgers Weekly*. There was a large painting of me - or someone who was supposed to be me - on the front cover, probably drawn from the family's official portrait. I looked about five or six years older, my skin a shade or two lighter. It was quite possible that anyone passing me in the street wouldn't *recognise* me, if that painting was all they'd seen. I supposed that wasn't a bad thing.

The article inside the covers was long on hyperbole and short on actual facts. Whoever had written it *clearly* hadn't been a witness to the duel. They'd heard everything at second or third hand, ensuring that the fragments of truth were mingled with exaggerations or blatant lies. I had *not* recreated the Emperor's Power Stone, nor had I blasted a giant hole in the school's walls. Castellan Wealden would have expelled me for *that*, I was sure.

There was a knock at the door. My mouth was suddenly dry.

"Come in," I managed.

The door opened. Sir Griffons stepped into the room.

He was *immense*, easily the largest man I'd met. His blond hair - a fraction too long for society's pleasure - framed a rugged face that had half the maids swooning whenever he came to call. The silver armour he wore, covered with protective runes, outlined a muscular body; his hands, scarred by countless battles, were large enough to make mine look tiny. I had never thought of him as particularly clever - his attempts at mending his own armour and weapons had frequently made matters worse - but he'd always been kind to me. That alone gave him status in my eyes.

"Lady Caitlyn," he said, gravely. His voice was deep, commanding. "I believe you summoned me?"

I swallowed. "Your blade is nearly ready, sir," I said. Sir Griffons *was* a Knight, a servant of King Rufus himself. I had no idea of his birth, but he deserved respect for his knighthood alone. "I just need your assistance with the final step."

Sir Griffons bowed. He couldn't hide the anticipation in his eyes. "It would be my honour, My Lady," he said. "What do you want me to do?"

"Exactly as I say," I said. I turned to open the door. "Come with me."

I couldn't help feeling concerned as I led the way into my workroom. Sir Griffons meant me no harm, I was sure, yet his mere presence could upset the magic. If he took a step too close to the unfinished blade…I wasn't *sure* what would happen then, but I had the feeling I wouldn't like it. Rose's mere presence had made a highly volatile potion explode so violently it had nearly killed both of us.

"You'll see the marks on the floor," I said, pointing to the lines. I'd measured them out carefully, carving them into the stone. "Do *not* step over them until I give you leave."

Sir Griffons nodded. I hoped he'd listen. He really *wasn't* the sharpest knife in the drawer. But then, he didn't have to be. Hacking away at enemies with a sword didn't require utter brilliance, merely strength, stamina and determination. I'd heard his brother was smarter - and a magical tutor in the capital. No doubt he'd inherited the brains, while Sir Griffons had inherited the brawn. Their parents weren't slouches either.

"The blade is almost ready," I repeated. It was easier to keep my voice steady when I started to talk about forging. "I have to trigger the spellform to finish the work. For that - in order to bind it to you - I need a sample of your blood."

I saw a shadow cross his face. I didn't blame him. We were all taught - from birth - to be very careful with our blood. An enemy who acquired a sample of my blood could use it to curse me from the other side of the world...perhaps. I wasn't entirely sure it was true of *me* - my nature might make it impossible for the curse to latch on - but it *was* true of everyone else. I used the blood rituals religiously, just like everyone else. There was no point in taking chances.

"Very well," he said. "But I'll want to take the knife afterwards."

"I can't use a salve to dampen the pain either," I said, as I picked up the knife and glass container from the workbench. I'd made both of them myself, washing the knife repeatedly until it was completely clean. I didn't dare risk contamination. "It will sting."

Sir Griffons lifted his bushy eyebrows. "Worse than having a sword slammed into your leg?"

I giggled, despite myself. Sir Griffons had been through hundreds of battles and suffered countless injuries, if half the stories were true. He wasn't likely to be bothered by me cutting his arm so I could collect some of his blood. But then, I had had paper cuts that had hurt worse than broken bones. I didn't understand how that worked, but it was true.

"No," I said. I passed him a cloth - I couldn't give him any potions or salves before the ritual was completed - and then stepped towards him. "Roll up your sleeve, then hold out your arm."

Sir Griffons did as he was told. I braced myself, then pressed the knife against his flesh. A droplet - and then a line - of blood welled up. I fought down the urge to recoil - blood was bad news, even for me - as the liquid started to drop into the glass. Sir Griffons showed no sign of pain. But then, he would sooner have cut off his own arm than show weakness in front of a girl. It would not have impressed the maids.

"Press the cloth against the cut, then wait," I ordered, once I'd collected enough blood. I'd seriously considered taking more, just in case there was an accident, but working with blood was enough to make me nervous. I would just have to ask him for a second contribution, if I needed more. "Do *not* use magic to seal the wound."

"Understood," Sir Griffons said. He sounded perfectly normal, as if we were discussing the weather instead of working on a ritual. I wouldn't have been so calm if we'd exchanged places. "I will wait."

I placed the glass on the workbench, then picked up the etching tool and dipped it in the blood. My heart started to beat like a drum as I pressed the tool against the blade, slowly carving out the final rune. If this worked…it would have been easier, far easier, to forge a sword that anyone could use, but Sir Griffons had wanted something special. The room grew warmer, again, as the rune took shape. I braced myself as I carved the last line. If I'd made a mistake…

The blade glowed, a brilliant white light that stabbed into my head and sent knives of pain slicing into my brain. I yanked the etching tool away, lifting one hand to cover my eyes as my head started to pound. Sir Griffons let out an oath - I decided it would be better to pretend I hadn't heard it - as the brightness increased, forcing us both to turn away. And then the brightness snapped out of existence, as if someone had blown out the candle.

I blinked, trying to get the spots out of my eyes. My head was ringing with pain, although I wasn't sure why. The light…the light hadn't been *natural*. My hands looked as though they were translucent…I blinked and the effect vanished, leaving my hands as solid as they always were. It made no sense. What had I done?

Think about it later, I told myself firmly.

The sword lay on the workbench, glowing faintly. I reached for the spectacles and put them on, swallowing a word I knew Mum would *not* have liked when I looked at the sword. It *glowed* with magic, a spellform that twisted up and down the blade…it had worked. I'd forged an Object of Power. But it wasn't quite finished yet.

I turned to look at Sir Griffons. "You have to take the blade," I said. "Pick it up with your sword hand and hold it in the air."

It would have daunted me, if someone had told *me* to do that. The blade was so large that it was hard to believe that a grown adult could have lifted it with only one hand. And yet, Sir Griffons took it in his stride. He stepped forward, held his hand over the grip and then picked it up effortlessly. Even *his* hand looked small compared to the blade, but it rose as if it were as light as air. The gemstone I'd worked into the pommel glowed brightly as he lifted it higher. Faint flickers of magic danced around the longsword as it bonded with its new owner.

"It's perfect," Sir Griffons breathed.

He stepped back and assumed a combat stance, slashing out at an imaginary foe. The sword darted forward and back as if it were made of pure light, flaring brightly as he thrust it outwards. It was so long he would have to wear it over his shoulder, rather than on his belt, but I had a feeling it wouldn't cause him any problems. The blade would practically *leap* into his hand when he called. And it might even have other powers too.

If it stays with him long enough to develop them, I thought. The ancients had insisted that a magical weapon *would* grow into the perfect match for its wielder, once it had grown used to him. But my calculations insisted that the spellform would remain stable unless someone damaged the blade. *And that would render it completely useless.*

I stepped back, sombrely, as Sir Griffons put the longsword through its paces. Magister Tallyman had shown us a similar blade, one forged in the Thousand-Year Empire. It had been a genuine Object of Power, one that had endured until some idiot removed one of the gemstones. Whatever the stone had been worth, the working blade had been worth far more. Now, it was just a piece of scrap metal. I might have been able to fix it, but - if it was bonded to someone else - I'd never be able to *use* it.

"This is brilliant," Sir Griffons said. He let out a deep laugh. "This is *fantastic*."

He bowed, deeply. "I thank you from the very bottom of my heart."

"You are welcome," I said, stiffly. My cheeks grew hot. I was thankful my skin hid the blush. I wasn't used to praise, not like that. "I designed a scabbard for you, but you'll have to wear it over your shoulder."

"I don't want to put it down," Sir Griffons said. His smile was so bright that I couldn't help thinking it made him look like a little boy. "What can it do?"

"Cut through almost anything, if you press it against something," I said. "You *do* need the intent to cut."

"It would be embarrassing if the blade was dropped on the floor," Sir Griffons said. His smile grew wider. "It might cut its way to the planet's core."

"That can't happen," I assured him. "Your intentions are important."

I paused, gathering my thoughts. "You should be able to block curses and hexes with the blade - the magic should give you some additional immunity, even if you don't manage to swat the curse before it strikes you. You should also be able to cut through wards, but a skilled sorcerer could probably design wards capable of trapping or reforming around the blade."

"I've met warlocks who did just that," Sir Griffons said.

"And you won't be able to hide the blade," I added. "The magic is quite distinctive. Once you take it out of the wards, anyone within fifty metres will probably be able to sense its presence."

Sir Griffons didn't look displeased at the thought of being made a target. If anything, the prospect of everyone *seeing* him coming seemed to delight him. And yet…I shook my head, feeling a flicker of disquiet. I couldn't sense the blade, not even if it was right next to me. The effect was predicable - my calculations had indicated that it would be there - yet I would never see it for myself. I was probably the only person in the world Sir Griffons *could* sneak up on while carrying the blade.

He took the scabbard and slipped the blade in and out, testing how it moved. "Who else can use it?"

"Anyone closely related to you," I told him. "A brother or sister, a child…anyone else would simply find it too heavy to lift. You *might* be able to give it to your cousin, but I don't know if it would work for him."

"Good," Sir Griffons said. He smiled, as one does at a particularly bad joke. "I wouldn't want someone to *steal* it."

"No," I agreed. "And don't let anyone steal the gemstone either. It would cancel the magic."

"I understand," Sir Griffons said. He swung the sword through the air. "This is…*brilliant*."

He reached out and slapped me on the back. "I owe you a boon, young lady," he said. "You may have anything, anything at all, as long as it is within my power to give it to you."

Within reason, I added, silently. Dad had taught me to be careful what I promised. Bad things happened to people who didn't keep their promises. Sir Griffons really should have known better. If I asked him for something that conflicted with his other oaths, I might put him into an impossible position. It might even kill him. *If I ask for the wrong thing...*

I pushed the thought aside. "If I need a boon, I will ask you," I said. It wouldn't have been *polite* to decline the promise. "And I hope you enjoy the blade."

"Oh, I enjoy it already," Sir Griffons said. He held it up in front of his face. "This is perfect, absolutely perfect."

I had to smile. He looked like an overgrown puppy.

"Thank you," he said, as he picked up the knife and bloodstained container. "And I meant what I said."

I rang the bell for Lucy, then sent Sir Griffons and her back to the guest wing. I had a feeling Sir Griffons wasn't going to stay, not after bonding with the blade. He'd probably start riding back to Tintagel, just to show off his blade to his fellow Kingsmen. They wouldn't believe it, not at first. And then they'd all want one too...

And I can make them, I thought, as I started to clean up the workroom. The thrill would fade, I knew, so I determined to enjoy it as long as I could. *And who knows what else I can make?*

CHAPTER SIX

"I trust you had a good breakfast," Mum said, in a manner that made it very clear that I was in trouble. "You have a lot of work to do."

I nodded, not trusting myself to speak. Mum had ordered me out of bed at stupid o'clock - the sun had barely been peeking over the horizon - and sent me to join the maids for breakfast before getting changed into gardening clothes. It was a very clear sign that I was in disgrace, even though I knew Mum loathed Great Aunt Stregheria as much as everyone else. I had been unforgivably rude and my parents were not pleased.

But it could be worse, I thought. *They could have sent me to clean the bathrooms instead.*

Mum looked me up and down, then nodded in grim approval. I concealed my amusement as she shoved a basket of gardening tools into my arms, before turning to march towards the door. Gardening was the only time I was allowed to wear clothes that would have shamed a beggar on the streets. The rough, ill-fitting shirt and trousers made me look like a tramp, but they could endure more abuse than my regular clothes. And when I came back to the house, covered in earth and mud, they could be dumped in the washroom for a thorough cleaning without worrying about damaging them. I tied my hair back into a bun, then followed Mum through the door and out into the garden. The warm air - tinged with a hint of the oncoming winter - brushed against my face as I closed the door.

"Don't dawdle," Mum snapped.

"Coming," I assured her, as I hefted the basket and walked after her. "What are we doing first?"

Mum didn't answer. I sighed and kept walking. I'd find out soon enough.

Our herbal gardens are my mother's pride and joy. Master Potioneers like Mum prefer to grow as many of their ingredients as possible, even though some of the rarer items - like dragon scales or octopus tentacles - can only be purchased from a handful of very high-class stockists. Mum insisted that being able to produce her own herbs helped keep prices down, although it *also* ensured that she knew everything about how the ingredients had been produced. Even something as simple as cutting herbs can cause problems if one uses a silver blade instead of an iron knife.

And that can make a difference, I thought. *Using a silver blade could make it harder to use a herb in a potion.*

I put the basket down as I reached the edge of the herbal garden, my mother chanting a handful of spells to unlock the protective charms covering the chessboard patchwork of herbs and other ingredients. Alana had once tried to break into the garden on a dare; she wound up hanging upside down until Mum had come along to free her, then rebuke her for daring to even *consider* trying to sneak through the wards. They were designed to keep out pests, but not all pests walked on four legs. Alana had never dared try to enter the garden without permission again.

The wind shifted, blowing towards me. I took a deep breath, enjoying the scent of dozens of herbs mingling together. Mum claimed that gardening was relaxing, and there were times when I was tempted to agree with her. We'd spent many happy hours planting seeds and cutting herbs, back when she'd been trying to use potions to bring out my magic. It had been futile, yet it had actually worked in my favour. I'd learnt the value of precision long before I'd needed to use it.

"Come inside," Mum said. She pointed to a barren patch of fallow ground. "You'll be breaking that for me today."

I picked up a shovel and carried it into the garden. Mum had left the ground fallow for three years, long enough to allow it to recover from whatever she'd been doing there. It had grown hard, unsurprisingly. Breaking it up so that something new could be planted wouldn't be exactly back-breaking labour, not here, but…it would be boring. And I'd wind up covered in mud.

"Make sure you put any stones to one side," Mum directed, as I pushed the shovel into the earth. It was hard, resisting stubbornly until I put all my weight on the shovel. "And dig as deep as you can."

The sun rose steadily as I dug, picking up pieces of earth and breaking them up before dropping them back on the ground. There weren't many stones, thankfully. Mum had cleared the area long ago, back before I was born, and kept it warded ever since. The handful I did find I put aside, save for one that looked like a long-lost gemstone. It was probably nothing, but Dad would want to take a look at it anyway. The hall was so large that we kept finding things former generations had lost or concealed over the centuries.

My hands and back were aching when Mum finally called a halt, passing me a bottle of sweetened lemon juice as I leaned on the shovel. I sipped it gratefully, feeling sweat trickle down my back. The clothes were starting to itch…I promised myself, silently, that I'd take a long bath when I got back to the hall. Mum would probably insist on it. I'd be washing off so many layers of dirt that I might clog up the pipes.

"Not too bad," Mum said, grudgingly. She studied my work for a long moment, then pointed me to a second patch. "You can start work there now."

I nodded sullenly. The sun hadn't even reached meridian, let alone started to descend. It felt like we'd been outside for hours. But there was no point in arguing. I walked to the next patch of ground and started to work. Mum stayed where I'd been, using a smaller towel to dig holes and plant seeds. It would be months before our labour bore fruit, but I was confident it would be worth it. The herbs we didn't use would be packaged up and sold to the local apothecary.

"What you said to Stregheria was cruel," Mum said, without looking up from her work. "You do know that, don't you?"

"Yes," I said. I knew better than to stop working. "But she was very rude to me…"

"Yes," Mum said. "And you shouldn't have let her get to you."

I looked up. "What would *you* have done if she'd been insulting Lady Meadows?"

"I might have pointed out that she was wrong," Mum said. "A common-born magician could make a good apprentice, as you know. Or find something else to do with her life that doesn't include grovelling in the dirt."

"Yeah," I said, reluctantly. "But I didn't think of it."

Mum stood. "I understand that you were angry," she said. "And I understand that you had reason to be angry. But you cannot let your anger rule your life."

"I know," I said.

"You are a child," Mum said. She dropped the towel back into the basket. "When you are an adult, such behaviour will have far more serious consequences."

I scowled. "Why doesn't it have any consequences for *her*?"

Mum smirked. She'd deny it, I was sure, if I asked, but I knew what I saw.

"Stregheria is welcome in very few halls," she said. "Hosts are very inventive when coming up with reasons why she shouldn't attend formal gatherings. She is very isolated, for all she pretends it doesn't bother her."

She met my eyes. "And while that doesn't excuse her behaviour," she added, "it may go some way towards explaining it."

"Hah," I muttered. I wasn't interested in explanations. The only way Great Aunt Stregheria could make me happy was if she never intruded on my life again. "She's a *crone*."

Mum shot me a warning look. "Be careful what you say," she said. "I dread to imagine what would happen if you had been an *adult*."

Feuds have started over less, I thought.

I broke the last patch of ground, then stepped back to admire my handiwork. It didn't look any different from the flowerbeds, but I knew it was bursting with potential. A few dozen seeds, some water and patience…it would soon give birth to new life. And the herbs we seeded would be turned into ingredients for potions in a few months. I wondered, idly, if any of them would be sold to Jude's. The school went through more potion ingredients in a day than my mother went through in a year.

"Very good," Mum said. "And just in time too."

I turned. Lucy was approaching, carrying a covered basket in one hand and a picnic rug in the other. I smiled at her as she laid the rug on the ground by the edge of the garden, then placed the basket on top and strode away. Mum walked over to the basket, opened it and produced a set of sandwiches. I followed her, shaking my head as I saw just how *much* food the staff had crammed inside: ham and cheese sandwiches, hard-boiled eggs, a selection of apples and oranges and a bottle of ginger juice. I couldn't help wondering if they thought they were feeding a small army.

"Sit down," Mum said. She passed me a sandwich, then took one for herself. "Are you looking forward to going back to school?"

I took a bite, feeling suddenly ravenous. Gardening had always left me feeling hungry.

"I don't know," I confessed. "I'm looking forward to seeing Rose again, but..."

Mum nodded. "I was pretty good at school," she said, "but I don't remember it with any fondness."

Pretty good, I thought, wryly. She was being very modest. Mum had been valedictorian for two years running, then gone straight into a brilliant potions apprenticeship that had catapulted her to fame and fortune. Dad had done very well too. *Are any of us going to live up to them?*

"It has its moments," I said. I *had* enjoyed some of the classes, as well as the chance to learn from some of the most experienced magicians in the world. It was just the other kids I disliked. They'd sensed my weakness and attacked. Perhaps I'd taught them a lesson, when I'd beaten Isabella, or perhaps not. "I just wish..."

I shook my head as my words trailed off. What did I wish? That I'd been born with power? Or that I'd been raised somewhere where my *lack* of power wasn't an issue? Or...I shivered as I remembered Rose's bare feet. The pockmarks from a childhood disease were too embedded to be removed without magic, yet Rose's family hadn't had the funds to hire a healer. And she'd been one of the lucky ones. She'd told me that far too many of her peers hadn't lived through their first decade.

"No magic can change the past," my mother said. Her dark eyes were sympathetic. "All you can do is make the best of it."

"Or not," I muttered. Did Great Aunt Stregheria make the best of it? "It just doesn't seem *fair*."

"The world is *not* fair," Mum said, flatly. "And sometimes bad things happen to good people."

She finished her sandwich, then pulled a bottle from the basket and put it to her lips. I felt an odd rush of affection, knowing that my mother normally wouldn't do *anything* as lowly as drinking out of a bottle. But then, she was wearing tattered old clothes and getting her hands dirty too. Dignity and gardening didn't really go together.

"I found several new potion recipes we might want to try," she said, as she passed me the bottle. "They all require *very* precise infusions of magic."

I took a long drink. The ginger tasted strong enough to make me cough. "And perhaps cannot be made by *real* magicians?"

"Perhaps," Mum agreed. "You *have* managed to answer a great many questions, Cat. But you have also given me far more."

I nodded as I reached for another sandwich. There were hundreds of potion recipes that no one, not even my mother or Magistra Loanda, had been able to make. I'd read the long-winded articles written and distributed by the potioneers guild. Every attempt had either failed completely - dissolving into a muddy sludge that was only *slightly* more magical than myself - or exploded violently enough to burn through wards and do serious damage. And yet, the promise kept potion masters trying to brew the recipes. A potioneer who managed to get just *one* of them to work would make his fame and fortune overnight.

Particularly the one that grants superhuman strength, I thought. The ancient tomes insisted that it had been invented in a tiny village, now long since wiped off the map. But no matter how one fiddled with the ingredients, the best anyone had managed to get was a reasonably tasty lobster stew. *Something must have been left out of the recipe when it was written down.*

"I can design a stirrer for you," I said. Mum had more than enough control over her magic to charge and use it, I thought. And even if she didn't, she could practice before she actually tried to use it. "And I'll forge it over the summer holidays."

"You could also help me brew them," Mum said. "This time, you won't fail."

I looked down at the ground. I'd brewed countless potions with my mother, but they'd all failed. Without an infusion of magic, a potion was just a collection of exotic ingredients in pure water. I knew now how I could *get* that infusion of magic, but the memory of those failures still haunted me. Alana and Bella had rubbed them in at every opportunity.

And Bella expects me to help her with her homework, I thought, feeling a flicker of tired amusement. She was just too lazy for school. I dreaded to think what her half-term report would say. Dad would probably hit the roof when he read it. *But if I help her, I can get her to help me.*

"I hope so," I said, finally. Mum wouldn't want to be anywhere near when I brewed 'Caitlyn's Boost'. The risk of an explosion was just too great. I didn't think Magistra Loanda would let me brew it in school either, not again. I might have to beg Dad to let me set up a potions lab in the summer house. "But…"

"You won't," Mum said. She gave me a smile. "We understand the problem now, dear heart. And we can learn to compensate for it."

"And find others," I said. I looked towards the thicket of close-knit trees, unwilling to meet her eyes. The opal garden was hidden behind the trees…a grim reminder that there were some things I would never be able to do. But it also offered a simpler way to find more people like me. "And who knows what will happen then?"

Mum offered me the last sandwich, then started to munch on a hard-boiled egg. "The world will change," she said. "And the family will, as always, prosper."

I took another sip of ginger. "I want to go back to school," I said. "And I *don't* want to go back to school. Is that normal?"

"I was born in Pontefract," Mum said. She jabbed a finger northwards. "For me, travelling to Shallot for my education was an experience. But I was also homesick, because even if I did manage to get out of the school there was no way to get home in a hurry. My guardians were kind enough, I suppose, but they didn't really understand me."

I looked up. "You were fostered?"

"In a manner of speaking," Mum said. "My parents had a friend in Shallot. They gave him and his wife guardianship, just in case something happened that needed urgent attention. It wasn't *bad*, but…they weren't my parents. And I didn't live with them, save for the occasional weekend. I can't say they ever really used their authority."

"Ouch," I said. I couldn't help feeling sorry for her. If *I'd* left Jude's, I could have walked straight home. "What happened to them?"

"They died shortly after I married," Mum said. She looked sombre for a moment. "They never had children of their own. I was the closest thing to a child they had - and they didn't really have me. They—" her lips twitched "—probably decided that I was too much work."

"You must have been naughty all the time," I said, mischievously.

"I was a very studious child," Mum said, primly. "My parents often had to chase me out of the house, just to force me to get some exercise."

"That's not what grandmother says," I countered. "*She* said you only studied so much because you were grounded all the time."

Mum smiled. "Grandchildren exist to allow grandparents to extract revenge on *their* children," she said, wryly. Her face fell. "My guardians barely knew me, to be honest. I was surprised when they remembered me in their will."

I blinked. "They did?"

"I was left a number of books," Mum confirmed. "You can find them in the library, if you wish."

"Oh," I said. That *was* a surprise. Books, particularly ones produced before the printing press had been invented, were worth far more than their weight in gold. Mum's guardians must have thought very highly of her. Unless they really *hadn't* had anyone closer to them who might inherit. "I'll look for them when I have a moment."

"Not for a while, I think," Mum said. She packed up the picnic basket, then rose. "Shall we get back to work?"

"Yes, Mum," I said. "How much more is there to do?"

Mum gave me an evil smile. "Guess."

CHAPTER SEVEN

"I hope you have enjoyed your unexpected holiday," my father said, as he surveyed the dinner table. "It will not happen again."

I kept my face expressionless as Alana and Bella groaned. A week off school probably wouldn't hurt their grades, not when they were already well ahead of a good third of their classmates. It wouldn't hurt Alana, at least. My sister might be a spiteful bully on her best day, but there was nothing wrong with her magic. She probably had some of the best grades in the year.

"They'll be looking forward to us coming back," Alana said, seriously. She shot me a taunting look. "My friends keep asking what happened to me."

Because you're the head of your little gang, I thought. Alana's name and position had ensured she had a gaggle of giggling cronies surrounding her at all times, once she'd gone to school. Isabella had had a gang too. *And if the head goes away for too long, the gang will go away too.*

"Pulling you out of school was the best of a set of bad options," Dad continued. "It was *important* that none of you were in a position to make the rumours worse."

"Hah," Bella muttered.

"You'll be going back tonight, then resuming classes tomorrow," Dad added, ignoring her. "I hope that you will take the time to reflect on your duty to the family, as well as yourselves."

I peered around the family room as the maids brought in the first course. It was far more comfortable than the formal ballroom, although

Great Aunt Stregheria would probably have considered it too undignified for her magnificence. A large fire burned merrily in the grate, a sofa and three armchairs were perched against the walls and lanterns hung from the ceiling, casting brilliant light over the scene. The portraits on the walls showed *us*, from birth to our last birthday. I couldn't help reflecting that we'd changed a great deal over the years.

Alana was looking at me, her gaze hooded. I wondered, suddenly, just *what* Dad had said to her while I'd been working in the garden. She hadn't said anything to me since Great Aunt Stregheria had stormed out, not even her usual mockery. And she hadn't tried to hex me either. It made me more than a little paranoid. Alana was bright enough to think of a way to get around my protections, if she put her mind to it. I was sure she was planning something.

We ate slowly, savouring every bite. The food at Jude's wasn't bad, but the school cooks were trying to feed over a thousand pupils. Henry and his apprentices only had to please the five of us. They could afford to take their time to craft a *truly* excellent dinner. The hunter's chicken was perfect, the mashed potatoes fluffy with a hint of cheese, the vegetables coated in something that made us want to eat them...I finished my plate and held it out for seconds. I definitely wouldn't eat so well at Jude's.

"I will be inspecting your grades, come winter," Dad said, as he placed his knife and fork on his plate. "I will not be pleased if your grades do not meet my standards."

Bella winced. I felt a flicker of sympathy. Even if she worked hard for the next two months, it was unlikely she could bring up her grades in time for the winter holidays. Dad was not going to be pleased, even if there was a good chance she could keep herself from having to repeat the year. Her tutors probably already had a good impression of just how lazy she could be.

"My grades are excellent, Dad," Alana said, airily. "*I* won't have to repeat a year."

"And *I* will be very displeased if that turns out to be an empty boast," Mum said. She signalled the maid to bring in the pudding. "I do not want to have to arrange summer tutoring for you."

Alana looked downcast, just for a second. For once, we were in perfect agreement. Summers were for playing games, for trying to forget that there was such a place as school. Dad had even promised to take us to the country estate, if we passed all of our exams. A summer of horse-riding, swimming in the lake and hiking through the cool mountains sounded very good to me. Alana probably felt the same way too.

And no one wants to spend their summers cooped up in a classroom, reviewing the material again and again, I thought. I'd learned to dread summer tutoring before I'd gone to boarding school. The tutors my parents had hired had been good, masters of their craft, but they'd been working with very poor material. *We have to pass our exams.*

"Cat cannot pass her exams," Alana pointed out. "She can't cast a single spell without help."

"We'll take that into account," Dad promised. "And so will her tutors."

"But that won't count," Alana insisted. "How can she be a magician if she doesn't have magic?"

I felt my temper rise and forced it down, remorselessly. "I might not get a high grade in practical magic," I said. I probably couldn't, even though I did very well with *theoretical* magic. "But does it actually matter?"

"No one asks an apothecary for his charms grade," Bella added.

Alana blinked in surprise. I felt the same way too. It was rare, very rare, for Bella to challenge Alana. I could count the number of times it had happened on the fingers of one hand. Bella had magic, unlike me, but she couldn't hold a torch to Alana. Alana would have no trouble hexing her into next week, if push came to shove.

"That is true," Dad agreed. "A single low grade doesn't make you a failure."

"How true," Mum commented. "I saw *your* potions grade."

Dad smiled, rather dryly. I kept my thoughts to myself. Dad's potion grades had been average, but his charms and defence grades had gone through the roof. Alana had a great deal to live up to, if she wished to impress her defence tutors. Mum hadn't done badly in either charms or defence, but potions had been her first love.

And I can't defend myself without Objects of Power, I thought. *I'd better be very careful in the shower.*

I touched my sore ear as Dad launched into a long lecture on what one could and couldn't do with the various grades. It hadn't burnt *that* badly - and I'd rubbed salve on the burn as soon as I'd left the table - but it was clear the earrings would need to be improved. Great Aunt Stregheria had cursed me so hard that the earring had been damaged, perhaps completely burnt out. I didn't want to think about what might have happened if she'd tried to curse me again, before Dad had ordered her to leave.

They have to be touching my skin, I reminded myself. I could lower the gemstones and their protective filigree a little, I thought, but that might risk losing the effect. Perhaps I should just stick with the simplest design. They might not reflect any incoming spell back at the caster, but they would last longer. *I'll have to do some more experiments.*

Lucy put a cake in front of me. I gaped at it in surprise. Vanilla sponge cake - my favourite - crammed with whipped cream and raspberry jam. A birthday cake? It wasn't my birthday…and, in any case, I shared my birthday with my sisters. I had never *liked* my birthdays…

"It is customary to celebrate when a child shows the first sign of magic," my father said, into the silence. "And what you have shown definitely *counts* as magic."

Alana opened her mouth, probably to say something cutting, but Dad fixed her with a look that would have intimidated Sir Griffons. My sister shut her mouth with a *snap*. Beside her, Bella was eying the cake eagerly. It might not be her favourite, but she'd eat it anyway. I had often thought, I reflected as I picked up the knife, that Bella was lucky that she was only a *little* pudgy. She just didn't get enough exercise.

I cut a reasonably-sized slice, placed it on a plate and passed it to Dad. By tradition, the head of the house had to be offered the first slice. Dad made a show of inspecting it, then passed the plate to Mum. She smiled back at him as I cut the next set of slices. Alana took hers with a sharp nod, while Bella was eager to start eating. I could practically see her salivating as I cut the final two slices.

"You may take the remainder back to school with you," Mum said, as I moved the cake into the centre of the table. "I'm sure your friends will enjoy it."

My one friend, I thought. Unless I counted Akin too. But he might not trust something that had come out of our kitchens. *There isn't enough for the entire dorm.*

I sighed as I started to eat my slice. There were nine girls in the dorm, all of whom knew - now - that I couldn't cast a single spell. They no longer doubted, they no longer believed I was a late bloomer...they knew I didn't have magic. And yet, I had a talent of my own. Who knew how they'd treat me? Perhaps I should share out the cake, but there wasn't enough left to give all *nine* a reasonably-sized piece.

And, by tradition, I have to share anything eaten in the dorm, I reminded myself. Jude's traditions were set in stone. A student who abused the code of honour would be shunned and abhorred by everyone else. Thankfully, some of the traditions worked in my favour. *But I'd need more cake.*

"This is very good," Bella said, as she finished her slice. "Can I have some more?"

"I think not," Mum said, firmly. She eyed Bella, warningly. "I really *do* hope you pass your exams."

Because then we could spend hours in the mountains, walking from place to place, I thought, wryly. Mum would stand behind Bella with a whip, if she tried to be lazy over the summer holidays. *And Alana won't be happy either, if we don't get to go.*

"Your trunks have already been returned to the school," Dad said. I wasn't sure why he'd bothered to have them sent home in the first place. "Go to your rooms and change into your uniforms, then meet me in the entrance hall. And *do* try not to be late."

I rose and hurried out the room, trusting that Mum would ensure that the cake was wrapped up and placed in a protective box for the journey. Alana followed me, but did nothing as we hurried up the stairs and into our rooms. I frowned as I stepped into my room and closed the door behind me. She was definitely up to something. But what?

The uniform, freshly cleaned and pressed, lay on the bed where one of the maids had left it. I felt oddly wistful, even though I'd hated the uniform the first time I'd worn it. A black skirt, reaching all the way down to my ankles; black shoes, shining under the light; a black shirt, a black blazer...a single white band wrapped around my right arm, marking me out as a first-year student. Other than that, everything was black.

I still look like a professional mourner, I thought, as I changed into the uniform. It felt normal, after having worn it for several weeks. I no longer felt ridiculous as I posed in front of the mirror, making sure everything was perfect. *All I need is the funeral.*

Someone had folded a cloak at the end of the bed. I threw it over my shoulder - there was no point in wearing it unless it was raining outside - and then picked up my bag. I'd made more than *just* the sword over the last few days, including a handful of Objects of Power that should make life at school a little easier. It was a shame, I reflected, that there was no way to miniaturise the spectacles, although I had managed to create a monocle. But it kept falling out every second minute.

I sighed, then took one last look around the room. It had been bare, only a few short months ago. Now, it was as finely-decorated as Alana or Bella's room. My parents *had* promised me that I would have a fine room, as soon as I cast my first spell. I couldn't help thinking as though I'd failed in some way, even though my talents were far more useful than either of my sisters' magic. Alana could spend the rest of her life in front of a forge, if she wished. It wouldn't let her craft an Object of Power.

The clock chimed, warningly. I turned and walked out of the room, closing the door behind me. I didn't bother to lock it. There was nothing in the room I wanted to keep secret, if only because I'd long since learnt how dangerous it could be to hide anything in a room my sisters tried to search every so often. Besides, the maids would need to clean it while I was at school. I just hoped they wouldn't mess up the bookshelves when they returned my books to the shelf.

My father was standing at the bottom of the stairs, wearing his formal cloak and holding a box under one arm. Alana was standing next to him, looking sullen. I joined them and waited, in silence, until Mum and Bella walked down the stairs and nodded to Dad. Mum checked our appearances, gave us all one last hug goodbye, then watched as we walked out of the hall and down the driveway.

"It's dark," Bella whined.

I rolled my eyes. Beside me, Alana snorted rudely. Dark or not, only a complete lunatic would dare to attack my father. His formal robes alone marked him out as a high-ranking member of Magus Court, which meant he was a powerful magician. And my sisters might have been young, but they were formidable too. I'd been told the streets of South Shallot were dangerous, yet few footpads dared venture into North Shallot. The City Guard would chase them out, if they weren't transfigured into toads by outraged residents first.

The air smelt of fish and brine as it wafted in from the harbour, down in Water Shallot. It made me feel wistful as we walked down the darkened streets. I'd dreamed of travelling, once upon a time, although my *real* motive had been more to escape my family than to see new places. My family owned several trading ships, but the crews needed magic to steer. I had always assumed that I'd never be able to join a crew. Female sailors, with or without a certain level of magic, were rare.

I saw a gaggle of young men emerge from a tavern as we reached the bridge and crossed the river. They chatted loudly amongst themselves, their words drifting on the air. I thought they were sailors, for a moment, before realising that they were students. Upperclassmen, then; upperclassmen who'd somehow escaped Jude's wards and gone out for a night on the town. My father sniffed in disapproval, but said nothing. Sneaking out over the walls was an old tradition, one that had never been snuffed out. The iron railings on the walls - designed to make life difficult for any would-be escapees - presented the sort of challenge that the school board felt built character.

And Dad probably slipped out from time to time too, I thought. It was difficult to imagine my parents being *young*. The portraits of Dad as a youngster might as well have belonged to my brother…if I'd had a brother. I'd inherited more than just the nose from my father. *I wonder if he knew Mum when they were both in school.*

I pushed the thought aside - there were things I didn't want to think about my parents - as we reached Jude's. The iron gates loomed ominously over our heads, topped with wrought-iron features that looked - in the semi-darkness - to be monsters, perched on the metal. I tensed, despite myself. There were formidable defences all around the giant school. If they decided we were unfriendly, we were in real trouble…

A shadow materialised near the gatehouse. "Report to the Castellan in the…ah, Lord Aguirre? I didn't expect you so late."

"We meant to be earlier, Skullion," my father said. He sounded oddly amused. "Can you not report us to the Castellan?"

"Of course, My Lord," the man - Skullion - said. I'd heard of the scowling gatekeeper who only came out at night, but I'd never met him. "I'm sure you're not up to any of your old tricks."

Dad laughed as Skullion opened a smaller door in the gatehouse, allowing us to walk into the grounds and up the drive. I glanced at Skullion as we passed, recoiling in shock. His face was half-cloaked in shadow, but what little I could see was hideously ugly. He looked as though someone had cursed him repeatedly until his face was a misshapen mess. I couldn't imagine a more intimidating figure on the gates.

We walked up the driveway, feeling a mixture of fear and trepidation. Jude's looked like a prison in the darkness, the shadows changing position whenever we weren't looking. The main doors were firmly closed, but a smaller door was open, a dark figure waiting inside. I told myself, firmly, that we were in no danger. Jude's wasn't *really* a prison.

It just feels like one, I thought.

"Greetings, My Lord," Castellan Wealden said.

"Thank you," Dad said.

"Alana and Bella can go straight to their dorms," Castellan Wealden added. "I need a word with Caitlyn before she goes to bed."

Dad nodded. "Here's the cake," he said, passing me the box. "Good luck, all of you."

He turned and walked back into the darkness. I wanted to call out to him, to ask him to take me straight home…but that would have meant abandoning Rose. I couldn't do that, could I?

"You two are dismissed," the Castellan said, addressing my sisters. "Caitlyn, come with me."

I sighed. "Yes, sir."

CHAPTER EIGHT

Jude's hadn't changed at all, as far as I could tell.

I walked behind Castellan Wealden, trying to calm the butterflies in my stomach. I wasn't in trouble. At least, I didn't *think* I was in trouble. But the empty corridors and dimmed lights couldn't help but feel ominous. It wasn't *that* late. The lowerclassmen would probably be in their dorms, even if they weren't in bed, but the upperclassmen should still be roaming the corridors.

The Castellan led the way up a flight of stairs, down a long corridor lined with portraits of Old Boys and Girls who'd made good and into his office's antechamber. His secretary sat behind her desk, eying me with an expression that suggested she'd smelt something disgusting. I didn't think she was one of my fans. Rumour had it that she was actually a golem the Castellan had brought to life, but no one dared to ask. Personally, I couldn't help wondering if she was related to Great Aunt Stregheria.

Which would make her related to me, I thought, as we stepped through the inner door and into the Castellan's private office. *And I don't want to be related to her.*

"Please, take a seat," the Castellan said. His voice was calm, as always. He seemed to have aged ten years since I'd last seen him, although he was still quite young for his post. "I assume you ate before you came?"

"We had dinner together," I confirmed, as I placed my bag on the floor and took a chair. The question surprised me. None of the staff had invited me for dinner before - or any students, as far as I knew. They preferred to have as little contact with us as possible outside the classrooms. "I should be fine until breakfast."

The Castellan sat, steepling his fingers in front of his face as he rested his elbows on the desk. My father had taught me that that was a sign of confidence, although he'd gone on to warn me that some men - and women too - were careful to project confidence even when they felt utterly unsure of themselves. I rested my hands in my lap and gazed back, trying to look as respectful as possible. There was nothing to be gained from being defiant, particularly when I probably wasn't in trouble.

"Your...nature has caused us some problems," the Castellan said. He nodded to a stack of papers on his desk. "The school board has had quite a lot to say about it."

I nodded, wordlessly. My father had told me that the school board was largely useless - they woke up long enough to confirm the *status quo*, had a good meal on expenses and then went back to sleep - but they *would* want to have a say when an important pupil managed to get themselves into trouble. Dad would have roused them from their slumber if I'd been expelled, after the potions incident...he might have threatened to do just that, after *Rose* had been expelled. The Castellan would not have wanted to get into an argument with a united board. They could overrule him if they wished.

And the Triad probably had a say too, I thought. *But what did they say?*

"It is evident that you cannot handle a regular course of study," the Castellan added, after a moment. "You cannot even *hope* to get through the practical exams, certainly not without help. On the other hand, you have a rare gift of your own and it is our responsibility to ensure that you have the opportunity to develop it."

He paused, clearly awaiting a response. But I didn't know what to say. I wanted to stay and I wanted to go. I wanted...I wasn't sure *what* I wanted. To be told that I couldn't pass the exams, no matter how hard I worked... it stung. And yet, I knew it was true. If I wasn't allowed to take Objects of Power into the testing chambers, I wouldn't last more than five minutes.

"We will be creating a customised course of study for you over the next few weeks," the Castellan said, when it became apparent that I wasn't going to say anything. "You'll stay in some of your regular classes, I think, and engage in private study for others. We'll be rearranging the timetables so you'll have the undivided attention of some of my staff. It will be difficult, at first, but they're quite looking forward to working with you."

It was hard to keep from wincing. In one sense, I'd had special treatment all my life; in another, I hadn't had anything different from my peers. I might have had private tutors, but so had Isabella and the rest of High Society. Now...I would be getting *very* special treatment, treatment that would not be offered to other magicians. Would having magic - and the ability to hex me at will - keep them from getting jealous?

Probably not, I thought.

"Your new timetable will be ready by the end of the week, I hope," the Castellan informed me. "We held back on a couple of classes so you and your sisters could attend from the beginning. You'll understand why when the classes begin."

I swallowed. "Thank you, sir."

"It is my duty," the Castellan said, gravely. He smiled, then leaned forward. "And that leads to a less pleasant discussion."

He met my eyes. "You are unique," he said. "That makes you valuable, at least until we locate someone else with your particular gifts. You will discover that a great many people will want to be your friend."

I didn't believe him, not really. People wanted to be *Alana's* friend, not mine. I'd grown more and more isolated from the rest of my peers as my lack of actual magic became apparent. No one wanted to be friends with a failure, for fear the failure might rub off. Rose had been the first person to show me real friendship. And *she* didn't have anything to lose.

"I advise you to be careful," the Castellan said. His voice hardened. "And I *order* you not to leave the grounds without an escort. You are *not* to try to sneak over the walls and through the wards. I know trying to sneak out is an old tradition - I've done it myself - but you are *not* to indulge in it. Do you understand me?"

"Yes, sir," I said. I'd never *planned* to sneak over the walls. A young student wouldn't have much of a chance of getting through the wards, not without help. Being trapped would be bad enough, but having the rest of the school laughing at them would be worse. "I won't leave the school."

"Make sure of it," the Castellan said, firmly. "You are too young to understand the dangers, Caitlyn. But rest assured, there *are* dangers out there."

I winced. Jude's was neutral ground. Anyone who tried something on the school's grounds would become an immediate pariah, uniting the rest of Shallot against them. But outside the grounds…suddenly, all the horror stories about family feuds seemed very real. It had been a while since the last true conflict - Magus Court tried to keep them from getting out of control - but that could change at any time.

"I understand," I said. Perhaps that was why Dad hadn't ordered me to stay home. The school was safer. Even families that detested mine would assist us if our enemies violated neutral ground. "And…I thank you."

"You're welcome," the Castellan said. He nodded to the door. "You may go. I believe your friend is waiting for you."

I rose, curtseyed to him, picked up my bag and headed for the door. Outside, Rose was sitting on a bench. I ran forward and hugged her, tightly. Tears prickled in my eyes. I'd missed her, more than I'd known. She was the one person who'd been there for me when I'd been utterly alone.

"Cat," she said, as she hugged me back. "Welcome back."

The secretary cleared her throat. "Go back to the dorms," she ordered, curtly. "You can catch up later."

I took Rose's arm and pulled her out of the office. "I wanted to be back sooner," I said, as I closed the door. "I'm sorry I didn't make it."

"It's all right," Rose said. "We've been quite busy."

I looked at her as we made our way down the corridor. Rose looked more…confident than I remembered, her long red hair glimmering under the lantern light. Her pale skin showed hints of makeup, carefully applied…her white nightgown fitted her perfectly, drawing attention to her face and bright green eyes. I frowned, puzzled. Rose had never used cosmetics - she'd never been able to afford them. How could she? And she had her hair down…

"Everyone has been surprisingly nice," Rose said, breaking into my thoughts. "Well, except Isabella. *She's* been very sullen."

"It's good to know that some things don't change," I said. I'd let Isabella stay in the dorm, after the duel. Perhaps that had been a mistake. "The others have been nice to you?"

Rose's hand brushed her cheek. "Henrietta helped me with my homework," she said. "And Ayesha taught me how to use powder on my face."

I felt a hot flash of jealousy, mingled with concern. Ayesha was one of Isabella's friends - or had *been* one of Isabella's friends, before the duel. No one liked a loser, as I knew all too well...and Isabella hadn't just *lost*. Her defeat had had repercussions that had echoed far beyond the school. I would have felt pity for her, if she hadn't been so horrible to me. Her father would have been utterly furious when he found out.

"I hope you're being careful," I said. Rose had a right to other friends, didn't she? It was good that she was finally making headway with the rest of the dorm. And yet...part of me wanted to keep her all to myself. "What about the others?"

"They've been nice," Rose said. She frowned as we descended the stairs. "It's been quite creepy, actually."

I had to laugh. "Maybe someone kidnapped our dormmates and replaced them with identical twins."

Rose giggled. "That would explain a lot, I suppose."

She elbowed me. "Akin was asking after you," she added. "But I couldn't tell him anything useful."

"He could just have written to me," I said, although I didn't know if I'd get his letter. Dad would have had a few things to say, none of them pleasant, about receiving letters from our family's great rivals. "How is he?"

"Doing well, as far as I know," Rose said. She rubbed her hand, gently. "He helped me out a lot in forging. I still haven't got the hang of it."

"I've been doing it for years," I reminded her. Maybe I should have felt jealous at the thought of *Akin* spending time with Rose, but it didn't bother me...not really. He was a good TA. Magister Tallyman had taken us both on as his Teacher's Assistants. "You'll have a one-star of your own by the end of your second year."

Rose sighed. "If I last that long," she cautioned. "I'm still behind in theoretical magic."

"I'll help you with it," I promised.

I wondered, sourly, why one of our dormmates hadn't offered to help her learn *that*. Perhaps it was a worrying sign. A student who didn't have a good grasp of magical theory would never become an upperclassman.

Rose could turn someone into a frog - I'd taught her that spell, even though I couldn't cast it myself - but she couldn't *keep* her victim that way without setting up the spell very carefully. And to do *that* she needed a working understanding of precisely *what* she was doing.

They might be pretending to be nice to her, I thought, *but they're not actually* being *nice to her.*

"I'm doing better at potions, too," Rose added. "But my potions are still not perfect."

"You just need practice," I assured her. The basic potions we brewed in class were easy. I'd seen Mum sweating over a steaming cauldron where *everything* had to be utterly perfect or the potion would explode. "And complete precision at all times."

I sighed. Mum had drilled those habits into me from Day One. It had surprised me that Magistra Loanda hadn't been *quite* so obsessed with precision, although most of the basic potions were quite forgiving. She might think that a prospective potioneer would have the sense to read the recipe and instructions - and then prepare the ingredients - *before* they started brewing the potion. And someone who didn't would learn the hard way when they had to scramble to find something before it was too late.

"I try," Rose said. "I think it's the magic that really makes it hard."

"We'll see," I said. I had a whole series of experiments I meant to carry out as soon as possible. Rose would help, of course. Perhaps I could talk Akin into helping too. That would *really* drive his sister up the wall. "You're just starting out, again."

Rose shook her head in frustration. "I used to cook on the stove at home," she said. "I should be able to brew a potion."

"I think it's a little more complex," I countered. Henry might insist that his cooking was as complicated as any potion, but I had my doubts. Roast beef didn't care if you cooked it over the spit for eighty-nine minutes or ninety-one. "And you're infusing magic into the brew."

We reached the bottom of the stairs and walked down a long corridor. I tensed, despite myself, as I heard footsteps echoing from the far end. A moment later, a pair of upperclassmen walked into view, glaring at us both suspiciously. Rose fished a pass out of her pocket and held it up before they could say a word. They inspected the pass, their eyes flickering over us, then passed it back and walked on. I allowed myself a sigh of relief. We might have permission to be out of the dorm, yet the upperclassmen would have been within their rights to question us. Sneaking out of the dorms was a bad thing, but only if you got caught.

"That was close," Rose said. "I wasn't sure if the pass covered you or not."

I had to smile. The Castellan would not have been pleased if two meddling upperclassmen had dragged me back to his office. I had permission to be outside the dorm, at least for as long as it took to walk back. But he would also have had to back up the upperclassmen's authority...I wasn't sure precisely *how* he'd react. I suppose I should have been glad that I wasn't going to find out.

"I'm sure it does," I said, reassuringly. Sandy would have given Rose the pass, ensuring that she could meet me without being given lines or sent back to the dorm by a prowling upperclassman. But even that might not have been enough, if the upperclassman was in a bad mood. Rose had no family to protest if she was given a particularly harsh punishment. "How is Sandy, by the way?"

"She seems to have mellowed a little, now that Isabella and you have settled your differences," Rose said. "But I don't know if that will change."

I shrugged. I hadn't spent a night in the dorm since the duel. Who knew *how* Isabella would react? I stopped long enough to open my bag and remove a couple of items, slipping them into my pockets, then closed the bag and slung it back over my shoulder. The earrings alone would give me some protection, if Isabella decided to hex me on sight, but I knew I'd need more. It was clear that there were limits to what the earrings could do.

I'll have to experiment with that later too, I thought. Rose would have to help. She could make up for my lack of magic. *And perhaps I can even improve on the design.*

We passed another group of upperclassmen, escorted by a teacher I didn't recognise. They didn't look remotely happy, something that suggested they'd been caught out of school and marched back to face the music. The City Guard must have caught them, I reasoned as we stepped to one side and tried not to be noticed. Normally, the Castellan and his staff would turn a blind eye to students who actually made it over the wall. I guessed they'd gotten into a fight in one of the bars and wound up being arrested.

And they'd probably be happier staying in the cells, I thought. The Castellan would be furious. They'd dragged the school's name through the mud. *They'll be in real trouble.*

Rose snorted. "That one in the middle," she said. "He gave me lines for skipping down the corridor."

I snickered. I hadn't seen the one she meant - upperclassmen all looked the same to me - but I could believe it. Even the responsible ones - like Sandy - acted as though us firsties were so far beneath them we might as well be on the other side of the world. They certainly didn't remember when *they* were firsties. Five years was quite a long time for a teenager.

"And now he's in trouble," I said mischievously, as we reached the door. "I wonder what will happen to him."

"A million lines, at least," Rose said. "His hand will drop off."

I grinned. Sandy had sometimes threatened us with a million lines, but there was no reason to be excessive. A few hundred lines was more than enough to make my wrists ache.

"And here we are," I said. The door to Raven Dorm looked as forbidding as I remembered, a solid dark mass covered in protective runes. "Shall we go?"

Rose nodded. I braced myself, then pushed open the door.

CHAPTER NINE

"Welcome home," Sandy called. I felt my mouth drop open as my dormmates greeted me. I'd never been popular, even amongst those who disliked Isabella and her cronies. But now, *everyone* was coming at me, everyone was greeting me. I flinched back as Clarian Bolingbroke and Gayle Fitzwilliam hugged me, while Ayesha and Zeya McDonald shook my hand. It was hard, so hard, to believe that their greetings were sincere. Their hugs might be cover for a hex…

"It's good to see you again," Henrietta Maria said. She smiled at me, charmingly. "I've been looking forward to discussing magical theory with you."

Ayesha ran her hand over my hair. "What did you put in it? It feels wonderful and soft."

I pulled back. It had taken me years to convince my mother that I didn't *need* elaborate hairstyles. A ponytail or plaits were enough, I thought, even though I apparently needed a fancy braid for formal occasions. I'd never been comfortable with the maids doing my hair for me, either. I knew Lucy and the others wouldn't deliberately set out to hex me, but my sisters had left me wary of being touched.

"Just shampoo," I said. I'd never really cared *that* much for my hair, either. "It's nothing special."

"You have to let me braid it," Ayesha said. "I could do a much better job with hair like yours." She jabbed a finger at Rose. "*Her* hair became more manageable after I gave her some proper shampoo and taught her a handful of grooming charms."

And you let her leave the dorm without tying her hair into a ponytail, I thought, sourly. It *was* late - and we *were* in school - but it was the sort of mistake that would have attracted some very *astringent* criticism from the old biddies of High Society. *Or did you think no one would care about her?*

"You're more than welcome to join us for study," Amber Alidade said. "You can teach us how to forge and we'll help you with potions and defence."

I shrugged, feeling a little overwhelmed. Sandy was sitting on her bed, brushing her hair and watching us with an unreadable expression on her face. Behind her, I could see Isabella pretending to be asleep. She was just too tense to be *actually* sleeping. Someone had moved her bed so she was right next to Sandy. I doubted Isabella appreciated it. Being so close to the older girl ensured she wouldn't get away with anything.

"Perhaps you could join us tomorrow," Amber pressed. "We're going to be spending the evening watching netball…"

Sandy smiled, rather thinly. "I think Caitlyn will have to catch up with her classes," she said, her voice cutting through the babble. "There'll be time for netball later."

"There's *always* time for netball," Amber said. Her voice became sweet with malice. "Isn't there, Isabella?"

Isabella rolled over and *looked* at me. The cold hatred in her eyes was terrifying. I knew the school's honour code forbade her taking revenge, now she'd lost a formal duel, but it still worried me. I hadn't *just* humiliated her. I'd knocked her right to the bottom of the dorm hierarchy. Her cronies - her former cronies - were above her now, peering down at their former leader with all the scorn and contempt they'd once heaped on me.

She'll recover, I thought. Isabella was *still* Isabella Rubén, *still* one of the heirs to a powerful family. Memories would fade as time went on, giving her a chance to start again. *And then…what will she do?*

Sandy cleared her throat. "It is time you all went to bed," she said. She clapped her hands, loudly. "Shower, dress, bed, sleep. I'll be dimming the lights in fifteen minutes."

I shot her a grateful look as I hurried to my bed. I had no sensitivity to magic at all, but I could *feel* Isabella's cold gaze watching me. If looks could kill - and there were spells for that - I'd be disintegrated into ash. Rose followed me, her footsteps echoing through the room. Someone had moved her bed too, putting it next to mine. With a little work, we could combine our curtains and share a bigger space.

"She's been *very* sullen," Rose whispered.

I put my bag down on the floor, then hastily checked the drapes for unwanted surprises before I pulled them closed. There were none, not even a single solitary hex. I frowned, concerned that I was missing something. Isabella might be barred from hexing me - although I was starting to think she didn't intend to abide by the honour code - but someone else might have decided to conceal a hex on my bed. It was the traditional way to welcome someone back to the dorm.

"I can tell," I whispered back.

I slipped one pair of spectacles from my pockets and perched them on my nose. The world changed colour at once, waves of light pulsing through the stone walls; blurs of light shimmering over the other beds. My dormmates had protected themselves thoroughly, Isabella most of all. My lips twitched. I had the sneaking feeling that even *she* would have to take several minutes to dismantle her protections before going to the toilet in the middle of the night. Sandy would probably have some problems getting Isabella up in the morning if she overslept.

But my bed was dark and cold. There were no spells; no hexes to zap me into a frog if I touched them with my bare skin, no charms to keep my dormmates from disturbing me with their snores. Even *Rose* had more protections on her drapes than I did. I felt oddly sure I was missing something, but there was nothing. My earrings didn't even get warm as I sat on the comfortable bed. Someone had taken the time to make up the bed and hide a pair of pyjamas under the pillow - and place my trunk at the end of the bed - but not to prepare an unpleasant surprise for me. I couldn't help feeling uneasy as I stood and pulled the drapes into position. Perhaps I *was* missing something.

"They were all pleased to see you," Rose said, after casting a basic privacy spell. I'd taught her to use it at all times. It was very basic, but the kind of spells necessary to break through it were banned in the dorms. "Are you...are you going to spend time with them?"

It struck me, suddenly, that *she* was just as uncertain - perhaps even jealous - as myself. We'd been the dorm outcasts, the powerless girl of noble blood and common-born magician who'd been raised in the countryside, herding pigs instead of learning magic. But now...now I could find friends from my own caste, if I wished them. I'd wondered if Rose would abandon me, now she'd found other friends, but she must have felt the same thing too.

"No," I said. Netball was boring, at least partly because I couldn't play. I could run and throw the ball with the best of them, but the spells? I'd be hexed out of the game within seconds. "I don't want to spend time with them."

I hesitated. "Did Ayesha say anything about wearing your hair down?"

Rose frowned. "No," she said. "Why...?"

"You're not *meant* to wear your hair down until you're old enough to marry," I said. It *was* late at night, and no one was expected to have their hair braided in bed, but someone would probably have said *something* if they'd noticed Rose outside the dorm. "When you go outside, make sure you tie it up into a ponytail at the very least."

Rose's cheeks reddened. "Thank you," she said. She touched her hair. "Did she...did she do that on purpose?"

I shrugged. I doubted Rose's family cared much for High Society's rules. They didn't have the time to learn them, let alone the money to spend on proper clothes, etiquette lessons and everything else a youngster needed if they wanted to be seen as a respectable member of society. It was possible that Ayesha had set Rose up for some embarrassment, but equally possible that she simply hadn't considered it important. Or noticed that Rose was leaving the dorm.

"I don't know," I said. I emptied my bag onto the bed, then picked up a focusing tool. It was a long wooden wand, decorated with carved runes. I'd thought it would be simple, when I'd decided on the gift, but it had been surprisingly tricky to make. "This is for you."

Rose took the wand and waved it in the air. Sparks flew from the tip, dancing around her fingertips. I watched, feeling an odd mixture of delight and envy. My gift made me practically unique - and my training would give me an edge, if I ever met another Zero - but I still didn't have magic. Rose would always have opportunities that I'd lack. But then, the reverse was also true.

"It's wonderful," she breathed.

"It's designed to help you modulate your magic," I told her. "With a little fiddling, you can use it to make sure you only use *precisely* what you need."

Rose smiled. "Thank you." Her face fell. "I didn't get you anything…"

"Don't worry about it," I said. "I…"

She gave me a hug, then settled back to watch as I opened my drawer. A punishment book - a new punishment book - sat there, waiting for me. I rolled my eyes as I picked it up, making sure that it *was* my name on the front cover. Someone had probably feared I'd leave the old book at home, out of sight and out of mind. They needn't have worried. Dad had made sure I'd packed it, along with the spellbook and a number of other textbooks. I put it on top of my clothes, then opened my trunk and started to cram my possessions into the drawer. They didn't seem to fit.

"If you have two punishment books," Rose asked, "which one is the *real* one?"

"Good question," I said. There was a complex linking charm binding *my* book to a master record, but I wasn't sure which one was the *real* one. Perhaps the punishments would appear in both books. Or perhaps the charm would get confused, rendering both books invalid. I'd have to experiment to find out. "If I stick my tongue out at Sandy, do you think she'd give me a hundred lines?"

"I don't know," Rose said. "She's been acting weird lately."

"*Everyone* has been acting weird since I returned," I muttered. I put the cake box aside - I'd share it later, outside the dorm - and then reached for my towel. "What's got into them?"

The weirdness only grew stronger as we walked to the shower. I'd expected a hex or two aimed at me - I'd kept the earrings on, just to be sure - but nothing happened. Instead, my dormmates smiled and waved as though we were the best of friends. I was almost grateful for Isabella's scowls and glares. At least *that* was reassuringly normal.

Maybe they're just glad Isabella got knocked down a peg or two, I thought. The showers didn't look to have changed much, if at all. The only real difference was the addition of a number of bottles of expensive shampoo. *Or maybe they're just trying to lure me into a false sense of security.*

I washed, changed into my pyjamas and walked back to the bed. Sandy was already dimming the lights, marching up and down the room and glaring at everyone who wasn't moving fast enough to suit her. Most of the students were pulling their drapes closed, trying to pretend to be asleep. I doubted Sandy was fooled, but she wouldn't say anything as long as they weren't blatantly defying her. A student who didn't get enough sleep would regret it the following day.

"Cat," Sandy said. She nodded to Rose, silently ordering her to her bed. Rose complied without argument. "A word with you, if you please."

I *didn't* please, but I didn't have a choice. Sandy led me to the front of the dorm, past a set of closed drapes. I hoped that Isabella was already asleep, instead of plotting revenge. The Objects of Power would give me some protection, but I was grimly aware that they didn't make me invincible. I'd grown up on too many stories of weapons that were supposed to do just that, but turned out to be flawed in some way.

"I had a long talk with Isabella, after the duel," Sandy said, once we were standing by her bed. She didn't bother to cast a ward to keep our conversation private. "I told her that I expected her to behave herself - and that I would take steps if she didn't."

I swallowed. Sandy hadn't intervened between Isabella and myself until matters had *really* started to get out of hand. On one hand, she wanted a quiet life; on the other, we were *both* from powerful families and alienating us - even just one of us - might have been bad for her future. And yet...I couldn't help wondering if I would have discovered the truth, if Sandy had squashed Isabella on the first day. I might not have. And if I hadn't, I would merely have been condemned to endlessly repeating the first year again and again, unable to pass the exams that would let me move into the second year.

"I expect the same from you," Sandy added, after a moment. "You won - well done. Now you and she can move on, without this petty little feud. I will *not* be pleased if you rub her nose in her defeat, nor will I be happy if she finds a new way to get at you. Do *not* defy me on this."

"She started it," I said. I knew it was childish, but I couldn't help myself. "I didn't want a rival…"

"I'm sure she's pleased to hear it," Sandy said, sardonically. Having a rival to match yourself against was another school tradition, but it generally only applied to upperclassmen. Besides, I'd always thought it was stupid. Why would *I* waste time challenging a rival? "And I'm sure you're pleased to hear that she doesn't want a rival either."

"Oh, *goody*," I said.

Sandy gave me a sharp look. "I don't care which one of you started it," she said. Her tone dared me to disagree. "And I don't care that your families have been feuding for the last umpteen billion years or whatever. You'll learn to tolerate each other, or I'll chain you together and put you to work scrubbing the floor."

"A fate worse than death," I said.

"How amusing," Sandy said, archly. Her lips curved into a humourless smile. "Isabella said the very same thing."

I smiled back, although it wasn't particularly funny. Rose and I had been forced to scrub floors after the potions incident, a task I'd rapidly come to detest. Doing it with Isabella would be far - far - worse. We'd keep exchanging barbs and insults until one of us snapped and tried to hurt the other. And then we'd both get in trouble for not cleaning the floor. I wasn't sure what was *worse* than being chained to my worst enemy and forced to cooperate, but I didn't want to find out.

"Now, go to bed and sleep," Sandy ordered. "I'll see you in the morning."

I started to turn, then stopped myself. "Sandy…why is everyone acting so *weird*?"

Sandy gave me a look that suggested she thought I was being stupid. "They're trying to get on your good side," she said, in a tone that *confirmed* she thought I was being stupid. "And they're trying to do it by buttering you up."

She jabbed a finger at my bed. "Sleep."

I walked back to my bed, my head spinning. They were trying to get on my *good* side? I'd never had *that* before, not after it was clear I didn't have much magic. Everyone had expected *Alana* to inherit the family name, title and wealth. They still did, I suspected. I might have a talent of my own, but I still lacked magic. And yet…I couldn't help feeling uneasy as I pulled the drapes closed. I'd grown used to people treating me as though I didn't exist. Now…

It might be fun, part of me thought. *What would Alana say if you had more friends and clients than her?*

It might be dangerous, another part countered.

I lay down on the bed and looked up at the ceiling. I'd never really wanted to be popular…no, that wasn't true. I *had* wanted to be popular, but I'd never *been* popular. And I wasn't sure how to handle it. Part of me was tempted to push it, to build a circle of friends that would support me; part of me figured that it was a very bad idea. I might be unique - now - but that wouldn't last. There would be other Zeroes.

And being popular didn't work out so well for Isabella, my thoughts pointed out. My blood ran cold as the thought sank in. *All her friends deserted her when she lost the duel.*

I could hear a faint sound, rising and falling in the night air. Rose was snoring…she'd forgotten to put up her wards. I felt a sudden rush of affection, driven with an awareness that Rose was a true friend. She'd seen me at my worst - and I'd nearly killed her - and she *still* put up with me. And I wouldn't have blamed her for leaving…

Goodnight, I thought. I yawned and closed my eyes as sleep beckoned. *I'll see you in the morning.*

CHAPTER
TEN

The weirdness only grew stronger the following morning. Rose and I got out of bed early, dressed in our uniforms and headed down to breakfast. No one paid much attention to Rose - she was just a common-born firstie - but me? People were staring, even upperclassmen who normally wouldn't have admitted to noticing me unless I was doing something they could punish. Girls and boys who were on the very edge of adulthood - old enough to live on their own, old enough to marry, old enough to walk away from their families if they wished - were watching me. It was...*creepy*.

None of them spoke to me, of course. *That* would have surprised me even more. An upperclassman wouldn't talk to a lowerclassman, not socially. If I'd had older siblings, they wouldn't have talked to me either, not in public. There were lines between the class years that couldn't be crossed on pain of the most sarcastic remarks from one's peers. But even paying *attention* to me was odd. It worried me more than I cared to admit.

We picked up our food, then sat down at a table to eat. The upperclassmen kept looking at us - at *me* - even as we ate, their gazes following me as I lifted the spoon to my mouth. I felt uneasy as I ate my porridge, feeling as though I was being confronted by a whole army of elderly relatives who wanted to criticise my table manners. I had never known that a young girl eating a bowl of porridge could be so fascinating.

Beside me, Rose ate with gusto and went back for a second helping. I didn't really blame her, even though the porridge tasted rather bland. She'd grown up in a place where the food was worse and second helpings were rare. A bad winter might make the difference between seeing another year and starving to death. I wondered just how many upperclassmen were silently criticising her table manners. Rose wasn't rude enough to chew with her mouth open, unlike some boys I could name, but it was clear she hadn't been given any formal instruction on how to eat in polite society.

Something we will have to consider, later, I thought. *Perhaps I can talk Bella into giving her lessons.*

The thought made me scowl. I hated etiquette, but Rose would have to learn if she wanted to pass as a well-born magician. People wouldn't question her birth if she wore fine clothes and spoke like an aristocrat, not unless they wanted to marry her. I had to smile at the thought, even though I knew it would horrify Alana and her peers. Rose was talented enough - as a magician - to be a very worthy prize for a lesser house. They'd overlook her birth if she did nothing to bring it to their attention.

I finished my bowl and sat back, watching as the dining room continued to fill. Jude's had students from all over the country, a mingling of people of different colours and creeds, united only by magic. A handful of students had even come from *outside* the country, including a pair of slant-eyed girls from Hangchow. I studied them with interest, trying not to make it obvious. Hangchow was on the other side of the world, their magical learning different enough from others to make sharing information potentially lucrative. It wasn't easy to get there and back, not in less than six months. I couldn't help wondering why the students had come to Jude's.

Probably to get an education, I thought, dryly. It wouldn't have been an easy trip. My father owned a handful of trading ships and held shares in several more, but the risk of losing a vessel - and the investment - was terrifyingly high. *And then go home to teach other students.*

Beside me, Rose stared at them in fascination. Tintagel, thanks to the Thousand-Year Empire, has always been a pretty mixed society as far as the races are concerned, but the Hangchowese still stood out. Their nation had never been a *part* of the Thousand-Year Empire: they don't speak the language, they don't share the heritage, they don't even share our faith in our ancestors. And yet, they had come to live and study in Shallot. They couldn't be *that* different.

I looked up as Magistra Haydon strode up to us. "Your timetable for the next two weeks," she said, holding out a sheet of paper. "I'll be seeing you this afternoon."

"Thank you," I said.

I scanned the timetable as the Magical Growth tutor walked away. It wasn't as bad as I'd feared. I'd still be sharing most of my classes with the rest of the year, although I'd be engaging in private study while they were practising magic. I was surprised I'd been included in defence classes at all...I could defend myself with an Object of Power, but I would be helpless without them. And there was a whole new class: Questioning Assumptions. I had no idea what *that* was...

"We haven't had it yet," Rose said, when I asked. "It'll be my first time too."

The bell rang, warning us that classes started in fifteen minutes. I glanced around the room, spotting Alana with her cronies and Bella reading a book. There was no sign of Isabella...I hadn't seen her at all, not since we'd gone to sleep. I wondered, absently, if she'd bothered to get up. Sandy wouldn't be pleased, but Isabella probably wouldn't care. I shrugged and led the way out of the hall. We had potions first thing, and Magistra Loanda would be furious if we were late. Her sharp tongue had been one of the first things we'd learnt to dread.

Rose nudged me as we picked our way through the maze of corridors. "Did you become a princess while you were away?"

"I don't *think* so," I said. I had to smile. King Rufus had three daughters, seven nieces and a number of other girls who were in the line of succession and technically had the right to be called *princess*. But I was unique. "They're just...being stupid."

Jude's maze of corridors, passageways and stairs never changed, I've been assured. But I didn't really believe it. The school had expanded outwards from the first building, swallowing up a multitude of others in its path. I couldn't help thinking, as we made our way down a flight of stairs that had clearly been designed for a smaller building, that warding the immense school had to be incredibly difficult. Jude's had just kept expanding to the point where it was threatening to knock down the outer walls. Finding one's way around was a chore. I'd studied maps, back in my first week, and I still wasn't sure I could confidently find my way from one side of the building to the other without getting lost somewhere along the way.

A handful of students were already waiting outside the potions classroom, reading books or mumbling prayers as they checked their homework for errors. They looked too busy to notice us, but when we joined the line they started to stare too. I braced myself - I wasn't sure for *what* - as they jostled forward. There was no social stigma in one firstie talking to another.

Magistra Loanda appeared, sweeping past us and opening the door. "Take your seats," she ordered, as she walked into her classroom. "Caitlyn, take the seat in the far corner."

I frowned as we followed her into the room. Magistra Loanda had given me a worktable of my own, instead of the table I normally shared with Rose. It wasn't any larger, but just having more space to myself would be wonderful. I'd grown too used to working on *my* giant workbench at home. An iron cauldron sat on top of a stove, a stove that reminded me of an oil-burning lantern I'd seen once. There had been no magic in it, my tutor had said, when he'd shown me the artefact. It had dated all the way back to the long-lost days before the Thousand-Year Empire. I'd never seen anything like it until now.

Rose took the table nearest to me, looking nervous. I didn't blame her. She would have been forced to work with someone else while I'd been away, someone who might not have worked so well with her. Magistra Loanda took a dim view of pranks played in her classroom, but she couldn't do anything about more subtle trouble. Rose was learning, yet no one could learn fast enough to match some of our classmates.

I reached into my pocket and recovered the stirrers. Two of them had been charged yesterday, with help from Mum and Dad; two of them didn't *need* to be charged, if the ancient texts were correct. They'd been harder to make too, I had to admit as I placed them by the cauldron. I'd wanted to make ten, but eight of the finicky little devices hadn't survived the forging process. I hadn't been able to figure out a way to lessen the strain on the wood.

Yet, I told myself.

Magistra Loanda clicked her fingers, a moment after Isabella and Rupert - the latter sitting down next to Rose - entered the room. The door shut with a loud *BANG*.

"We will be brewing something more complex today," she informed us, as she strode back to the front of the class and nodded to the blackboard. A complicated recipe appeared on the board. "How many of you can tell me what sort of potion *this* is?"

I studied the recipe for a long moment. A base composed of common herbs, the ones that could be found in almost any garden, but active ingredients that included snake eyes and fish scales? A healing potion was the most obvious answer, yet…two of the ingredients would make the drinker be sick almost at once, while a third would…unless the different ingredients balanced each other. And that meant…?

Isabella stuck up her hand. "A precautionary potion, Magistra."

"Correct," Magistra Loanda said. She shot Isabella an approving smile. "Druid's Draught, to be precise. And what - if I may ask - does it *do*?"

"It strengthens the body against viruses and poisons," Isabella told her. "And it forces an immediate reaction if someone *is* infected."

"Very good," Magistra Loanda said. She leaned back, addressing the entire class. "Druid's Draught is useless, I should add, if the victim has already been infected - or poisoned. It is generally only taken when explorers head into the wildlands to the south, where all sorts of deadly diseases can be found. Some people *have* reported effects when the potion is given, in desperation, to someone who has clearly been infected, but they have been minimal."

She paused. "So why are we learning to brew it?"

Bella waved her hand in the air. "Because it teaches us skills we need to learn?"

Magistra Loanda raised her eyebrows. "Correct," she said. "Druid's Draught is odd because it is unforgiving, yet doesn't have a habit of exploding when the ingredients are mixed up or not properly treated. But don't get complacent! Anyone caught being careless will regret it."

Her eyes swept the classroom. "You have ninety minutes. Begin."

I read and reread the ingredients, making sure I had them memorised before I went to the supply cupboard. Magistra Loanda would not be happy if I had to run back while I was trying to brew the potion, no matter how minimal the danger. Rose joined me a moment later as we went to gather our supplies, joining the throng jostling for space inside the giant cupboard. I made a face as I saw the cockroaches in their cage - they weren't poisonous, but the ones raised for the apothecaries gave nasty bites - and breathed a sigh of relief that we wouldn't be killing and dissecting them for ingredients today. They weren't the worst creatures we had to harvest, but they were certainly the least pleasant.

Rose nudged me. "Will you be alright?"

Isabella overheard. "Will you be alright? Will you be alright?"

I felt my cheeks grow warm. "Yes, thank you," I said, as politely as I could. Isabella would know I was mocking her, but...so what? "I'm sure I will be fine."

We carried the ingredients back to the table, then divided them out. It was important to have everything ready, right from the start. I weighed the seeds, checked the herbs for any unexpected surprises and then finally lit the stove with the firelighter. A firelighter without magic was rare too, as far as I knew. I couldn't help wondering where it had come from.

Magistra Loanda watched us like a hawk as we prepared the base liquid, snapping out instructions, corrections and detentions whenever one of us made a mistake. She was a harsh woman - it was something of a tradition among potioneers - but my mother wasn't much better, when she was trying to teach us the basics. I didn't really blame her. A single explosion could do a great deal of harm, despite the wards protecting the classroom. I didn't want to think about a cauldron of boiling water being blasted in all directions.

I picked up the first stirrer as the liquid started to bubble and, bracing myself, lowered it into the cauldron. The stirrer grew warm in my hand, an instant before a faint light blazed through the boiling liquid. I pulled the stirrer back and watched, my eyes going wide with relief, as the base liquid shimmered into existence. It was perfect.

"Very well done, Caitlyn," Magistra Loanda said.

"Cheat," Isabella muttered.

Her voice was just loud enough to be heard. The room went quiet, very quiet. I had a sudden flashback to the moment I'd insulted Great Aunt Stregheria, the moment when she'd attempted to curse me...

"Stay behind after class," Magistra Loanda ordered. Her voice was very cold. "And if your potion isn't perfect, you'll be redoing it until you get it right."

I tore my attention away from the scene and started to prepare the second half of the potion, carefully dropping the active ingredients into the liquid one by one. The shimmer grew stronger as the potion started its transformation, but it was hard to be *sure* it was perfect. I wished - not for the first time - that I could sense magic. The spectacles could help me to *see* magic, but not sense it. I couldn't manipulate it as effectively as any of my peers.

Bracing myself, I picked up the second stirrer and dropped the final ingredient into the cauldron. The liquid turned green and started to bubble. I lowered the stirrer into the liquid and stirred, carefully counting each clockwise and anticlockwise stir. A normal magician could *feel* when she'd infused enough magic into the brew, but *I* couldn't do that. I'd just have to hope my calculations were correct.

There was another shimmer and the potion started to turn into a sickly yellow colour. I took a breath and regretted it, instantly. The stench was awful. That wasn't uncommon for healing potions, I knew from bitter experience, but this one was particularly bad. I wasn't sure I could have forced myself to drink it, even if I *needed* it. The explorers in the wildlands - which had been left devastated after the Sorcerous Wars - were definitely brave men.

Or they have no sense of taste or smell, I thought, wryly. *Perhaps they numbed it deliberately so they could drink the potion.*

"Good work," Magistra Loanda said. "That would be suitable for the healers, I think."

I jumped. I hadn't noticed her standing there. She moved so silently I hadn't heard her approaching.

"Thank you," I stammered. "Is it drinkable?"

"It should be drinkable as long as the drinker holds their nose," Magistra Loanda said. She picked up the used stirrer and examined it, thoughtfully. "I look forward to considering other uses for these."

I swallowed, suddenly unsure what to say. I'd dreamed of the day I'd be useful, the day people would listen to me…and now it was here, I wasn't sure what to do with it. Magistra Loanda wanted to play with something only I could provide. I was unique and yet…I wasn't sure what I wanted. But I had the rest of my life to figure it out.

"I can make more," I said. "But it will take time."

"We have time," Magistra Loanda said. "There are some potions that you might be able to brew using them - or *not*, without them."

"My mother said the same thing," I said.

"I'll discuss it with her," Magistra Loanda said. She glanced at Rose's potion, which was rapidly shading from yellow to purple. "A little too much magic, I think. The cascade reaction is out of control."

She walked the room. Isabella had managed her potion perfectly - I admit I was a little annoyed about *that* - but most of the others had failed to brew the potion successfully. I watched and listened as Magistra Loanda pointed out what had gone wrong each time, then explain how to avoid it. Most of them hadn't been precise enough when measuring out the ingredients.

"I need to practice," Rose said. "How do I do that?"

"Carefully," I said. I could tell her the theory, but actually doing it…? Bella wanted me to help with her homework. I could get her to teach Rose in exchange. "We'll review the theory in the library."

"Isabella, remain behind," Magistra Loanda said, as the bell rang. "The rest of you can go."

"Let's go," I said, rising. "We can get something to eat before the next class."

"Coming," Rose said. She nudged me as we headed for the door. "You're looking forward to forging, aren't you?"

I nodded. "Oh, yes."

CHAPTER ELEVEN

Forging wasn't *just* my favourite class, I admitted to myself as we made our way down to the giant workroom. It was the only one I'd ever been any good at before discovering how my talents actually worked. I'd *earned* the two-star ranking I held. My sisters had leant the basics, of course, but neither of them had actually *worked* at it. The only first-year student I knew who'd earned a similar ranking was Akin.

He was standing by the door when we approached, surrounded by a gaggle of hangers-on. It was hard to believe he was related to Isabella, even though they looked very similar. They had the same blond hair, the same blue eyes, the same pale skin…but their personalities were very different. He'd been friendly to me, although we were technically competitors. I liked him more than my parents would have found comfortable.

"Cat," he said, stepping away from his cronies. Like Isabella, he'd acquired a circle of friends and allies. "How have you been?"

"Well enough," I said. I'd enjoyed working with him, but I wasn't going to say too much in front of listening ears. "It's good to be back."

"It's good to have you back," Akin said. He sounded sincere. "I've been very busy."

I had to smile. We were both TAs, charged with assisting our fellow students *and* teachers, but Akin had been on his own for the last week. I doubted he'd had any time to forge for himself, not when his workload had doubled. I had no idea what that would mean for his final scores, when the exams were held, but I wouldn't have blamed him if he felt overworked. Teaching requires a kind of patience that neither of us really possessed.

The door opened before I could think of a response. Magister Tallyman stood there, looking amused. He still wore a workman's outfit, rather than teaching robes, but I couldn't help noticing that *this* one was new. And yet, it already had a large and growing collection of burn marks, patches and stains that no amount of magic could remove. His face seemed to have acquired a couple of new scars too, although it was hard to be sure. A lifetime in forgery had left him with little of his original face and hands left. I couldn't help wondering, as we trooped into the classroom, if I would end up like him. My hands were already scarred in places. How much of my face would still be *mine* when I turned thirty?

I pushed the thought aside as we took our places at the workbenches and surveyed the giant workroom. Magister Tallyman had been busy. Large bags of gemstones, pieces of wood and chunks of metal had been placed against the far wall, waiting for us to sort them into bins for later use; a dozen new tools had been positioned around the room, including two I'd never seen before. I figured they were devices Magister Tallyman had made himself. If they were in common use, Dad would have bought them for our workrooms at home.

"Welcome back," Magister Tallyman said, softly. He raised his voice as the doors slammed closed. "How many of you have yet to complete last week's project?"

Nearly everyone - Akin and a couple of the other boys were the only exception - put up their hands. I hesitated, unsure if I should raise mine too. I hadn't even *started* the project. I didn't even know what it *was*. But at least I had a good excuse for not doing anything...

"Those of you who haven't finished should be able to complete it over the next couple of days," Magister Tallyman said. His voice boomed around the room as he jabbed a finger at yet another workbench. "Those of you who *have* finished can join me over here."

I nudged Rose as Akin hurried to the workbench. "What are you doing?"

"It's supposed to be a focusing device," Rose said. One hand dropped to the wand at her waist. "But it isn't working very well."

"Ouch," I said. I knew several designs for focusing devices. I'd made them myself. But I had no idea which design Magister Tallyman wanted them to follow. "Do you have the plans?"

"In my locker," Rose said. She stood. "I'll just go fetch them."

She hurried off, leaving me feeling at a loose end. I didn't *think* Magister Tallyman would want me to work on a simple focusing device, not when I had a two-star. Did he want me to assist the other students? Perhaps...but he'd dragged Akin over to the workbench instead of putting him to work. Magister Tallyman wouldn't want the TAs to be *too* helpful. First-year was all about developing the skills magicians needed to build more complex devices in later years.

Rose returned, carrying a large wooden box. She put it down on the workbench, allowing me to see a cat's cradle of string, metal wire and wood. I recognised it instantly, even though I hadn't seen the plans. The focusing device was perhaps the crudest known to exist, and one of the least forgiving, but it did have the advantage of being relatively easy - and educational - to make. And it was easier to repair, too. There was no way one could say *that* for an Object of Power.

"It's not channelling magic properly," Rose told me, as she placed it on the table. "It keeps coming apart."

I studied the connections for a long moment. "You're not putting them in place carefully enough," I said. "The stress is causing the wire to pop out of the wood."

"I see," Rose said. She sounded doubtful. "But if I put in too much pressure, I break the wire."

"Practice," I said. I made a mental note to source some pieces of scrap wood and wire for her to practice *on*. Magister Tallyman wouldn't complain if I salvaged them from the waste bin, provided I made sure to cleanse them of magic before I took them out of the room. Akin could help me do that, if he wanted. "Right now, concentrate on getting the first ones into place before you do the others."

Rose nodded and went to work. I watched her, torn between admiration and envy. She'd learnt her lessons well, even though her touch wasn't sure. I offered a few words of advice as she broke down some of her earlier pieces of work and refitted them, but otherwise let her get on with it. I wanted to be doing something for myself. And yet, Magister Tallyman was still talking to Akin and the others. I didn't know what to do!

"It hasn't connected properly," Rose said. "Why?"

I peered down at the wire. "You've blunted the nub," I said. Whoever had threaded the metal hadn't done a very good job. It was starting to come apart. "Strip that whole piece out and start again."

Rose looked pained, but did as she was told. I watched, sympathetically. I didn't really blame her for being annoyed - the project was finicky - but there was no choice. She had been strikingly lucky. If she'd left the mistake unfixed, the device would have come apart when she tried to use it. Or exploded in her hand. And it would take weeks for anyone to get used to a new hand.

Magister Tallyman strode over to our table. "Caitlyn," he said. "Come with me."

I followed him into a makeshift office. It looked as though someone had built a small shack in the workroom, perching it against the stone wall. Inside, there was a workbench, a pair of stools and rickety-looking supply cabinets and a single lantern, casting an eerie light over the scene. The scent of carved wood was suddenly much stronger. Magister Tallyman must have put the private workroom together in a hurry. I hoped that meant it was safe. The walls looked as if one cough would blow them down.

"I hear you made a sword," he boomed. I knew what he meant. Anyone could make a sword if they put in the time and effort to learn how to forge, but only one particular sword would interest *him*. "Congratulations!"

"Thank you, sir," I said. I'd heard that Sir Griffons had told everyone. If anyone had doubted my talents, when they'd first heard the stories, they didn't any longer. "It was a very complex piece of work."

"So I hear," Magister Tallyman said. "You couldn't even include a maker's mark!"

I nodded, ruefully. Forgers were meant to include a mark on their work, just to claim it as *theirs*, but I hadn't been able to attach mine to the sword. It would have disrupted the spellform, according to my calculations. I'd carved a mark into the scabbard - the scabbard wasn't particularly magical - but it wasn't quite the same. And yet, the ancients had had *some* way to do it. The Family Sword had been marked by a long-forgotten maker. We knew nothing about him, not even his name.

"I had to leave it off," I said, finally. "And the sword worked."

"Yes, it certainly did," Magister Tallyman said. He reached into his apron and produced a set of plans. "Do you think you could make *this*?"

I took the paper and examined it, carefully. It was odd, both more and less complex than the sword. I'd need a number of potions as well as an ample supply of metal and at least seven gemstones. I would have taken it for a Device of Power if the notation at the bottom hadn't made it clear that no one had managed to modify the original design to the point where a forger could make it work.

"I'm not sure," I said. I'd have to break it down into a series of manageable chunks, then try to do them one by one. The entire project would have to be carefully planned. "What does it do?"

"It's a flying machine," Magister Tallyman said. "Or, at least, it is the *core* of a flying machine. Or so we have been told."

I frowned. "Sir...do you want me to forge something without knowing what it does?"

Magister Tallyman looked irked. "Yes."

I tried to keep the doubt off my face. Dad had warned us, time and time again, that we should *never* cast a spell without knowing what it did. There were thousands of horror stories of young magicians who'd accidentally killed or wounded someone because they'd cast the spell without taking it apart first. Even *Alana* hadn't dared to cross him on *that*. And I... it hadn't mattered, I supposed. I could recite a spell until my face turned blue and nothing would happen.

And yet...a *flying* machine?

The Thousand-Year Empire had been a place of wonders. All the stories agreed that the Eternal City had mastered the secret of flight, as well as many others. There had been flying machines exploring the globe, cloud-castles floating in the air, ships prowling the oceans, going where they willed without paying heed to wind or rain...I knew there were sailors who would have killed for *that* secret. Dad's clipper ships looked good, but they were terrifyingly flimsy when a gale blew up out of nowhere. A ship that could go *anywhere* would change the world.

"I'd have to work out the spellform," I said. The spellform - perhaps more than one - would be far more complex than the sword. "And then we'll have to see if I could put it together."

"Of course," Magister Tallyman said. "I'm not expecting you to do it in the remaining" - he made a show of checking the clock - "fifty minutes."

I nodded, smiling. "When *do* you want me to do it?"

"I don't think there's much point in keeping you in the basic class," Magister Tallyman said, bluntly. "You and Akin are already two or three years ahead of your peers. I think it would be better if you were to work here during lessons. And you'll also have access to the workroom later in the day."

"I understand," I said. I felt…I wasn't sure *how* I felt. On one hand, I was going to be isolated from my peers; on the other, I was going to get to use my talents. "Am I still your assistant?"

Magister Tallyman gave me an odd smile. "I think, rather, that I will be assisting *you*," he said. "And that leads neatly to a different question. Do you remember the sword I showed you?"

I nodded, wordlessly.

"It would be nice if it could be repaired," Magister Tallyman said. "Would you like to try?"

I blinked. The sword had once been worth a king's ransom, before someone had thought it would be a good idea to pry out one of the gemstones. Now, it was a worthless chunk of metal that would shatter if someone crashed it into a mundane blade. I supposed the remaining gemstones might be worth something…

"I might," I said. In theory, the sword could be repaired. In practice…I wasn't so sure. I had managed to prove, at least to my own satisfaction, that the spellform could not be adjusted once it was in place. Everything had to be preset before the final rune was cast or everything would go horribly wrong. "But I don't know if it would work."

"You may try," Magister Tallyman said. "And if you succeed, you may keep the blade."

I gaped. "Sir?"

"It's useless at the moment," he reminded me. "And if you're the only one who can get it to work…"

I wondered, numbly, what my father would say to *that*. A sword that was worth a king's ransom...perhaps *more* than a king's ransom. And it would be mine, if I managed to repair it. I had no idea if I could, let alone if I could *use* it. The blade might well be blood-bonded to a family that had no connection to ours, making the sword unusable. I might not even be able to *carry* the blade if I didn't have a trace of their blood in me.

But we could sell it to them, I thought. *And they'd want it...*

"I can try," I said. "Do you know anything about its history?"

"The blade was sold to me years ago," Magister Tallyman said. "It passed through several sets of hands before coming to rest in mine. Whoever originally owned it..."

He shrugged. "I don't know."

I frowned. There might be no way to find out, either. The family might not even be *based* in Shallot. Or it might have died out in one of the wars. Or...the blood might have become so diluted that the blade wouldn't recognise the descendents of its original owner. There was no way to know, save for having everyone in the school try to lift the blade...

And that assumes we can actually repair it, I thought, ruefully. *It may be impossible.*

But I didn't blame Magister Tallyman for wanting to try. The sword wasn't the *only* Object of Power that was broken beyond repair. My family had a small collection in the vaults under the hall. If we could mend one, we could mend others. And who knew where *that* would lead? Dad would certainly want me to try too. The family would have a very definite advantage if *we* were the only ones who could repair otherwise-useless artefacts.

"I'll try," I said. I'd have to be careful. The sword might be dead...or there might be enough magic left in the blade to cause an explosion, if I did the wrong thing. "Thank you, sir."

Magister Tallyman nodded. "Work on the project plans now," he said, nodding to the worktable. "And good luck."

I sat down and studied the plans closely. They were fascinatingly complex, so complex that I suspected there was a simpler way to channel the magic. It was how it always worked, according to the tutors. Someone made a discovery by figuring out a very basic way to do something, then someone *else* improved on it until the original design was lost under the bells and whistles. I'd have to work out how the design channelled magic before I could determine what was truly important and what wasn't. There were just too many additions and offshoots that didn't quite seem to make sense.

The bell rang...I jumped. Had it really been an hour since I'd sat down to work?

Someone knocked on the door. I rose, putting the papers to one side and stepped out of the workroom. Akin stood there, looking tired and hungry. Behind him, I could see Rose clearing away her tools. The rest of the class was already heading out of the door. Isabella was the last. She shot me a nasty look before leaving.

"Dad gave her a proper roasting," Akin said. He sounded oddly amused. "He said it was all her fault."

"Oh," I said. I wondered if I should feel sorry for her. But how *could* I? She'd been maximally mean to me ever since we discovered we were sharing a dorm. "What did you say?"

"Nothing," Akin said. "I was two rooms away and I could *still* hear the shouting."

"Ouch," I said. "What did he say to you?"

"Not much," Akin told me. "He just said he expected me to do well at school."

Rose joined us. "Lunch?"

"Lunch," I agreed. I had a free period afterwards, while the rest of the year went to Protective and Defensive Magic. Maybe I'd come back to the workroom and start inspecting the sword. "How did you get on?"

"She's doing fine," Akin said, before Rose could answer. "She just needs a little more confidence."

I nodded. I'd been nervous too, when I'd started. The prospect of seriously hurting myself had never been far from my thoughts. But I'd learnt to overcome it.

"Let's go," I said. "Or else there'll be nothing left for us."

CHAPTER TWELVE

"My techniques did not fail, at least," Magistra Haydon said, calmly. Her green eyes were pensive. "That is some small consolation."

I said nothing as I sipped my herbal tea. Magistra Haydon *had* tried to bring out my powers...but she'd been thwarted by the simple fact that I *had* no powers. She had to have found her apparent failure more than a little frustrating. Not everyone took Magical Growth seriously as a subject, even though she had had some successes. Her enemies must have taken heart from her problems.

"And I understand that you are now embarking on a course of study tailored to you," she added, after a moment. "How do you feel about *that*?"

"I feel it will be useful," I said. I'd already used some of the theory I'd been taught to design and forge the sword. "It gives me a chance to achieve something of my own."

"It also isolates you from your classmates," Magistra Haydon pointed out. "How do you feel about *that*?"

I sighed. "I was always isolated," I said. Rose had been the only real exception and even *she* had enough magic to make a name for herself. The others had been more interested in hexing me than making friends. "That has not changed."

"You have a very cynical view," Magistra Haydon said, lightly. "Why do you feel that way?"

I shrugged. It wasn't something I wanted to discuss.

"You're now the most famous child of your generation," Magistra Haydon added, when it became apparent that I wasn't going to answer her question. "How do you feel about *that*?"

"Odd," I said. The upperclassmen had *kept* staring as I walked past them. Whispers followed me everywhere I went. "It feels...*strange*."

I took another sip of the tea. "I didn't do anything to earn it," I admitted. "And yet...I don't know how I should feel."

"That isn't uncommon," Magistra Haydon said. "But you *did* do something to earn it, did you not?"

I shrugged. I'd worked hard to earn my journeyman qualifications in forging. But Akin had done the same and *he* couldn't forge Objects of Power. There was no way he could match me, no matter how hard he practiced. It didn't seem fair. And yet, there was no way I could match him at magic either. The wands and other focusing devices might allow me to *use* magic, to some extent, but they didn't give me anything like as much flexibility as a trained magician. I'd caught Isabella by surprise, in the first duel. It wouldn't be so easy if she challenged me to another.

She might argue that using Objects of Power is cheating, I thought. She'd made the same suggestion in Incantations and Geomancy, after I'd used a focus to craft a spell. *And she might just convince the upperclassmen she's right.*

Magistra Haydon cleared her throat. "Are you listening to me?"

"I don't know," I said. I shook my head. "I just don't know what to make of it."

"Time will pass," Magistra Haydon assured me. "Someone *else* will do something that will steal the magelight. And then things will go back to normal."

Or they'll find another Zero, I thought. It *was* a possibility, after all. *And then I might have some competition.*

I had to smile. Demand for Objects of Power had always been high. A *thousand* Zeroes couldn't meet it, even if they worked from dawn until dusk. Another Zero wouldn't change things *that* much, would it? And I'd have someone to talk to who would actually *understand* what it was like to lack magic. Rose did her best, but she'd been able to sense magic from birth. She wasn't the blind man in the kingdom of the sighted.

"I hope so," I said. I finished the tea and put the cup back on the saucer. "We shall see."

Magistra Haydon didn't smile. "We'll be having these talks every week," she said. "It is *important* that we design a course that suits you, as well as any others we discover with your...particular talent. The Castellan has stated that he wants your opinion of everything."

"I understand," I said. Was it a good idea to teach Zeroes alongside regular magicians? I had my doubts. But I knew the Castellan wouldn't want to open a whole new building, not when it would weaken his control. It might even lead to demands for a whole new school. "And I'll tell you how I feel after we settle in."

"Please feel free to tell us anything," Magistra Haydon urged. She smiled, warmly. "We'll see each other again in a week."

It was clearly a dismissal. I rose and headed for the door. Hopefully, I'd be able to find an excuse to avoid the next meeting. I didn't like talking about my feelings, even to someone who was oathbound to keep my secrets to herself. Rose was perhaps the only person I felt I *could* confide in, particularly now. She wouldn't have any *reason* to share them further.

An upperclassman was waiting outside, leaning against the wall in a manner that suggested she wasn't meant to be there. She straightened as I approached, her dark eyes fixed on me. I tensed, unsure if I was in trouble or not. It wasn't Lights Out - we hadn't even had *dinner* yet - but it was odd for a student to visit a classroom outside teaching hours.

"Caitlyn Aguirre," she said. Her voice was soft, too soft. And yet, the High Society accent was very pronounced. "Walk with me, please."

I sighed, inwardly. I didn't have a choice. An upperclassman's word was law, as far as we lowerclassmen were concerned. I followed her down the corridor and into a smaller room, an office that clearly wasn't in use. The cleaners hadn't bothered to visit either, I noted as she pointed me to a chair. Dust lay everywhere. Someone had written an unimaginative comment about a teacher's body odour on the table. I hoped whoever had done *that* had left the school by now. The teachers would not see the funny side.

She closed the door and cast a pair of privacy spells. "Do you know who I am?"

I studied her for a long moment. She was tall and pale, with long dark hair that was braided into a tight ponytail. Her uniform marked her out as a seventh year, which made her somewhere between eighteen to nineteen. I guessed, judging from her accent alone, that she was from one of the families, but I didn't know her name. She was at least six years older than me, too old for us to have played together when we were younger.

"No," I said, hoping she wouldn't take it as an insult. I'd heard stories of upperclassmen who'd handed out lines to juniors they felt hadn't shown the proper respect. "I don't think we've met."

"I am Jeannine D'Arcy," she said. "Do you know me now?"

I forced myself to think. The D'Arcy Family was neutral in the ongoing struggle for power in Magus Court, which - if my father was correct - meant they wanted to hold back until a clear winner emerged. I thought I'd met Lord D'Arcy at some point, when he'd visited the hall for discussions with Dad, but I'd never met any of his children. Unless I was much mistaken, that probably meant he didn't have any children who were around my age.

"I think I've met your father," I said, slowly. "I don't think I've heard much about you."

Jeannine looked relieved. I wondered, absently, just what I was supposed to have heard. But it wasn't really a surprise that I'd heard nothing. She was from a whole different generation to myself...old enough to marry, old enough to be treated as an adult in her own right. We simply didn't move in the same circles. I doubted *Alana* had heard much about her either.

"I want you to make something for me," she said, leaning forward until our heads were practically touching. Her voice was hushed, even though she'd used *good* spells to give us privacy. "And I will pay very well."

My eyes narrowed. I didn't like people who came so close to me. "What do you want?"

"There is a design for a charm - an amulet - that dispels lingering spells," Jeannine said. She lowered her voice still further. "I want you to make one for me."

I shuffled my chair backwards. "You can forge something similar in the workrooms," I pointed out. An upperclassman would have access to a workroom of her own, as long as she behaved herself. "You don't need me to do *that*."

"I need a *perfect* amulet," Jeannine said. There was a hint of desperation in her voice. "It must dispel *everything*."

"I see," I said. I'd forged a couple of necklaces that dispelled spells. Forging an amulet wouldn't be *that* much harder. But if she wanted a genuine Object of Power, it would be easy - far too easy - for anyone to trace it back to me. Where *else* would she have obtained it? I wasn't sure I wanted to get involved until I knew the full story. "What do you want it for?"

"I can pay," Jeannine said, with ill-hidden desperation. I felt a flicker of alarm. *Most* upperclassmen would have told me to shut up and do as I was told, or else. "I could give you around…around seventy *guilders*. Or maybe a hundred, if you gave me time to save…"

I blinked. Seventy *guilders* was a *lot* of money. Maybe not enough to use as the down payment for a shop, somewhere in Water Shallot, but enough to buy a considerable number of potions ingredients or forging supplies. And whatever I made with them, with or without my talents, would be enough to turn a healthy profit. Jeannine *had* to be desperate. She was offering me enough money to be noticeable.

And that worried me. An amulet like the one she wanted could be used for all kinds of malicious purposes. Someone could easily use one to break the protective wards on a roommate's bed - or worse. I'd used something similar to break into Alana's room, snapping her wards rather than cracking them. Jeannine might have something similar in mind. And seventy *guilders* might not be enough to make the consequences worthwhile.

"I need to know what you want it for," I said, hoping I could spot a lie. Jeannine seemed to be poor at hiding her reactions, but that could easily be an act. Dad had told me that he'd met a couple of total nincompoops who'd actually been very slippery customers, relying on a facade of idiocy to keep their victims from realising that they were being duped. "What do you want to do with it?"

Jeannine bit her lip. "Between you and me?"

"I won't tell anyone," I said, although I was unsure if I could keep that promise. My father would demand answers, if the whole affair exploded in my face. "What do you want it for?"

She looked down at her hands. "My mother...has laid a number of protective spells on me," she said. "I want those spells *gone*."

I blinked. Mum *had* tried to lay protective spells on *me*, but they'd never lasted. It hadn't been until I'd come to understand my talents that I'd realised *why*. Mum - or any magician - could put a spell on me, but the spell would only last as long as it had power. And I had no power for the spell to draw on. For once, it was Alana and Bella who had reason to complain.

"They'll be gone completely," I said, as I forced my tired brain to *think*. "There's no way you could rebuild them."

"I don't care," Jeannine said. "I just want them *gone*."

I winced. A spell cast by a blood relative, her *mother*. It would linger, all right. And it would be so tightly wound into Jeannine's magic that it would be nearly impossible for her to remove. Her father or siblings *might* be able to remove it, but anyone else would probably discover that the spell was designed to counter any threat to its existence. There were no shortages of curses designed to attack anyone who tried to remove them. I could easily write a somewhat more benevolent spell that would have the same effect.

"These spells," I said. "What do they actually *do*?"

Jeannine reddened. "Does it matter?"

"I don't know," I said. I'd overheard a number of stories from the maids, stories they'd told when they thought they couldn't be heard. Mum would not have been pleased if she'd heard them for herself. If they'd been telling the truth...I winced. There were some things I refused to believe. "The amulet would dispel *every* spell on you. You couldn't protect yourself while you were wearing it."

"But the spells wouldn't come back," Jeannine said. "Would they?"

"Not until they were recast," I agreed. There were *some* spells that had to be completely dispelled or they rebuilt themselves, but that wouldn't be a problem. Jeannine could wear the amulet for a few minutes, once I had made it, and the spells would be *gone*. "But it would be very noticeable that they were gone."

"I won't be seeing my mother again until winter," Jeannine said. "It will be fine."

I swallowed. "I don't want your money," I said, after a moment. "I want...a favour, a favour to be redeemed at my discretion."

Jeannine eyed me for a long moment. She knew the rules as well as I did. A favour...I could ask for anything, as long as it was of roughly the same value. But a working Object of Power was almost priceless. I could ask for anything and she knew it. And yet...she might prefer to owe me a favour, rather than surrender what *had* to be a large percentage of her life savings. She might need the money if her family disowned her.

"Very well, saving only my obligations to my family," Jeannine said. Her voice turned cold and hard. "I trust that will be acceptable?"

"It will," I confirmed. I couldn't ask her to betray her family. The family magics would probably turn on her if she tried. "When do you want it?"

"As soon as possible," Jeannine said. "And if you could bond it to me, I would be very appreciative."

I nodded. An upperclassman owing me a favour would be cool. A graduated magician owing me a favour would be even better. I wouldn't call it in at once, either. Who knew where Jeannine would end up by the time I graduated? And it wasn't as if I'd need to charge her for the materials, either. I could take anything I wanted from the workroom stockpiles.

"I'll see to it," I promised. "But I'll need you there when I bond it to you."

Jeannine nodded. "Keep this to yourself," she said. She pointed a finger at my chest. "If anyone asks, I dragged you in here to berate you about your jacket being covered in dust."

I rose. "My jacket wouldn't have been covered in dust if you hadn't dragged me in here," I pointed out. I didn't think Magistra Haydon would have been too impressed if I'd walked into her office with dust sifting from my clothes. She'd have sent me right back to change, after assigning detention. "Do you think anyone will notice?"

"Probably not," Jeannine said. "And besides, no one will really care."

I nodded in agreement. I'd found out, fairly early on, that if there was a dispute between an upperclassman and a lowerclassman, the upperclassman would always win. They were assumed to be more...*honourable* than their juniors, although I rather doubted that was remotely true. But then, Sandy hadn't hexed us all into complete silence by now. I supposed that said good things about her self-control.

And no one will care that Jeannine got me covered in dust, I thought, sourly. *They'll just congratulate her for telling me off.*

Jeannine turned and strode out of the door. I waited several minutes, then followed her to the stairs. If I was lucky, I'd make it down to the dorms in time for a shower before dinnertime. Rose and I had made plans to spend the rest of the evening in the library, before we finally got kicked out. Akin might even join us, if he wasn't busy with his cronies. I couldn't really blame him for putting them first. People would talk if they saw us spending too much time together.

Sandy raised her eyebrows when I walked into the dorm. "Why are you covered in dust?"

"I went into the wrong office," I said, with a wince. "Jeannine D'Arcy already told me off for it."

"You can sweep the floor after your shower," Sandy told me. Thankfully, she didn't seem inclined to do anything else. "Go now before you get it any further."

I sighed. It would be easy for her to use a simple spell to clean up the dust. But I could see her point. Casting the spell wouldn't have taught me a lesson, would it?

But I didn't ask to walk into an office of dust, I thought. *That was her idea...*

I shook my head. Jeannine had been willing to pay through the nose for a single Object of Power, one that only *she* could use. And it made me wonder just how many *other* upperclassmen would be interested in making the same deal?

And if I wind up with a dozen upperclassmen owing me favours, I thought as I walked into the shower, *who knows what else I could do?*

I smiled. It was a very promising thought.

CHAPTER
THIRTEEN

I was still contemplating the possibilities the following morning when Rose and I walked into Questioning Assumptions and stopped, dead. The classroom had the usual collection of chairs and tables, but otherwise it was completely bare. There was no fire in the grate, no bookshelves or portraits lining the walls…nothing, save for a single shelf near the front of the room. A single book sat on the shelf, out of reach. The tallest boy in the class couldn't have reached it. Even my father would have had trouble.

Rose looked at me. "Do you think we went to the wrong classroom?"

I checked the timetable, then the plaque on the door. Room 6B, Building Seven. It was the right room, just…empty. No teacher and no students, save for us. I was wondering if there was a problem with our timetables when Alana and Bella arrived from breakfast, the former looking grim. I wondered, as we slowly picked our seats, what was bothering them. It probably wasn't a missing teacher. I touched the earring absently, making sure it was clearly visible. The last thing either of us wanted was to get hexed in the back.

The room filled up slowly. Akin and Isabella entered together, Akin heading towards me while Isabella sat at the rear of the room. I did my best to ignore her gaze, burning into the back of my neck, as Akin sat next to me. She'd get over it eventually, wouldn't she? She had six years to rebuild her position, then a guaranteed place in High Society. I knew I wouldn't be so lucky, unless I built a massive network of my own. The lack of power would prove a major impediment when I grew to adulthood.

"It's five minutes after we were due to begin," Akin muttered. "Perhaps we're in the wrong room after all."

"Our timetables say Room 6B, Building Seven," I said. "What about yours?"

"The same," he confirmed. "But..."

The doors swung open. I turned to look as I heard a rattling sound. An upperclassman was pushing a wheelchair through the doors, carefully manoeuvring it past the desks and up to the front of the room. He turned it slowly, bringing the passenger into view. I stared in disbelief as my mind tried to grapple with the sight before me. The passenger - the tutor, I assumed - was...was *strange*.

He - or she? I couldn't tell. He was strikingly androgynous. The face was neither masculine nor feminine; the hair a shade too long to be a man, but too short to be a woman. The clothes were baggy, a bizarre mix of colours and styles...it took me a moment to realise that even the *materials* were mixed, a blend of noble silks and rough commoner cloth. I wasn't even sure of his - or her - *age*. The tutor had to be in his twenties, at least, but it was hard to be certain. My gaze seemed to slide over the tutor's features. I couldn't tell *anything* about him for sure.

It could be a glamour, I thought, as the tutor's assistant strode past me and left the room. I reached into my pocket and found the spectacles. *Perhaps if I look at him through them...*

I lifted the spectacles out of my pocket, only to have them yanked out of my hand by an invisible force. The tutor held up a gloved hand, caught them neatly and placed them on the desk.

"Naughty, naughty," the tutor said. Even the *voice* was androgynous. Too deep to be feminine, too light to be male. "Talk to me after class."

I tensed as I heard snickers from behind me. Alana, Isabella...probably the rest of the class too. A detention barely five minutes after class had been due to start...it was a new record, probably. Maybe the teacher was just establishing his - or her - authority. Or maybe he - I decided I'd consider him a *he*, until I knew better - wanted to keep his secrets to himself. I wondered, sourly, just what I would see if I had a chance to look at him through the spectacles. His true face, perhaps?

He's in a wheelchair, I thought. *What happened to him?*

I couldn't think of an answer, save for a particularly horrific curse. A magician capable of teaching at Jude's would have no trouble paying for a pair of new legs, if whatever had happened to them couldn't be fixed. Perhaps there *was* a curse on his legs that had wielded itself so tightly into his magic that it couldn't be removed. It was the only answer I could think of that made sense. And yet…there were all kinds of experts at Jude's. Surely, *someone* could have come up with an answer.

"Let us start with a question," the tutor said. His wheelchair squeaked loudly as he rolled forward. "There is a book on the shelf above my head. How can I reach it without magic?"

"Use a summoning spell," Alana muttered.

"I said *without* magic," the tutor snapped. The class snickered again, louder this time. "No magic. How do I reach the book?"

I silently considered the problem. No magic…*I* could have pushed a table into place under the bookshelf, then climbed on it, but a man trapped in a rickety wheelchair couldn't hope to get out without help. Get someone else to do it? That might work, if he found someone tall enough. He'd dismissed his assistant, but I assumed he could call the assistant back. Or…

"Use a bat to knock it down," Gayle Fitzwilliam suggested.

The tutor smiled. "Do I have a bat?"

No, I thought.

I stuck up my hand. "You ask one of us to do it," I said. "We put a table under the bookshelf and climb up to get the book."

"Good thinking, I have to get it for myself," the tutor said. "No magic. How do I get it?"

I glanced at Rose, who shrugged. No magic…? I couldn't see any way a wheelchair-bound man could reach the bookshelf, not without help. The problem seemed unsolvable, unless he was hiding a walking stick somewhere around his person. I certainly couldn't *see* one…

"Watch and learn," the tutor said.

He stood. We stared at him in shock as he walked over to the shelf, reached out casually and picked up the book. And then he turned to face us.

"The solution was obvious," he said. "And yet, none of you realised it because of the flaw in your thinking. You *assumed* that I was stuck in the wheelchair. And you were wrong."

He dropped the book on the desk. It made a satisfying BANG.

"*Assume*, as the saying goes, makes an *ass* out of you and me," he added. "If you learn nothing else from me, learn this. The assumptions you make, the assumptions you don't think to question, will eventually get you into trouble."

I nodded, slowly. How many people had assumed I had magic? And how many people had assumed that the secret of Objects of Power was something other than the truth?

"This class is *Questioning Assumptions*," the tutor added. He waved a hand at his outlandish garb. "Why did I choose to dress like this? To wear my hair like this? To shave my face and hide my wrinkles? Why?"

There was a long pause. No one wanted to try to answer. I thought I knew the answer, but I wasn't sure. The tutor - he still hadn't given us his *name* - had deliberately set out to mess with our minds. Our clothing presented us as young students; male and female; *his* clothing presented a collection of very mixed messages. Male *or* female, noble *or* peasant, rich *or* poor…he simply didn't fit into any of the established patterns. I felt an odd flicker of envy as I touched my braided hair. No one cared about the colour of my skin or my eyes or my hair, but if I wore it a centimetre too short I could be sure of some very *astringent* criticism indeed. A girl who shaved her head - or a boy who grew his hair too long - would be shunned by High Society.

Alana stuck up a hand. "Because you wanted to confuse us."

"*Precisely*," the tutor said. He clapped his hands, loudly. "If I'd worn tutoring robes, you would have drawn one set of assumptions about me; if I'd donned golden silks or sackcloth and ashes, you would have made two *different* sets of assumptions about me. And your assumptions would have been badly flawed. What's to stop a commoner wearing noble clothes?"

I felt Rose stifle a laugh beside me as an uneasy mummer ran around the classroom. In theory, commoners were barred from wearing silks; in practice, if the commoner could obtain noble clothes, what was to stop him wearing them and claiming to be nobly born? There were so many noblemen in the kingdom that a commoner who looked and acted the part could probably get away with it for years, as long as he was careful.

Who was going to write to someone on the other side of the country, just to check a low-ranking nobleman's *bona fides*?

"It's against the law," Isabella said.

"Yes, it is," the tutor agreed. "But tell me…how is the law enforced?"

"The Guardsmen or the Kingsmen would arrest a fraud," Fredrick said. "He'd be hung."

"But how would they *know* that a man with a noble bearing, with all the social graces of a born aristocrat, is a fake?" The tutor's gaze swept the room. "Their eyes would see a man who fitted the part and they would look no further. Why would they? Their assumption would be that anyone who looked the part actually *was* the part."

"No one could do that for long, surely," Isabella said.

The tutor smiled at her. "It's been done," he said. "There have only been a handful of cases, but it has happened. A person would step into High Society, claiming to be minor nobility from the other side of the country…as long as they looked and acted the part, no one would be suspicious of them. Ah, there was even a father and daughter team who conned a number of society ladies before they absconded with their ill-gotten gains. How did they get away with it? No one thought to question them before it was too late!"

He paused. "Any questions before we continue?"

Akin stuck up a hand. "Yeah," he said. "How do we know you're the *real* tutor?"

I fought to hide a smile. Akin was probably going to be in detention for the rest of his life, but…it *was* a good thought. How *did* we know the tutor was a *real* tutor? Sure, he'd walked into a classroom he'd clearly prepared for us, but that didn't prove anything…did it? If someone could walk into High Society and fool all the society dames like Great Aunt Stregheria, why couldn't a fake tutor walk into Jude's and convince the Castellan that he was qualified to teach?

The tutor surprised us by laughing. "Very good, young man," he said. "You'll go far."

His voice was suddenly serious. "For the record, I am Magister Niven. And, also for the record, I'm not always going to be honest with you. You will get into trouble if you take everything I say seriously, without checking it for yourself. Why? Because some of the things I will tell you will be true and some will be lies. Your grades will depend on just how good you are at telling the difference."

Bella choked. "That doesn't make sense!"

Magister Niven smirked. "Why not?"

"You're the teacher," Bella protested, when no one else tried to answer. "You *have* to tell us the truth."

"I don't recall seeing *that* line in my contract," Magister Niven informed her. "But let us consider your argument. I am a teacher, therefore I am authority. And authority should always be straight with you, right?"

Bella hesitated, then nodded.

"Wrong!" Magister Niven clapped his hands, again. "Authority can be wrong. Sometimes, a person in authority can be mistaken. A person who believes a lie, and who repeats the lie, does not do so out of malicious intent! And yet, he is repeating a lie! You force him to drink a truth potion and he will *still* repeat the lie, because he does not *know* it is a lie. There are books, books written as recently as five years ago, books you can still find in the library, which include untruths. Did those writers lie to you?"

I shook my head. They'd told the truth, as they'd known it. But future generations had discovered that their concept of the truth had been very limited. Magical knowledge was still advancing...

"And that is just the milder form," Magister Niven added. "*Authority* is also often more interested in maintaining itself than determining the truth. A person who clings to his authority - which may or may not be based on a known lie - is unlikely to want to do anything to weaken it. You may discover that proving your tutors wrong is a good way to get into trouble.

"Earlier, I mentioned that con men had been known to pose as nobles - and successfully fool people who had been raised from birth in High Society. And yet, many of you found it impossible to *believe* me. Perhaps, after I told you to take everything I said with a pinch of salt, you thought I was lying. And the reason you thought I was lying, I suspect, was because you had been told from birth that the noble-born are special. You didn't want to believe that a commoner could fool you because that would suggest that you *weren't* special.

"And yet, there is another reason. The Grand Dames of High Society wouldn't want to admit, not even in private, that they were fooled. Their authority rests on their ability to decide who is in and who is out, who has the right bloodlines and who doesn't, who is suitable marriage material and who isn't...they don't want you to think that their abilities might be flawed because that would call their authority into question. Authority works to preserve itself."

He paused. "Can any of you give me an example of authority acting to preserve itself?"

Great Aunt Stregheria, I thought. *She doesn't want to give up a shred of her power either.*

I kept that thought to myself. Magister Niven had steered us into uneasy - if not *dangerous* - waters. I found it hard to believe that High Society *knew* what he was teaching us. The Castellan would be in trouble if the Grand Dames ever found out. And yet...the secret would be out, the moment one of us wrote home. What did *that* mean? Did the Castellan *know* what we were being taught?

"Three hundred years ago," Magister Niven said. "John Lollard."

There was a collective intake of breath. The tutor ignored it.

"A poet and preacher during the time of the Peasant Uprising, a man many called mad," he said. "Lollard asked a simple question, time and time again; *when Rome built and Rime sowed, who was then the gentleman?* Authority - in the form of King Rickard and his aristocracy - made no attempt to answer the question. They could *not*. Instead, they killed Lollard and his followers. The copies of his poems were rounded up and burnt. Only a handful survived the purge."

He paused. "Lollard was not executed for writing bad poetry. He was executed for pointing out that the king and the aristocracy had no *natural* authority over the kingdom, when they claimed otherwise. Authority chose to perpetrate a lie rather than have a honest debate. They believed they would lose. Perhaps they were right."

I swallowed, hard. It wasn't safe to question the king's right to rule. I'd been brought up to believe that the king *did* have a right to rule, gifted by our ancestors. And yet...why *did* he have the right to rule? *Did* he have the right to rule?

"This class will teach you how to isolate and question your assumptions," Magister Niven said, moving back onto safer ground. "You will be graded by your ability to back up your assertions with facts, figures and reasoned arguments..."

Akin nudged me. "I can argue with the teacher!"

"Yes, you can," Magister Niven said. He clearly had very sharp ears. "But you had better put forward a coherent argument. As amusing as it is to read an essay that consists of nothing but insults aimed at me, I'll still fail anyone who writes it. I don't want you to parrot what you've been told back at me, either. I want you to actually *think* about the material."

I felt torn. I liked the idea of arguing and debating with the teacher, but...I couldn't help feeling a little nervous. What would we be discussing? I wasn't sure I wanted to know.

Magister Niven reached under his wheelchair and produced a stack of envelopes. "There is a sheet of paper in each of these," he told us. He clicked his fingers. The envelopes flew into the air and darted towards us. "I have written a specific statement on each of them - a *different* statement. Your homework, due on Friday, is a short essay proving or disproving the statement. Use as many words as you feel appropriate. You are *not* to collaborate on this. I *will* know and you *will* regret it."

I caught an envelope and held it. It felt surprisingly light.

"I think I've taxed your brains enough for one session," Magister Niven added. "You are dismissed. Except you, Caitlyn. Remain behind."

"Hah," Alana muttered.

"I can wait behind," Rose said.

I hesitated. "It might be a while," I said. We had potions immediately after Magister Niven's class. And there was no clock in the room. I wasn't sure what time it was. Rose might only have a few minutes before the bell rang. "Get something to drink. You might need it."

"Okay," Rose said. "Good luck."

CHAPTER FOURTEEN

Magister Niven waited until the rest of the class had left the room, then sat back down in his wheelchair. "Do you know," he said as the door closed, "why I asked you to remain behind?"

A number of smart answers ran through my head. I dismissed them.

"Because I wanted to see through your glamour," I said. He was turning my spectacles over and over in his hands. "I would have known what you were trying to hide from us."

His lips curved into a sly smile. "Here," he said, passing me the spectacles. "What *do* I look like?"

I donned the spectacles and peered at him. There was no visible magic, not even a standard protective spell. He hadn't used a glamour…he hadn't used anything. The appearance he'd presented to us was real.

"You didn't hide your appearance," I said, dully. "I don't understand."

"I wanted you to stay behind because I wanted a chat with you," Magister Niven said. "You gave me the opportunity to hold you back without raising too many eyebrows."

"Oh," I said. I could see the logic, but I wasn't pleased. "What do you want to chat about?"

"Take a seat," Magister Niven said. He sat back in his wheelchair, resting his hands in his lap. "Those spectacles are really quite fascinating. Do you know just how many of your classmates touch up their appearance with a little glamour?"

I nodded, shortly. My mother had tried to teach me basic cosmetic spells, but - of course - I'd never been able to get any of them to work. She'd taught Alana and Bella too, then warned them to be careful. Anyone who didn't like them could easily cast a cancellation charm at their glamours, popping them at the worst possible moment. Lazy magicians had been publically humiliated because they'd tried to hide everything under a glamour. A *smart* magician would use the glamours to improve their appearance, but they wouldn't rely on them.

"And genuine Objects of Power, at that," Magister Niven added. "The first *new* Objects of Power in over a thousand years."

"Yes, sir," I said, wondering if he was going to get to the point. I was due in potions soon…how soon? I didn't even know the time! "I made them myself."

"Indeed you did," Magister Niven agreed. He leaned back in his wheelchair. "Over the past thousand years, countless magicians have sought to forge Objects of Power. They all *assumed* that it required a level of precision that few magicians could muster. It never occurred to them that they were going in the wrong direction. Why do you think they never saw the truth?"

"Because people with *no* talent for magic at all are very rare," I said, dully. I'd assumed the same myself until I'd been sent to school. "They might have believed that they simply didn't exist."

"There's no *might* about it," Magister Niven said, sternly. "Everyone has magic, at least at some level. A person who cannot cast a single spell might still have some level of magic - we know that to be true, don't we? It is a *rule*. But you seem to be a complete exception to the rule."

I nodded. "And that means that the rule is bunk."

"Correct," Magister Niven said.

He leaned forward. "Now, here is the question," he said. "Forgers always assumed that they were required to *infuse* magic into their workings. And - historically - they used their magic to create Devices of Power. They took their limited success as proof that the whole mystery would be cracked, one day, when someone managed to muster the precision necessary to carve Objects of Power.

"But tell me...if you need magic to forge, how can *you* forge?"

I stared at him. "What do you mean?"

"You have no power," Magister Niven said. "So tell me...where does the power *come* from?"

"I..." I stopped, unsure how to answer. Everyone knew that carving the right runes into metal - or wood or whatever - allowed a forger to infuse magic into the object. I'd done it...I'd done it, even before I was sent to school. And Magister Niven was right. Where *had* the power come from? "I don't know."

He met my eyes. "Can you brew a potion?"

"Not without help," I said. I thought of the stirrers in my bag. "Or without the right tools."

"And you need magic to turn a smelly concoction into a potion," Magister Niven said. "Why can you forge Objects of Power, but not brew a potion?"

"I don't know," I repeated. I'd never thought about it before. And yet... it made no sense. I was powerless. If I couldn't brew potions, I couldn't forge. But I *could* forge. I'd made a number of Devices of Power before I'd discovered I could make Objects of Power. My head hurt. It made no sense. "Sir..."

I tried to gather my thoughts. "I carve runes into the metal," I said, after a moment. "Don't *those* have power?"

"Maybe," Magister Niven said. "But if runes have power, why is it safe to sketch out a runic diagram in a textbook? And if words have power, why can't you cast a spell simply by reciting the magic words?"

"I...I don't know," I said.

I'd recited spells until my throat had started to hurt. I'd whispered incantations, I'd roared and chanted spells that would have daunted magicians more advanced than either of my sisters...I'd even touched on Words of Power so dangerous that only a handful of sorcerers had dared to write them down. And it had been pointless, utterly pointless. There hadn't even been a glimmer of power.

Dad didn't even reprimand me for looking at those books, I recalled. *He was too desperate for me to show even a spark of magic.*

My thoughts ran in circles. Logically, I shouldn't have been able to forge. And yet, I knew I *could* forge. Why couldn't I *brew*? Or cast spells? Except...

"It makes no sense," I protested. "It's impossible."

"The word *impossible* is only a reflection of the unknown," Magister Niven said. "We have been told stories about flying buildings and castles that were bigger on the inside. The stories are so prevalent that they are impossible to dismiss. And yet, we don't know how it was done."

"The Empire knew how to do it," I said. "Unless...the stories grew and changed in the telling."

"It's possible," Magister Niven agreed. "But it's equally possible that the secret of flying buildings was lost when the Eternal City fell."

I remembered Magister Tallyman's flying machine and felt cold. If one could produce a flying machine, why not a flying building? What were the upper limits? *Were* there any upper limits? Magister Niven was right. My sisters cast spells - regularly - that our ancestors would have said were impossible. And yet, I knew how easily a rumour could grow and change until it became unrecognisable. It had been a thousand years since the Eternal City had fallen. Who knew how the stories might have changed as they were passed down the years?

Magister Niven pressed his fingertips together. "You forge Objects of Power," he said. "I believe that makes you unique, for the moment. Or is there a technique that your family has decided not to share?"

I shook my head, firmly. Dad wouldn't have hesitated to sell the secret, if there was a secret to sell. It would have secured our position, once and for all. No, there was nothing different about my forging, nothing Akin or Magister Tallyman couldn't match. The only real difference lay in the person doing the forging. I could follow the ancient instructions and get an Object of Power. Akin could follow the same instructions and get nothing, but a piece of scrap metal. Or an explosion.

"So tell me," Magister Niven repeated. "Where does the power come from?"

I had no idea. From me? I was wary of that, simply because I wanted to believe it. The thought of having power...it had been my dream, ever since I had started to realise that I had *no* magic. And yet, if it didn't come from me, where *did* the power come from? The runes?

"A rune needs to be carved into the metal for it to work," I said, slowly. "Perhaps the diagrams simply don't trigger the magic."

"I've seen active runes drawn on paper," Magister Niven countered. "A sorcerer who *wanted* to protect his spellbook would need to work runes into the cover, just to lock the spell in place."

"Maybe my intent shapes the runes," I said. But that didn't make sense either. Someone *could* cast a spell without knowing what it did. It was stupid, but it wasn't impossible. "I have to be very careful to make sure the spellform doesn't take shape until the last possible moment."

"Which leads us right back to the original question," Magister Niven said. "Where does the power *come* from?"

I looked down at my dark hands. I'd never considered the question, not really. And yet, in hindsight…why hadn't I thought about it?

Because I assumed…I assumed what? The thought taunted me. *That there was magic inherent in the materials?*

"When we brew a potion," I said, "we take care to pick ingredients that have magical properties…"

My voice trailed off. *That* couldn't be right. I'd been careful, very careful, to keep my workroom free of magical contamination. The cold iron I'd used to forge the blade - and the layers of gold and silver I'd laid on top of the iron - had been as close to magically dead as myself. Potioneers might break down the magic in different ingredients to produce a single spellform, but I…I couldn't do that. Magister Niven was right. Where *did* the power come from?

"It makes no sense," I protested.

"Nor would a spellform from our era, if you showed it to your great-grandfather," Magister Niven said. "We assume that one requires magic to forge. But you forge - and forge well - without magic. Or at least magic of your own. So…where does the power come from?"

"I don't know," I said. I was starting to be sick of that question. It wasn't something I wanted to look at too closely. And yet, it nagged at my mind. Where *did* the power come from, if it didn't come from me? "Magister…I don't understand."

"Nor do I," Magister Niven said. He gave me something I *think* was meant to be an encouraging smile. "But we will figure it out, eventually."

"I hope so," I said. I wasn't sure that was true. If someone figured out the secret, if someone found a way for normal magicians to forge Objects of Power, what would happen to me? "I...why do *you* think I can forge?"

Magister Niven cocked his head. "You lack active magic, yet you can forge Objects of Power," he said. "Simple logic indicates that those two facts are connected. Your lack of magic is actually an asset, under the right situations. Can you name others?"

"Spells don't linger on me," I said, slowly. I could be turned into a frog, but not for longer than a few hours. "They just don't stay in place."

"Another piece of the puzzle," Magister Niven said. "We will solve the rest, in time."

He rose. "We'll be talking again, later," he said, as he walked over to the desk. "Are there any questions *you* want to ask, before you go?"

I hesitated. There *had* been something I'd been wondering about, but I wasn't sure I wanted to ask. And yet..."Will you get in trouble for...for talking about John Lollard and King Rickard?"

"There are always complaints," Magister Niven said. He sounded amused. I realised I wasn't the first person to raise the issue. "But the authorities understand the importance of my class."

But you told us that authority moves to stamp out anything that brings its authority into question, I mused. Was that a lie? Or was he lying to me now? Or was I missing something? *Why did you caution us against believing everything you said?*

I took a breath. "I think I understand why you want us to question assumptions," I said, slowly. I wasn't sure what I wanted to say, let alone how I wanted to say it. "But why do you want us to question everything? Should we not have something to rely on?"

"Last year, everyone knew that everyone has magic," Magister Niven pointed out, coolly. "How many people got into trouble because they believed something that was demonstrably untrue?"

"They didn't *know* it was demonstrably untrue," I countered. "Did they?"

"No," Magister Niven said. "But does that make a difference?"

He sat down at his desk. "Everything we *know* to be true may be untrue tomorrow," he said, wryly. "Our assumptions may be proven wrong at any moment. And when that happens...we need to maintain the flexibility to *adapt* to a whole new world."

His lips quirked. "It takes nearly three months to sail from Shallot to Hangchow," he added, after a moment. "Why can't we do the trip in one month, by sailing through the Inner Sea and passing through the Corvallis Gulf?"

"Because no ship has made it past the Eternal City," I said. I'd heard the stories. Storms, tidal waves, sea monsters...even the stoutest sailor would mutiny instead of trying to sail through the Sea of Death. "They have to go the long way around."

"Quite," Magister Niven agreed. "What happens if - tomorrow - the Sea of Death became passable?"

I thought about it. Trade between us and Hangchow has always been limited, if only because it took *months* for a ship to reach Hangchow and return. Silks, spices, fine wines...there weren't many other trade goods worth carrying all the way from Hangchow. A handful of travellers had headed south to visit Hangchow - I'd dreamed of joining them, once upon a time - but there was no such thing as tourist trips to such distant lands. Noblemen on the Grand Tour didn't *think* about taking a year out of their lives to go to Hangchow, particularly when the risk of death was so high.

But if travel times were cut, sharply...

"It would be easier to get a return on one's investment," I said, slowly. Sailing ships were expensive. "And there would be more ships heading there and back."

"True," Magister Niven agreed. "But if transit times were shorter, it might be economical to ship *different* goods from Hangchow to Shallot. What might happen to us if *something* was imported from Hangchow? Or if it became easier for Hangchow to project military power over here? Or for us to project power over there?"

"It would be a change," I said. I wasn't quite sure what to make of it. "I don't know *what* would happen."

"But it might," Magister Niven said. He jabbed a finger at me. "The world changed, the moment you discovered you could make Objects of Power. Your family now has access to a game-changer. Worse, anyone who finds another like you will have a game-changer of their own. And if we cannot adapt to the new world, we will go the way of the terrible lizards."

He met my eyes. "Always question what you are told," he said. "And always question what you *know*. Because someone might be lying to you - for reasons of their own - or what you know may simply be not so. I think my opinions are correct, for all sorts of reasons, but I need to hear it if I'm wrong. Does *that* answer your question?"

"Not everyone likes to hear they're wrong," I said. I'd corrected Alana's work, once. She'd turned me into a snake and stormed off. "You could be getting some of us in trouble."

Magister Niven snorted. "Would you rather get into trouble or believe a lie? A truth can always be *proven*, young lady; a truth can be defended, even against a vigorous attack. But a lie will not hold up to scrutiny. And anyone who refuses to allow vigorous debate is *not* on the side of truth. It is better to fight and refight the battle over truth, time and time again, rather than let a single lie - or mistruth - go unchallenged."

He smiled. "A year ago, everyone believed that using dragon scales in a potion was asking for trouble. And what did you manage to prove?"

My face itched. "That I could use them safely, with care," I said. That *I* could use them safely. Rose and I had nearly been killed because Rose had stood too close to the boiling cauldron. "I don't know if anyone else could use them."

"Not in the same way, no," Magister Niven said. "But it does prove that the original theory was wrong, doesn't it?"

The bell rang. I groaned. There would be no chance of getting something to drink before the next class. I had a bottle of water in my bag, but it wasn't the same.

"We'll talk later," Magister Niven said. "Dismissed."

I nodded, scooped up my bag and hurried out of the room. The corridors and passageways were already filling with students, trying to get to their next class before the second bell. I felt eyes following me as I walked down the stairs, picking my way through the building. No one spoke to me...

The homework envelope felt heavy in my pocket as I walked down the corridor. I pulled it out and opened it, my eyes going wide as I read the single line. A MAN WITHOUT MAGIC IS WORTHLESS. I blinked. Prove or disprove? My mere existence disproved it.

But that, I reflected, might be the point.

CHAPTER
FIFTEEN

"Magister Niven is crazy," Akin said, after classes had finished for the day. "How many students are already writing home?"

I shrugged as I looked around the chamber. Magister Tallyman had told us both to join him - barely giving either of us enough time to snatch a drink before we walked back to the workroom - but there was no sign of him. The wards on the door had opened at our touch, allowing us to step inside. He must trust us, I decided. But then, he'd know who to blame if something went missing from his classroom.

"He wouldn't be discussing such matters without approval," I said. The sword - the broken sword - was positioned on a table, cocooned in a cobweb of silver wire. "No one is going to pay attention to the complaints."

Akin made a rude face. "This isn't us whining about being given too much homework on the first day," he said. "This is..."

"Questioning assumptions," I finished.

I heard the door open and turned, just in time to see Magister Tallyman stride into the workroom. He looked to have picked up a couple of new facial scars in the last few hours, although they didn't seem to have slowed him down. So little of his face was *his* any longer that I couldn't help wondering if he'd lost all feeling. I'd splashed molten metal and boiling liquid on my bare skin and the pain had been agonising.

"Caitlyn, Akin," Magister Tallyman said. "I trust that you are both well?"

We nodded, in unison. Not that we would have said otherwise no matter how we were feeling. Being asked to assist Magister Tallyman was a great honour. A stint as his TA would look very good on our resumes. And besides, the chance to work on his projects was an even *greater* honour. Neither of us wanted to waste it.

"Very good," Magister Tallyman said. He indicated the sword. "What do you make of it?"

I walked around the table and peered down at the blade. It still *looked* sharp, but there was a sense of brittleness that suggested a single solid blow would shatter the metal beyond repair. The runes were dark, almost burnt out; the metal was stained too, as if it had been allowed to rust for too long. There were dark marks - darker marks - around the gemstones, as well as scratches that suggested that someone had tried to extract one of the *other* stones. The pommel, where the missing stone had been, was a blackened ruin.

"It's a mess," I said, slowly. I could replace the gemstone, but what then? Would that trigger the spellform? "The layers of metal are badly scorched."

I looked closer. Whoever had made the blade, originally, had done a fantastic job. They'd layered gold and silver over the iron, just like I'd done, but they'd added frills I couldn't hope to match. It had been a work of art, once upon a time. But whoever had stolen the gemstone had damaged the sword, perhaps beyond repair. I wondered, absently, if the vandal had been caught before he tried to sell his ill-gotten gains. There was no punishment too cruel and unusual for a man who'd destroyed a priceless sword.

"The spellform would have to be rebuilt from scratch," I said, carefully. "And if the metal is too badly warped, it won't take."

"It might be easier to build a new sword from scratch," Akin mused.

I glanced at him and nodded. He had a point. If the spellform took, the sword would be back to normal; if it refused to settle, the whole exercise would be worse than useless. There was no point in taking the sword apart, then putting it back together again. I couldn't even melt the blade down and recycle the metal. The warped magic would have tainted the blade beyond repair.

"I'll have to do some calculations," I mused, finally. The spellform would need to be perfect, absolutely perfect. "And it might take some time."

Magister Tallyman smiled. "I've spent years on it, one way or the other," he said. "You can have as long as you like."

And the blade itself, if I succeed, I thought. It was a tempting prize - or it would have been, if I hadn't been able to make a similar sword for myself. I *could*...Dad wouldn't object if I wanted to design and forge a weapon more suited to a young lady. And yet, if I did manage to repair a broken Object of Power, it would be a remarkable achievement. *But it might just be a waste of time.*

"I'll work on it," I promised.

Magister Tallyman nodded, then led Akin away. I bent back over the sword, trying to memorise every last inch of the blade. The magical discharge had caused quite a lot of damage. I'd have to hope the internal damage wasn't so bad, although I was fairly sure that was just whistling in the dark. I honestly wasn't certain just how much damage the blade could take before the spellform failed completely. If it was too far gone, I was simply wasting my time.

I reached for my notebook and started to make a note of every imperfection. If I accounted for them all, when I devised the spellform, I might be able to make everything snap back into place. But if I didn't...I was torn between a desire to prove I *could* do it and a reluctance to waste time. I had too much else to do over the next few weeks. Writing an essay in response to Magister Niven's statement was the least of it.

And yet, I mused as I worked on the blade, *where does the power come from?*

The question had bugged me ever since I'd left Magister Niven's classroom. I'd brewed a potion to infuse magic into *other* potions, but I hadn't used it when I'd made my stirrers. I knew who'd charged half of them, yet...the others hadn't been charged. They'd been designed to work without being charged. But that thought took me right back to the original question. Where did the power come from?

I finished sketching the sword, then sat down on a stool while I reread my notes. I'd need Magister Tallyman - or someone - to check my work before I started trying to repair the blade. And then I'd have to plan out every step...it wouldn't be easy. I knew better than to start at once, even though part of me wanted to. I needed to sleep on it before doing anything else.

Magister Tallyman walked back over to me. "Any luck?"

"Just a little," I said. The more I thought about it, the surer I was that I could repair the blade. But a tiny mistake would ruin everything. "I'll have to finish the calculations first."

"Leave it until later," Magister Tallyman suggested. "Why don't you work on the flying machine instead? Or a project of your own?"

It wasn't a dismissal. He knew, as well as I did, that sometimes you had to step back from a project for a while, just so you could look at it with fresh eyes. I pocketed my notebook - I'd write out the calculations completely before I asked him to check them - and then headed for my workroom. Magister Tallyman had put the fear of detentions into most of my fellow students. *No one* was allowed to enter the makeshift workroom without my permission. I was surprised that someone hadn't hexed the doorknob as I stepped inside. It was the sort of trick I'd come to expect from my sisters.

And yet, everyone is being nice to me, I thought. It still felt odd. I'd been running in the corridors earlier, just to get to my next class in time, but none of the upperclassmen had given me lines to write. *What do they want?*

I lit the lantern, then sat down at the desk. The flying machine plans lay where I'd left them, broken down into their component sections. Whoever had designed it, I felt, had been a genius, or a madman, or both. And yet, the more I studied the plans, the more I felt there was a logic to them that made sense. It was a levitation spell on a colossal scale. I couldn't imagine any magician, no matter how powerful, holding it together for long. The power requirements would keep rising until the magician fell out of the air.

And yet, there are stories about magicians who used to fly halfway around the world for lunch, I reminded myself. *They must have known how to make it work.*

I rubbed my head, then forced myself to work. The runic diagram was insanely complex, but it had the same internal logic. One set of runes provided the lift, I thought; others provided steering and...and what? I wasn't sure *what* they did...I groaned in frustration as my head began to hurt. I was going to have to go to the library after dinner and dig out some new reference tomes. Magister Tallyman *might* let me experiment with runes without a solid idea of what they actually *did*, but he'd be the only one. Everyone else would demand my immediate expulsion.

The power runs through the runes, I thought. *Where does it come from, and where does it go?*

An idea struck me and I reached for a sheet of paper. Perhaps the design wasn't complete, after all. Perhaps...I tried to imagine a flying machine, something bigger than a full-grown dragon. It would be the same size as a clipper ship, perhaps. The Object of Power that provided the lift might not be in the same room as the control spells, just like a ship's steering wheel wasn't right next to its rudder. What if...

The equations made a certain kind of sense, I supposed. And yet, I suspected it would take months to fine-tune my calculations to the point I could take flight. A mistake might keep me grounded, but it might also throw me right off the planet. Coming to think of it, could anyone else even *fly* the machine? A random surge of magic might prove devastating.

I rubbed my forehead again as I peered down at my notes. They would have to be checked and rechecked time and time again before I started to forge, just in case. Forging a sword used far less effort...this time, there would be two or three spellforms interacting together, spellforms that could *not* be brought into existence at the same time. A single mistake in my calculations would almost certainly cause an explosion.

Pushing my notes to one side, I stood and walked to the workbench. I'd collected all the tools and materials I needed to forge Jeannine's amulet during class, when Magister Tallyman hadn't been paying so much attention to me. He *had* said I could draw on his stocks for my own projects, true, but I wasn't sure I wanted to discuss my private commissions with him. He'd probably prefer that I worked on the sword or the flying machine. But I needed a change.

The amulet design was simple enough, thankfully. Spellforms designed to break down or simply absorb other spellforms were easy to forge, although some of the more complex spells were designed to resist any attempt to dispel them. Devices of Power could be easily countered if the original magician had the power and skill to work countermeasures into their spell. And yet...that wasn't a problem with Objects of Power. Jeannine could be covered with so many spells that she couldn't use her own magic and my amulet would *still* dispel them.

I gathered my tools, then hesitated. Jeannine would be grateful, of course, but her mother would be furious. If, of course, she realised what Jeannine had done. Jeannine might *just* have managed to find a way to untangle herself from her mother's spells. Jeannine certainly wouldn't want to admit what she'd done. Who knew? Anyone capable of undoing such a spell would certainly be considered a formidable magician, in the days and weeks to come.

She has every incentive to keep it to herself, I told myself. *And she has every incentive to keep her side of the bargain.*

I reached for the silver wire and began to compress it into shape with practiced ease. *Rose* wouldn't have found it relaxing, but *I* did. It was a simple piece of forgery after the two swords and the flying machine. I could have done it in my sleep, although I knew better than to try. The scars on my hands bore mute testament to just what could happen if I allowed myself to become distracted. And yet...

I'd always been told that I'd have to build a patronage network of my own. Dad had insisted on it, long before my lack of magic had become all too clear. My sisters and I would take over the family affairs when our parents died, after all. One of us would be the Head - the position couldn't be shared - but the other two wouldn't be pushed out of the family. Or would we? Alana wasn't the sort of person who wanted to share. And we'd always assumed that *she* would inherit Dad's title. She was the only one of us three with the power and drive to take his place.

But if I had a patronage network of older magicians, I wondered, what could I do?

The thought nagged at my mind as I wrapped the filigree around the gemstone, then linked it to the chain. A simple addition to the original spellform would make it difficult for anyone to see, unless their attention was called to it. I didn't *think* it would trigger any household wards, if Jeannine took it back to her house, although it was impossible to be sure. Dad had told me that *our* wards noted and logged anything our guests carried that might be dangerous.

I'll have to ask her after she goes home for the holidays, I thought. I carved the runes into the metal, one by one. The spellform wouldn't take shape until the last one was in place and I couldn't do *that* until I managed to get Jeannine into the workroom, but I could get the amulet as close to finished as possible. *I wonder what will happen if someone else wears the amulet.*

I puzzled over it for a long moment as I finished the second-to-last rune. It seemed to glow, just for a second. I stared, then donned my spectacles. There was nothing, not even a flicker of magic. Magister Tallyman had worked hard to keep the tiny workroom as magic-less as possible. Maybe I'd just imagined it. Maybe...

Or maybe there was some magic already infused into the metal, I mused. It should have been impossible, but I knew it wasn't. *And that might mess up the spellform...*

I examined the amulet carefully, turning it over and over in my hands. There was nothing, no flicker of magic at all. And yet, I was sure I'd seen a glow. I was tired, perhaps too tired to think straight. Maybe I should go straight to bed after dinner. But I'd promised Rose I'd meet her in the library...

The bell rang. I put the amulet in a drawer, then picked up my notes and hurried out of the tiny room. Magister Tallyman was standing by the table, watching Akin as he worked on a complicated-looking Device of Power. I was careful not to step too close as Akin carved runes into the metal. Who knew what my presence would do?

Nothing, I thought. It was a bitter thought. *I stood next to Dad as he forged and Mum as she brewed and nothing happened.*

And yet...if Rose's presence had caused a cauldron to explode, who knew what *my* presence would do if things were reversed? The thought bothered me, more than I cared to admit. If I had power, why could I do nothing but forge? Surely, I could do more. And if I *didn't* have power, where did the power come from? The question ran through my mind, time and time again. I had a feeling I'd never forget it until I found a satisfactory answer.

"Very good," Magister Tallyman said. He looked up. "Caitlyn. Did you make any progress?"

"I think I'm starting to understand some of the equations," I said. It was true enough. "But I'm going to need some time in the library to really come to grips with it."

"Take your time," Magister Tallyman said. He smiled. "The Triad would not be amused if the entire school took flight."

Akin snickered as he stepped back from the workbench. "The entire building would come crashing down," he said. "It would be worse than the South Wing."

Magister Tallyman looked distantly unamused. *Someone* had blown up the South Wing, a year or two before I'd been sent to school. No one knew what had happened, but even *I* had heard the rumours. There had been threats of inquiries from Magus Court, perhaps even a Royal Inquest. And yet, the truth - whatever it was - had been firmly buried. I wondered, suddenly, just what Magister Tallyman knew about it. He'd been a teacher for decades.

And he wouldn't tell, if we asked, I thought. I didn't think the teachers were obliged to swear oaths of perpetual secrecy, but talking out of turn could cost them their jobs. *Whatever it was, it had to have been bad.*

"Go have your dinner," he said, curtly. He sounded distracted, as if he was thinking about something else. It was a bad habit in a forger. "We'll finish up later."

We nodded and made our escape.

CHAPTER
SIXTEEN

"This equation doesn't make sense," Rose said, as we settled into our study room. "Why can't I understand it?"

I took the sheet and scanned it. "You're mixing up two of the variables," I said. Rose had progressed by leaps and bounds, but she had a long way to go before she matched anyone who'd been raised in a magical household. It didn't help that she'd only started studying magical equations a few months ago. "This one needs to be separated from *that* one until you're ready to cast the spell."

Rose made a face. "Why don't they just *say* that?"

"It's one of the points that everyone is expected to know." I groaned in frustration. How many things did I take for granted? How many things did I know that just weren't so? "We may need to go over the basics again."

"Or practice with newer spells instead," Rose said. "Did your head hurt when it was pounded into your skull?"

I winced. I'd studied magical theory extensively, believing that understanding how magic actually worked would allow me to use my talents. And I'd been good at theoretical magic, good enough to win prizes if I'd been able to *use* what I'd learned. I could devise a spell, if I wanted, but I couldn't cast it. Rose couldn't devise a spell, yet she could make one work if I gave it to her. Between us, I supposed we would make a pretty fair team.

"I had more time to study the basics," I said. I'd spent two years learning the basics, as well as several languages that were useless outside magic studies. Rose...had less than six months to learn enough to let her pass the exams. "And I had better tutors."

Rose shot me a warm look. "You're a good tutor."

I shook my head. I couldn't demonstrate the spells. And I couldn't demonstrate how theory fitted into practical spellcasting. I could teach Rose a great deal - and I *had* taught Rose a great deal - but I had my limits. Rose really needed an upperclassman - or a private tutor - to make sure she had a solid grounding in theory before it was too late.

"You need to restart the equation," I said. I could have done it for her and I was tempted to do just that, but Magister Von Rupert might just call on Rose to explain her work. She'd be in trouble if she couldn't explain what she'd done. "This time, keep all of the variables separate until the very end."

I reached for a stack of reference books and picked up the top volume. I'd found every book within reach on the subject of old runes, although Magister Tallyman had warned me that a number of runes on the flying machine diagrams weren't included in modern textbooks. I had no idea if that was because the runes were useless or their original meaning had been forgotten long ago, but it didn't matter. If I was lucky, I might find something close enough to the mystery runes to give me a good idea what they did. And if I wasn't lucky...

It might just be time for some experiments, I thought.

My fingers touched dust as I opened the book. No one had looked at it in years, I guessed. It shouldn't have surprised me. There were more modern textbooks, ones that detailed every rune and sigil we knew. And yet, I knew just how hard my parents - and every other magician in the city - worked to mine secrets from the past. I was surprised that an older student hadn't found the ancient book and studied it intensively.

But they wouldn't have left the book here if they thought it still held secrets to unlock, I told myself, as I parsed out the text. *Dad has volumes that he will never share with anyone outside the family.*

The book felt *old* against my bare fingers. It lacked even basic protective spells. The runes - one to a page - were faded, some so faint that it was hard to be sure they were complete. And yet, most of them were known runes. The ones that didn't have a known purpose might be useful...or they might be maker's marks that had been mistaken for ancient runes. I parsed them out one by one, cursing the writer under my breath. I'd been taught the language, but whoever had written the book seemed to delight in elliptical statements that confused me more often than not. I had to reread each section several times to be sure I understood the meaning.

"This is a pain," I muttered.

Rose looked up, sympathetically. "Do you *have* to parse out the runes?"

"Unless I want to start experimenting," I said. Magister Tallyman would let me experiment, wouldn't he? We could go somewhere well away from the school...there was a campus somewhere in the hills, wasn't there? I'd been told there was a secondary building at the South Pole, but I didn't believe it. "It would be better to have a good idea of what I was doing first."

I felt a flicker of envy for the original designer. He'd have *known* all the secrets, all the little tricks I had to figure out for myself. I'd advance, I was sure, and so would the school...Jude's *wanted* a program to train Zeroes, didn't they? But I would have cut off my hair for a chance to study with the ancient magicians. They could have told me everything I needed to know.

The door opened. I looked up, alarmed. If a bunch of upperclassmen wanted to turf us out...

Bella stepped into the room. "Cat," she said, shortly. She held a large sheaf of papers under her arm. "I was told I'd find you here."

"Oh," I said. "Who told you that?"

"The librarian," Bella said. She walked over to the table. "And *you* told me you'd help me with my homework."

"As long as you help us with ours," I said. I gave her a pleasant smile. "Rose needs some practical assistance."

Bella frowned. "And you think I can help her?"

"Yes," I said. I reached for the papers. "Why don't you show her how the equations translate to real life while I look at your homework?"

Bella nodded and motioned for Rose to join her at the worktable. Rose didn't look happy - Bella hadn't been as bad as Alana, yet she'd bullied Rose too - but she followed Bella anyway. I opened the papers and skimmed them. Bella had been trying, I supposed, but it was clear that she'd written the essays in a hurry. Magister Von Rupert would *know* it, too. It was hard to imagine him handing out detentions and punishment essays with a free hand, but his partner was punitive enough for both of them. Bella would be in deep trouble if she didn't rewrite at least two of the papers before her next class.

"Each of the equations determine a different variable," Bella was saying. She sounded marginally surer of herself. "This one determines the amount of power you push into the spell, this one determines the range, this one determines precisely what happens when the spell is triggered. Changing even one of the variables will get you a different result."

"Like you need to change the geometric diagrams you've drawn out here," I called, without looking up. "The spellform isn't very stable."

"I can balance the spellform," Bella pointed out, crossly.

"Not unless you keep your mind on it," I countered. It wasn't something I'd actually *done*, of course, but I knew the theory. "You won't be able to cast a second spell until the first one is completed."

Bella made a rude sound. "Seconds, at best. Even *you* couldn't dodge a spell indefinitely."

"It would cost you the chance to get a second spell off," Rose put in. "Is that why I managed to tag Drina?"

I nodded. I'd forced Rose to practice casting spell after spell in quick succession, even though it had drained her. My sisters might have gotten far too used to hexing a target that couldn't hex back. I wondered, sourly, if Isabella actually had an advantage over Alana. She would have tried to hex Akin, who was perfectly capable of throwing spells *back* at her. If nothing else, she'd know how to dodge…

"You need to balance the spellform for later," I said. I drew out a set of pencil lines on her diagram. "You can compensate for poor planning now, I think, but later…something more advanced will just come apart when you try to cast it."

"Hmm," Bella said.

I read through the rest of her essays one by one, trying to ignore the moments of envy - even jealousy - when I heard her demonstrating the spell time and time again. I had a talent of my own, didn't I? I had a unique talent. And yet, it was limited. I'd never be casting spells from my fingertips or breathing words that would change the course of entire nations.

I'll just be forging the tools, I thought, instead.

"I think I understand it now," Rose said, when Bella had finished. "But why do the variables need to be altered?"

Bella shot me a challenging look. I scowled back.

"The original spell is designed for a very specific set of circumstances," I said. We'd gone through something similar before, hadn't we? "You need to understand the theory so you can modify the spell to suit your needs."

I took a breath. "For example, transfiguring someone into a frog takes less energy than turning them into a donkey. But you can change the spell so that it does turn someone into a donkey, yet if you do the power requirements suddenly become a great deal higher. If you don't change those, the spell will either fail or simply not last as long as you might wish."

Rose looked blank. "Why does turning someone into a frog take less energy than turning someone into a donkey?"

I glanced at Bella, who shrugged. I'd never really thought about it. Being turned into a small hopping thing was a hazard of growing up in my family's hall. It was just part of life. I really hadn't stopped to consider why the power requirements might be different…it was something to think about, perhaps. I wondered, absently, what Magister Niven would say if I asked him.

"I don't know," I admitted. The answer *might* be somewhere in the theory books. I made a mental note to look when I had a moment. Dad and his tutors hadn't discussed it with me, but that proved nothing. "It just…*does*."

"Magister Niven would not be happy with that answer," Bella said. We shared a giggle. It gave me a warm feeling inside. "He'd want you to come up with a better theory."

"Perhaps," I said. "But why…?"

I shook my head. I wasn't going to solve *that* problem overnight. I needed to figure out, first, if anyone else had already solved it.

Bella cleared her throat. "What did you make of my essays?"

"You need to rewrite these two, at least," I said. I passed them over to her. "And I've already told you about the diagrams."

"Joy," Bella said. "Thank you, I suppose."

"You're welcome," I said.

She left, closing the door firmly behind her. I shared a look with Rose, then went back to my runes. The bell rang, thirty minutes later. I put the book aside for further study and followed Rose out of the library. The rest of the students were checking books out or pleading to be allowed to stay longer. I wondered what they'd do when exam season rolled around. They still had several months before their progress was formally tested.

Rose shot me a sidelong look as we walked down the corridor. "Are we going to be spending all of our time in the library?"

I looked back in surprise. There wasn't much else to do, was there? Jude's grounds weren't *that* big - and besides, they were dominated by upperclassmen. I'd been cautioned against leaving the school and I wouldn't have left in any case. We were in Water Shallot. Family name or not, it wasn't the kind of place I wanted to explore without an escort.

I could try and talk an upperclassman into escorting us, I thought. *We might be able to go for a walk.*

The thought tempted me for a few moments, before I dismissed it. An upperclassman who took us over the walls would probably be unceremoniously expelled on the spot. *Dad* wouldn't help her either. He'd be more likely to want the offender hung, drawn and quartered.

"I don't know," I said. Netball wasn't my thing - or hers, either. I'd done my best to stay away from social clubs. Even chess could turn nasty if one player was a magician and the other was a zero. "Where do you want to go?"

"There are parts of the school that I've never seen," Rose said. "We should go exploring."

I had to smile. Jude's was immense. There *were* entire wings that hadn't been used for decades, secret passages and chambers that hadn't seen the light of day. We *could* go exploring, if we wished. I was tempted, even though I had far too much to do. We'd certainly have far less time to explore in the years to come.

"Why not?" It *was* a pleasant thought. "We might find the lost treasure of Master Jude."

"Or a secret passageway leading out of the school," Rose said. "How much would *that* secret be worth?"

I shrugged. If there was a secret passage like that, I would be very surprised. The staff might turn a blind eye to upperclassmen sneaking over the walls - if they made it through the network of wards and traps - but they'd never tolerate a secret passageway. I wasn't even sure the wards would *notice*, if there *was* a passageway. The building was so poorly designed that warding the whole complex had to be an absolute nightmare. A secret passage would just make matters worse.

"It would be fun," I said. I didn't *think* we'd find anything new, but... it would be fun. And we would learn more about the school. Jude's had secrets. Perhaps we'd discover some that had been lost long ago. "I..."

A flash of light darted up the corridor. Rose let out a yelp, throwing up her hands an instant before she shrank and became a frog. A second spell struck me, only to rebound back in the direction it had come. I heard someone cry out, an instant before she was silenced. But she wasn't alone.

Isabella stepped out of the shadows. "Well," she said. She didn't look at her friend. I wondered, absently, just who she'd talked into supporting her. "The *cheat*."

I slipped my hand into my pocket. I'd stowed a couple of artefacts there.

"I didn't cheat," I said. I felt a flash of cold irritation. *She'd* demanded satisfaction, not me. "There's no rule against bringing Objects of Power into a duelling circle."

Isabella glared at me. "Only because no one thought it might be necessary!"

I probably shouldn't have baited her, but...I couldn't resist.

"Then they really should have paid more attention in Magister Niven's class," I said. The thought made me smile. "They *assumed* I couldn't bring an Object of Power - let alone more than one - into a circle. How *careless* of them."

"My father is working on changing the rules," Isabella snapped. "Soon, no one will be able to bring anything into the duelling circle! And then I will challenge you again. And again."

I felt my blood run cold. I did my best to hide it.

"I can't cast spells," I said. If I had to face her without my earrings, if nothing else, I was doomed. "You know it."

"And you shouldn't even be here." Isabella sneered. Her voice hardened. "You can't even fight fair!"

Rose croaked. I didn't dare take my eyes off Isabella, let alone draw the dispeller from my pocket and free Rose.

I forced myself to face her. "You're a coward, aren't you? You'll hex someone who can't defend herself, but when she finds a way to fight back it's *unfair*..."

Her face flushed bright red. "You utter..."

An upperclassman walked around the corner. "Fighting in the halls," she said. Her eyes flickered over us, resting on me for a long moment before she pointed a long finger at Isabella. "Report to the janitorial staff. I'm sure they'll find work for you to do."

Isabella gaped. Her face turned pale. "I..."

"Go," the upperclassman ordered. Her voice was utterly unyielding. "Now."

I watched as Isabella turned and scurried off. The older girl hadn't seen the struggle begin, I thought. She hadn't known - she couldn't have known - which of us had started it. And yet, she'd come down hard on Isabella. I wasn't sure if that was a good thing or not.

"Caitlyn," the upperclassman said. She snapped her fingers at Rose, who froze. "I would like you to forge something for me."

She sounded, I reflected, as though she thought she was the first person to have thought of asking me for a private commission. I wasn't going to tell her otherwise.

"I see," I said, instead. She could at least have turned Rose back before freezing her. But I suspected she wanted this discussion to be private. "What would you like me to forge?"

The upperclassman beamed. "I want something very simple," she said. I had the feeling it wasn't going to be remotely simple. "And I will pay very well."

CHAPTER SEVENTEEN

It turned out, I discovered over the next few days, that quite a few students were having the idea of asking me for a private commission or two.

Their requests surprised me, although I suppose they probably shouldn't have. Everyone wanted an Object of Power. And yet...I made a list of requests, then started to plan out how best to meet them. The prospect of dozens of upperclassmen owing me a favour was too tempting to resist.

"Perhaps you should offer to provide services instead," Rose said, when I told her about the latest request. A student wanted an Object of Power that would protect him from hexes while playing football. "You could rent out your work and make more money."

I touched one of my earrings as I thought about it. It might work. It certainly *should* work. An Object of Power that wasn't blood-bonded would be less effective than something I'd made for a specific person, but if all they wanted was to cleanse themselves of spells...it should work. I could give Jeannine or someone like her an hour with a necklace, then reclaim it. They wouldn't pay me so much - and I didn't just want money - but it might be worthwhile.

But no one is going to give me an open-ended favour merely for an hour with an Object of Power, I thought. *They'll insist on paying in cash or smaller favours.*

"I don't need money," I said. "Favours would be more useful."

"Maybe for later," Rose said. "But money would buy you favours, wouldn't it?"

I shrugged. Objects of Power were priceless - no, they'd *been* priceless. My father was one of the richest men in the city, yet even *he* couldn't have bought one of the rarer Objects of Power. He'd have had to practically bankrupt himself to purchase a smaller one. And a family sword - something blood-bonded to a specific line - would be priceless to its owners and worthless to everyone else. Dad wouldn't waste his money purchasing something he couldn't use.

"It depends on the favour," I said. "There are some things money just can't buy."

Rose snorted. "Which matters very little to those who struggle to put bread on the table," she said. She pointed a finger at me. "What will you do when you run out of supplies?"

She had a point, I admitted as we made our way to the next classroom. Magister Tallyman *had* said I could draw from his supply cupboards, but that wouldn't last. I doubted I'd ever become an upperclassman, even if the staff *did* rewrite the curriculum for me. It was more likely they'd put me in an independent studies course, once they worked the kinks out of the system, or let me leave school after completing my fifth-year exams. After that...

I'll have to raise prices, I thought. Buying the raw materials to make Objects of Power would be very expensive. *And it will be harder to pick and choose my clients.*

I spent the rest of the day mulling over it, feeling a little unsure of myself. I wanted - I needed - a patronage network. And it was good to have students - particularly upperclassmen - paying attention to me. I hadn't had so many people trying to get into my good books since the rumours about my magic - or lack of magic - had started to spread. I *wanted* Alana and Bella to see their "useless" sister doing well for herself. I owed them for every hex, for every cruel taunt, for every snide remark detailing what would happen to me when my parents died.

It still nagged at me as I walked into the workroom at the end of the day. Akin was already there, working on a Device of Power. I nodded to him and strode over to the workbench, silently running through Magister

Tallyman's planned set of experiments. I wasn't too pleased about *him* getting involved - I'd been happier trying to parse out my talents on my own - but I knew I should be relieved. Magister Tallyman had more than earned his reputation.

And you were glad enough of the prospect of studying under him, a little voice whispered at the back of my head. *Weren't you?*

"I'm sorry I'm late," Magister Tallyman said, striding into the room. "I trust you weren't too bored."

"No, sir," Akin said. "I was just finishing my work."

Magister Tallyman glanced at it, then nodded curtly. "Come with me, both of you," he ordered. "I've set up an experimental chamber for us."

We followed him through a series of passageways and into a larger workroom. It looked oddly bare, even though there was a wooden worktable and a set of supply cupboards. The walls were plain stone, without even a single rune linked to the ward network. A small selection of tools - and a single sheet of instructions - lay on the table. I scanned them quickly and frowned. The Object of Power was really nothing more than a set of interlocking discs on a horizontal axis that were - apparently - supposed to spin in unison. If it had a purpose - beyond decoration - no one had been able to figure it out.

"Cat," Magister Tallyman said. "How quickly could you make this?"

I calculated it, quickly. "Not long," I said. "Half an hour, perhaps."

Magister Tallyman nodded. "Then start making one," he said. "Akin and I will be in the next room."

"Yes, sir," I said.

I felt my fingers tingle in anticipation of the challenge as I opened the storage cabinets and started to assemble the materials. Sheets of copper, iron and a surprisingly flimsy gold foil, all wrapped in cloth to keep them pure. I wiped them down anyway, just to be sure, then picked up my tools and went to work. The Object of Power was astonishingly simple, almost as simple as the fan I'd built weeks ago. And yet, we honestly didn't know what it did.

But it shouldn't be anything dangerous, I told myself. The runes made the discs spin - and that was it. I'd checked again and again, just to be sure. *It's nothing more than a piece of art.*

The Object of Power took shape in front of me, piece by piece. I took a long breath as the last of the runes fell into place, the object glowing briefly as it started to spin. A faint light flared up as the discs spun faster and faster, casting an eerie radiance over the scene, but nothing else happened. I guessed I'd been right. It *was* nothing more than a piece of art.

Unless it's part of a greater design, I speculated. There were hundreds of Objects of Power that had no discernible purpose. Magister Tallyman's flying machine was actually a trio of interlocking Objects of Power, if my calculations were correct. *Perhaps it's only useless because we don't know what the other parts are meant to look like.*

I puzzled over it as Magister Tallyman stepped back into the room. "Very good, Cat," he said, examining the spinning discs. "You may keep it, if you wish."

"Thanks," I said. I remembered Magister Niven's words and frowned. Where *was* the power coming from? "What do you want me to do now?"

"I want you and Akin to build a second Object of Power," Magister Tallyman said. "But he's going to be the one to shape the discs."

I felt an odd rush of emotion as I carried the Object of Power into the main workroom and then returned. It was important - I knew it was important - to know just how much of the work could be done by someone else, by someone who lacked my talent, but I couldn't help feeling conflicted. What if Akin managed to forge his own Objects of Power? Cold logic told me that it was unlikely that a twelve-year-old would solve a puzzle that had baffled the greatest minds in sorcerous history, raw emotion reminded me that *I* had cracked the mystery. And what one magician - or whatever I was - could do, another could duplicate. My heart clenched as I watched him go to work. What if…?

Akin worked with practiced ease, cutting the discs out of the metal and placing them gently on the workbench. I kept my distance, torn between admiration for his obvious skill and a deep ache that tore at me. I liked Akin, perhaps more than I should, but his sister was a very different matter. And our families had been enemies for *decades*. Outside Jude's, would we still be friends? Or would he hex me the moment he saw me?

His father would expect him to do just that, I thought, sourly. I'd only seen Lord Carioca Rubén once, but he'd worried me. I would have felt sorry for Isabella if she hadn't been so horrible to me. Her father had good reason to be *very* annoyed at her. *And if he really can get the rules rewritten…*

I pushed the thought out of my head as Akin finished the third disc. Magister Tallyman checked them, using a compass and ruler to make sure they were perfect. I watched, unsure what I felt. It would be easier, much easier, if someone else could do some of the work, but it would diminish my value. I gritted my teeth as Magister Tallyman pronounced the discs perfect. I wasn't going back to being useless. I *wasn't*.

"Cat," Magister Tallyman said. "See if you can put them together."

I took the discs. A sour feeling rose up within me, urging me to make a tiny error that would render the Object of Power nothing more than a piece of scrap metal. It wouldn't be hard, either…but Magister Tallyman would notice. He was watching me like a hawk, silently noting everything I did. And I admired him too much to want him angry at me.

And Dad wouldn't be pleased either, I reminded myself. Dad and Mum took experiments seriously. Outright sabotage would get me in real trouble, whatever the motive. *I'd be grounded for the rest of my life.*

I carved out the runes, one by one. It felt…odd, although I couldn't put my finger on *how* or *why*. I ground my teeth in frustration. I'd been told that experimental magicians often had odd feelings when something was about to go spectacularly wrong, but nothing they'd been able to describe to me. Perhaps something was about to go wrong. Or maybe I was just imagining it. The feeling seemed to fade the moment I concentrated on it.

The discs and axle assembled perfectly, of course. I fought to keep my face impassive, despite an uneasy feeling in my gut. Akin had done a very good job. And then they started to spin…

"Get down," Magister Tallyman snapped.

He slammed into me. I yelped in pain as I toppled over and landed on the floor, his huge body landing on top of me. A second later, the room shook violently. I heard pieces of debris flying in all directions, smashing into walls and crashing to the floor. Akin said a word I *knew* my mother would have washed my mouth out with soap for *thinking*, let alone *saying*.

Magister Tallyman rolled off me a second later. He looked deeply worried.

I forced myself to stand on wobbly legs. The workbench had been solid wood. It wasn't any longer. The wood was cracked and broken, scorched so badly that it could have been converted into charcoal with very little effort. Fragments of metal lay everywhere; some embedded into the wood, others lying against the walls where they'd fallen. The discs had shattered…

"I sensed a surge of magic," Akin said, picking himself up. "It failed, didn't it?"

Magister Tallyman gave him a sharp look. "Yes."

I nodded, slowly. "I made everything, from start to finish, and it worked. You made the discs and it failed."

"It looks that way." Magister Tallyman strode across the room and opened one of the cupboards. "The question is simple. How much can Akin do before it explodes?"

"Rose was standing close to the cauldron when it exploded," I said, carefully. My face itched. We'd both been badly wounded when the potion destabilised. "Maybe Akin was standing too close."

"I was on the other side of the room," Akin pointed out. He sounded shaken. "Magister Tallyman was closer."

"You weren't when you were making the discs," I countered. "Perhaps your touch was enough to render the discs useless."

"Perhaps," Akin said. "But anyone can *touch* an Object of Power."

"A working Object of Power," Magister Tallyman said. He sounded pleased, even though we'd come far too close to being injured. "It seems that we need to carry out more experiments."

Akin looked as though he wanted to say something biting. "The discs exploded," he said, instead. "Doesn't that mean the whole experiment failed?"

Magister Tallyman was too enthusiastic to reprimand him for his tone. "*Something* happened," he said, patiently. "We now know that you cannot make all three of the discs without causing an explosion. That is a *datum*. Now, we see if you can make *one* of the discs."

"Or if Cat can make the discs and I can put them together," Akin offered.

I had my doubts. If Rose's mere presence was enough to cause an explosion, Akin's craftsmanship certainly would too. And yet…I rubbed my forehead in frustration. The puzzle seemed unsolvable. I wasn't sure I *wanted* it solved, but still...

"I'll need to get a new workbench," Magister Tallyman said. He looked down at the wreckage, shaking his head in amusement. "And probably tighten up the wards."

Akin pointed upwards. "And maybe do the next experiment in the open air," he added. I followed his gaze. Hairline cracks were clearly visible in the stone. "We don't want to bring down the building."

"Or even the roof," Magister Tallyman agreed. "They'll take it out of my salary."

And what will they do, I asked silently, *if one of us gets killed?*

Magister Tallyman glanced at the clock. "You may as well go back to your workrooms or straight to dinner," he said. "I'll plan out the next experiment and we can carry it out next week."

I exchanged a look with Akin, then followed him out of the room. "That was interesting," Akin said, when we were alone. "What did you make of it?"

"I don't know," I said. I needed to carry out more experiments. Perhaps Akin should have left the discs alone for a while, long enough to let the magic fade. If it did fade...it should fade, I told myself. Runes gathered and shaped magic, but unmarred metal shouldn't have anything holding the magic in place. "Perhaps we can just keep asking questions."

"Yes," Akin said. "I..."

He broke off. Jeannine was loitering at the door.

"Go to dinner," she told Akin. "Caitlyn, I want a word with you."

Akin frowned, but hurried out of the room without comment. I met Jeannine's eyes and realised, to my surprise, that she was nervous. It wasn't as if she didn't have an excuse to be here, did she? She was an upperclassman, with access to workrooms specifically set aside for them. Magister Tallyman wouldn't say a word if he caught her in the workroom. But she was still nervous.

"This way," I said, leading her over to my makeshift workroom. "Don't use magic once we're through the door."

Jeannine muttered something under her breath as I opened the door. I chose to ignore it as I rooted through the drawers, eventually digging the amulet out of its hiding place. It glittered under the light, even though it wasn't quite finished. Jeannine leaned forward, admiringly. It wasn't my best work, but that didn't matter. All that mattered was that it was an Object of Power.

"It will dispel every spell tied to you," I said. I wasn't quite sure what it would do if someone tried to hex her. I'd have experimented, if I could have cast the spell. "I just need some of your blood to anchor the spellform."

She looked reluctant, but held out her hand anyway. I cut her gently, collected a little of her blood and wove it into the final rune. The amulet glowed brightly - it dawned on me, a second too late, that I probably should have asked her to step well back - as the spellform blazed into existence. I let out a breath I hadn't realised I'd been holding. My first commission...if it had failed, I wouldn't have received many others.

"Done," I said, quietly. I picked up the amulet and passed it to her. "Wear it for at least an hour, then take it off. It may interfere with your ability to cast spells."

Jeannine draped it over her neck. "It feels *dead*," she said, slowly. I frowned. *That* didn't sound good. "But...I think it's working."

"Good," I said. The spellform wasn't *difficult*. I'd have made one for myself, if spells clung to me longer than an hour or so. "And make sure you don't show it to anyone."

"Of course," Jeannine said. She reached out and patted my hand. "And I will give you that favour."

I nodded. The favour would be worthless now, but later...who knew where Jeannine would end up? I'd looked her up in *Who Is Who*. Jeannine had the connections to go far, if she escaped her overbearing mother. And even if she didn't, the amulet had still cost me very little to make. I'd come out ahead.

And this is just the first commission, I told myself, as the dinner bell rang. *The sky's the limit.*

CHAPTER EIGHTEEN

"And so...ah...we can devise a runic network to *keep* a spell in place," Magister Von Rupert said. He sketched out a set of patterns on the board. "This is...ah...a key concept in protecting a building...ah..."

I hastily copied down the diagram as Magister Grayson's eyes swept the classroom. I didn't want to get in trouble, not with him. Magister Von Rupert was too focused on his work to care much about what we were doing - I'd never heard him issuing detentions to *anyone* - but Magister Grayson believed in ruling with an iron hand. I didn't really blame him, either. A careless student who miscast a spell during practicals might easily hurt someone.

"The network has other uses, of course," Magister Von Rupert added. The Incantations and Geomancy teacher glanced at us, looking as if he were faintly surprised to find himself in a classroom. "Can anyone name one?"

"Turning someone into a frog and *keeping* them that way," Alana said. I didn't miss the hard edge to her voice. She'd probably try to test the runic diagram on me as soon as she could, if she actually managed to make it work. "Or preventing someone from using magic."

"Correct," Magister Von Rupert said. He didn't seem to have noticed the malice in Alana's voice. "A spell does not remain in place unless held there by a network of runes. For homework—" I heard a groan echoing around the classroom as we reached for our notebooks "—you will devise a runic network that will hold a single spell in place."

"Do *not* attempt to test it," Magister Grayson added, as we jotted down the assignment. He crossed his arms, daring us to defy him. "The network needs to be checked and rechecked before you actually try to use the spell."

Rose nudged me. "Would that work on you?"

I shrugged. I didn't know. I'd discovered that spells fed on their target's magic, which was why they never lingered on me. I simply didn't *have* any magic. And yet, how could a runic network hold a spell in place past the point it ran out of power? I was starting to realise, between experiments, that a lot of what we *knew* about magic was incomplete. Perhaps it wasn't even *so*. Magister Niven's habit of poking holes in our assumptions only underlined it for me. We didn't know as much as we thought.

"We'll probably find out, later," I said. I wouldn't mind if *Rose* wanted to test her runic diagram on me. "But for now…"

Magister Grayson cleared his throat. "We'll be holding the practical lesson next door," he growled. "Move it."

The room emptied, rapidly. Rose shot me a worried look before following the others into the next room. I half-wished Bella - or Akin - would stay close to her, but I knew neither of them would be interested. Bella couldn't be seen with Rose, not publicly, if she wanted to remain one of the popular girls. And Akin had the same problem, only worse. I was mildly surprised that he was talking to me outside class.

And Alana would hex them both if she thought they were becoming friends, I thought. My sister had driven off anyone who'd wanted to be *my* friend, at least until the rumours had started to spread. *Bella isn't happy about defying her.*

Magister Von Rupert cleared his throat. "Ah…perhaps you would like to come with me," he said. "This classroom is not conductive to private study."

I could go straight to the library, I thought, as I rose. It was too early for me to be out of class, even if Magister Von Rupert wrote me a pass. The upperclassmen *might* let me go - I was working my way through a whole list of commissions - but the librarians would ask pointed questions. *It isn't worth the hassle.*

I followed him through a hidden door and into a small office. No, I realised slowly; it was larger than it seemed, but it was utterly *crammed* with boxes, paper sheets filled with handwriting, manuscripts and books. The only visible wall was lined with bookshelves, all bulging under the weight of yet more books. *Mum would have gone through the roof if I'd left my bedroom in such a state,* I thought, as Magister Von Rupert removed a pile of books from a chair. There was hardly any room to breathe. And yet, there was something about the room I found endearing.

"I do…ah…know where everything is," Magister Von Rupert said, as he sat down at his desk. It was covered with papers too, including a class schedule that was dated five years ago. I wondered if he was still trying to teach to it. "Please don't move any of the boxes."

I looked at the pile of boxes - some taller than I was - and shuddered. I'd always *liked* the idea of digging through archives, but I had my limits. Besides, some of the really old archives had nasty protections. Dad had told me that he'd helped excavate one, back before I'd been born. He'd come far too close to death before the ancient chamber had finally been cleared.

"I won't, sir," I promised.

"Very good," Magister Von Rupert said. "I…ah…I was wondering what you would make of this."

He picked up a roll of paper and held it out to me. I took it carefully, looking around for an empty table. There was none, not within view. If there was one buried under the boxes and files…I pushed the thought aside as I carefully unrolled the paper and examined the runic diagram. It looked like a ward network, but I'd never seen anything so complex in my life.

"It is very detailed," I muttered. "What *is* it?"

"The school's defences," Magister Von Rupert said. "Or some of them, at least."

I looked down at the diagram. "Are they really this complex?"

Magister Von Rupert looked surprised. "The school just kept expanding," he said. "Ah…we really should consider moving to purpose-built premises, but…ah…no one wants to pay for it."

I struggled to recall the theory I'd had drilled into my head over the last six years. Warding an entire house was a tricky piece of work, all the more so if the building grew bigger over the years. Aguirre Hall was so big precisely because we might need the space, one day, without having to worry about rebuilding the ward network from scratch. I'd heard of buildings so old that the wards had practically taken on a life of their own. I wasn't sure if Aguirre Hall was old enough for *that*, but only a fool would challenge the master of the wards on his territory. Aguirre Hall was our fortress as well as our home and the centre of our power.

"It would have to be a very big building," I said, after a moment. Aguirre Hall was huge, but I doubted we could fit everyone from school into our walls. "Sir...this network is a mess."

"It was put together...ah...over many years," Magister Von Rupert informed me. "I don't believe...ah...that any of the original designers set out to make it *that* complex, but it grew with the school. There are parts of the school that are very well protected indeed and other parts with very limited coverage."

I made a face. "Can't someone find a weak point and break into the school?"

"The outer wards are solid," Magister Von Rupert said. "But fixing the problems throughout the inner network may take years."

"Oh," I said. I looked down at the diagram for a long moment. "Why are you showing me this?"

"Because some of the really old parts of the building are based on Objects of Power," Magister Von Rupert said. "They may need to be replaced."

That caught my attention. No *wonder* successive administrations hadn't dared to grasp the nettle. A mistake, perhaps something as simple as moving the Object of Power, might cause part - or all - of the network to collapse. They'd built layer after layer of wards on top of an artefact that dated all the way back to the Thousand-Year Empire. I didn't blame Magister Von Rupert for being concerned about what might happen if the wards were updated. The entire school was at risk.

"And you want me to replace it," I said. I didn't even know where to begin. There *were* protective Objects of Power included in the books in

Dad's library, but they'd all struck me as an order of magnitude more complex than the flying machine. And if I had to build them alone...I wasn't sure I could do it. "It might be hard..."

"Ah...we do understand," Magister Von Rupert said. He let out a sigh. "But...ah...we must find a solution soon, before it is too late."

I nodded in understanding. The family wards were tied to a specific bloodline, allowing a degree of direct control and sophistication the school's wards lacked. There was no way to *tie* them to a bloodline too, not without rebuilding the entire network from the ground up. It would be a nightmare. And who would take control of the school? Jude's was neutral ground. Whoever took control would be in a position to shatter that neutrality beyond repair.

"I'd have to study the plans carefully," I said. It was a *very* long-term project. "I think it might take years."

"I understand," Magister Von Rupert said. "Ah—" he cleared his throat "—what did you make of today's class?"

I frowned as I slowly wrapped up the diagram and placed it on his desk. "I think I understand," I said, slowly. "But why do the runes keep the spell in place?"

"The magic is locked into the spellform," Magister Von Rupert said. "It is really very simple."

I frowned. I knew *something* was wrong - or at least misunderstood - but I wasn't sure how to put it into words. And yet...

"When you set fire to wood for heat," I said slowly, "the fire burns as long as it has something to burn. You have to feed it a constant supply of wood if you want to keep the fire going. And that's true of spells too, isn't it? A spell remains in being as long as it has a supply of magic."

And it doesn't care where the magic comes from, I added, silently. I'd proved *that*, to my satisfaction, but I hadn't discussed it with anyone apart from Rose. Our names on a research paper would go a long way towards ensuring that she had a satisfactory future after she graduated. *But how does locking it in place keep the spell active?*

I struggled to put my vague concept into words. "The spell should still be burning magic," I said. "So why doesn't it run out of magic, even with the runes holding it in place?"

Magister Von Rupert frowned. "It is generally believed that magic *doesn't* work like firewood," he said, slowly. "Ah...the magic is concentrated in one place, rather than being *burnt*. One might...ah...compare several men working together to lift something, instead of each man trying to lift the object on his own. The runes keep the magic from leaking away."

He reached for a folder and started to flick the pages. "That may be why the runes on Objects of Power and Devices of Power are different in many ways," he said. "The latter are more focused on preventing magic from leaking, once it has been infused into the Device."

"But I don't *have* any power to infuse," I pointed out. "Where does the power come from?"

"Ah...a very good question," Magister Von Rupert said. "You may be unlocking previously unknown magical aspects of metal and wood. It was not until recently that we discovered that the common or garden...ah...worm had uses beyond the obvious. And you yourself proved that dragon scales *can* actually be worked into something useful."

I nodded, slowly. Dragon scales weren't actually *useless*, but they require very careful handling indeed. I hadn't been the only one to realise that they could be used to produce a burst of raw magic, merely the only one to make it work. And yet...when I'd tried to show the trick to Rose, I'd nearly killed both of us.

It did make a certain kind of sense. The potions my mother brewed would have seemed impossible to my ancestors, at least as far back as the empire. They would have stared in disbelief as Mum brewed a potion involving spells they *knew* to be dangerous when mingled with potion ingredients. Maybe there *was* something about wood and metal that could only be unlocked by a Zero. But...something told me that wasn't the answer. There were simply too many unanswered questions.

"It might be true," I said. "But..."

"You will uncover more secrets as you work," Magister Von Rupert assured me. "And you will lay the groundwork for your successors."

He gave me an odd little smile. "You might as well do your homework now," he said, as he turned his attention to an ancient crackling manuscript. "And if you have questions, you can ask."

I would have preferred to do my homework in the library or even the dorm, but it was clear that I wasn't going to be allowed to leave until the bell rang. Opening my notebook, I reread the assignment and then went to work. The runes were simple enough to draw, yet getting them into the right pattern was a little harder. A mistake might not be a complete disaster - it would keep the spell in place for a few hours longer, not indefinitely - but it would be annoying. Magister Grayson wouldn't hesitate to call any particularly brainless mistakes out in front of the class.

"I was wondering," I said, as the runic network took shape. "If someone uses a network of runes to turn their victim into a frog and keep them that way, what's to stop the frog from hopping out of the network?"

"Nothing," Magister Von Rupert said, simply. "Unless, of course, you…ah…add a *secondary* set of runes to keep the frog in place. Or you put a ward-line around the network. But it can be difficult to draw out the line without weakening the runes."

I nodded. I had a feeling that I'd need to know that, sooner or later.

"The prisons have a more complex set of spellforms to keep the prisoners under control," Magister Von Rupert added, after a moment. "We'll be looking at that when you become an upperclassman."

"If I do," I said. I looked down at the runic diagram I'd drawn, feeling a sudden flash of irritation. I could plot it out, but I couldn't make it work. "Is there any *point* in trying to pass my exams?"

"Ah…theory is important," Magister Von Rupert said. "Many poor spellcasters can still add to our body of knowledge, simply by devising newer and better runic diagrams. You are still on simple runes, for all your advanced knowledge. The more complex networks are beyond you. Ah…for now."

For a moment, he sounded sterner. "And you…ah…have a talent that makes you unique," he added. "Ah…do you think your exam results matter?"

"Alana will lord hers over me for years," I predicted, gloomily.

"She can't make Objects of Power," Magister Von Rupert reminded me. The bell rang, loudly. "Try to focus on your advantages instead of your disadvantages."

I closed my notebook - I'd have to finish the diagram later - and headed for the door back into the classroom. An upperclassman was sitting at one of the desks, looking bored. He smiled at me as I approached, a smile I *hoped* was his best attempt at seeming friendly. It looked rather like he was out of practice.

"Caitlyn," he said. "I was wondering..."

"...If I could do a private commission for you," I said. I'd heard it before. I wondered, absently, just what I was going to be offered this time. Money? A favour? Or something else? "Tell me what you want and I'll see if I can do it, for the right price."

His face shadowed, just for a second. "I want an improved focusing device," he said. "If you can make one that stores and releases multiple spells at once..."

I made a show of considering it. I couldn't *rent* a focusing device, not one bonded to a specific person. He'd have to pay very well. And perhaps not in money.

"Maybe I could," I said. "What are you offering?"

I felt someone *looking* at me. I looked up. Alana was standing in the doorway, her eyes wide. Us juniors - us *firsties* - didn't *talk* to upperclassmen. They only noticed us when we'd done something wrong. Or when they wanted to take their bad mood out on us. Even brothers and sisters wouldn't socialise, publicly, in school. But an upperclassman was talking to me...

I smiled at her. Alana, for all of her magic and the family name, didn't have upperclassmen asking her for favours. Even those who wanted to apprentice under my father didn't ask *us* for help. But an upperclassman was *still* talking to me. For once, I was the favoured one. I'd pulled off a social coup she couldn't hope to match. I allowed my smile to grow wider, daring her to say something. But she seemed too flabbergasted to say a word.

And then she withdrew, as silently as she'd come.

CHAPTER NINETEEN

Weekends had never really been *quiet* days for me. At home, there had been the ever-present threat of waking up to discover that I'd been turned into something small and slimy; at school, there had been the same problem combined with a complete lack of concern for our personal welfare. And *then* there had been a series of detentions that had kept me from sleeping in...

"Wake up," someone shouted. "Wake up!"

I jerked awake, one hand reaching for the dispeller. I'd protected myself as best as I could, but my defences weren't perfect. If Isabella had decided to sneak through the drapes and cast spells on me...I could hear people outside the drapes, but no one seemed to be trying to break through. I checked myself quickly with the spectacles, then stood. Whoever was shouting seemed to want us *all* out of bed.

"Come on," someone said. It *sounded* like Isabella. "Hurry!"

I checked my nightgown, brushed my hair out of my eyes and stepped through the drapes. Isabella was standing in the centre of the room, holding a large paper bag in one hand. She held it out to Henrietta as I watched, offering her a chocolate...no, a sweet. There was a single sigil on the bag, confirming that it had come from Sweetmeats. I stared in awed disbelief. Isabella had slipped out of the school?

"I brought them back myself," Isabella said, catching my eye. She held the bag out to me. "Try one?"

I hesitated. Sweetmeats was the best sweetshop in the city. Everyone said so. And yet, I wouldn't have taken one from Isabella if there had been any other choice. But it was rude to decline food, when offered. I took a raspberry drop and palmed it, unsure if I actually wanted to put it in my mouth. Isabella could easily have hexed the sweet when I wasn't looking.

Although she would have had to know which sweet I'd take, I thought. Henrietta was sucking hers with every evidence of enjoyment. *And she would have had to keep the other girls from taking it...*

Rose took a sweet before I could stop her and popped it into her mouth. I tensed, expecting Rose to turn into a chicken or start croaking like a frog or something else humiliating. I'd seen countless sweets that had...*interesting*...effects on people foolish enough to put them in their mouths. But nothing happened. I eyed my sweet warily, then pocketed it as Isabella offered the bag around. I didn't think I wanted to eat it.

"That was good," Rose said. "What *was* it?"

"A caramel surprise," Isabella said. "I slipped out at dawn and bought them."

"Hah," I said. "You had them shipped to you..."

Isabella held out the bag. The date on the seal was today. "Not so clever, are you?" Isabella said. "You're a cheat! And nothing, but a cheat!"

I swallowed several nasty responses. Isabella couldn't have gone out of the school, could she? Sneaking through the building might be tacitly ignored, as long as the student in question wasn't actually *caught*, but actually leaving the school? Isabella should have been caught before she had a chance to cross the grounds. I glanced at the clock and frowned, again. Isabella would have had to get up at least a couple of hours ago to get out of the school, make her way to the sweetshop and then get back before her absence was noticed.

Although if she kept her drapes closed, Sandy might not notice she was gone, I thought, slowly. *She might have made it out...*

I dismissed the thought as Isabella passed out the rest of the sweets. It was a trick. It had to be a trick. Alana was the most advanced student I knew in my year and *she* couldn't have broken through the school's wards. Magister Von Rupert had insisted that the outer wards were secure, hadn't he? And if a firstie could break them...I looked at the raven badge on my blazer, waiting for me to put it on, and frowned. Someone might *just* be able to use the badge to get inside.

"We'll discuss this later," Sandy said, quieting the chatter. Everyone but me wanted to congratulate Isabella on her success. "Everyone else, go back to bed or clear out. I don't care which."

I looked at Rose, then headed for the shower. Isabella had tricked everyone, it seemed. How had she done it? I couldn't wrap my head around her mastering a trick that had defeated a number of upperclassmen...I groaned as it hit me. It was obvious. It should have occurred to me at once. She'd bribed an upperclassman to buy the sweets, then claimed to have bought them for herself.

We showered quickly, then headed down to breakfast. The giant hall was almost empty, save for a handful of upperclassmen who looked somewhat the worse for wear. I guessed they'd been caught by the City Guard and marched back to the school, although there was no way to know for sure. We tried to avoid attracting attention as we ate our breakfast. Akin joined us as we finished, looking tired. I wondered, absently, what had kept him up half the night.

"We're going exploring," Rose said. "Do you want to come?"

Akin looked surprised. "Exploring *what*?"

"The school," I said. "All the sections that haven't been visited for decades."

"Cool," Akin said. He looked wary, for a long moment. "Shouldn't we be in the workroom?"

I shook my head. I'd spent the last few afternoons and evenings in the workroom, forging various commissions *and* experimenting with Magister Tallyman. It had been interesting, but both reassuring and frustrating. Akin couldn't touch the discs - or anything, really - without risking an explosion. He'd forged a set of discs and left them alone for a couple of days, but they'd exploded as soon as I'd tried to work them into an Object of Power. Magister Tallyman seemed to believe that we were getting closer to something we could actually turn into a research paper...

I wasn't so sure, really. The more I thought about it, the more I was sure we were missing something. But what? Did Akin's mere *presence* contaminate the discs? Or was it something to do with his work? I just couldn't understand it.

"I think I've done enough forging for the week," I said. "Shall we go?"

"Your sister said she sneaked out of the school," Rose said, as we left the dining room and headed for the lower levels. "Is that true?"

Akin shrugged. "She doesn't talk to me that much, these days," he said. "She's too busy brooding."

The school felt emptier and emptier as we made our way through the passageways and into sections that hadn't been touched for years. There were entire wings and floors of Aguirre Hall that were effectively abandoned - we'd played hide and seek there when we'd been children - but they didn't feel so *old*. Dust hung in the air as we pushed through a half-open door and walked down a darkened corridor. It was clear that no one had been in the area for years. The dust was so thick that it was interfering with Akin's light spell.

We stopped outside an old classroom and looked inside. The room seemed frozen in time, utterly unchanged from the day it had been abandoned. Someone had stripped the walls bare, but otherwise left it alone; someone else had written an unflattering comment about Magister Nortel's body odour on the blackboard. I'd never even *heard* of Magister Nortel. He might well have left Jude's before I was born, let alone gone to school.

"I've never heard of him either," Akin said, when I asked. He moved from desk to desk, flipping open the table tops. All he found were dust bunnies, some moving under their own power. They'd been left alone so long that they'd absorbed some of the background magic from the wards. "He must have left a very long time ago."

Rose snickered. "Perhaps he saw the note and felt too ashamed to return."

I shrugged. Very few students would be brave enough to tell a teacher that he smelt bad, no matter how bad it was. I rather suspected that the note had been written *after* the classroom had been abandoned and then forgotten. If no one had returned for years, the writer might *also* have left school. Perhaps it had been Dad. I found it hard to imagine Dad writing rude notes on the wall, but I supposed it was vaguely possible.

We walked out of the classroom and made our way further along the corridor. Rose and Akin both felt uneasy, insisting that they could feel fluctuations of raw magic in the air. I felt nothing, save for the feel of dust in my throat. Faint sounds echoed through the air - rats and mice, disturbed for the first time in years - reminding me that the whole area had been exposed to magic. Who knew *what* was breeding down here?

"It reminds me of the old sewers under the city," Akin said. "My father told me that all sorts of creatures live down there, warped and twisted by loose magic."

I nodded. The old sewers dated back to the days before the Sorcerous Wars. Dad had told me that every magician had poured the remains of his experiments into the sewers, allowing hundreds of different brews to mingle together. By the time Magus Court had discovered that there actually *was* a problem, when some of the mutated creatures had started to climb to the surface, it had been too late to do more than seal off the old sewers and enforce newer and stricter laws about disposing of one's potion residue. Mum hadn't been pleased about some of the requirements, but she had to admit they were necessary. Allowing so many potions - and worse - to mingle had been a *seriously* bad idea.

"I don't think it will be quite so bad down here," Rose said, as we reached a fork in the corridor. "This isn't a sewer."

"Someone *did* blow up the South Wing," Akin reminded her. "It wasn't pleasant."

We walked through a dozen more classrooms before the dust started to make my hands feel old and withered. I'd thought we'd hit pay dirt when we discovered a handful of textbooks in one classroom, but on closer inspection they turned out to be a mere thirty years old. I glanced at the titles anyway, then dismissed them. There were copies of these - and countless others, besides - in my father's library. I could read them whenever I wanted.

Slowly, we made our way back to the inhabited parts of the school. Dust billowed from my uniform, leaving me feeling thoroughly uncomfortable. Rose and Akin didn't look any better. Akin's hair was so covered with dust that he looked old enough to be his great-grandfather. I was silently glad that no one was around as we reached the exit and stepped back into the corridor. We looked terrible. Anyone who saw us would probably send us for a shower, then give us thousands of lines to write.

Akin held up a hand, then muttered a spell. A wind sprang up, lifting the dust away from Rose's clothes. It blew around me too, but faded before it could actually remove the dust. I felt the earring go warm and whispered a rude word under my breath. Akin was trying to help, but the spell wouldn't work…

"You'll have to take it off," Akin said. He cleaned his own clothes with another spell. "You can't walk back to your dorm looking like that."

I hesitated. I'd been careful not to remove the earring when someone else was around. Did I trust him enough to take it off? I knew he wasn't like Isabella, but…

There's no choice, I thought.

I reached up and removed the earring, passing it to Rose. Akin repeated the spell, blowing a wind through my hair. My braid threatened to come loose - I put up a hand to hold it in place - as a small storm of dust blew away from me. The wind failed a second later, allowing me a chance to tie my hair back into place. I still felt unclean - I'd have to go for a shower before lunch - but it was a vast improvement.

"I'll see you in the workroom later," Akin said. "Bye."

He gave us a jaunty wave and strode off. I exchanged a look with Rose as she gave me back my earring, then shrugged as we started to walk back to the stairs. It was probably pretty close to lunch time, although I had no way to be sure. Our dormmates would probably be up by now. We could slip back into the dorm, get a shower and then go for lunch. And then…

Alana stepped out of the shadows. "Cat," she said. Her gaze fell on Rose. "Scram."

I glared. "She's my friend."

"And this is *family* business," Alana said. "Send your friend away."

I hesitated, unsure what to do. If Alana was right - if this *was* family business - Rose shouldn't be hearing it. She wasn't family. She wasn't even one of our trusted retainers. And yet, I didn't want to send Rose away either. She deserved better than to be pushed around by my sister.

"I'll see you in the dorm," Rose said. She squeezed my hand. "Good luck."

I crossed my arms and glowered at Alana. "What?"

Alana looked back at me. "Why are you spending time with Akin Rubén?"

"He's a friend," I said, although I wasn't entirely sure that was true. I liked him, but our families were bitter enemies. His *sister* was a bitter enemy. "And who are you to care who I spend my time with?"

"I'm your sister," Alana said. She leaned forward, her eyebrows narrowing in a way I knew portended a hex. *That* didn't worry me, not now. "And I have a duty to you."

I laughed, harshly. "Where was your…*duty*…to me when we were younger?"

Alana opened her mouth, but I pushed on.

"You made sure I didn't have any friends," I reminded her. "You made sure that I could never relax, even in my room. You made sure that I was the laughing stock of the entire city…"

"That was then," Alana said, ignoring what I said. "This is now."

I met her eyes. "Oh? This is now? What has changed? Oh! I know! Little Zero Cat is suddenly *useful!*"

Alana's fingers slipped into a casting pose, then relaxed. I knew that meant nothing. Alana could cast spells with surprising intensity without moving her fingers, if she wished. And yet…I had the earring. She would freeze herself again, if she cast a spell. It felt so *good* not to be scared any longer.

"I never thought you were useless," Alana said, slowly. "I…"

"You thought I was completely useless," I snapped. I wasn't going to let her rewrite family history. She'd been horrible to me - and Bella and anyone else she could get away with bullying - for the last five years. "You said you were going to turn me into a frog permanently when our parents died, remember?"

"It was a mistake," Alana said. She took a breath. "What are you doing with those upperclassmen?"

"Building a patronage network," I said. Upperclassmen? Alana had discovered that there was more than one? Who had talked? And why? "You know…what we're *supposed* to be doing."

Alana rested her hands on her hips. "Akin Rubén is just trying to use your talents," she said, icily. "And so are those upperclassmen."

I felt a flare of hot anger. "And you're *not* trying to use me?"

"They're not interested in *you*, Cat," Alana said. "They're only interested in what you can do for them. What you, and you alone, can provide. They wouldn't give you the time of day if you didn't have your unique talents."

"I *do* have my talents," I protested. My voice rose. "Why shouldn't I use them?"

"And why should they be allowed to use you?" Alana asked. "You shouldn't be talking to our family's enemy, let alone students who will be graduating in a year or two..."

"And why not?" I demanded. "You were surrounded by a circle of cronies the moment you walked into the school. They didn't sign up with you because you have a nice personality, did they? Why shouldn't *I* use my talents to build up a patronage network too?"

"Because they're using you," Alana snapped. "Cat, as your sister, I order you..."

"You're not the boss of me," I snarled. "I *don't* have to do what you say!"

Alana's hand lanced out. Before I could stop her, she grabbed the earring and yanked as hard as she could. I screamed in pain as the earring came free, blood dripping to the floor. Alana cast a spell a second later, slamming it right into me. I froze, instantly.

"You have your tricks," she said, as panic gibbered at the back of my mind. The pain was suddenly gone, but it didn't matter. I was defenceless. She could do anything to me. "But what are you without them? Nothing."

Her voice hardened. "They're just using you," she warned. "And don't you ever forget it."

She dropped the earring into her pocket, then turned and walked away. I struggled to move, but my limbs refused to budge. It felt like every muscle had locked solid. All I could do was wait, silently praying to all the ancestors that no one would come along until the spell wore off. She hadn't cast a very powerful spell, had she? I didn't know.

It felt like hours before the spell broke. I dropped to the ground, every muscle aching. My ear hurt...I touched it, lightly. It wasn't as bad as I'd feared - I'd thought the whole earlobe had been torn off - but it was still pretty bad. I'd have to go to a healer.

I forced myself to stand. She was wrong, wasn't she? They weren't using me, were they? I was trading favours, just like Dad and the other high lords...

I clung to the thought as I made my way to the infirmary. Alana was wrong. I was sure of it.

And I was certain, too, that I was right.

CHAPTER
TWENTY

Alana hadn't just frozen me, I discovered as I reached the infirmary. A *normal* freezing spell wouldn't have had quite so many side effects. Instead, she'd used a spell that locked my muscles solid, holding them firmly in place. I had pins and needles everywhere, making it increasingly hard to walk. It felt as though I was walking through neck-high water.

"That looks bad," Healer Risdon said, as he examined my ear. He was a young man, one of the healers who'd saved my life after the dragon scales potion had exploded. "What were you doing?"

Stupid question, I thought. I wasn't going to tell him. I wanted to take revenge myself, rather than be thought a sneak. And I *had* to take revenge. Alana wouldn't hesitate to walk all over me if she thought she'd cowed me into submission. *What do you think I was doing?*

"I accidentally pulled my earring free," I said. "And I broke the skin."

He gave me a look that suggested he knew perfectly well I was lying - he'd probably seen quite a few students suffering from the after-effects of hexes and jinxes in the corridors - but said nothing. Instead, he rubbed a salve on my earlobe and offered me a potion to drink. I hesitated before taking it - I couldn't afford magical contamination - but there really was no choice. The pins and needles were becoming unbearable.

"It doesn't seem too bad, now I've wiped away the blood," he told me. I took the tissue and put it in my pocket for later disposal. "But I suggest you give it time to heal before you put on another earring."

I nodded, curtly. I'd had to argue for hours to convince Mum and Dad that I should have my ears pierced, particularly after Mum had thrown a fit about Bella getting *her* ears pierced a year or so ago. But it was the easiest way to keep an earring safely attached to my person. I made a mental note to design other protective Objects of Power. A bracelet, an amulet... even a belt buckle. Alana wouldn't be the last person to think of simply tearing the earring off and *then* hexing me.

And she has one of my earrings now, I thought. *What am I going to do without it?*

The question worried me as I slowly made my way back to the dorm. I felt naked. If someone decided to hex me, I was defenceless. It was all I could do to walk normally, as if I didn't have a care in the world. I'd hated the etiquette lessons Mum had drilled into our heads, but I was grateful now. Mum had taught me to remain calm and dignified, whatever the situation. High Society would have been proud of me.

Rose looked up from her bed as I entered. "Cat? What happened?"

I glanced around, making sure we were alone. It was lunchtime. Everyone else would have gone to lunch before the netball game. Isabella had been making herself obnoxious about it, bragging about her place on one of the teams. She'd even told me that she was going to humiliate Alana...Alana, who'd *also* bribed her way onto one of the teams. A thought occurred to me and I smiled. Getting into Shark Dorm might be impossible, but...

"Cat?" Rose asked, urgently. I'd zoned out. "Are you all right?"

"Alana thought it would be a fun idea to grab my earring," I said, sourly. I kept the rest of our discussion to myself. I'd developed a talent that put hers in the shade. All of a sudden, people were paying attention to me, not to her. She was jealous. She wanted the spotlight back. "And I need to plan revenge."

I walked over to my bed and searched through my trunk for the spare earring. Dad would have reprimanded me for not thinking ahead. I'd never anticipated someone actually *grabbing* the earring and I *should* have. But then, most magicians used their magic, rather than their hands and fists. I'd punched Isabella in the nose and everyone had been shocked by the sight of blood.

Score one for Alana, I thought. I was going to make her pay for that - and all the other humiliations. *She is not going to get away with this.*

I clipped the spare earring over my other earlobe, then dug through to find a handful of very special ingredients. Alana knew to be careful, of course. She didn't sit down until she'd made sure to check the seat for concealed hexes. And she wouldn't leave her own possessions undefended. I could dispel her charms, of course, but she'd notice they were missing. I'd have to be very careful, too.

"We'll go to lunch," I said, once I'd pocketed a handful of supplies. Alana had been imaginative enough to realise she didn't *need* to use magic. But did she understand all the implications? "And then I need you to help me."

Rose frowned. "Is it a good idea to strike back?"

"I have to," I said, surprised. I felt a pang. I'd spent too long trying to stand up to her before I'd discovered my talents. "Or else she'll just walk all over me again."

"Yes, but..." Rose struggled for words. "What's to stop her from just snatching the earring again? Or catching you in the shower? Or...why don't you just stop this feud?"

"Because she won't leave me alone," I said. I understood the dangers. But I also understood my sister. When I'd been powerless, I'd been a threat to her reputation; when I'd discovered my talents, I'd become a threat to her future. People who had scorned Alana for having a powerless sister now paid court to me instead. "I can't let her get away with it."

"And she has your earring," Rose said. "What can she *do* with it?"

I shrugged. The earring wasn't blood-bonded to me. Alana could wear it too, if she pierced her ears. Maybe she could rig up a clasp, if she didn't want to risk Mum's displeasure. And the earring would work for her, if she didn't accidentally destroy the spellform. But anyone *wearing* it wouldn't be able to use magic themselves. It wasn't a problem for me, of course, but her? Alana would feel crippled without her magic.

And yet...I rubbed my earlobe as we headed down to lunch. There would have been traces of my blood on the earring, wouldn't there? Could Alana do anything with it? I honestly wasn't sure. Blood magic was banned for a reason. Alana would have to be insane to risk something that would get her expelled, from polite society as well as the school. And even if she did...I didn't know if a spell focused on my blood would strike me. I had no magic running through *my* veins. It was quite possible that Alana would merely waste her time.

I should find out, I thought, grimly.

But I wasn't sure how. Dad wouldn't use blood magic on me, not even as part of an experiment. And anyone else would be in real trouble if they were caught. Magus Court was unlikely to sanction any experiments involving blood magic. The only thing they'd take a dimmer view of was left-hand magic. Dad's political enemies would use it to tear down his position and destroy the family.

The dining hall was crowded, hundreds of students stuffing their faces before the games. I glanced at the football teams - jeering at each other - and then sought out my sister. Alana, surrounded by a gaggle of older girls, was making rude faces at Isabella. Isabella was making them back, surrounded by her own teammates. I exchanged glances with Rose as we collected our food and sat down with the handful of sane students who paid no attention to the games. We ate slowly, even as the bell rang. No one would care if we stayed behind when the players and their supporters went to the arena. Sandy - mercifully - had stopped insisting that everyone should attend the games.

And she wouldn't know who she wanted me to cheer for either, I thought. I didn't want to cheer for Isabella *or* Alana. *Maybe I should go check out the football game instead.*

"The library will be empty," Rose pointed out. "We wouldn't be fighting for the books."

"We'll go there later," I promised. I understood Rose's reluctance to make an enemy of my sister, but I couldn't stop. I *needed* to make Alana pay. "Let's go."

We returned our trays to the staff, then headed down to the arena. The noise-dampening charms had weakened, if someone had bothered to put them up at all. I could hear the roar of the spectators shaking the walls themselves. The announcer was giving a running commentary so loud it could probably be heard on the other side of the city. I didn't *have* to attend to know what was happening.

The changing rooms were deserted, as I had expected. There were four: two for the girls and two for the boys. The gym teachers preferred to keep the two teams separate while they got changed, knowing that one player might decide to hex another player and remove her from the field before the game began. I pulled on my spectacles and examined the half-open door suspiciously. There was a very generalised ward drifting over the entrance, but nothing else.

Designed to make note of who enters rather than anything else, I thought, as I pulled on one of my bracelets. I'd designed it myself, then tested it against Dad's wards. It wouldn't break down the ward, but it *should* conceal me from its unblinking gaze. *They should have just locked and warded the door.*

"Stay here," I muttered. "And cough loudly if someone approaches."

My heart started to pound as I stepped into the changing room. There *was* a toilet at the far end, giving me the barest fragment of an excuse if anyone *caught* me in the changing room, but I doubted anyone would believe it. Sabotaging the other team was a long-standing tradition. So was hexing anyone caught in the act. I looked around, silently noting the team banner on the wall. Whoever had designed the ugly thing *must* have bribed the team to accept it, I thought. It was a hodgepodge of colour and crude patterns.

I found Alana's clothes and peered at them through the spectacles. There were no less than five hexes guarding them, all nasty. I wondered, absently, if her teammates hadn't been too pleased when she'd joined the team. Alana hadn't really had time to develop her skills. I could easily understand why some of her teammates might resent her presence, no matter what she'd offered them. Losing because of a first-year student would turn them into a laughing stock.

And they'll probably hex her today if she loses, I thought. Alana was good, but she was no match for someone three or four years ahead of her. *I wouldn't want to be in her shoes.*

I briefly considered dispelling the hexes, but I knew she'd notice at once. Instead, I looked around for the bottles of juice. Isabella had bragged about the juice - brought in from Sweetmeats by older students - often enough that I knew they had to be there. And they were, resting on a bench and carefully labelled with each student's name. I walked over, checking carefully. There were no hexes guarding them from theft.

Because while hexing one's opponents is allowed, theft is not, I thought, wryly. *It isn't tradition.*

I picked up Alana's bottle and opened it, then removed the syringe from my pocket. I didn't dare put too much in the drink - she might notice the taste - but a few drops should be more than sufficient. I closed the lid, returned the bottle to the others, then hurried out of the changing room. Alana *might* realise that someone had opened the bottle and cast detection spells, but it wouldn't matter. What I'd done didn't rely on magic.

Rose was outside, looking pale. "Are we done?"

"Nearly," I said, as we hurried towards the arena. "We just want to wait and see the results."

No one bothered to question us as we took seats in the stands and watched the game. Alana, Isabella and the rest of their teams were throwing a ball around, hexing and jinxing each other when the referee's back was turned. I'd never really liked the game, even as a spectator. It was just another reminder that there were things I'd never be able to do. And besides, who was *I* meant to cheer for?

I watched Alana running around, dodging hexes and tossing the ball to her teammates. She wasn't *bad*, I admitted sourly; she was smart enough to keep moving, rather than trying to hex her older opponents. And she was fast, faster than I'd realised. I'd always thought she'd never had the time to learn to play, but perhaps she'd played with her friends. I hadn't attended those parties.

The whistle blew for half-time. I leaned back in my chair and waited, patiently. The die was cast. Alana would drink the juice or she'd smell a rat and pour it down the toilet. I wasn't sure how long the potion would take to take effect - my calculations had been imprecise - but I was fairly sure it would work quickly. And then...

She won't even know who to blame, I exulted. No, that wasn't entirely true. Alana would have a very good idea who to blame. But no one else would listen to her. *They'd be more inclined to think she accidentally drunk the potion herself.*

Isabella's team returned to the field, took up their places and waited. And waited. I waited too, impatiently. No team captain would leave their opponents on the field for long, not when the opposition would take advantage of the opportunity to scatter hexes all over the place. The referee might not even bother to object. But where were they?

Rose nudged me. "Are you sure you didn't hurt her?"

I nodded, curtly. And yet...had something gone wrong?

Alana's team reappeared. I knew, immediately, that *nothing* had gone wrong. Alana's mouth was tightly closed, her lips and teeth clenched together. And yet, it looked as though *something* was trying to come out of her mouth. The referee blew the whistle, startling everyone...and Alana brayed like a mule. I laughed, along with the rest of the audience, as she clamped her mouth shut. She'd be braying like that for hours, perhaps days.

I tried not to giggle as the game resumed. Alana's captain must have threatened her with something truly awful to make her take the field. I could tell she was furious and humiliated - and who could blame her? Her mouth kept opening and emitting donkey sounds. And she was perplexed, too. There were quite a few hexes to make someone talk like an animal - she'd used them on me, far too many times to count - but no one had hexed her. She would have noticed.

"Let's go," Rose said, firmly.

I followed her out of the arena and back up the corridor. It was hard to contain my giggles. I wanted to throw back my head and cackle insanely, like a character in a mad play. My entire body shook with the effort it took to keep myself under control. Alana had been hexed and humiliated and she didn't have the slightest idea how it had happened!

Serves her right, I thought. She'd humiliated me, often enough. *And it will teach her a lesson.*

Rose caught my arm. "What did you do?"

"I put the potion ingredients in her juice," I said. The potion itself was quite simple, so simple that a child of five could brew it. I *had* brewed it. I'd just never been able to get it to work. "There wasn't any magic, you see. She couldn't detect it with her spells because there was no magic."

"I see," Rose said. "And yet it worked."

I smirked. "Her magic triggered the potion," I said. It was a simple trick, so simple I was surprised no one else had thought of it. Perhaps I just had a unique perspective. "The juice didn't *become* potion until she drank it, at which point it took effect. And then she started talking like a donkey."

Rose didn't seem so amused. "And how long will it last?"

I looked back at her. "Are you feeling *sorry* for her?"

"I'm worried about you," Rose said. "What happens if she *keeps* talking like an ass?"

I reflected that Alana had *always* talked like an ass, but I kept that thought to myself.

"It will wear off, soon enough," I said. "I'd be surprised if it lasted till evening."

But I wasn't really sure how long it *would* last. It depended on how much of the potion Alana had actually drunk. If she'd realised it tasted odd and stopped, she might only have swallowed a drop or two. But then, we *had* tried to drink Dad's black coffee under the impression it would make us more adult. And *that* had tasted foul.

"Be careful," Rose urged. She didn't seem as pleased as I had expected. Alana hadn't been nice to her over the last few months. I'd thought she'd be glad to see the other girl humiliated. "She's going to want revenge for this, isn't she?"

"Probably," I agreed. Alana would know who to blame. She knew she hadn't been hexed. It wouldn't take her long to deduce my involvement. "And then I will take revenge myself..."

Rose sighed. "Be careful," she said. She squeezed my arm, lightly. "Feuds never end well."

"No," I said, tartly. The potion wouldn't last. "But nor does letting someone else walk all over you."

CHAPTER
TWENTY-ONE

As it turned out, I was wrong.

Alana was at dinner that night, braying like a mule. She had to struggle to eat her dinner, then hurry back to her dorm with the entire hall laughing at her. And she was *still* braying the following morning, when we went down for breakfast. Even I might have started to get a little worried, at this point, if it wasn't clear the potion was wearing off. By lunchtime, she was back to normal. I was sure she was plotting revenge of her own.

I took Rose down to the workroom after lunch, intending to work on a few of my commissions while she practiced her forging. Magister Tallyman didn't need much persuasion to convince him to let Rose work, although he insisted that either Akin or myself had to keep an eye on her at all times. Akin didn't try to argue. I'd never been sure how he felt about Rose - she might not have been an enemy, but she was still a commoner - yet he seemed happy enough to help. Perhaps he just wanted the teaching credit.

"I'll have more experiments for you, later in the day," Magister Tallyman told us. "Make sure you're back here after dinner."

I nodded as I went to work. None of the commissions were particularly complex, but they were satisfying. I was building up a network of favours that I'd be able to call in, one day. I'd even started working on an Object of Power that would cleanse someone of magic - all magic - without being blood-bonded to them. If I offered to rent it out to students like Jeannine, who knew *what* they'd pay for it? I was midway through the fifth commission when there was a knock at the door.

"Hang on," I called, as I moved my current project out of the way. "Come in."

The door opened. An upperclassman peered in and smiled. "Lady Caitlyn?"

I nodded, slowly. He was handsome enough, although his face had a rugged look that suggested he'd spent too long playing football or rugby instead of studying. His brown hair was grown out a shade too long, something that would probably earn him his mother's displeasure when he returned home. His blue eyes studied me for a long moment, just as I studied him. I couldn't help thinking that he simply didn't have the polish to be part of High Society, even though he clearly wasn't commoner-born. A merchant's son, perhaps. He wouldn't have been raised to treat the whims of High Society as iron commands.

"I am Rolf," he said, with a half-bow. Definitely a middle-class student, then. "I was wondering if I could have a moment of your time."

"If you wish," I said. I racked my brain for the proper formalities, then decided to forget them. "What can I do for you?"

"And what am I prepared to pay for them?" Rolf finished. "I'd like you to help me - us - with a project. And we can make it worth your while."

I nodded, slowly. A merchant's son, almost certainly. High Society's older children would be a little more subtle about wheeling and dealing. Dad had told me that it was the same thing, just dressed up differently. I had no reason to disbelieve him. Rolf's approach was...refreshing.

"I see," I said. "And what would you like me to do?"

"We want to get over the back wall," Rolf said. "And if you help us, we'll bring you back a mountain of chocolate from Sweetmeats."

I blinked, surprised. "You think I can help you break through the wards?"

"I think you can make something that can help us slip through," Rolf said. "If some of the old stories are true..."

I considered it, carefully. "I might be able to make something that would help you get through," I said. The chance to share a mountain of sweets myself...*that* would give Isabella a nasty shock. "But wouldn't it be considered cheating?"

"There's no rule against using Devices of Power," Rolf pointed out. "And there's certainly no *tradition* against using Objects of Power."

"True." I had to smile. By tradition, anyone who managed to get over the walls was free to roam the city...although they could expect to be in hot water when they finally returned to the school. Dad's apprentices had told me that the smarter ones brought back a bottle of wine or two to bribe the gatekeeper. Sneaking *into* the school was a great deal harder than sneaking *out*. "But would that count as *you* getting over the wall?"

"You could come with us," Rolf said. "You'd be the youngest student to cross the walls in a thousand years."

It *was* a tempting thought, I had to admit. The youngest student who'd crossed the walls had been a third-year, nearly a hundred years ago. A number of second-years had tried to match his feat, but they'd all wound up entangled in the wards. Isabella would never be able to sneer at me for crossing the walls, unless she decided to accuse me of cheating again. But Rolf was right. There was no rule against using Objects of Power.

There probably will be soon, I thought. I'd sold over a dozen Objects of Power to various students. *The prospect of someone using one in school is greater now.*

I wrestled with my conscience for a long moment. Dad - and the Castellan - had told me to stay in the school. And yet, I was tempted. If I had an escort, I would be safe...right? But I didn't think Dad would see it that way. He might pull me out of school altogether if I defied him so blatantly. Or he'd crush Rolf and his friends...

"I'll help you get through the wards," I said. I didn't have to make them something specific for the job. "But it'll cost you more than just the chocolate."

We haggled backwards and forwards for nearly ten minutes before agreeing on terms. I was mildly impressed, although a merchant's son *should* know how to bargain. And yet, he *needed* me. Getting over the rear walls was supposed to be *very* hard. I was in a strong position and I knew it.

"Meet us by the Blasted Oak in an hour," he said, when we'd finally agreed on terms. "And bring at least one of your friends. We don't want to be seen with you alone or people will start asking questions."

I nodded. Every upperclassman who'd asked for a commission had worked hard to get me alone, just to make sure no one saw them socialising with a firstie. If I'd had an older brother, *he* wouldn't have talked to me too. I was surprised that rumours had started to leak out, let alone reached Alana's ears. The upperclassmen had every reason to keep their private commissions a secret.

"You'll have to give whoever I bring chocolate too," I said, firmly. "They need a reason to keep their mouth shut."

Rolf looked pained. "Very well," he said. "But no more than three friends."

I shrugged as he turned and left the workroom. I didn't *have* three friends. Rose and Akin were the only ones I'd consider inviting. Rose deserved a chance to share chocolate too, while Akin probably wanted to show his sister that she wasn't the *only* one who could bribe upperclassmen into fetching chocolate.

And if I invited Bella, she'd eat all the chocolate, I thought. *Mum would not be pleased.*

I walked out into the main workroom. Rose was bent over a workbench, carefully carving runes into a piece of wood. Akin stood on the other side of the table, whispering advice as she worked. I felt a flicker of jealously, mingled with relief. Rose was already considered part of my patronage network - my only client, as far as most students were concerned - and that put her on my family's side. Her being friends with Akin might just keep her from being automatically classed as an enemy by *his* family.

"Nearly done," Akin said, without looking up. "Rose is doing very well."

Rose blushed. "Thanks," she managed. "I...I think it's ready."

Akin held up her work for inspection. "It's definitely going to last for quite some time," he said. "Make sure you make good use of it."

I smiled. "Well done," I said. "Very well done."

Akin nodded. "What did *he* want?"

I didn't have to ask who *he* was. "He wants my help." I explained, as quickly as possible. "And I need you two to come too."

"Clever of him." Akin looked oddly amused. "A Device of Power would probably be unable to get through the wards. But an *Object* of Power..."

Rose cleared her throat. "Is this actually a good idea? I mean...we're talking about leaving the school."

"No one would dare to harm us," Akin said, confidently.

I wasn't so sure. Akin had magic and a family name, Rose just had magic. And I had the name. But it didn't matter.

"We're not going to leave the school," I said. "We're just going to help them get out."

"It's tradition," Akin agreed. "And if we were to sneak out too…"

I shook my head. "Let's just get them out, shall we?"

Akin looked rebellious. I understood, all too well, just what he must be feeling. The chance to leave the school and roam around for a few hours…he'd get in trouble when he returned, but he would still have done something that would never be equalled, let alone bettered. And he had magic to protect himself. *His* father would probably laugh and make snide remarks about boys being boys rather than demanding immediate punishment. *Mine* would be much less sanguine.

"You can go," Rose said. "But we'll stay here."

"I'll bring you back some chocolate," Akin said. He winked at me. "It should be fun."

I went back to my workroom to gather my supplies. The outer edge of the school's wards - the one configured to block anyone *leaving* the school - wouldn't be that strong, not compared to some of my father's wards. Jude's was just too big and unwieldy to be protected properly. And while I might not be able to knock the wards down without setting off alarms, I could weaken them enough to let Rolf and his friends get out. They could take the blame, while we took the chocolate.

And if Akin wants to go, I thought, *why not?*

We made our way out of the building and walked slowly around the school. Jude's had just kept expanding until the outer walls were a mismatch of styles, ranging from stone buildings that dated all the way back to the empire to more modern brick and clay. The gardens were a mess too, a strange mixture of rock formations, tiny pools and overgrown hedgerows. I'd heard that older students liked to pick herbs from the gardens, but I doubted it. Mum's herbal garden was perfectly regimented, everything in its place. Jude's gardens would make any gardener weep.

Rose cleared her throat. "Why is this such a…a mess?"

"It provides cover for students climbing over the walls," Akin said. "It's tradition."

I nodded in agreement. There were hundreds of traditions in Shallot, some of them so old that the original purpose had been forgotten long ago. It was possible that some previous Castellan had decided to let the gardens lie fallow, I supposed, but it was equally possible that he'd reasoned that the school would be expanding again soon and there was no point in trying to keep the gardens tidy. He might have been right, I thought. There *were* some buildings on either side of the school that might wind up being absorbed, sooner or later.

"The walls aren't very high," Rose pointed out. She sounded as if she wanted to be somewhere - anywhere - else. "Our fences back home are higher."

"The walls aren't the real protection," I said, suppressing a pang of guilt. The walls surrounding my family's hall weren't that high either. "A single blasting spell could put a hole through the walls, if they weren't crawling with wards. They're only really there to mark the school's territory."

I slipped my spectacles on as we reached the rear of the building. It was practically a jungle, dozens of trees competing viciously for the same space. I could see flickers of raw magic passing through the woods, blurring into the faint haze surrounding the school. Rolf was standing by a path, doing his best to pretend he was ignoring us. I suppose it would have fooled me, too, if I hadn't known we were supposed to meet him. Rolf would become a laughing stock if his fellows thought he was talking to us.

And yet, he wanted to take a few friends over the walls, I thought, as we walked into the jungle. Insects flew past us, the buzzing setting my teeth on edge. *But they'd all have a vested interest in keeping their mouths shut.*

I looked around with interest. The jungle would have made my mother throw up her hands in horror, but there was something about the green wildness that appealed to me. I *knew* the jungle really wasn't very big, yet…I couldn't help feeling that it went on forever. Paths appeared and disappeared as we walked on, twisting so I couldn't tell where they led; a handful of statues peered out of their leafy disguise; strange fruits hung from some of the trees, slowly ripening before they fell to the ground. The smell was strange, almost heady. I took a breath as the wind shifted and regretted it, instantly. The smell grew sour, utterly vile. And yet, it was oddly familiar. I wondered, absently, if some of the fruits were used in potions.

Rolf caught up with us. "That's the edge of the walls," he said, pointing. His voice was hushed, although I have no idea who he thought would overhear. The sound of insects buzzing through the trees was overwhelmingly loud. "Can you see the wards?"

I nodded. I could see the stonework at the end of the path. The walls were lower than before - I could have climbed over them without difficulty - yet they weren't unprotected. The wards were invisible to the naked eye, but I could see them through my spectacles. A *real* magician wouldn't have been able to see them either, yet…they'd be able to sense them. I wondered, as we moved closer, if I actually had an advantage. I could see the spellform - and the ward's structure - in far greater detail than any magician.

As long as I have the spectacles, I reminded myself. I touched my earlobe, gingerly. The pain had largely faded, but it still ached. *Without them, I wouldn't even sense the ward until it was too late.*

"You came," a dry voice said. I looked up to see another upperclassman standing there. Two more stood behind him, their faces nervous. I understood. Getting caught as they tried to sneak out of the school would get them laughed at, nothing more. "Welcome."

Rolf put a hand on my shoulder. "Can you weaken the ward?"

I studied the ward for a long moment, then nodded tersely. I'd have to work fast. The longer we stayed here, the more likely someone would come to investigate. I had no idea how well Rolf could spin a story, but I didn't think there was *any* good reason for four upperclassmen and three lowerclassmen to be in the same place. It wasn't as if Rolf was my brother, having a private chat with his sister. Someone would definitely ask a lot of hard questions.

"Be careful," Rose murmured.

I nodded as I went to work. The ward was beautiful, in a way. I could see magic ebbing and flowing around the walls. And yet, it was clearly weak…it had been designed to provide a deterrent, rather than an actual barrier. The other wards, the ones designed to stop people entering the school, were far stronger. I could see them too. They wouldn't turn on us as long as we were actually *leaving*.

And we might be in some trouble if we got caught between them, I thought. *We'd be stuck until someone came to get us.*

"This should tear a hole in the wards, just for a few seconds," I informed them, once my Object of Power was in position. I didn't *think* the ward was directly monitored. If it was, we were in trouble. Bending the ward out of shape would probably not set off an automatic alarm, but a living mind would definitely notice. "Get ready to get over the walls and out."

Rolf moved forward. "Do it."

I pushed the Object of Power forward. The ward sparkled into visibility, a sheet of blue light that danced in front of us. I pressed harder, bracing myself. A Device of Power would have shattered at this moment, unable to cope with the feedback. But an Object of Power...I heard someone breathe an oath behind me, a word I wasn't supposed to know, as a gap appeared in the wards. It rapidly grew big enough for a grown man.

"Now," Rolf said.

His voice was sharp, different. I glanced back, just in time to see him slam a stunner hex into Akin. Akin tumbled, hitting the ground with a terrifying *thud*. Rose fell a second later, blasted down by one of Rolf's friends. I grabbed for the speller in my pocket, but it was too late. Rolf brought a small club down on my head...

...And I knew, as I fell into darkness, that I had made a terrible mistake.

CHAPTER
TWENTY-TWO

My head hurt.

I fought my way back to wakefulness through a haze of pain. My memories were a jumbled mess. Something had happened, but what? A potions explosion? *Another* potions explosion? Or something else…

"Welcome back," an unfamiliar voice said. Panic shot through my mind. "Open your eyes."

I tensed as my memories snapped into place. Rolf had lured me to the walls, talked me into opening the wards, then…then he'd *hit* me. And then…where *was* I? Rolf had to be out of his mind if he thought he could kidnap me. Where were Rose and Akin? What had happened to them? Did Rolf really want *two* of the most powerful families in the city for enemies?

My eyes opened, slowly. I was lying on a comfortable bed, in an unfamiliar room. A young woman - probably about nineteen - was sitting by my bedside, watching me through worried eyes. I didn't know her, which meant…I wasn't sure *what* it meant. She wore a long black shirt and trousers, a style that had never quite gone out of fashion among Shallot's magicians. And her hair fell down her back and brushed against her waist.

I studied her, thoughtfully. She looked Hangchowese, with almond dark brown eyes, but her face was pale enough to suggest she was mixed. The child of a sailor and a local woman, perhaps. There simply weren't many other Hangchowese in the city. And a magician…I wondered, grimly, if she really *was* a trained magician. It was illegal to dress like a magician without proper training, but kidnapping was also illegal. Wherever I was, I was a long way from home.

I could be on the edge of the city, I thought, slowly. *Or maybe in a nearby country home.*

"I apologise for the rough treatment," the girl said. Her accent definitely *suggested* Shallot, although there was a hint of something different. "Please rest assured that it was I who tended to your wounds, removed your remarkable artifices and dressed you."

I looked down at myself. My uniform was gone. Instead, I was wearing a simple white nightgown that itched against my skin. I felt naked without my protections…she'd taken everything, even the dispeller. And I'd been kidnapped…I swallowed, hard, as the implications struck me. If I was behind a set of sealed wards, it was unlikely I'd ever be found.

And how long, I asked myself, *was I asleep?*

Panic bubbled at the back of my mind. I forced it down, ruthlessly.

"Thank you," I managed. My voice sounded croaky. My throat was dry. "Who…who are you?"

"Call me Fairuza," the woman said. "It's as good a name as any."

And definitely not your real name, I thought. Fairuza had been a popular name, once upon a time, before Queen Fairuza committed some kind of treason against her husband. I didn't know the details, but she must have done something terrifyingly bad. The name had gone out of fashion with remarkable speed. *Who are you really?*

I looked around the room. It was a simple bedroom; bare stone walls, no windows…the only illumination came from a lantern, hanging high over my head. There were three doors: one made of solid metal, the other two made of wood. I guessed that one led to the bathroom, but the other two were a mystery. There weren't even any runes, as far as I could see. The walls were completely bare. It was a prison designed for someone without magic.

"There's no way out," Fairuza told me, calmly. "This place is very secure."

"Oh," I said. I forced myself to think. "You *do* realise that my family will be looking for me?"

"I'm afraid they have no conception of where we've brought you," Fairuza said. She leaned forward, threateningly. "There's no way they'll find you here."

I swallowed, hard. I was alone, I was defenceless...I didn't even know where I was. And I doubted she'd tell me, if I asked. Knowledge was power...a bitter swell of defeat threatened to overcome me. She could simply use magic to *make* me do whatever she wanted, if she wished. I couldn't even jump her without being frozen mid-leap.

"My family will pay for my return," I said, trying not to panic. Dad would ransom me, wouldn't he? I was sure of it. Alana might be pleased at the thought of me never returning home, but no one else would agree. "He will..."

"He can't pay what we'd want," Fairuza told me. "You're our servant now, our slave. And the sooner you come to terms with that, the better."

I stared. Me? A servant? A *slave*? It was unbelievable. And yet it had happened...

Fairuza stood. "Get up," she ordered. She nodded towards one of the wooden doors. "Use the washroom, if you wish. And then I have some things to show you."

I didn't move. "I'm not your servant."

Fairuza snapped her fingers. The bed lurched, then tipped on its side. I rolled over and fell, landing hard on the stone floor. It felt cold and hard against my bare skin.

"Get up," Fairuza repeated. "I will not ask again."

I glared at her. I wanted to resist, I wanted to force her to pull me to my feet, but it was clear I had no choice. Moving as slowly as I dared, I stood and tottered towards the washroom. It was simple, very simple. A bath, a shower, a washbasin and a single mirror. I peered at my own reflection, trying to guess how long I'd been asleep. My hair, hanging down in an unwashed mass, didn't seem to have grown any longer. Maybe I hadn't been asleep for more than a few hours.

They would have had to get me well away from the school, I thought. Rolf and his friends might well have attracted attention, if they hadn't moved quickly. *And how long would that have taken?*

I worked the problem as I splashed water on my face. Assuming they'd had a carriage waiting, they could have whisked me to the docks and loaded me onto a ship...or driven me out of the city before the hue and cry was raised. How long would it have taken the school to notice I was missing? Magister Tallyman would have noticed when *none* of us showed up for his experiments, right? Sandy would definitely have noticed when I didn't sleep in my bed...

Despair howled at the back of my mind. I was a prisoner, a helpless prisoner. No one knew where to find me. And escape was impossible.

Nothing is impossible, I told myself, firmly. *I'm not trapped until I surrender all hope.*

"Come on," Fairuza ordered. "Now."

I brushed my hair back - Fairuza didn't seem to have supplied anything to tie my hair into place - and walked back into the bedroom. Fairuza was holding a porcelain jug of water in one hand and a drinking glass in the other. I took the glass and hesitated, a moment before tasting the water gingerly. It tasted normal, as far as I could tell.

"If I wanted to force something down your throat," Fairuza said, "do you think I couldn't do it?"

I scowled. Fairuza was a magician. I knew that, now. And that meant she could force me to drink whatever she wanted. There was no point in trying to limit my intake. Besides, I felt dehydrated. It was a sign, if I recalled correctly, that someone had fed me sleeping potion to keep me unconscious. I supposed I should have been grateful that they hadn't used nastier spells.

"Drink whenever your body tells you that you need to drink," Fairuza said. She passed me the jug as I finished the first glass of water. "You need to listen to it."

"Yeah," I said. "I know."

She turned away from me, exposing her back. I lifted the jug instinctively, then brought it down on her head. Or tried to. A flash of light sent me flying backwards into the wall. I hit the stone hard enough to knock the wind out of me, then fell to the ground, nearly breaking my legs when I landed. Pieces of porcelain crashed down around Fairuza, none of them actually touching her body. She'd woven powerful protections around herself.

Fairuza turned to face me. "I do trust that that will be the last such attempt on my person," she said, in a manner that reminded me of my grandmother. She'd always sounded more irritated than shocked by childish naughtiness. "The next time, I will be forced to take more…unpleasant…steps."

"You want me for something," I said. I didn't bother to get up. "You won't hurt me."

"You will be surprised, I am sure, by just how much pain you can suffer without being crippled or killed," Fairuza said. "Get up."

I struggled to my feet. My legs hurt and I tottered when I walked, but I didn't seem to be seriously hurt. Fairuza led me though the second wooden door and into what was clearly a private workroom. A large workbench sat in the centre, surrounded by a number of forging tools. Bookshelves and cupboards leaned against the walls…I had no doubt that they were crammed with reference materials and supplies. The pattern was familiar. The room had clearly been laid out by an experienced forger. Tools within easy reach, materials on hand, smaller tables that could be moved around for best advantage…it was practically identical to the workrooms at school. I glanced at Fairuza as she moved around the room. Had *she* gone to Jude's? With a face like that, she would have been remembered.

Remain calm, I told myself. Dad had taught me what to do, if I was ever kidnapped. *Gather information and wait.*

I allowed my eyes to roam the room. There were no windows here, either. Five lanterns hung from the ceiling, all out of my reach. Three more doors, one metal, were clearly visible in the stone walls. There were no runes, as far as I could tell, but that meant nothing. The wards might be positioned further away from the suite. Fairuza waited, patiently, for me to finish my survey. It struck me, suddenly, that she wasn't in any hurry. *That* wasn't a good sign.

Rolf and his friends must have vanished already, I thought. He would have covered his tracks as best as possible, but *someone* might well have seen him with us. What could he possibly have been offered that made the certainty of incurring my father's anger a good thing? *They threw away their schooling, for what?*

Fairuza smiled. "Why do you think we brought you here?"

I bit down a sudden flash of pure hatred. A formal exchange of hostages was purely ceremonial, with the 'hostage' being treated as one of the family. He wouldn't be supposed to actually *escape*. But someone who had been kidnapped *would* be expected to try to escape…I didn't think *they'd* be put in a suite attached to a forge. It was more likely they'd be hexed into submission or simply chained to a wall.

"I don't know," I said. I was playing dumb. There was only one thing that possibly justified the risk of kidnapping me. "You want to force my father to part with thousands of gold sovereigns?"

Fairuza gave me a sharp look that reminded me of Magistra Loanda. "You're not stupid, young lady," she said. "Why do you *think* we brought you here?"

I looked at the forge. "You want me to forge something for you."

"Correct." Fairuza's voice was loaded with sarcasm. "It was blindingly obvious, was it not?"

"Yeah," I said, in a tone that I knew got under my mother's skin. "I suppose it was."

Fairuza didn't show any signs of anger. "As it happens, we want you to forge a great many Objects of Power for us," she told me. "And you *will* do it for us."

I rested my hands on my hips. "No," I said. "I won't."

"Yes, you will," Fairuza said.

"Or you'll hurt me?" I challenged. "How far can you go before I lose the ability to work?"

Fairuza met my eyes. "Do you really want to find out?"

The honest answer to that was *no*, but I knew better than to say that out loud.

"You can't compel me to do anything, either," I added. I wasn't entirely sure that was true, but I didn't want her trying to experiment. "A compulsion spell would make it impossible for me to forge."

"I assumed as much," Fairuza said. I had the sudden sense I'd fallen into a trap. She raised her voice. "Akin! Rose!"

One of the doors opened. Akin and Rose stepped into the room. I stared in horror. Both of them were moving with strange, jerky motions… they were under a *geas*! My blood ran cold. Whoever had planned the kidnapping had managed to start a feud with *two* houses, not just one. My father and Akin's father might loathe each other, but they'd work together to find their missing children. And very few others would be able to stand against their power combined.

I looked at Fairuza. "What have you *done*?"

"I thought you might need incentive," Fairuza said. She indicated Akin and Rose as they came to a halt. "You might be immune to compulsion spells, but they…they are not."

I swallowed, hard. Akin was seeing me in a nightgown, with my hair down…I felt a hot flush of embarrassment, even though he was wearing something similar. And Rose…she was wearing a nightgown too. I cursed myself as I saw my horror reflected in their eyes. If I'd been more careful, if I'd been more wary, they wouldn't be in this mess. I'd dragged them both into immense danger.

"You've picked a fight with Magus Court itself," I stammered. There wasn't a single family in the city that would risk uniting everyone else against it. Merely kidnapping someone from Jude's was quite enough to start a war. "Who *are* you?"

"That is none of your concern," Fairuza said. Her voice hardened, suddenly. "You are aware of how *geas* spells work, aren't you?"

"No," I said. I knew a little, but not enough to be useful. Dad had banned us from learning anything about such spells. "What have you done?"

"Your friends will be their normal charming selves soon enough," Fairuza said. "But they will do as I tell them - and they will do as you tell them, as long as you don't order them to ignore my standing orders. They'll assist you with your work, while keeping an eye on you…just in case you devise a cunning plan. If you do, they'll tattle on you at once."

"You…" I stopped myself before I said something she'd make me regret. My friends weren't puppets, but they'd been turned *into* puppets… no, they'd been turned into something worse. They would betray me at once if they thought I was working on an escape plan…even though they'd want to escape too. "This is…this is outrageous!"

"I suppose it is," Fairuza agreed. She crossed her arms under her breasts. "I have two other things to tell you. For starters—" she jabbed a finger towards the wall "—you don't have the slightest idea of where you are, and I'm not going to tell you. What I *will* tell you is that we are miles from civilisation. If you somehow manage to get out of this place, you'll be in a very dangerous land indeed. I wouldn't care to bet on you reaching the closest town alive."

Assuming you're telling the truth, I thought. We could be in a Family Hall in Shallot, for all I knew. The risk of keeping three prisoners in such a place would be staggering, but whoever was behind the kidnapping had already crossed the line. *You'd want me to remain here, held by my own fears.*

"How nice," I said. I tried to sneer, like Alana. "And what else do you want to tell me?"

"Just this," Fairuza said. Her voice turned nasty. "Akin? Hit her."

I barely had a second to react before Akin slammed his fist into my chest. I doubled over, gasping for breath. Akin was strong…I'd known he was strong, but I hadn't known *how* strong. He'd certainly never *hit* me before. I staggered backwards, grunting in pain. It was hard, so hard, to breathe.

"I…" Akin said. "I…"

"Be quiet," Fairuza said. Akin's mouth snapped shut. "Rose? Hit her."

Rose slapped me. I twisted, catching her blow on my shoulder instead of my face. It still hurt. Rose was strong too…she'd slapped me once before, when I'd needed it. Now…I looked up and saw horror written all over her face. My best friends had become my unwilling jailors.

"I could make them hit each other, instead," Fairuza said. There was a hint of heavy satisfaction in her tone. "Or I could torture them myself."

"No," I managed. It was still hard to breathe. Maybe I could have held out, if it was just me, but I couldn't bear the thought of my friends being hurt. Or being forced to hurt me. "I'll do as you say."

"Very good," Fairuza said. She turned towards the door. "I'll have food sent to you. After that, I'll give you your first assignment."

She stopped and looked at me. "You are our prisoner, but it doesn't have to be unpleasant," she added. I resisted the urge to snort. She sounded as though she was trying to be sincere, but it wasn't very convincing. "If you behave, you will be treated well."

Too late for that, I thought. My mind raced, trying to come up with a solution. *We have to get out of here.*

CHAPTER
TWENTY-THREE

"I'm sorry," Akin said, as the metal door closed. "I...I'm sorry."

"It's alright," I lied. The pain was fading, but the shock would linger for a long time. "It wasn't your fault."

Rose was crying, great heaving sobs that tore at my heart. I reached out and wrapped my arms around her, trying to give what comfort I could. Akin and I had some protection because of our family names, although I had no idea just how much it counted for now; Rose had none. No one would feel any need to placate a commoner family. And, I supposed, if you'd already made enemies of the two most powerful families in the city, you wouldn't really care about a commoner.

I held Rose tightly, trying to think. Guilt overwhelmed me. It was all *my* fault. If I'd thought twice about helping Rolf and his friends...but who would have expected them to kidnap us? They had to be out of their tiny minds. The sheer audacity of the plot staggered me. No one breached Jude's neutrality, no one. Dad had been more concerned with someone trying to take me from the hall than school. I should have seen it coming, but I hadn't. It had been in my - our - blind spot.

Whoever did this has to be very powerful, I thought. And yet, who *did* have that sort of power? The king? I couldn't imagine King Rufus making enemies out of everyone in Shallot. He could just have ordered me to Tintagel, if he'd wished. Everyone else would be far more concerned, surely, about uniting the city against them. *What if...*

My blood ran cold. What if we'd been taken right out of the kingdom? I'd never really considered the possibility, but I should have. Tintagel had enemies, enemies who feared us as we feared them. They wouldn't be happy about Tintagel producing new Objects of Power, would they? A single Object of Power, used properly, could change the course of a war. And yet...there was something about Fairuza that suggested she was from somewhere a little closer to home. I didn't think we'd been taken *that* far from the city.

But there's no way to know how long we were asleep, I reminded myself. A regular dose of sleeping potion would keep us asleep for weeks, if they were careful. They'd have to feed us, somehow, but that wouldn't be a problem. *We could have been asleep for quite some time.*

My mind raced, suggesting possibilities. A week...someone could have carried us out of the kingdom by that time, either in a carriage or on a boat. Or simply moved us to a hiding place in Shallot and waited to see if we could be traced. Dad - and Akin's father - had our siblings, didn't they? I didn't know if Dad could use Alana or Bella to track me - I still had no idea if my blood could be used for magic - but Carioca Rubén had Isabella. *Her* blood could be used to track Akin. Unless we were very heavily warded...

I looked up. The roof was bare, but that meant nothing. We could be in a very small part of a very large building. The wards could be blanketing the outer walls, making it impossible for someone to track us down. And yet, blood magic was hard to keep out entirely. I wouldn't have cared to take the chance...I shivered. They had to be *very* sure they'd blocked Akin's connection to his sister. If they couldn't be sure, keeping him prisoner was dangerous - and stupid. They'd have let him go or cut his throat by now.

"We'll get out of this," I said, patting Rose's back. But I didn't know how. My friends were my jailers. I couldn't share anything with them without having it passed on to Fairuza and her allies. "How much do you remember?"

Rose said nothing. It was Akin who answered.

"When I woke up, the *geas* was already in place." His voice was raw with anger - and bitter helplessness. "Fairuza gave me my orders, then told me to wait."

I nodded, slowly. Someone smart might be able to find a way to subvert the *geas*, but it would take time. And Akin would have to convince himself that he wasn't cheating. *That* wouldn't be easy. Until then, I didn't dare rely on him. He was too smart to be tricked easily - and if he caught on, he'd report me. The *geas* wouldn't let him do anything else.

And Rose will be the same, I thought. Despair threatened to overcome me, again. I'd only just started to have friends and now...*I can't count on either of them.*

I helped Rose to a chair and told her to sit down, then started to go through the cupboards. As I'd expected, they were crammed with raw materials: wood, metal, everything a forger might need. The layout was definitely familiar. Whoever had set up the workroom had gone to Jude's. The tools were well-made, but lacked a maker's mark. I puzzled over that as I inspected an etching tool. Most forgers and artificers would have passed up on a contract rather than produce work that didn't carry their name. And it didn't look as though the mark had been removed. Someone must have shelled out a lot of money to get the tools.

"Dad will find us," Akin said, firmly. He sounded as though he was trying to convince himself. "He'll be looking."

I hoped he was right. Enemy of the family or not, I would have given a great deal to see Carioca Rubén. But I wasn't so sure.

Fairuza must be someone's client, I thought. It was unlikely her family had enough money - or a title - to overcome the prejudice she would have faced. A girl with no lineage to speak of wouldn't have many prospects, not in Shallot. But someone had clearly seen her potential and given her a job. Maybe she hadn't been trained at Jude's. That didn't make her useless. *I wonder if I could talk to her...*

I considered the possibility as I peered into the second bedroom, Akin following me like a lovelorn dog. The *geas* wouldn't let him do anything else, I feared. *One* of my friends had to be with me at all times. They couldn't escape on their own...I wondered, slowly, if Fairuza *had* left such an obvious chink in their armour. But I doubted it. Anyone willing to use a *geas* on children would have practiced first.

The second bedroom was smaller, but had the same basic layout as the first. I guessed I was meant to share my room with Rose, which wouldn't have been so bad if she hadn't been bespelled into spying on me. She wouldn't sleep well at all…I made a mental note to see if I was allowed to sleep without being chained to the wall. If not…I might be able to sneak around while they were sleeping. Rose had slept in a dorm. She'd be used to sleeping through loud noises.

Although she would have been nervous about someone sneaking into her drapes and casting spells on her, I thought. I'd rarely slept deeply, even after I discovered ways to protect myself from my sisters. *She might sleep very lightly indeed.*

I kept my thoughts to myself as I checked the bathroom, then walked through the third wooden door. The room was barren, completely bare save for a lantern hanging from the ceiling. There was no window, nothing except empty walls and a featureless ceiling. I guessed it had been a bedroom, once upon a time, but there was no way to be sure. Maybe Fairuza used it as an office. Or…or something. It wasn't as if there weren't hundreds of unused rooms in my family's hall.

"I'm sorry, Cat," Rose said, as we walked back into the workroom. "I just couldn't *stop* myself."

"I understand," I said. I knew enough about *geas* spells to understand that resistance was pretty much impossible. A skilled magician *might* manage to break the spell from the inside, but Rose was only a firstie. The spell would keep her from even *starting* to resist. "Don't worry about it."

"But you…" Akin stopped dead. "I…"

I winced. He'd clearly wanted to say something the *geas* didn't like. An idea to get us out of the trap, perhaps? Or something cutting about our captors? I wondered, sourly, if I was truly as safe as I believed. If I was wrong about a *geas* making it impossible for me to work…she might try to find out. I shivered at the thought. If I was wrong, it was over. I wouldn't have a hope of escape.

But a geas won't linger on me, I told myself. *Goading her into enchanting me might be a possible way out.*

"Don't worry about it," I said, out loud. I couldn't risk sharing my thoughts with either of them. "We'll just have to make do."

I heard a dull *THUNK* and turned, just in time to see the metal door open. A young man was standing there, carrying a large tray. I wanted to try to jump him, but I knew it would be pointless. Even if I could knock him out before he could cast a spell, Akin and Rose would freeze me at once. A desperate bid for freedom would only end badly.

The young man showed no expression as he strode into the room. I peered past him and saw a long corridor, leading down into darkness. The walls were stone, as unmarked as the walls in the suite. And that meant... what? Where were we? Somewhere that hadn't been designed for magic? Or somewhere that was so immense that no one had bothered to carve runes on the walls? I tried to think of a building in Shallot that might fit that description, but came up with nothing. I'd visited many halls, before my lack of power became apparent, yet I'd only seen the public areas. Our hosts had barred us from the rest of their halls.

I turned my attention back to the young man. His features were... indistinct, as if my eyes kept slipping over his face. A glamour, then. Oddly, I found that reassuring. Our captors were clearly not as confident in their security as Fairuza had implied. And yet...*she* hadn't worn a glamour. Or had she? Someone who'd grown up in Shallot would know what her particular combination of features meant.

"Here's your dinner," the young man said. His accent was pure Shallot, although there were hints of something different in the way he pronounced his words. Not Rolf, then. Maybe he'd spent time out of the city. "Bang on the door when you're done."

"Thank you, sir," I managed. It galled me to be polite to kidnappers, but Dad had warned me to keep a civil tongue in my head if I was ever taken prisoner. "May we ask what time it is?"

"You may," the young man said. I thought I heard a hint of resentment in his voice. I didn't understand why. "But I will not answer."

He put the tray on the workbench, then turned and strode out of the room. The door closed with an ominous *thud*. I listened carefully, but I didn't hear any locks. There must be wards on the far side, I decided, or bolts. They wouldn't hold a magician for long, but they would be more than enough to hold me. I couldn't cast a spell to save my life.

"We'd better eat," I said. Fairuza and her fellows might have slipped a potion into the food, but there was no point in worrying about it. They'd have no trouble forcing us to drink something, if they wished. "What do we have?"

Rose inspected the tray. "Bread, butter, cheese and ham," she said. "And a pot of tea."

Akin made a face. "Commoner food."

"*Farmer* food," Rose shot back at him. "It may not be *fancy*, but it is filling. Make sure you eat plenty. You'll need it."

I walked over to join them. The food was very basic, but there was plenty of it. I took a piece of bread and made myself a sandwich. Our captors had told us something important, I realised, as I ate the ham and cheese slowly. We were quite some distance from the city. A poor family in Shallot would eat fish, not ham and cheese. Did Fairuza realise what she'd told us? Or was she deliberately trying to confuse us? I had no idea.

"It tastes good," Rose said. She sounded more like her old self, now she'd had something to eat. I wondered, grimly, if Fairuza had bothered to feed Rose while she was asleep. "The cheese is definitely from a farm."

Akin snorted. "Where else would it come from?"

"A dairy," Rose said. Her voice suggested she thought it was a stupid question. But then, Akin had probably never been on a farm. "Farm cheese is richer, but it doesn't get sold very often."

I puzzled over it for a long moment. If someone powerful had taken us from Shallot…were we on a country estate? Surely, they'd be searched…wouldn't they? But Dad would have problems convincing aristocrats they needed to open their mansions. My heart sank as I started to make a second sandwich. Searching the city alone would take months. Searching the entire country would be impossible.

"If it doesn't get sold," I said slowly, "where *does* it go?"

"The farmer's family eats it, normally," Rose said, dryly. "My father has an arrangement with the local innkeeper to supply *him* with milk and cheese, but we don't sell it any further."

"I'm sure your cheese is better than this," Akin said. He didn't look as though he was enjoying his food. And yet…he finished his sandwich and looked around. "What are we going to do?"

"We have to do as Fairuza says," I lied. I'd have to come up with the escape plan on my own, then carry it out. And then I'd have to find a way to free them from the spell. "We appear to be trapped."

Rose poured tea for the three of us as I inspected the door. It was solid metal, firmly held in place. I pushed at it experimentally, but nothing happened. It didn't budge at all. Locked in place by magic, then. I allowed myself a grim smile. The more I knew about our prison, the more planning I could do. And who knew what I could do, given time and tools?

The tea tasted odd, too. I sipped it, wondering if I'd been wrong about our captors putting potion in the tea. But nothing happened…it just tasted different. Perhaps we were in another country after all, or perhaps…we were just drinking a different blend. My father and most of the nobility wouldn't drink cheap tea if their lives depended on it. And yet… coffee shops and teahouses had been all the rage in Shallot after explorers brought home coffee beans and tea leaves. *Everyone* drank tea.

"I'm going to have a lie down," I said, putting my mug back on the tray. "You can stay here, if you like."

"I have to come with you," Rose said, dully. She shook her head. For a second, I saw terror in her eyes. She was helpless and she knew it. "Cat…"

"I understand," I said. I wasn't going to be alone, was I? "Akin, you start looking at the reference books. See if you can figure out what they want us to make."

What they want me to make, I thought, as we walked into the bedroom. Rose followed me, standing so close that I wanted to push her away. *They wouldn't have gone so far if they hadn't had a reason to snatch me.*

There was no second bed, I noted. Perhaps Rose and I were expected to share. I cringed at the thought and made a mental note to ask for a second bed - or at least some blankets. I could sleep on the floor, if necessary. I'd sooner sleep on hard stone than share a bed with anyone, even my closest friend. Rose sat down on the chair and watched me as I puttered around, her eyes hard and wary. The *geas* had to be pushing her hard.

I lay down on the bed and tried to think. We would have access to tools, wouldn't we? And I knew more about Objects of Power than anyone else. I should be able to improvise an escape, right? And if I couldn't…I gritted my teeth. How much did Fairuza actually *know*? There were details

I hadn't told anyone apart from Dad and Rose...my blood ran cold as I realised the implications. Fairuza had Rose under a spell. All she had to do was interrogate her...

I just have to hope she doesn't think of that, I thought. Rose was a commoner. An aristocrat wouldn't think much of her. But would Fairuza make that mistake? *Or trying to extract answers from me by force, either.*

I closed my eyes. My thoughts ran in circles. Someone had done this, but who? I couldn't think of any suspects. They'd somehow convinced Rolf and his friends to throw their lives away, for...for what? I couldn't think of anything - money, power, patronage - that would make the risk worthwhile. Perhaps Rolf had a patron too...it would make sense, him being a merchant's son. Dad would find out, given a chance. It wasn't as if anyone would dare stand in his way.

And Akin's father will be looking too, I told myself. *Who would dare to hide from both of them?*

Slowly, unwillingly, I drifted off to sleep.

CHAPTER
TWENTY-FOUR

"Cat," Rose said. She shook me, not gently. "You have to get up."

I groaned as I fought my way back to wakefulness. Rose was shaking me harder now, driven by the *geas*. I suppose I should have been grateful she didn't simply blast me out of bed. She didn't look good either, I discovered as I opened my eyes and peered at her. Dark rings lined her eyes, suggesting she hadn't slept a wink. I wondered, sourly, just how long the *geas* would keep her from resting. She'd collapse eventually, *geas* or no *geas*.

"I'm coming," I managed. My throat was dry. "What happened?"

"She's outside, waiting for you," Rose said. It took a moment for me to realise that Rose meant Fairuza. "She wants you outside now."

I swung my legs over the side of the bed and stood. The lanterns seemed dimmer somehow, although I knew it could be just my imagination. I hadn't slept well. I'd dreamed…I couldn't recall my dreams. But I knew they'd been bad. My legs felt wobbly as I tottered towards the door, Rose walking behind me and jabbing her fingers into my back every time I slowed. I knew she didn't want to do it, but I still felt angry. And yet, there was nothing I could do about it.

Fairuza was standing by the workbench, wearing a long black dress and looking surprisingly imperious with her hands clasped behind her back. She looked striking, I had to admit. She would have been the belle of the ball in High Society, if her family lineage had been well-established. Instead…her eyes tracked me as I made my way towards her, feeling as though I hadn't slept a wink. Akin stood by the wall, unnaturally still. I'd have thought he'd been frozen if I hadn't seen him breathing.

"Good morning," Fairuza said. "I trust that you had a pleasant sleep?"

"No," I said, stiffly. "Rose and I require more blankets." I tugged at the nightgown. "And we also require more clothes."

"They will be provided," Fairuza said. I'd expected an argument. Maybe she'd just been waiting for us to complain before she found newer and better clothes. "Are you ready for your first assignment?"

I glared at her. "Do I have a choice?"

Fairuza shrugged. "Not really," she said. She tapped the workbench, indicating a sheet of paper. "I want you to forge *this* for us."

I took the paper and inspected it. I'd seen the design before, several times. A wardcracker...a *powerful* wardcracker. I didn't think there was a single ward that could stand up to it, if the wardcracker was shoved into the spellform. There were Devices of Power that were designed to knock down wards, but they tended to shatter if the magician using them didn't get the spells *exactly* right. I'd heard stories about incompetents who'd blown off their own hands while trying to rob magicians.

"It will take some time," I said, carefully. "And I will also require tools."

Fairuza's eyes narrowed. "You *have* tools," she said. She pointed at the selection on the table. "Is this not sufficient?"

"I need better tools," I told her. "I'll have to forge them for myself."

"Really," Fairuza said. She looked at Akin. "Is that true?"

"...Yes," Akin said. His voice was curiously flat. The *geas* was in full control. "Her tools are designed to assist in forging Objects of Power."

Fairuza looked back at me. "And you can forge these tools here?"

"Yes," I said. It wasn't hard, given the right materials. The *real* question was what she'd do with them, when I wasn't working. I could do more with my homemade tools than outsiders might realise. "That will take a couple of days, then I can start work on the wardcracker."

"Very good," Fairuza said. She eyed me, sharply. "What else do you need?"

Privacy, I thought. But I wasn't fool enough to say that out loud. *I have to ask her for things I can justify.*

"My spectacles, if you kept them," I said. "And any of the other tools I was carrying when you kidnapped me."

"They weren't brought here," Fairuza told me.

I winced. I thought she was lying, but I wasn't sure. She'd be unwise to just *give* them to me, in any case. The dispeller alone would have been worth its weight in gold. She would certainly have wanted to ask more questions before letting me have them.

"Then I have to build some of them too," I said. I did my best to pretend to be cooperative. "But after that, I can get started on the wardcracker."

Fairuza never took her eyes off me. "Why do you need them?"

"I can't sense magic," I reminded her. I was fairly sure she knew that already. "And if I can *see* the magic, it's easier to forge."

Whatever else Fairuza was, I decided as she bounced question after question off me, she was definitely a trained forger. I'd had vague thoughts about forging a suit of armour and breaking out, once I managed to find a way to put it together without my friends noticing, but Fairuza was too well-trained to miss what I was doing. Anything I built would have to be more subtle. The thought made me smile. I could do subtle.

"You may as well start now," Fairuza finished. "Unless you have something else you need?"

Her tone suggested, very clearly, that I better hadn't. I made a show of looking around the room, then shrugged. I'd need more materials - and potion ingredients - sooner or later, but I didn't have an excuse to demand them *now*. I made a mental note to come up with a list, the more outrageous the better. It would be interesting to see what Fairuza could and could not provide.

"I need them to keep their distance," I warned, slowly. Akin and Rose could help, of course, but they couldn't do the work for me. "If they get too close, the spellform will be distorted."

"Really," Fairuza said. Her voice was biting. "And do you think I'm going to let you work unsupervised?"

"They can watch from a distance," I said. I would have bet my share of the family inheritance that she had the suite under constant surveillance. There were plenty of ways to spy on someone, particularly if you knew where they were. "But if they stand too close, the spellform will not take shape."

"And nor will the Object of Power," Akin said. I wondered if he was trying to help. Maybe he was. He'd be helping her too, on the face of it. "I wasn't able to help her build a simple Object of Power."

"I see," Fairuza said.

"They can brew potions for me," I said, quickly. I didn't want her thinking that Akin was useless. "They just can't stand too close when I'm working."

"Very well," Fairuza said. She waved a hand at the cupboard. "You can start making your tools now. If you need anything else, just tap on the door."

So someone is right outside, I thought. Fairuza was the *second* person to tell us to knock on the door. *Unless...*

I watched as she turned and left the workroom. Was there only one person? The waiter could easily have been Fairuza, her face hidden under a glamour. But...Rolf and his three friends were also involved. Fairuza probably wasn't alone. I simply had no way to be sure.

"Akin, take one of the cauldrons and start brewing a cleansing potion," I ordered. I doubted I could get either of them to make something dangerous, but combining two otherwise innocuous potions could have interesting effects. "Rose, brew an etching solution and..."

Rose's face went blank. "I have to watch you," she said. "I..." - she stumbled as her face returned to normal - "Cat, I can't..."

"Don't worry about it," I said. I pointed at the wall. "Just stand there and watch."

I was going to have to be careful what I said to them, I reflected, as I walked to the cupboards and started to gather my supplies. They'd do whatever I said, as long as it didn't interfere with their standing orders. I didn't know if Fairuza wanted to give me servants or give them incentive to be angry at me, but it didn't matter. I'd have to be very careful indeed.

Akin went to work with practiced ease. I felt a flicker of envy, then turned my attention back to the workbench. It didn't normally take *that* long to devise and forge my own tools, but this time I was going to stretch it out as long as I could. I needed time, time to think...time to plot an escape.

They definitely spent a great deal of money on this place, I thought, as I stacked up a number of gemstones. Did Fairuza *know* I'd found a way to produce stirrers that didn't actually need to be charged? I hoped not...Rose knew, but she wouldn't say a word as long as she wasn't asked directly. *And if I can charge a number of gemstones with magic, I can do quite a bit with them.*

The door opened, revealing the glamoured young man. He passed Rose a stack of clothing, then departed as silently as he'd come. I put my work aside and hurried to change into something a little more suitable. The nightgown wasn't bad, but I was uneasily aware that it would provide no protection whatsoever if I splashed hot liquid - or molten metal - on myself. Rose followed me, changing as well. The clothes were definitely not from the richer part of Shallot.

And completely impossible to trace, too, I thought, as I eyed myself in the mirror. I'd grown too used to tailored dresses and school uniforms. I looked like I was wearing a sack a demented tailor had turned into a shirt and trousers. It was the sort of thing a tradesgirl would wear, not the daughter of a great house. *Would anyone recognise me if I managed to escape?*

It was a chilling thought. People *would* recognise me in Shallot, but anywhere else? I was just another young girl. If I didn't wear noble clothes, would anyone recognise me as a noble? Or anything? It was just something else that cut me off from my former life...I caught myself, sharply. I was not going to give in and surrender. I was going to escape and I was going to take my friends with me.

I walked back into the workroom, just in time to see Akin finish his potion. I took the cauldron gratefully, then let him get changed himself while I started to work on the rest of the tools. They took shape one by one, while Akin and Rose took turns brewing different potions and watching me. I had Rose charge a handful of gemstones for later use, hiding them in the stirrers. With a little effort - if I was very lucky - I would never have to drain the gemstones until I actually *needed* them.

It would be fascinating to see what happens, I told myself, *if I combined the two designs...*

The minutes turned into hours and the hours slowly turned into days. We stopped working long enough to eat and sleep, then returned to our work. I took two days - I thought it was two days - to design and forge a number of tools, then ran out of stalling tactics. The wardcracker design lay in front of me, mocking me. It was complex, but nothing I hadn't done before. The sword I'd forged had been a great deal harder.

"Rose, cut me nine strands of gold wire," I ordered. I wasn't *sure* that her cutting the wire would weaken the design, but it was worth trying. "And..."

Akin hexed me. I fell forward, hitting the stone floor hard enough to hurt. My hands and feet were suddenly stuck to the floor. I looked up, just in time to see Akin's fingers - clearly moving against his will - casting a spell. The world went dark. I couldn't see a thing. He'd blinded me...

"You may not sabotage your work," Akin said. It was the *geas* talking. "If you try, you will be punished."

I fought down the urge to cry, helplessly. I was trapped...my hands and feet were stuck to the floor and I couldn't see a thing. The spell wouldn't last, I knew, but it didn't have to last very long. I thought I could hear footsteps...someone walking towards me. Akin and Rose didn't *want* to hurt me, but the *geas* didn't give them a choice. If they wanted to kick me while I was down...

"I won't try that again," I said, desperately. Someone was right behind me, weren't they? I could hear...*something*. "I'll cut my own wire."

The world suddenly blazed with blinding light. I squeezed my eyes shut, then opened them slowly. The spell blinding me had broken...or been removed. I wasn't sure. The spell holding my hands and feet to the stone vanished a moment later. I collapsed to the floor, shaking. I'd known I was vulnerable, but now...I wasn't sure I could get *anything* past Akin and Rose. The horror on their faces didn't help. They might have been unwilling gaolers, but they were gaolers nonetheless.

"I'm sorry," Akin said. He was babbling...I honestly wasn't sure who he thought he was talking to. Me? Or his family? "I'm sorry..."

I picked myself up, carefully. *He* was sorry? I was trapped and he was my jailer and he was sorry and...I told myself, firmly, that it wasn't his fault. But it was hard to believe it.

Rose passed me the wire, wordlessly. I cursed my mistake under my breath as I started to cut the golden thread, hoping her mere presence would be enough to cause problems. *Rose* might not have realised the problem, not when she hadn't been there for Magister Tallyman's experiments. But Akin had...I should have made sure he hadn't overheard the order. It was too late now.

The wardcracker took shape, piece by piece. It was an elegant design, I had to admit; it looked almost like a wire hand, with gemstones trapped in a silver lattice instead of bones. And yet, it was dangerous. Someone using it could break through almost any ward in the city. I *thought* that the wardcracker wouldn't survive contact with a really powerful ward, but it would still take the ward down too. The City Guard was supposed to have a wardcracker that dated all the way back to the Thousand-Year Empire and was still functioning. I couldn't help wondering how the original forgers had compensated for the magic surge...

"Stay well clear," I ordered, as I pushed the final pieces into place. It should work...Akin had watched me like a hawk, nudging Rose away whenever she got too close. But if I was wrong...I *thought* the spellform would still take shape. It just wouldn't be perfect. "Here we go..."

I carved the final rune into the handle. The wardcracker blazed with light. It was so bright that I had to cover my eyes and turn away, although it didn't help. It felt as though the light was burning into my very skull. There was something about it that felt...*wrong*. And then the light snapped out of existence, leaving the wardcracker lying on the table. I reached out gingerly and picked it up. It felt...*ready*.

"It's perfect," Akin breathed.

I hoped he was wrong. I hoped it wouldn't survive its first encounter with a powerful ward. But I had no way to know...I had no way to know, either, if Fairuza would believe I'd sabotaged it somehow or if it was just a problem with the design. I'd done the calculations in my head - Akin had checked the ones I'd written down - but I knew they were far from precise. Too much could go wrong with the design.

Rose touched my shoulder. I leaned into her embrace, feeling bitter. It would have been great, if I'd done it for myself. A working wardcracker would have been a remarkable achievement. But now...Fairuza was going to take it and...and what? A wardcracker could be used for all sorts of things. Very few of them were *good*.

She could try to break into the family hall, if she wished, I thought. Dad's wards were strong - and he had good reason to know that there might be new Objects of Power on the way - but I wasn't sure how well they'd stand up to my work. *Or even break into the palace itself.*

The door opened. "Very well done," Fairuza said, as she stepped into the room. She sounded amused. "You did a very good job."

I glared at her, sullenly. "Can we go now?"

"I'm afraid not," Fairuza said. "But I will consider a few other requests."

"Something to play, when we're not working," I said. "A chessboard, perhaps."

Fairuza smiled. "We'll see what we can find," she said. I had the odd feeling she meant it. "Anything else?"

"Books," Akin put in.

"I want to write a letter home," I said. "You can sneak it out..."

"I'm afraid not," Fairuza said. "It would be far too revealing."

"You could read it first," I said. "And you could take care with any reply..."

"No," Fairuza said. Her voice was firm. "And that's the end of it."

And we have to get out of here, I thought. *Or we'll go mad.*

CHAPTER
TWENTY-FIVE

I would have enjoyed the next few days, if we hadn't been prisoners.

It was what I'd wanted, I knew all too well. The chance to be *useful*, to be the sort of person others asked for help. And yet, I was a prisoner. Fairuza came every day with a new request, a new demand for an Object of Power. And I had no choice but to forge it for her. I had no idea what she intended to *do* with them - or what whoever was backing her wanted to do with them - but I doubted I'd like it when I found out. I *had* to find a way to get us out of the trap.

And yet, it was hard to prepare an escape when I was being watched like a hawk. Rose stayed with me all the time, even when I was in the bathroom; Akin watched and checked my work, alert for even the *slightest* hint of sabotage. If he'd known everything, I was fairly sure that there would have been no hope of escape. As it was, gathering the tools, charged gemstones and potions I needed was difficult. He certainly wouldn't have let me get away with what little I was doing if he'd noticed.

"That was a good game," Akin said. He'd been playing Rose. Chess was supposed to be a nobleman's game, but Rose had admitted that she'd learnt to play a long time before she'd gone to Jude's. "You're getting better at this."

"She beat you three games to two," I pointed out. Akin didn't seem to take it personally, but there were some noblemen who'd be horrified at the thought of a commoner beating them at anything. "Shall we have some tea before we go to bed?"

I rose as Akin reset the board and poured hot water into the teapot, then added a tiny splash of makeshift sleeping potion. It wouldn't be enough to send them to sleep - not immediately - but once they were asleep, it would keep them out for at least five hours. I'd be drinking it too, yet…if I was right, the magic would fade before it managed to take effect. And if I was wrong…well, I'd just have to come up with something else.

"We should have another game," Akin said. "Winner takes all."

"I'm still ahead of you," Rose said. "You'd have to beat me at least twice."

I smiled, pouring three mugs of tea and passing them around. Akin took his and sipped it, gently. I did my best to pretend I wasn't watching as he drank. If he noticed something funny about the taste, he'd alert Fairuza. And then I'd be in deep trouble. Rose drank her tea quickly - I was less worried about her noticing something wrong - and then headed for the bedroom. I waited until she'd finished in the bathroom, then moved to follow her. Akin already looked tired as he headed for his own bedroom. He didn't seem to notice when I left the bedroom door slightly ajar.

Rose lay down on her mattress, looking tired. I hoped she didn't realise that she was *too* tired as I lay down myself. I'd have to stay awake, somehow, until her snores told me she was deeply asleep. I forced myself to design newer and better Objects of Power in my head, trying to think of something that might get us out of the trap. It was a shame that Akin was so good at forging. Someone who didn't know so much might miss what I was doing until it was too late.

But even a complete novice would notice if I was forging a suit of armour, I thought, as Rose began to snore. *And I have to hope they're not watching the suite too closely.*

I forced myself to wait until Rose's snores became regular, then slipped out of bed as quietly as I could. For once, my sisters had been useful. I'd had a great deal of practice in sneaking around. I listened carefully at the door for several minutes, then crept into the workroom and checked Akin's door. It was firmly shut. I picked up my spectacles and peered at the wooden door. It was crawling with nasty-looking wards.

Clever, I thought. I felt a flash of warm affection. Akin hadn't managed to beat the *geas*, but he'd found a way to subvert it, just a little. Even *he* would need several minutes to take down his wards in the morning. I'd have plenty of warning if he decided to get up and check the workroom in the middle of the night. *That's something I'll have to exploit for myself.*

I kept the spectacles on as I walked to the metal door. It was glowing faintly, confirming my suspicion that it was barred by magic. I couldn't see enough of the spell to see the spellform, but it didn't matter. I knew how to take it down, if I wanted. But I had no idea what else was on the far side of the door. I wasn't sure of *anything*, except for one thing. We had to get out of the trap before it was too late.

And we don't even know what time it is, I thought. I'd asked for a clock, but Fairuza had flatly refused to provide one. It *felt* like the middle of the night, yet…was it? I'd been told that people who took too much sleeping potion often lost track of the time, their bodies insisting that it was the middle of the night while the sun insisted it was midday. *We don't even know how long we've been here.*

I pushed the thought aside as I walked back to the worktable. I didn't have much time. If Akin or Rose woke up, I was in deep trouble. I'd done as much as I could in the open - I'd explained that I was preparing additional supplies for future projects - but I knew I was about to start something I couldn't explain. If I was caught, I was dead.

The ancients had done wonders, I reflected, as I pulled the spellcasters together. I wasn't entirely sure I understood the calculations, but it allowed me to rig up wands and focusing devices without asking Rose or Akin to cast the spells for me. The spells lacked the finesse of a trained magician, yet it wouldn't matter. All that mattered was that it would give me the ability to cast spells without magic of my own.

And yet, I asked myself, *where does the power come from?*

Magister Niven's question nagged at my mind. I'd built Objects of Power that were using magic, some very *intense* magic. A wardcracker might just feed off the ward it cracked - and some of my protections drew their power from the spells they absorbed or redirected - but where did the spellcasters get *their* magic? And how could I even use them? Jabbing the pointy end towards the target seemed to be more than enough. I had the strangest feeling that I was on the verge of a breakthrough, if I had time to plan some experiments, carry them out and then sit down and think about the results. But I didn't have time. I didn't even dare write anything down for later.

I put the spellcasters aside - it was lucky that I *had* convinced Akin that he shouldn't touch my prepared supplies, as it allowed me to hide something on the top shelf of the cupboard - and started to work on a new set of protections. The earrings were too noticeable, I felt, but I could work the same design into makeshift bracelets and ankle chains. Wearing several would allow me to balance my protections, even making them stronger. It ran the risk of one of them overheating - it couldn't reflect the spell back if it was covered - but I'd just have to live with it. Thankfully, they were flimsy enough that I could just break one of them off if necessary.

It was tempting, very tempting, to slip one on and wear it. But I didn't dare. Rose and Akin *knew* I didn't have any jewellery. They'd certainly report it if they saw me wearing a bracelet, even if it wasn't apparently an Object of Power. Instead, I put them next to the spellcasters and concealed them behind random supplies. They'd just have to remain hidden for a day or two.

And I could break the spells on them, if I dared, I thought, sourly. A dispeller - like the one I'd forged for Jeannine - would probably break the *geas*. But Fairuza would notice immediately. I knew she spoke to Akin and Rose every day, conversations they hadn't been allowed to share with me. *I'll have to stun them too before I get them out of here.*

I put a dispeller together anyway and concealed it with the rest of the gear, then walked back to the door and listened. There was no one outside, as far as I could tell, but that meant nothing. The door was solid metal, effectively soundproofed. There was probably a silencing charm or two on the far side of the door too. Rose or Akin might be able to sense it, but I couldn't. The spectacles couldn't tell me enough to be useful. There could be *anything* on the other side.

I cursed under my breath. I could go now - I could get out - but where would I go? I didn't know. I knew nothing about the layout of the building, let alone where we were in the wider world. It wouldn't be *that* hard to build a compass that would point to Shallot - or Akin's family, at least - but we might be hundreds of miles away. Fairuza had told us that it was a very long way to civilisation…she might be lying, of course. And yet, keeping us close to the city would be incredibly dangerous. An alert guardsman might just realise that a country house was suddenly buying more food than before...

And she wants us to keep forging for her, I thought. *She intends to keep us prisoner permanently.*

I rubbed my tired forehead. Fairuza *couldn't* be the person in charge. If nothing else, her superior wouldn't want to show himself - or herself - to us. Proving that someone wealthy and powerful had been behind the kidnapping wouldn't be easy. And yet...if someone started selling new Objects of Power, it would be a red flag to Dad. Whoever was selling the items certainly wouldn't be able to produce a second Zero, when asked.

The yawn crept up and took me by surprise. I leaned against the wall for a long moment, then slowly walked back to the bedroom. I'd prepared most of the potions I'd need, but the remaining elements would have to be put together on the spot. And if I was wrong...I'd be in deep trouble. But there was no reason to hope for ransom. Fairuza and her unknown superior had more to gain from using me than selling me back to my family.

And they won't return Rose and Akin either, I thought, numbly. I sneaked back into the bedroom and checked Rose. She was still sleeping, snoring loudly. I felt a flicker of envy, combined with fear. I was too valuable to kill and Akin was too *dangerous* to kill - his family might notice his death - but Rose was useless. Her only value lay in supervising me...

And if they catch us trying to escape, they might decide to be a little stricter, I thought, grimly. *Rose would become expendable.*

I shuddered as I crawled into bed, silently promising myself that I'd do everything in my power to get Rose out. She'd tried to stop me from allowing my emotions to guide me...and she'd been right. And she was the one most at risk. Fairuza could order her to hurt – or kill – herself, and she would obey. I just couldn't save her unless I got her out before it was too late.

And it is worth the risk, I told myself, firmly. *Whatever the risk, I have to take it.*

Rose was shaking me, a second later. I started, utterly confused. Rose...? I must have dozed off. What time was it? It felt like I hadn't slept at all. How long had I been asleep? I wasn't sure.

"It's morning," Rose said. She reached out and touched my forehead. "You feel hot."

I groaned. My head felt thick as well as hot, a grim reminder that I *really* hadn't had enough sleep. I'd never been any more likely to get sick than my sisters - my mother had dosed us all with potion whenever something started going around - but now…? I shuddered, fighting down the urge to retch. Maybe I'd accidentally swallowed something I shouldn't have, or breathed in the wrong fumes. Or…I remembered the sleeping potion and scowled. I might have accidentally poisoned myself.

"Bad dreams," I said, sitting upright. "Can you pass me a glass of water?"

Rose shot me a grateful look - I'd worded it as a request - and headed for the bathroom. I kept my eyes firmly fixed on the bed, breathing hard. I couldn't get ill, not now. If Fairuza called for a qualified healer, he might find traces of the sleeping potion in my blood and then…Fairuza would ask questions. Neither Rose or Akin would have the answers, but it wouldn't matter. She'd keep digging until she found out the truth and then…

…I didn't want to know.

Rose came back, carrying a glass in one hand. I took it and sipped gratefully. Water would help, I thought. It would certainly be better than asking Fairuza for a painkilling potion or something else. I could brew one for myself, or get Akin to brew it for me, but even that would be risky. Fairuza would probably be informed.

"That's better," I said, slowly. "Thank you."

I touched my forehead. There *was* a sheen of cold sweat on my forehead. I rubbed it gently, then climbed out of bed. My legs felt unsteady, but I made it to the washroom without incident. Rose watched, silently, as I splashed water on my face. I wanted a shower - or a hot bath - but I doubted I had the time. Akin was probably waiting for us already.

Breakfast was already waiting when we stumbled into the workroom. Bacon, eggs, freshly-baked bread…it confirmed Rose's suspicion, I supposed, that we were near a farm. I took heart from that, even though there was no way to know if the farmers were friendly. My family could offer enough money to raise a farming family into the nobility. If nothing else, they'd be able to alert the Kingsmen.

Akin smiled at me as we ate our eggs. "Did you sleep well?"

"Bad dreams," I said, tartly. I didn't dare say anything that might be misinterpreted - or interpreted all too well. "How about you?"

He looked down at his food. I didn't blame him. We were prisoners. We couldn't afford to forget it. Playing chess and chatting about nothing was meaningless, when our lives could be ended at any moment. I would sooner have been in jail. There was something honest about a jail cell.

But you've never been in a jail cell, I reminded myself. Alana had locked me in a room once, but it hadn't been quite the same. *A jail might be worse.*

I sighed. I really *could* have enjoyed spending all my time in a workroom, if I hadn't been a prisoner. But I *was* a prisoner.

The door opened. Fairuza stepped into the room. She looked disgustingly fresh and alert, as if she'd just had a good night's sleep, a shower and a hearty breakfast. I felt a flash of pure hatred, mingled with bitter rage. I could break the spells on my friends - now - but Fairuza wouldn't have any trouble stopping them in their tracks. I'd seen enough to know she was a powerful magician. The only way to stop her would be to take her by surprise.

"I have a special task for you today," she said. She held out a scroll. "I want you to make *this* potion."

I scanned the recipe, then blanched. I'd seen it before, in one of Mum's old books. The Thousand-Year Empire had devised it to knock down city walls - heavily-*warded* city walls - but the secret of its production had been lost long ago. And yet...I knew, now, that the potion needed someone without magic to make it. I could do it. Akin - and Mum - couldn't get through a third of the recipe without causing an explosion.

"I could bring down the building," I said, carefully. "This could go wrong..."

"Not if you brew the potion," Fairuza said. "And you will, won't you?"

I looked at her, nervously. There was no *use* for the potion, but widespread devastation. I wouldn't want to be anywhere near the potion when someone lit a match and tossed it into the liquid. It would burn down Aguirre Hall, or Rubén Hall, or even Tintagel Castle itself. And then...it would keep burning until it had consumed all the magic in the vicinity. I couldn't do it.

"You will," Fairuza said. She pointed a finger at Rose, who cringed back. The *geas* wouldn't even let her defend herself. "Or do I have to take steps to *make* you?"

"I will," I said. "But they have to keep their distance."

Fairuza nodded, slowly. "Very well," she said. She placed a small bell on the table. "Summon me when you are done. And have fun."

I kept my face impassive. It would take a day - perhaps two days - to brew the potion. It was a *very* complex piece of work. And then...

I shook my head. We couldn't let her take something so dangerous to her superiors. We had to move. There was no longer any time to plan. I'd have to put the escape plan into action and hope for the best.

And if we fail to get out before the potion is ready, I told myself, *she'll unleash a nightmare.*

CHAPTER
TWENTY-SIX

The potion looked deceptively simple.

I felt sweat running down my face as I watched the multicoloured liquid bubbling over the stove. It might have looked simple, but it was anything but. I had to prepare multiple cauldrons of various potions, all within a very short space of time. And I couldn't even brew each of the liquids separately, then use freeze charms to keep them in stasis until I was ready for them. They couldn't touch active magic without either going bad or exploding.

"I'm going to need more room," I said. The third cauldron was changing colour now, shifting from green to brown. I could see sparks within the mucky liquid...I *hoped* that was normal. No one had brewed this potion successfully for hundreds of years. "Can you push the table into place, then get into the back room?"

Akin looked doubtful. I didn't really blame him. The *geas* demanded that he let me work, but it also insisted that he had to keep an eye on me. Moving the table would force him and Rose into the back room, where they couldn't watch me. But there was no choice. A magician who stood too close to the cauldrons would trigger an explosion.

My calculations suggested that the resulting blast, combined with the potion's magic, would be more than enough to destroy the Royal Palace of Tintagel. Fairuza wasn't being careless, leaving me alone. I had a potion that could take out the entire building - wherever we were - at the cost of killing everyone, including myself. She knew I'd never kill my friends.

And she was smart enough to leave as soon as I started, I thought. My body ached with the memory of just how long I'd been working on the potion. *She just left us a bell to call her when we were done.*

"Hurry," I said, as the liquid bubbled furiously. "I need this away from the other cauldrons."

Akin hurried to do as he was told. I breathed a sigh of relief - Fairuza really should have left me completely alone, although she wasn't that foolish - as he put the table into place, then slipped into the backroom. He left the door open so he could watch me, but it didn't matter any longer. He couldn't come into the room without risking an explosion.

If nothing else, the geas will have problems deciding how to react, I thought. I didn't think the spell was *that* clever, particularly if it had been forced on an unwilling victim. It wouldn't know what to do if it was faced with an unanticipated problem or a conflict between two different sets of orders. *He might be unable to move until it was too late.*

I hoped that was true as I moved from cauldron to cauldron, inspecting the liquid. The timer ticked, counting down the last few minutes. I wiped my brow, cursing the original alchemists under my breath. What sort of mind would see potential in such a brew, let alone work their way through the thousands of variants? Mum had been known to mutter that some of the ancients must have been insane. I was starting to think she was right. Who could possibly have imagined that such a complex potion was workable?

They knew more than we did about alchemy, I reminded myself. The stories talked of potions and magics well beyond anything we knew. Flying machines were the least of them. *They must have understood alchemy at a far greater level.*

I wiped my forehead and took a breath. The air smelled funny, a sickly-sweet smell that made me feel unwell. I forced myself to breathe through my mouth, wishing I'd had the foresight to don a mask. I could have asked for one too, I was sure. Fairuza had been quite accommodating with everything I said I needed, save for freedom. She hadn't let me out of the suite since I'd arrived.

Which would have told me more about where I was, I thought. I'd tried hard to keep track of the days, but I honestly wasn't sure just how long I'd been a prisoner. Maybe three to four weeks, perhaps. Akin had found my makeshift calendar and hexed me. *We just don't know what is on the other side of the door.*

I eyed the door grimly, knowing I didn't have time to wait any longer. I *had* to get out - and take the others with me. And I couldn't rely on them, not as long as they were enchanted...I cursed Fairuza, once again. Perhaps using my friends as jailers was a sign of weakness, a sign that she really didn't have many people working for her. Or perhaps it was just a ruthlessly practical solution to a problem. Even Magister Tallyman would have problems telling the difference between the work I'd been forced to do for my captors and my escape plan.

Putting two more cauldrons on the table, I rapidly filled them with ingredients and lit the stoves. It didn't need magic, not yet. If I'd done my work properly, the two potions wouldn't need magic at all. And if I hadn't...I eyed the potions in the cauldrons, nervously. A misjudgement now would get us all killed.

The timer rang, loudly. I jumped, then scrambled to the first cauldron and tipped its contents into the second. The liquid blazed with white light, then faded back into a simmering blue. It looked beautiful, I thought, as I reached for the third cauldron and started to pour it into the second. Steam exploded upwards, making me swear as I took a step backwards. Mum would have exploded - with rage, I hoped - if she'd heard my language. If I'd made a mistake...

There was a final flare of light, then the liquid subsidised into a viscous oily fluid. I let out a sigh of relief as I checked it carefully, before pouring it all into a fourth cauldron and putting it on a table of its own. I'd fudged the figures a little - just to keep Akin and Rose out of the workroom - but I couldn't help eying it nervously. I wasn't sure what would happen if I took the spellcasters too close to the cauldron and I didn't want to find out the hard way.

I sat on the chair, fighting to gather my breath. It had worked, barely. The first stage was completed, the second stage was on the way. Whoever had come up with the recipe must have had more than one Zero under his command, I decided. I'd worked myself ragged trying to brew all the different components on my own. I hoped - prayed - that Dad would find another Zero soon enough, if only so I had assistance. But it would take years to train my new partner up...

And what, a little voice asked at the back of my head, *if you're truly unique?*

I shivered. What if I was a throwback to some long-gone past, when magic wasn't universal? What if...what if I was just a freak? What if I was truly alone?

The second timer rang. I sprang to my feet and hurried over to the next set of cauldrons, pushing my thoughts to the back of my mind. The three liquids had to be mixed together, but in a precise order...I checked my notes, just to be sure that I knew what I was doing, then started to empty the first cauldron into the second. This time, there was no flash of light, just a faint shimmer as the two liquids blended together. I reached for the stirrer and stirred carefully, unsure what was going to happen. Nothing did, as far as I could tell. It was inert...

It's meant to be inert, I reminded myself. I'd done my best to work out how all the different ingredients interacted, but...I wasn't sure I'd done my calculations correctly. Mum would have done a better job, I felt. She'd have checked and rechecked everything obsessively before letting me get to work, if she'd let me brew the potion in the first place. *She certainly wouldn't have wanted to brew it anywhere near the family hall.*

I kept stirring, carefully counting the stirs. Fifty-one stirs; no more, no less. It was a *precise* infusion of magic, so precise that no one short of a Potions Master could have hoped to muster it. I wondered, idly, if I was cheating. The stirrers I'd designed made it so much easier to measure the infusion, assuming - of course - that I had magic.

Or a source of magic...the wretched question nagged at my mind, again. Where *did* the power come from?

The third cauldron bubbled, loudly. I poured the contents into the second, stirring rapidly to mix the liquids together. It shimmered for a long moment, then turned an eerie green colour that made my head hurt. The smell changed too, turning into something foul and thoroughly unpleasant. I gritted my teeth, resisting the urge to stagger backwards and retch loudly. If I moved away from the cauldron before the liquid was ready, everything I'd done would be wasted. I didn't want to start from scratch...

We really need to find help, I thought. Akin's idea of humanoid automations might have potential, if they didn't need magic to run. *But it's just a matter of chance.*

I raised my voice. "I'm going to do the final step now," I called. "Stay as far from the door as you can."

Akin's voice was strangled. "Will do!"

I winced in sympathy. The *geas* was pulling him in two directions at once. Rose had it easier, I supposed. She simply didn't know enough to fear what I might do, if left unobserved for long enough to forge something dangerous. But Akin didn't know I'd already prepared most of my tools. He clearly assumed - and the *geas* would read it in his mind - that I wouldn't have had enough time to prepare something he couldn't handle.

And he would be right too, I admitted sourly. *All someone has to do to keep me prisoner is tie me up or throw me into a locked and empty cell.*

I sighed. Being kidnapped had proved a learning experience - and a grim reminder of my own vulnerability. All young magicians learnt basic cantrips for untying knots and opening locks, but I couldn't make them work.

"Be careful," Rose said. She'd watched as I'd done the calculations. She knew how dangerous the potion was, even though I'd done my best to exaggerate the dangers...insofar as that was possible. Thankfully, Akin hadn't taken a close look at the figures. "Don't get us all blown up."

"I won't," I promised. Rose had good reason to remember the *last* time I'd made a potion explode. "Just stay well away from the danger zone."

"We will," Akin said. "And you tell us what you're doing."

"I don't think I can do two things at once," I said. Mum had told me never to multitask when I was brewing. "The potion needs all my concentration."

I contemplated the possibilities of disaster for a long moment, then lifted up the full cauldron and carried it over to the one I'd made earlier. The steam grew stronger, but nothing else happened. I braced myself, then picked up a ladle and lowered a *precise* amount of the first fluid into the second. There was a bright shimmer, then nothing but steam. We hadn't reached critical mass, not yet. I nodded - my calculations had said as much - then ladled two more spoonfuls into the second cauldron. Things started to happen as soon as the third ladleful was lowered into the liquid.

I jumped back as blinding white light filled the room. It...it felt badly wrong, as if it was burning through my skin and gnawing at my bones. I thought I saw my flesh turn translucent, just for a second; I turned away, taking what cover I could. The potion hadn't exploded yet, but...but I didn't know what was about to happen. There was a *lot* of magic wrapped up in that cauldron, slowly going critical.

And there's quite a bit of the activator left, I thought. I'd planned as much, making twice as much of the first potion than I needed. I'd had a number of ideas about how it could be used in our bid to escape. *All I have to do is bottle it up.*

The light slowly faded. I turned my head, half-covering my eyes. Light seemed to be hovering over the cauldron, blazing so brightly that I couldn't make out anything on the far side. I hoped Akin and Rose were cowering in the backroom, keeping their magic well away from the unstable potion. I crept to the supply cupboards, picked out a handful of bottles and then recovered two of the spellcasters. I'd only get one shot at using them. Akin was remarkably quick to cast spells and Rose wasn't a slouch...

And if they cast a spell in here, they'll blow us all up, I thought, as I slipped one of the protective bracelets onto my wrist. I'd told them that the danger zone grew exponentially as more and more cauldrons were added, although I didn't think that was true. My calculations suggested that there were actually a number of danger zones, one per cauldron. But it didn't really matter. *They'll still be able to overpower me physically.*

The light was dimming rapidly now, leaving spots dancing behind my eyes. I concealed the spellcasters in my sleeves as I walked to the door and peered inside. Akin was leaning against the far wall, reading a book; Rose was sitting on the bed, drawing runes on a sheet of paper. Akin had started to teach her some of the more complex runes, the ones that had been drilled into my head when I was younger. I rather thought he was a better teacher than some of the tutors Dad had hired.

I pulled the first spellcaster from my sleeve and jabbed it at Akin. His eyes went wide, a moment before he shrank rapidly and turned into a tiny statuette. Rose let out a gasp and threw a hex at me, which sparkled out of existence as the bracelet worked its magic. I jabbed the spellcaster at her a second later, transfiguring her too. They were going to hate me when they returned to normal, I knew. I wasn't sure if the spell would leave them conscious in those inanimate forms or if their thoughts were frozen. If the former, they were about to have a very unpleasant time of it. Alana had turned me into something inanimate far too often.

"I'm sorry," I said, as I picked them up. They seemed to stare at me, accusingly. "I can't see any other way to get you out of here."

I put them into my pocket, then walked back into the workroom. I was careful to keep my distance from the cauldrons as strode around to the supply cupboards and opened them. I'd planned what to do carefully, very carefully. It only took me a moment to fill a bag with everything I thought I might need. I slung it over my shoulder, stuck the remaining spellcasters into my belt, then strode over to the door. Fairuza shouldn't be able to see what I was doing - the surge of magic from the potion would have damaged any spying spells she was using - but I knew better than to count on it. I dropped the bag by the wall, then walked back to the potions and matched the activator with one of my private brews. It shimmered to life, then waited. I poured some of the liquid into the bottles and added them to my bag, then splashed the rest of the liquid on the floor. It would make life interesting for anyone who wanted to recover the brew.

Here we go, I thought, as if I hadn't been committed the moment I'd shown Akin and Rose the spellcasters. I poured a third potion by the door, then reached for the bell and took cover behind a table. *Let's see what happens...*

I rang the bell. There was a long pause, long enough for me to wonder if Fairuza wasn't waiting for me to ring. She wouldn't want to be anywhere near the brewing, for fear that her mere presence would trigger an explosion. Or in the danger zone, if I accidentally messed up the recipe and caused an explosion myself. I told myself, grimly, that I *could* break down the door if I had to, but...my one shot at Fairuza would be lost. And yet...I hesitated, unsure what to do. What if...?

Someone started unlocking the bolts on the far side. My blood ran cold. If this went wrong...I'd kill myself and my friends. A single mistake would be disastrous.

Dad wouldn't approve of me trying to escape, normally, I thought. I had to smile at the thought, even though time was fast running out. *It would be dangerous.*

But now…I shook my head. I didn't have a choice. Fairuza wasn't a common kidnapper. She and her cronies - and her superior - hadn't taken me for ransom, but for what I could do for them. There was no hope of freedom if I stayed with them, no matter what I did. They wanted me to work, not to sit and wait to be free. They were irrecoverably committed the moment they'd taken Akin as well as me.

And if they can't have me, I reminded myself, *they'll make sure that no one else can have me either.*

The door opened. A second later, an explosion shook the room.

CHAPTER
TWENTY-SEVEN

I jumped up, spellcaster at the ready. Fairuza stood in the doorway, flickers of light blazing around her. She'd taken the brunt of the blasts on her wards - she'd clearly had more protections than I'd realised, even though I'd managed to take a look at her with my spectacles - but she'd been shocked. I jabbed the spellcaster at her, blasting her back through the door and down the corridor. There was no way to fine-tune the spell, but it shouldn't matter. The force should have knocked her out.

Jamming my spectacles into place, I grabbed my bag and ran forward. The suite opened into a network of corridors, leading in all directions. The only light came from a series of lanterns, hanging from the walls. I threw another blasting spell after Fairuza, then picked another corridor at random. The walls were cold stone, but there was a style about them that was oddly familiar. It nagged at my mind as I ran, keeping one hand on my spectacles. Wards and protective spells would be invisible to me, without the spectacles, until I actually ran *into* them. Flickers of magic danced along the walls - very *odd* flickers of magic - but there were no actual wards.

That makes no sense, I thought. I reached an intersection, listened carefully, then picked a direction at random. If I could find a window, or a map, or something else that showed me the layout of the building, escape would be a great deal easier. *They have to be hiding us behind heavy wards.*

I puzzled over it as I ran, listening carefully for signs of life. How big *was* the building? The family hall was big and Jude's was bigger, but...this building felt immense. There were dozens, perhaps hundreds, of empty rooms, all coated with layers of dust. A thought struck me and refused to go away, even though I *knew* it was nonsense. Were we in Jude's? That couldn't be true, could it? Rolf and his friends wouldn't have had to lure me out of the school if they'd meant to conceal me *inside* the school... right?

Don't be stupid, I told myself, sharply. *We're nowhere near the school.*

A ward flared to life in front of me, an instant before I would have run straight into it and gotten trapped - or worse. I didn't *think* kidnappers would have bothered to make their wards *gentle*. I yanked the dispeller out of my pocket and pushed it against the ward, holding my breath as the ward glowed with light. It shattered, snapping out of existence with a loud BANG. I wasn't reassured. I'd taken down the ward, but anyone monitoring them would know *precisely* where to find me.

And they might be able to track me too, I thought, as I darted past the broken ward and hurried down the corridor. *I may not be magic, but I'm carrying magic...*

I heard...*something*...behind me and threw myself against the wall, an instant before a hex flashed past me. I spun around, spellcaster raised; two men were running towards me, their hands casting spells. I jabbed the spellcaster at the nearest and blasted him, throwing him back into his companion. Their wards took the brunt of the blast, part of my mind noted dispassionately, but they were still stunned. I jabbed the second spellcaster at them, then turned and ran. They'd have problems breaking the spell before it wore off.

But I don't know how long it will last, I reminded myself. The spell could be cancelled, if someone found them before the spell wore off on its own. I'd read stories about Objects of Power that transfigured or controlled people, Objects of Power that had been lost long ago...if the stories were true. Their spells could be cancelled by someone else, but not broken by the victim. I wondered, as I glanced at the spellcaster, if I'd just reinvented them. *It's just a pity they really can't be fine-tuned.*

The air grew fresher as I ran up a flight of stairs. I felt as though I was underground, although I wasn't sure. The walls still felt oddly familiar, even though I couldn't place them. Where was I? Where were we? I ran around a corner and nearly crashed into a young man wearing brown robes. I shoved the spellcaster into his chest before he could react. He froze, held in place by fear rather than magic.

"I can see magic on you," I said. It was true, thanks to the spectacles. I'd see a spell if he started to cast it. "You start to cast a spell and I blast your chest. Understand?"

He nodded, frantically. He didn't seem *that* much older than me. I wished, suddenly, that I had time to ask him more questions, starting with whoever was behind the whole plot. But I rather suspected he wouldn't know. Dad had taught us about setting up patronage networks and *satellite* patronage networks. The people who were part of the secondary network might not know that their boss had a boss of his own.

And their ultimate superior wouldn't want them to be able to betray him, I reminded myself, grimly. Even Fairuza might not know who she worked for. Or she might be under a *geas* of her own to keep her mouth shut. I'd heard horror stories - mainly from spying on some of Dad's meetings - about spells that ensured that criminal masterminds could never be betrayed. *He won't know that much.*

I glared at him, trying to make it clear that I would hurt him if necessary. "I will know if you lie," I told him. "Where *are* we?"

"Aragon," he said. "Let me go!"

"Stay still," I growled. Aragon? It meant nothing to me. But I hadn't heard of everywhere within the kingdom, let alone outside it. "Which way to the exit?"

His body started to shake. I swallowed a savage word. A *geas*, then. He couldn't tell me anything useful, not even to save his life. And yet, he *had* given me a name…hadn't he? Or was it false? I didn't know. Dad had interests in a place called Celadon, but that was right on the edge of the kingdom. I didn't know anywhere else that sounded remotely close to Aragon.

"Tell me where the nearest window is," I said, instead. Perhaps I could give him enough leeway to fool the *geas*. Or maybe…"Show me…"

He inclined his head down the corridor, an instant before his entire body collapsed. The *geas* had knocked him out, rendering him comatose until his comrades found him. I felt a flicker of pity, combined with disgust. Who was he? What was he doing here? I studied his robes for a long moment, but nothing came to mind. He looked like some kind of priest. There was nothing about his face to suggest a specific origin.

I heard the sound of running footsteps, hurrying towards me. I yanked one of the potion bottles out of my bag as I moved, splashing the liquid on the floor as soon as I was several metres from the comatose man. Someone shouted behind me as I straightened up; I fled, running as hard as I could. A second later, another explosion shook the building. I heard the sound of pieces of falling masonry hitting the ground. Wherever we were, it clearly hadn't been designed for magicians. Or perhaps whoever had lived in the building, once upon a time, had known better than to brew unstable potions...

The air grew colder as I made my way along the corridor, spellcasters at the ready. More flickers of magic darted through the air, but they didn't seem to be doing anything. They weren't wards, as far as I could tell, nor were they seeking spells. I studied one of them, trying to parse out the spellform, but it was so warped as to be beyond recognition. It didn't seem to have *any* purpose, as far as I could tell.

I felt a brush of wind against my face and grinned, my legs starting to ache as I pushed myself onwards. If - when - I got home, I promised myself that I'd go for a run every day until I was fitter. I'd never been as pudgy as Bella, but I clearly wasn't a fast runner. But wind...I turned the corner and ran into a large room. A giant window dominated the scene, revealing utter darkness. I stared, trying to see something - anything - in the gloom. If the cold air hadn't smelt of the outside world, I would have wondered if I'd found something else instead. A balcony, perhaps.

The darkness was near-absolute, yet...I looked up and saw the stars. The constellations were largely familiar - Dad had taught me to watch the skies - but out of place. I tried to parse it out, slowly...we'd moved east, I thought. And that meant...my blood ran cold as I digested the implications. I might be on the edge of the kingdom or I might be outside it altogether.

I peered down as my eyes slowly adapted to the darkness. The walls were crumbly, with plenty of handholds, but I had no idea how far it was to the ground. I kicked myself, mentally. There were Objects of Power that would let me see in the dark, like my namesake, but I hadn't thought to make one. If I started to climb down, what then? If I fell...

A hex struck my back. The bracelet grew warm, just for a second, as it absorbed the spell. I spun around and jabbed the spellcaster towards the oncoming men, forcing them to take cover. Panic gibbered at the back of my mind as I tried to think of a plan, but there was nothing. There was only two ways out of the room - the corridor or the window - and both of them were dangerous. Or I could just stay where I was...

I looked from side to side. The room was bare, completely empty. There was nothing I could turn into a weapon, nothing I could forge to save myself. If I'd stayed in the suite...I gritted my teeth, unsure what to do. The longer I waited, the greater the chance that my captors would find a way to get to me that didn't involve magic. Or simply cast spells that got around my defences. Or...

"You can't escape," a male voice called. "You don't even know where you are. Drop the focus and give up."

My bracelet heated. I blinked in surprise, then smiled. A compelling voice...Alana had been fond of that spell, at least until I'd developed the willpower to overcome it. But it wasn't *normal* for twelve-year-olds to be able to do that, was it? I made a mental note to ask *Akin* if *he* could resist the spell. Not that it mattered, not right now. My bracelet protected me from direct mind manipulation.

A head poked up. I jabbed the spellcaster at him. It vanished, abruptly.

Got him, I thought. It wasn't much of a victory, but I clung to it. They should have made their wards stronger, although I wasn't sure if they *could* make them strong enough to stand off an Object of Power. My makeshift spells weren't *precise* and they were somewhat inflexible, but they were *strong*. *What will they think of next?*

I worked the problem in my mind as I tried to divide my attention between the corridor and the window. If I was considering climbing down, someone else could consider climbing *up*. Or...I kept trying to look into the darkness, but it was too dark to make out much beyond faint glimmers of magic. I couldn't help finding the sight disturbing. Where *were* we?

"Cat," a quiet voice said.

I tensed. Fairuza was standing at the bottom of the corridor, holding a large scutum shield in one hand. I gritted my teeth as I parsed out the runes on the shield. It wouldn't be hard to blast the shield - or shields, once the others picked up their own - but the runes would give them some protection. They'd just keep advancing until they caught me or I jumped out the window.

"You don't understand what is at stake," Fairuza said. She sounded as though she was trying to be reasonable, although the nasty bruises on her face made her look angry. I wasn't too concerned. A few minutes with a healer would patch up the scars, if there was a healer nearby. One of the magicians might have *some* healing training, even if they didn't. "You need to work with us."

I pointed the spellcaster at her with one hand, while pressing the bracelet into my bare skin with the other. If it got hotter...

"You took me and my friends from school, then cast forbidden spells on us," I charged, angrily. "Where are we?"

Fairuza rested her shield against the wall, exposing herself. "You are quite some distance from civilisation," she said, coolly. "I know we haven't kept you in the best of conditions, Caitlyn, but you don't want to go out there."

"Why?" I challenged. "What *is* out there?"

"Dangers," Fairuza said. She sounded tired. "I can return your friends to their loving parents, Cat, if you come back and stay with us."

I was tempted, just for a second. Akin and Rose had seen enough to help Dad track down Fairuza and her superior, hadn't they? But I didn't trust Fairuza to keep her word. She could offer to swear all the oaths she wished, yet it would be easy for her to trick me. I wouldn't have trusted her to do anything. Akin and Rose would probably have their throats slit, as soon as they were outside the building. The *geas* wouldn't let them resist.

"Why should I trust you?" I racked my brain for options. Going out of the window was starting to look like the best of a set of bad choices. "What could you possibly say that would actually manage to convince me that you're telling the truth?"

Fairuza looked irked. "I won't let you leave, Cat," she said. "Either stay with us or die."

I swallowed, hard. That was it, wasn't it? What Dad had seen and I had missed. My mere existence was a shift in the balance of power. Anyone who wanted to restore the balance could do it simply by killing me. Dad had believed that Jude's was safe, too. He hadn't realised, not really, that the balance of power had shifted too badly for the school's neutrality to be left alone. Old certainties were falling everywhere.

My mind raced. Lord Carioca Rubén had every incentive to restore the balance of power, hadn't he? But he wouldn't allow his son to be kidnapped, right? Unless it was a cunning double-bluff. Perhaps he'd always intended to arrange for Akin to be ransomed back to himself, once I'd served my purpose, or maybe he'd decided that Isabella was a better heir after all. And yet…it didn't seem quite right. Too many things didn't quite add up.

I peered down at Fairuza. "Why do you want the potion?"

"None of your business," she said. "Come here. Now."

"You're just a minion, aren't you?" I knew taunting her was dangerous, but it might provoke her into doing something stupid. Alana had taunted one of the maids - lesser family - until the maid had snapped and hexed her into silence. "Do you really believe that whoever gives the orders cares about you? You'll be killed the moment you outlive your usefulness."

"Come here, you little brat," Fairuza ordered. Her eyes were dark with rage. I didn't want her anywhere near me. She'd probably hex me into next week, even though it meant I wouldn't be any good for forging for a few days. "Now."

She lifted her shield and started forward, holding it in front of her. I jabbed the spellcaster at her, but the magic slammed into the shield and flashed out of existence. The blast had barely knocked her back. Whoever had forged the shield had done a very good job. Fairuza's minions stood, raising their own shields. I braced myself, then lifted the spellcaster and started jabbing it at the ceiling. They stumbled backwards, a second before the roof caved in with a deafening roar. I hoped none of them had been caught by the debris as I turned and ran to the window. There was a faint glimmer of dawn in the distance, but otherwise the world was still wrapped in darkness. Fairuza had been right, I realised as I swung my leg over the windowsill. We were a very long way from civilisation.

Scrambling down the wall was an utter nightmare. I'd done stupid things before, but this was the worst. I had to struggle to find handholds, slipping and sliding as my fingers brushed against smooth parts of the wall. The wind blew gently, mocking me; I tasted faint hints of seawater as I breathed in and out. I lost track of time as I crawled down, finally landing on solid ground. But it couldn't have been that long. The world hadn't gotten much brighter.

I leant against the wall for a long moment, trying to catch my breath. There was very little magic in the air, according to my spectacles…save for faint flickers that were as enigmatic as always. My eyes slowly became accustomed to the gloom, picking out hints of trees and buildings in the semidarkness. Where *were* we?

A nasty thought lingered at the back of my mind. There was *one* place they might have taken us, one place we could have been hidden indefinitely…

I heard a faint sound in the distance. They were coming.

Pushing the thought aside, I spilled my last potion bottle on the ground under my feet, then turned and fled into the darkness.

CHAPTER TWENTY-EIGHT

I thought I heard an explosion behind me as I scurried through the shadows, but I didn't dare look back to see the flash. That would make them a little more careful about chasing me, I hoped. Fairuza *might* be able to go through the supply cupboards and figure out how much I'd made, but I doubted it. I'd fudged the figures as best as I could, overusing some ingredients and under-using others. Mum would have been furious if I'd done that in her potions lab, but Fairuza would have worse problems. She couldn't be sure just how much I'd made of *anything*.

I probably should have set the suite on fire when I left, I thought. In hindsight...it had been a mistake, although setting fire to some of the potions ingredients would have had unpleasant consequences. *That would definitely have made it impossible for her to tell what I'd made.*

The darkness closed in around me as I hurried through the enigmatic buildings. Flickers of magic shot past me, growing stronger and stronger...I really *didn't* think they were spells at all. I'd heard of bursts of raw magic - there had been a sudden magical surge two hundred years ago when a large stockpile of potions ingredients had been destroyed - but this was different. The nasty thought I'd had about where we were surfaced, again. There weren't many places with such odd magical fields.

I glanced from side to side, listening carefully for sounds of pursuit. The shadows seemed to move when I wasn't looking - I nearly blasted a shadow before realising that it was *just* a shadow - but I couldn't hear anything behind me. And yet...I felt a growing unease that nagged at my mind. What were Fairuza and her comrades doing? Tracking spells might not work on me, but they might work on my friends. And if they had dogs...

I'd read stories about dogs that had been thrown off the scent by pepper, or running water, but I didn't *have* any pepper. And I wasn't sure I would have trusted the water either, if I'd stumbled across a lake. My stomach growled, reminding me that I'd be hungry soon. I'd stowed *some* supplies in my bag - there were advantages to a steady diet of bread, ham and cheese - but they wouldn't last long. I hadn't been able to prepare enough sandwiches for all three of us.

I'll need to turn them back, sooner rather than later, I thought. The path sloped upwards, taking me up a hill. *Keeping them inanimate for so long will have side effects.*

I shuddered as I stopped outside a darkened building and peered inside. It was deserted, as far as I could tell. There didn't even seem to be any rats, let alone any other vermin. I didn't like rats much, but I *really* didn't like the implications. Come to think of it, I hadn't heard owls or any other night bird either. The whole region seemed to be utterly lifeless. I braced myself, then inched inside. The air smelled...musty, as if the building had been abandoned a very long time ago. I was starting to think that that was true.

And yet...I turned my head from side to side, thinking hard. There was...*something*...there, wasn't there? It was calling to me, a gentle pull...I touched the bracelet, but it was cold. And yet, the air seemed pregnant with possibility. I knew it might well be dangerous - I'd been warned to be very careful of subtle traps, although most of them didn't seem to have any effect on me - but...but it was hard to believe it. It spoke to me personally...

And that's the danger, I told myself, as I sat down on the stone floor. The light was a little brighter now, bright enough to show me that the room was empty. Everything that wasn't stone had rotted away a long time ago. *It wants me to come to it.*

I reached into my pocket and pulled both of the statuettes out, placing them on the floor. The dispeller should be able to free them from the *geas*, but only if it had time to work. I rested the dispeller next to

Akin, then pulled the third spellcaster from my bag. I hadn't dared use it earlier - the spell it cast was too easily countered - but neither Akin or Rose would have time to fight. Pointing the spellcaster at them, I triggered the dispeller. They returned to normal, sitting upright with terrifying speed. I stunned them both before they could cast a spell.

Sorry, I thought. I didn't dare speak out loud. The air was so still that I was sure that even a whisper would go quite some distance. *You'll both have headaches when you wake up.*

I tied their hands and feet together, then put the dispeller to work. Hopefully, the *geas* would be gone by the time they woke up, but if it wasn't...I shook my head. Akin could get out of the ropes like lightning, if he didn't freeze me first. All I could really do was slow them down a little, unless I was willing to transfigure them again. And doing *that* might be dangerous. I had no idea just how aware they'd been while they'd been trapped.

And no way to test it either, I thought. *I couldn't even cast it on myself.*

I shivered as I waited. The spells Alana and Bella had been taught were designed to cushion the victim's mind, making it easier for them to cope with being turned into a frog. Or a statue. Or merely being unable to move. My spell didn't have any of those safeguards. It had more in common with Great Aunt Stregheria's spells than I cared to admit. But I hadn't had a choice. Even engraving a basic spell into an Object of Power was immensely difficult, particularly when I hadn't had much time to prepare.

The light grew brighter, steadily. I looked at the door, wondering if I should go check on our surroundings. Or even find out what was in the nearby rooms. But I could still feel the pull at the back of my mind. Whatever it was, it was still calling to me. And I didn't dare give it any satisfaction or it would just get stronger. I stood and started to pace, trying hard to keep my churning thoughts under control. If I'd got something wrong, we were in deep trouble.

My body ached. I checked my legs - dozens of scrapes and scabs where I'd banged my skin during the climb - but there was nothing I could do about it, not now. Fairuza hadn't given us any medical supplies, beyond the basics for a potions lab. I didn't think any of *them* would come in handy now. I'd just have to put up with the discomfort until we made it home.

I took a long breath. The sensation - almost a smell - was stronger now, a faint tingle that sent shivers down my spine. And yet...it wasn't a smell at all. It was...I struggled to describe it, even to myself. I would have thought of it as a modified repulsion ward, if I'd been able to see the spellform. Dad used them to deter people from trying to climb our walls. It kept most apple-scrumpers out of our orchards. There were nastier defences further inside for thieves who didn't take the hint.

No focused magic, I thought. *Just...*

Akin jerked, his eyes snapping open. I raised the spellcaster, ready to stun him again. I'd have bare seconds, if that, before he hexed me. I was tempted to strike first, despite the risk...if I was wrong, he was going to hex me and then take me back to the cell. And we wouldn't have a second chance to escape.

"Cat," Akin managed. "I..."

He turned to one side and retched, hard. I allowed myself a moment of relief, then helped him into the recovery position. Retching was a good sign, I'd been told. It was proof that whatever ailed him was on its way out. And yet...I watched him, warily. If he made a single false move, I'd stun him first and give him another go with the dispeller. He'd hate me for it, but it was better than being recaptured.

"That was...that was bad." Akin's voice was practically a croak. I relaxed, slightly. "I...I...I couldn't stop myself."

"It's alright," I said. I pulled the bottle of water out of my bag and passed it to him. We'd have to ration it carefully. I had no idea if the water here, if we found a river, was safe to drink. "How much do you remember?"

Rose groaned before Akin could answer. I helped her to lie on her side, trying to split my attention between both of them. The *geas* seemed to have vanished, but...but it would be a long time before I relaxed. I'd read too many stories where someone was secretly enchanted, appearing perfectly normal until the spell took effect. But if Akin and Rose *had* been enspelled like that, the dispeller should have removed it too...right? I could only hope I *was* right.

There are no certainties any longer, I thought, as I passed Rose the water. She drank, carefully. I took it back before she could empty it. *Everything we thought we knew is wrong.*

Akin pulled his hands free and rubbed his forehead. "Where are we?"

"An abandoned settlement," I said. I eyed him, worried. *Geas* or no *geas*, his senses would be sharper than mine. "What do you sense?"

"Magic," Akin said. "It feels…weird."

Rose looked up at me. "We shouldn't be here," she said, with the earnestness of a child half her age. She sounded as though she'd hit her head. "This is a bad place."

"Don't try to cast spells, not yet," I said, firmly. I freed Rose's hands and left her to release her legs. It would give her something to focus on. "How much do you remember?"

"You…you did something to us," Rose said. She concentrated. "Everything after that is something of a blur."

"Probably for the best." I stood. Tiredness nagged at my mind, but…I had to force myself to move. We were still far too close to our captors for comfort. "Can you two stand?"

"Barely," Akin said. His eyes opened wide. "What happened to you?"

I looked down at myself and blinked. My shirt and trousers were torn and stained with blood. *My* blood. And I hadn't thought to pack a change of clothes…I giggled, despite the seriousness of the situation. My clothes were a ruin, my hair was a mess, my hands and face were dirty… High Society would throw up its collective hands in horror if they saw me in such a state. Mum would order me thrown in the bath and viciously scrubbed by the maids.

"I had to climb down from our prison," I said, wryly. I didn't know just how far *down* I'd climbed, either. My scars bore mute testament to my feat. "You two got the easy part."

Akin nodded, then stopped and looked around. "Rose is right," he said. "We really shouldn't be here."

"Yeah," I said. If *I'd* sensed that something was wrong, it had to be bad. I might not be able to sense magic, but I could sense its effects. "We really need to start moving."

I returned most of my tools to my pack, but kept the dispeller and the spellcasters in my pockets. I'd need them, if we had to fight. I briefly considered giving some of my protective bracelets to Akin and Rose, but they'd only make it impossible for them to use their magic too. I didn't think the trade-off was worth it. Instead, I walked to the nearest door and peered through into the next room. It was as bare and barren as the first.

Rose caught my arm. "What do you think this place was?"

"I don't know," I said. The stone walls had survived...however long the building had been abandoned, but everything else had long since rotted away. Carpets, wooden furnishings...everything was gone. "It could have been a house or a forge or..."

"A house," Akin said. He sounded disturbed. I wondered if he'd had the same thought as myself. Rose hadn't been raised on the old stories, but *we* had. "And one built quite some time ago."

I frowned as we glanced through the remaining rooms. It *could* be a country villa, I decided; there were bedrooms, storage rooms, a giant dining room and an indoor swimming pool that was deep enough to worry me. If I'd fallen into the water-less pool in the darkness, I'd have broken my legs. There wouldn't have been any hope of climbing out, either. My eyes trailed over a set of headless statues - I couldn't tell if they'd decayed over the years or had been designed to look that way - and rested on a plinth. It was... odd. It reminded me of the shrines we raised to our ancestors, but...but it was different. A whole set of faded designs were carved into the stone. They were so faded that I couldn't be sure I was seeing the whole thing.

The air felt...*odd* as we stepped out of the building. I couldn't put my finger on it. The wind blew, yet...yet it felt dead. And yet...there was something timeless about the whole region, as if the world had slowed to a halt. No birds sang in the trees, no insects buzzed through the air, no small animals burrowed through the undergrowth...it was eerie, even to me. Both Rose and Akin grew increasingly jumpy as we looked around. I didn't blame them. It must have been far worse for them.

"This place is wrong," Rose said.

I nodded in agreement. The buildings had looked bad enough in the darkness, but they looked far worse in the day. They looked ancient, yet frozen in time; decayed, yet intact enough to be made liveable with very little effort. And yet...my head hurt, every time I looked into the darkened doorways. It was very hard to escape the feeling that the darkness led in directions the human mind wasn't equipped to understand. Rose was *definitely* right. There was something fundamentally wrong about the whole place.

The buildings looked...old. I'd seen buildings like them in Water Shallot, buildings that dated all the way back to the Thousand-Year Empire, but these were different. My head started to pound as I tried to come to grips with what I was seeing. Stone walls, covered with stone heads... human heads, monstrous heads. Gargoyles stood on every wall, peering down at us. The buildings were ancient and decayed, yet preserved...preserved like flies trapped in amber. All of a sudden, I understood *precisely* why Fairuza had been so confident she could keep us hidden here. There was so much wild magic in the area that even *blood*-linked magics would be unreliable.

I glanced at Akin. "We have to go up," Akin said. "We need a view."

Rose didn't look happy, but she followed us upwards anyway. The wind blew hot and cold; hot enough to make me sweat, cold enough to make me shiver. I gritted my teeth and forced myself onwards, trying to remember the stories about my very distant ancestors. I'd been told they'd lived in sunlit lands, where they'd walked out in the noonday sun while visitors cowered under the shade and rain was a myth.... But then, very few of those stories had survived the Empire. I had no way to know which of them - if any - were actually true.

My sense of unease grew stronger and stronger as we reached the top of the hill. The trees were pretty, in a way, yet...yet they were twisted, as if they'd been warped by powerful magic. I wasn't even sure they were *alive*. I certainly didn't dare touch them. How could they even survive without insects? The whole region was as silent as the grave. Perhaps the trees, too, were simply frozen in time.

"There are no weeds," Akin said. We peered into a garden. It was as neat and regimented as my mother's garden, yet...yet there was something eerie about it. Nothing moved, not even when the wind blew. "This place is creepy."

I nodded, peering down into the distance. The entire region was nothing but ruined city. I could see wreckage stretching in all directions, piled high as far as the eye could see and somehow frozen in time. And yet, I saw a harbour below me…it had clearly been a harbour. I'd seen it before, on yellowed and dusty maps the ancients had preserved for us. A giant inland lake, connected to the sea through a canal…four hills, looming over the city they guarded…

…And us, standing on the fifth hill, some distance from the rest.

"Parnassus Hill," Akin whispered, quietly. His words echoed in the stillness. "We're on Parnassus Hill. We're a very long way from home."

I sucked in my breath. We were on Parnassus Hill. The thought I'd had - the thought I hadn't wanted to admit - snapped back into my mind. There were very few places as tainted with wild magic as the city below us. We were on Parnassus Hill.

And that meant that the ruined city below us was none other than the Eternal City itself.

CHAPTER
TWENTY-NINE

I'd heard the stories. But none of them came close to the reality.

The Eternal City had been the city of light, once upon a time. Flying machines…flying buildings, castles in the sky. The entire city had been paved in gold and silver, the buildings lit up so brightly that the city could be seen for thousands of miles. There hadn't been any lighthouses in the harbour, if the stories were to be believed. The glow had been bright enough to let sailors work day and night. Now…

Now…it was rubble, yet…

I stared, trying to parse out what I was seeing. The rubble looked… odd, great shifting patterns that made little sense. It struck me, as I inspected what might once have been the Imperial Palace, that the buildings *had* been floating, if they hadn't been simply been held up by magic. Dad had told me that it *was* possible to build a house using magic, instead of a more mundane framework, but it was dangerous. A single cancellation spell might bring the entire building crashing down. Looking at the remains of the city, I couldn't help feeling that *something* had happened to the magic. The entire city had crashed down into rubble.

Worse than that, I thought, numbly. *The floating buildings would have crushed anything underneath when they hit the ground.*

Rose shivered. "Can't you feel it?"

Akin nodded in agreement. I glanced from one to the other, feeling blind. A faint haze hung over the city, but otherwise…nothing. And yet, the sense of unease grew stronger the more I stared at the rubble. It called to me, yet repelled me. Whatever had been unleashed here, in the heart of the Thousand-Year Empire, had been thoroughly unnatural. I'd never felt anything like it, ever. None of Dad's protective wards came close to matching it.

"Whatever happened here was *bad*," Akin said.

Rose caught my arm. "What *did* happen here?"

I kicked myself, mentally. *Rose* wouldn't know, of course. *She* hadn't been raised with the old tales. Her family knew very little about the kingdom's past or about the world outside their village. The king certainly wouldn't want to encourage commoners to think about the time before the kingdom took shape and form. Who knew what they'd think when they heard the empire hadn't been so invulnerable after all?

"This was once a village," I said. It was hard to believe, but all the stories agreed on it. "The original name was lost long ago. Magic...someone living in the village was the first to codify the principles of magic, to bind it to his will. He taught others, who taught others still...soon, he had an army. They set out to conquer the world."

"They succeeded," Akin said, bluntly.

I nodded. The Thousand-Year Empire hadn't known about Hangchow - maybe they hadn't realised the world was round - but they had swept over most of the known world. If the stories were true, the first set of conquests had been effortless. And why not? The ancients hadn't known what magic could do until it was too late. Resistance had been crushed before the village's enemies could copy their techniques for themselves.

"Somewhere along the line, they discovered how to make Objects of Power," I added. *That* secret had been kept, even as more common magical techniques leaked out. But then, there were very few spells that could only be cast by a handful of people. "And then they were unstoppable. Their armies marched from one end of the continent to the other, north and south, east and west. They united the entire known world under their rule."

I tried to think how my distant ancestors must have felt, when they'd seen the flying machines and marching armour. They'd had magic, of course, but they'd never codified it into something usable. So many records from that time had been lost, yet I was sure I knew how the story had gone. Resistance had been crushed, a new ruling elite had been installed; slowly, surely, my distant ancestors had been integrated into the empire.

"They absorbed talent," I remembered. It was one of the stories Dad had made sure to tell us, when we'd been younger. "Smart and capable magicians were invited to the Eternal City to study, to learn magic and improve on it. Others...were offered a chance to join the ruling class. And all the benefits slowly filtered down to the rest of the population. Food and drink, health and education...even public toilets! It was a golden age."

Rose looked pensive. It struck me, suddenly, that *she'd* been snatched up because of her talent, but she wouldn't be going back to her village to improve it. I felt a pang as I realised that Rose, when she graduated, would have very little in common with her family. The poorest citizen of Shallot would still have a better life than a commoner out in the countryside. I wanted to hug her, to tell her that it would be better, but I couldn't. I didn't think it *would* be better.

"And then it fell," Akin said. "We don't know what happened, Rose. No one knows."

I looked into the haze, remembering the stories. The city had fallen, they'd insisted, but there had been very few details. The wars that followed the collapse had seen to that, tearing apart all the institutions the empire had so painstakingly built. By the time the dust settled - and a hundred kingdoms had taken the empire's place - the Eternal City lay in ruins. Very few people dared venture into the once-great city. It was believed to be cursed.

And we were brought here, I thought. Fairuza had nerve. I'd give her and her backers *that* much. But then, they'd had fewer options than I'd realised. Being *here* would confuse the blood magic our families would use to trace us, *without* using wards that could have no other purpose. *But what did they want us for?*

My eyes traced the rubble, remembering the old stories. Was that the Imperial Palace? Or was it the Commandery, where the conquest of the known world had been planned? Was that massive building the hospital where the empire's medical magics had been developed? Or was it a temple? A strange angular shape could be seen near the water...was it the remains of a giant oceangoing ship? I'd heard stories of wreckage sailors had seen, half-hidden under the waves. The ancients had built ships that made our largest clippers and galleons look tiny. And was that framework part of a flying machine?

There was something...despondent about the whole scene. I felt sad, almost mournful; I felt as if I was on the verge of tearing up. I was looking down on a thousand years of history, smashed to rubble in a moment. The Eternal City looked to have been easily five or six times the size of Shallot, perhaps more, yet it now lay in utter ruins. And Shallot was one of the largest cities in the kingdom. Would my city die the same way, one day?

I caught my breath. "We can't stay here all day."

"No," Akin said. He was staring at the city, his eyes wide. "But where do we go?"

"And where do we find food?" Rose didn't seem to have any trouble dragging her eyes away from the city. "We don't have anything like enough to keep us going for more than a few days. And we really need water."

I nodded, even though I didn't have an answer. We *could* slip down to the sea, I thought, and scoop up some water, but even with purification spells I wasn't sure we could drink it. There were stories about the waters around the Eternal City, tales of monsters and strange apparitions and *things* below the waves. Sailors would sooner round the horn and risk death there than sail near the Eternal City. I'd never believed the stories, but now...I believed them. I didn't know if we could risk eating or drinking *anything* from the Eternal City.

"We'll head north," Akin said. He jabbed a finger away from the city. "That should get us on the way home."

I felt myself torn between the urge to laugh and cry. We were over a thousand miles from Shallot. We'd reach the border sooner...I started to giggle, helplessly. If we started walking now, we might *just* reach the border in a couple of weeks, assuming we didn't get caught on our way home. Or lost...I'd seen a handful of maps, but none of them had been particularly detailed. Very few people visited the Eternal City. Even fewer returned.

Akin glanced up, sharply. A second later, a hex flashed over our heads.

"They're here," he snapped.

I followed his gaze. Two men were standing at the bottom of the hill, pointing their fingers at us. A hex snapped towards Rose; I caught it on my hand, feeling my bracelet growing warm as it absorbed the spell. Akin cast two spells back, but the men had no trouble blocking them. I wasn't surprised. Whoever they were, it was clear they were fully-trained magicians.

"This way," Akin snapped. He caught Rose's arm and yanked her to the side. "Hurry!"

I drew the spellcaster and jabbed it towards the men, several times. Flashes and bangs filled the air, resounding oddly in the haze. I didn't think I'd *hit* them, but it should force them to duck...I *hoped* it would force them to duck. They might have upgraded their protection spells after my escape, after they'd seen what I could do. But there was no way to know.

"Come on," Akin called.

I followed him, clutching the spellcaster with one hand. The air grew hotter and thicker as we descended the hill and ran through a maze of old buildings, each one creepier than the last. I heard shouts behind me, but there was no sign of pursuit. I wondered, idly, just how many men it would take to search the area properly. Alana and Bella had played hide-and-seek with their friends, but I'd never been able to take part. My lack of magic would have kept me from hiding, let alone ambushing anyone who came too close.

At least their hunting spells won't work so well here, I thought, as the haze grew thicker. The thought made me smile. *They'll have to set eyes on us.*

I glanced back as we paused behind a stone house. The aura from inside was so dark that even *I* could feel it, something so eerie that I wanted to turn tail and run. No one was behind us, yet...I felt as though we were being watched by unseen eyes. I looked up. A stone gargoyle was looking down at us, its teeth bared in a grimace of pure hate. Others were looking at us too...I told myself, sharply, that any enchantments animating the gargoyles would have decayed long ago. But I wasn't sure that was true. There were plenty of stories of cursed tombs that had killed anyone foolish enough to defy the warnings and step inside.

The shouts grew louder. I looked around, trying to place them. But I couldn't. They seemed to be coming from all around us, echoing off the buildings and blurring together into a terrifying whole. Sweat poured down my back as Akin started to lead us around the house and into another frozen garden. I couldn't go back to that cell! I wouldn't...I drew one of the other spellcasters from my pocket and held it in front of me, looking around for targets. I knew the *theory* of magical hide-and-seek...

We reached the garden and ducked low, shuffling towards a frozen hedgerow and the concealed ditch - the ha-ha - in front of it. My eyes started to hurt as we inched forward, the spectacles showing me flash after flash of raw magic...and something indistinct, something I couldn't quite understand. Whatever forces had been unleashed in the Eternal City - and no two stories agreed - they'd warped the landscape forever. The entire region was a death-trap! I just hoped it was confusing Fairuza and our enemies as much as ourselves.

Akin paused as we reached the hedgerow and crawled along the ha-ha. I wondered if we should inch down into the ditch - it looked safe - but some instinct told me it would be a very bad idea. Whoever had designed the garden had clearly not shared my mother's belief in regimenting everything. Rows of herbs contrasted oddly with sections that had been allowed to run wild and free, perhaps in an attempt to see which plants would survive and thrive in such a competitive environment. Mum had never liked the concept. She'd always believed it would induce random mutations in potion ingredients.

"We need to keep moving north," Akin whispered. "I don't want to go any closer to the city itself."

I nodded, although I wasn't comfortable with the decision. The ruins might give us shelter...I shook my head, remembering the tales. People would go into the Eternal City and come out *changed*, if they came out at all. There was a *reason* the entire region had been abandoned, after all. Maybe I'd be safe - I didn't know. My friends *wouldn't* be safe.

"Keep inching north," I whispered back, as we reached the edge of the ha-ha. Its designer had clearly believed in catching unwary trespassers in the ditch. Anyone who managed to scramble over the hedge would fall into the ha-ha and get stuck. "Once we're out of the city, we can decide what to do next."

I glanced back at Rose. She was pale, but bringing up the rear with a determination that surprised me. I told myself I was being silly. Rose had been brave to go to Jude's, leaving everything she knew behind. She was one of the bravest people I knew.

"Keep moving," she muttered. Dry mud crunched as we pushed our way through the hedge, deafeningly loud in the eerie silence. I hoped the hunters hadn't heard. "Don't stop for anything."

The road on the far side of the edge looked...odd. Akin glanced at it, then led the way down the pavement. I didn't blame him. There was no visible threat, yet the aura of *danger* was growing louder. I looked down the road, towards the city and saw...*something*. The road seemed to bend in a way my mind refused to grasp. The buildings behind us shifted and changed, as if they were illusions...or worse. I forced myself to look away as my head started to pound. We had to get out of the city before it was too late. Even here, on the outskirts, we were at risk.

Akin picked up speed as the shouts grew louder. They seemed to be coming from further away, but it was impossible to be sure. Fairuza wouldn't let us go, not when there was a very real chance we'd make it out of the city. I smiled as the implications dawned on me. My family - and Akin's - wouldn't stop trying blood magics until they found us. The moment we were out of the city, they'd be able to locate us. And then...

Keep moving, I told myself. *If we're so far from home, it will be days before someone comes to rescue us.*

I looked around as we reached a crossroads. A large villa sat at the far end of one of the roads, calling to me. I could *feel* the call, stronger now. And yet...neither Akin nor Rose seemed to perceive anything. I frowned, puzzled. They should be *more* vulnerable, not less. I didn't know what I was feeling. It was just...*there*.

There was a flash of light. Akin froze.

I jumped. A young woman stood there, holding a focusing device in one hand and a small club in the other. She wore the same brown robes as the boy I'd frightened...had it really been only a few short hours ago? I jabbed the spellcaster at her, but her protections deflected the spell. Ice trickled down my spine as I realised we were in trouble. The bracelet grew warm, a second later. The woman was casting a spell...

No, I thought. *I am not going back...*

I yanked the dispeller from my pocket and threw myself forward. The woman's eyes went wide and she cast a spell, a moment before I shoved the dispeller into her. Her protections vanished in a flash of light. She slapped me hard, knocking me to the ground. I tasted blood in my mouth as she lifted her hand, then collapsed. Rose had stunned her an instant before she could hex us.

"Well done," I said, as I pushed the dispeller against Akin. Rose wouldn't have stood a chance against an older magician, not normally. But the dispeller had destroyed *all* of the woman's protections. "She nearly had us."

My cheek throbbed, but I had no time to tend to it. Instead, we studied the woman's unconscious body while Akin searched her. She was in her early twenties, I estimated, although I couldn't tell much else about her. Her face was a rich chocolate colour, shades lighter than my own; her clothes were cheap, probably completely untraceable. She would have been attractive, if she hadn't been trying to recapture us.

"Nothing much," Akin said. He held out his haul. A couple of Devices of Power and a simple gold chain she'd worn as a bracelet. I took the chain and inspected it, then waved the dispeller over the metal. "What do you think it means?"

I shrugged. The chain hadn't been magical, as far as I could tell, but it would be costly. And yet, everything else about her was *cheap*.

"I don't know," I said. I looked up and saw more people running towards us. "But we have to move."

CHAPTER
THIRTY

"They're everywhere," Akin said. "Where do we go?"

I glanced at the villa. The call was getting stronger, yet…yet I felt no threat. And besides, Akin was right. The hunters were closing in rapidly. We *might* be able to hide in the villa, or find a place we could defend, or…I caught Rose's hand, trusting that Akin would follow us.

"This way," I said. "Come on!"

The shouts grew louder, intermingled with whistles, as we raced down the road towards the villa. It was massive, yet there was something about it that nagged at my mind. Two stories, as far as I could tell; surprisingly intact, despite its location. And there were no gargoyles, nothing to suggest defences…I told myself, sharply, that I could be running straight into a trap.

There's no choice, I thought. *We don't dare let them take us prisoner again.*

The gate was open, inviting us into a tiny courtyard. It looked odd to my eyes - there wasn't room for a carriage to turn unless the driver was prepared to scrape the walls - and there were no plants within view. Perhaps it was meant to be empty, I thought, or…perhaps we were about to sneak in through the servants' entrance. The other side of the villa might be far grander. Or…I pushed the thought out of my mind as we reached the wooden door, temptingly ajar. I was surprised it had lasted so long, despite the location. The wood should have decayed long ago.

I paused, forcing myself to *think*. The call was coming from *inside* the villa. And that meant…we could be walking into very real danger. There was still no sense of threat, but there wouldn't be. A trap wouldn't *look* like a trap, would it? I'd heard of plants and animals that had a hypnotic effect on their pray. There were spells that did the same thing, drawing their victims in and holding them until it was too late. None of them *looked* like deadly traps.

The sounds from behind decided me. I pushed the door open, then led Akin and Rose into the villa. The inside was cool, so cool that I found myself shivering. There were no windows, yet...yet it wasn't dark. Light seemed to fan through the room, coming from...I couldn't see *where* it came from. Dad's warnings rang in my mind as I closed and bolted the door, cutting off the outside world. I didn't think it would slow the hunters down for long. They wouldn't want to go into the buildings, but they didn't have a choice. They'd have to find us before we made it out of the city.

"The magic here feels wrong," Akin said. He tried to cast a spell, but the spellform refused to take shape. "Cat...where have you brought us?"

"I don't know," I said, truthfully. The villa didn't feel *bad*, not to me. But Rose looked uneasy, clutching my hand as through it was a lifesaver. Akin didn't look much better. "I think..."

The door shook. I said a rude word, then led the way into the next room. The villa was large enough for us to sneak to the far side, surely... unless the hunters had already surrounded the building. I forced myself to keep going, anyway. We couldn't keep second-guessing ourselves until we froze, unable to decide what to do. The noise seemed to quiet down as we entered a passageway and vanished altogether as we entered a third room. Somehow, I didn't feel that was a good thing.

"Someone lives here," Akin said. "And we shouldn't be here."

I frowned. The room was a dining room, utterly frozen in time. There were plates on the table, plates covered with food...it looked as though whoever lived in the villa had just stepped out for a moment, as though they would be back at any moment. My eyes swept the room, noting the wooden cupboards, the large portrait on the wall and the tiny stuffed donkey sitting on one of the seats. I felt a pang of grief for the child who had owned the toy, centuries ago. She - or he - would be nearly a thousand years dead by now.

Rose made an odd sound. "Why is the portrait so weird?"

I followed her gaze. There were twelve people in the portrait, five of them women. The men were facing outwards, their faces clearly drawn; the women had their backs to the painter, their figures barely recognisable as feminine. One of the girls was clearly younger than me, yet she had her back turned. I couldn't help wondering what it meant. Dad had never insisted that I turn my back when I sat for a family portrait.

"I've seen it before," Akin said. "My family has a collection of ancient paintings from the empire. They never depicted female faces, not once."

Rose and I exchanged glances. "Why not?"

Akin shrugged. "Isabella asked," he said. "My father didn't know."

I considered it for a long moment. The empire had given us so much of our culture - everything from clothes to etiquette - that I found it hard to understand why *our* portraits were different. Perhaps it was something that hadn't survived the collapse, a holdover from the days before the empire had conquered most of the known world. My ancestors had lost most of *their* culture when they'd been brought into the empire, but the founders might have kept something of theirs. There had been a belief, if I recalled correctly, that knowing someone's *face* was enough to cast a spell on them.

But that makes no sense, I told myself. *They wouldn't be making portraits of anyone if that was true.*

I reached for the stuffed donkey, only to have it crumble to dust the moment it touched my hands. My fingers tingled; I brushed away the dust, feeling another pang of bitter guilt. The toy had been perfect, frozen in time until I'd tried to pick it up. Cold logic told me that the original owner was dead, but…but it was hard to believe it. I didn't really *want* to believe it.

"Don't touch the food," Akin said.

Rose smiled. I hesitated, then nodded grimly. Who knew what would happen if I touched the food? I didn't want to find out the hard way. Instead, I looked around the room again, trying to see if there was anything else we should look at before we hurried onwards. There were books on the shelves, locked in a glass-fronted cabinet. I wanted to take them, but I didn't dare try. They might crumble the moment I touched them too.

A crash echoed through the building. I exchanged glances with Akin and Rose, then led them out of the eerie room. The hunters seemed to be moving slowly, but that wouldn't stop them catching us. I wondered if we could defend the room, yet...it didn't seem likely. We'd beaten one by sheer luck, but there were too many ways in and out of the dining room for us to hold it for long. And they'd know about the dispeller by now.

Another crash, directly ahead of us. I cursed. They'd delayed long enough to surround the villa, then break in from both sides at the same time. It was likely to work, too. If they kept pushing from the front and the back, they were going to catch us between them. I looked from side to side, then led the way up a set of stone stairs. It might buy us more time.

And I went down the wall once, I thought, as we crept up the stairs. *We can do it again.*

The call seemed louder, somehow, as we reached the top of the stairs and glanced around carefully. Everything still seemed suspended in time. The carpet under our feet was intact, even though it should have rotted away hundreds of years ago. I led the way down the corridor, peering into the four bedrooms. Two of them were definitely for children, judging by the size of the beds. I wasn't the tallest girl in my year, but the beds were still too small for me...if I could have slept on the beds without breaking whatever magic was holding them suspended in time. The other two were either for older children or adults.

And that one is for a woman, I thought. A half-opened wardrobe was clearly visible, crammed with dresses and scarves. I couldn't help thinking that much of what we knew about the empire was clearly wrong. Why had the women covered their hair, perhaps even their faces? *What else have we forgotten over the years?*

I heard voices from down below. The hunters had found the stairs. They might not know for *sure* we'd gone up, but they'd put a guard on them anyway. And...when they figured out we weren't on the ground floor, they'd go up themselves. I wondered, sourly, if we could ward the stairwell, but I knew it would be pointless. Akin presumably could cast a dozen different wards - Dad had drilled them into Alana and Bella from a very early age - yet I doubted he could cast anything that could stand up to an adult magician. And none of the Objects of Power I'd forged could help.

We slipped down the corridor as the voices grew louder. One room was clearly a playroom, crammed with toys; another was probably a small office, the walls lined with bookshelves. I promised myself that we'd come back, if we made it home. The books needed to be recovered before... before what? The glee of discovering something new was tempered by the awareness that thousands of books had survived, in libraries or collections all over the known world. Their owners had parsed them out, trying to figure out the secret. But none of them had deduced the truth.

"Crap," Akin muttered. "They're coming up the stairs."

I barely heard him. The call was suddenly very loud, leading me - leading us - into another office. It was larger than Dad's office, yet...there was something regal about it. The walls were lined with gold and covered with portraits, a couple of which I recognised from the ancient tomes. Emperors, dead and gone years before their empire had crumbled into dust.

And yet, the room was oddly bare. No bookshelves, no fireplace, no windows...just a couple of chairs, a solid wooden desk and a door on the far side of the room.

Rose gasped. "We're trapped!"

I glanced at her. "What?"

"There's no way out," Akin said. I could hear people coming down the corridor towards us, searching every square inch of the building. "Cat, we're trapped."

"There's a door there." I pointed to the door. A faint light shone through the opening. "We can go out that way."

Akin stared at me. "There's no door there."

I looked back, stunned. I'd never been able to see through illusions; I'd never even been able to *sense* them, not until I'd forged my spectacles. Alana had made me walk into walls or closed doors a couple of times, just by casting illusions she knew wouldn't fool anyone else. But now...why was *I* the only one who could see the door? Was it because I was the only one who could hear the call?

"There's a door there," I insisted. I walked around the desk, wishing I had the time to go through it. The office looked as if it belonged to someone important. But maybe it was just for show, a place to hold meetings with visitors. Dad didn't do his important work in any of the offices he showed to outsiders. "Come on."

I reached out and waved my hand through the door, half-expecting a spell to bite me. Alana had done that too, hiding a hex under an illusion. But there was nothing. My fingers met empty air. Akin stared at me, perplexed. It dawned on me, slowly, that he really *couldn't* see the door. Rose seemed more inclined to take my word for it. But what was on the far side...I saw a corridor, I thought, but...but there was something odd about it. I didn't really know what I was seeing.

"Come on," I repeated. The sounds from outside were getting louder. "We have to move."

Rose hurried over to join me. Akin cast a quick spell on the doorway, then walked over as I led the way down the corridor. I noticed he had his eyes shut as he walked through the hidden doorway. To him - and Rose - it must have seemed as though I had stepped right into a wall. And yet... his eyes jerked open as we passed through, clearly shocked.

"The magic..."

The floor vanished. We fell, crying out in shock. I had a brief impression of utter darkness washing towards us, then...then I squeezed my eyes closed. A trap...I'd led my friends right into a trap. Perhaps it had been configured to snare me, or someone like me, rather than a magician. The Thousand-Year Empire had known about us. They'd probably had ways of dealing with us.

I felt solid ground below my feet. We'd landed...we'd landed so gently I hadn't felt the impact. I opened my eyes carefully and looked around. We were in an underground chamber, illuminated by a single glowing orb. My friends were standing beside me, utterly unmoving. I poked Akin in the arm, but felt...I wasn't sure *what* I felt. My finger *skittered* over his shirt, as if there was something isolating him from me. I turned to Rose, but she was just the same. They were trapped like flies in amber.

Panic crashed against my mind. I clutched the spellcaster tightly, even though there was no visible threat. The dim light made the shadows look nasty...I couldn't even see the chamber's walls. And...the only thing I could see was a scroll, sitting on a small wooden desk. It was surrounded by a faint haze of yellow light.

The call snapped off the moment I saw the scroll, as if it had never been. It had wanted me to *see* the scroll, I realised dully. I pulled the dispeller out of my pocket and pressed it against Akin, but nothing happened. The panic grew stronger, threatening to overwhelm me. If my friends were trapped, again…what could I do? What had happened to us? Where *were* we?

I looked up. The gloom was all-consuming, but…I couldn't see any way up. I didn't even know how we'd gone down…I'd heard stories about teleport gates and other fantastic magics, but none of them seemed plausible. The power it would take to teleport a grown man from one side of Shallot to the other would be beyond a hundred magicians working in unison. And yet…I knew we'd fallen…maybe I was just over-thinking it. It wouldn't take more than a handful of spells to slow our fall, then lock my friends in place…

Maybe I was frozen too, I thought. It felt like paranoia, yet…yet there was no way I could disprove it. There were spells that froze a person's thoughts as well as their bodies, trapping them until they were freed. I could have been frozen like that too, but…the thought nagged at my mind. *The spell simply couldn't hold me for long.*

I touched Rose's cheek. It didn't feel like flesh. My fingers touched, but didn't touch…as if there was a barrier between us. It wasn't something I recognised. Time itself seemed to run oddly within the chamber…no, within the entire city. The villa had been unchanged until we'd blundered our way into the building. I wondered, as I turned to look at the scroll, just what had happened to the original owners. They'd left in a hurry.

We're on the outskirts of the city, I reminded myself. The Eternal City had been *huge*. I had problems grasping the sheer size of the city, no matter how hard I concentrated. *They might have had time to leave before whatever ruined the city reached here.*

I inspected the scroll through my spectacles, but there was nothing. The yellow haze didn't seem to be quite real…as if it wasn't magic. And yet…it was there. I held my hand over the haze, unsure if I should touch it or not. It didn't feel threatening, but…I knew from grim experience that I couldn't sense a threat until it was too late. If there was a nasty spell just waiting for me, I was in trouble. And yet…

Bracing myself, I plunged my hand into the haze. It snapped out of existence at once, as if someone had cancelled the spell. I yanked my hand back, but nothing else happened. The scroll just lay there, waiting…waiting for me. I peered down at it, yet…there was nothing. It was just a scroll. I told myself I was being silly and reached for the scroll, half-expecting it to crumble the moment I touched the parchment. Instead, it was easy to open it and read the top line.

Greetings.

I frowned. It was written in Old Script, but a very archaic *form* of Old Script. I supposed it shouldn't have surprised me. The more modern languages hadn't even *existed* when the Eternal City had collapsed. And yet…it still *felt* odd. I'd had the ancient language drummed into my head from birth, but I still had to work to translate every line. The writing was tiny, so tiny I had to squint to read. And the phrasing was archaic. Even the most hidebound of my tutors had clearly spoken an imperfect version of the tongue…

Putting the thought to one side, I started to read.

CHAPTER
THIRTY-ONE

Greetings.

If you're reading this - if you gained admittance to this chamber - you're a Zero.

I assume - I hope - that you know what that means. You have no link to the magic field. You can no more cast a spell than I can - and I was taught my trade in the Eternal City. But you should be aware of your own talents. I have done everything in my power - working complex runes into the stone walls - to ensure that you would not be able to enter this chamber without you knowing something of your talents. But too much can go wrong over the centuries for me to be entirely sure.

I don't know just how much time has passed between my sealing the chamber and your arrival. Decades, at least; centuries, perhaps. I certainly intend to ensure that no one returns to this complex for months, long enough for my work to take effect. And I don't know how much you know of the underlying truth behind magic, the truth we discovered...the truth that eventually wrecked the empire. Knowledge of us - the Zeroes - was kept hidden, even as the empire conquered most of the known world. You may be staggeringly ignorant, by my standards; you may look upon me as a child, struggling vainly to impress his elders and betters. It doesn't matter. I know you don't know why the Eternal City fell because I am the sole survivor of the disaster. No one else, in these terrible times, knows the truth.

There have been times when I considered taking the secret with me to the grave. Would it not be better for the truth to remain buried? But it is the way of things that secrets never remain undiscovered indefinitely. And so I have left this letter for you, my successor. If you read this, you will know the truth. May the gods have mercy on you.

My name is Tyros of the Eternal City. I am the last of the Zeroes.

I was born in a simple farming hamlet, several hundred leagues from the Eternal City. Magic was a rare thing there, largely because none of us had access to anything more than shamanic knowledge passed down from parents to children. I certainly didn't know any spells, which - coincidently - kept me from realising my true nature. There was no reason to expect anything other than following my father and grandfather onto the farm. I would marry young and have children, keeping the farm in our family. As it happened, the gods had a different fate in mind for me.

I was thirteen when we were summoned to the village school, all of us. Boys and girls alike, from eight to eighteen. My father grumbled, saying that we would soon put on airs and graces and forget the farm, but we had no choice. The empire had ordered that all of us were to have at least two days of schooling per week. I didn't like it. What was the point of learning to read, I ask you, when there was literally nothing to read? Only a handful of second sons professed to enjoy learning and they wouldn't have a hope of inheriting anything from their fathers. I didn't begrudge them their chance to leave the village for good.

My brother and I walked down to the schoolhouse with Cynisca, a girl from the neighbouring farm. She was the same age as me, her body just starting to show signs of curves that caught my attention and held it. Her blonde hair seemed to shine in the sunlight. I was, I believed, hopelessly in love with her. My father had even promised to talk to her father, once we both came of age. We did our best to chat, but I was tongue-tied. I never quite knew what to say to her.

The schoolmaster greeted us as we entered the schoolhouse, then pointed towards the main hall. He was a stern man, always willing to apply vigorous correction to any miscreants, but on that day he looked almost fearful. I realised why when I stepped into the hall. A grim-faced man wearing black was standing at the front of the room, watching us. His outfit - black, covered in silver runes - marked him out as a quaestor. He had the power to do anything in search of the truth, we knew. We stayed quiet, like mice before the cat, as the last of the schoolchildren trotted into the chamber. I don't think it had ever been quite so full.

I watched, fearfully, as the quaestor rose to his feet and brandished a wand at us. My head seemed to go dull, just for a second. I felt tired, too tired. And then the sensation was gone, as if it had never been. I stared at him, wondering just what had happened, then glanced at my brother. He was standing beside me, his eyes dull and vacant. His hands hung helplessly at his sides. The entire room was silent, utterly silent. I was the only one who seemed to be able to move.

"You," the quaestor said. "Come here."

I obeyed, fearfully. Up close, he was a truly fearsome man. I wanted to run, but I knew it was futile. All I could do was wait, trembling, as he cast spell after spell over me.

"You're coming with me," he said, once he'd finished his tests. "Now."

I swallowed. "Sir, my parents..."

"Will be informed," the quaestor said. "Come."

He turned and strode out of the hall. I hesitated, glancing back at the rest of the schoolchildren. They stood there, unmoving.

"Go," the schoolmaster hissed.

I took one last look at Cynisca. She was standing there, as helpless as the rest. Her hair was as shiny as ever, but her eyes were blank...

By all the gods, I wish I'd never lived to see that!

The quaestor took me back to the farm and had a long chat with my parents. I learnt later that he'd paid them for me, as if I was a cow he'd bought at the market, but at the time all I could think of was that he was taking me away. I didn't even have a chance to say goodbye. He ordered me onto his flyer and carried me off, casually. I was on my way to the Eternal City before I even knew it!

Ah, the Eternal City. Do they tell tales of it in your time? Do they tell you that the streets were paved with gold? That a man could walk a hundred miles without ever touching the ground? There was truth in many of the stories, too. Half the buildings hung in the air, balancing on strands of stone or floating, held up by magic. The walls glowed with a pearly white light, illuminated night and day. Even the poorest amongst the city-folk dwelled in luxury, a luxury made possible by the empire and its magicians. And, of course, the Zeroes.

I hadn't quite realised it, but my life was now devoted to the empire. Until, of course, it wasn't.

The quaestor and his comrades searched every year for children with high magic potential and no magic potential. We Zeroes were rare, it seemed. There were only two others in my class at the Eternal City, Tristan and Helena. They would both shape my life and, ultimately, change it.

Helena was a young woman, a year younger than myself. She came from a senatorial family and had been raised in the expectation of marrying someone who would cement her father's grip on power. Or she would have, if she hadn't been attacked by a werewolf two months ago. One half of her face was stunningly pretty; the other half was scarred, despite her father's doctors. She'd been shunned in polite society, everyone expecting that she'd turn into a wolf at the next full moon. When she hadn't, they'd known she was a Zero and sent her to us. She was a very bitter girl, understandably. Her parents had told everyone that she'd been disowned.

Tristan was an angry young man, a year older than me. He would be calm and composed at one moment, then snapping and snarling the next. It was never easy to tell what would set him off. I watched him bite his forearm weekly, just to burn off some negative energy. He acted as though he'd been cheated by life, even though he was a Zero. I never knew much about his background, but from what little he'd let slip it was clear that he hadn't had a happy childhood. His older siblings had tormented him with their magic, I believe. It certainly made him bitter, too. I used to think that Helena and Tristan were well matched. As it happened...

Well, I'll get to that in due time.

I won't bore you with the details of my training. I doubt you'd find it interesting. I had a great deal to learn, but so did Helena so at least I wasn't alone. Tristan knew more, yet he was always willing to help - to help both of us, it turned out. He was calmer, somehow, while he was explaining things. The three of us grew to maturity together, remaining friends even as we graduated. None of the older Zeroes had much time for us.

It was Helena, oddly enough, who started asking the obvious questions. Why were we different? What separated us Zeroes from the average low-magic user? Why could we make Objects of Power? And why, perhaps most importantly to her, did the werewolf curse have no effect on us? Tristan and I struggled to answer her questions, delving deeper and deeper into the true nature of magic. Dare I say that I miss those days, even now? We sat in our workroom, drinking and chatting and theorising and devising experiments to confirm our theories...we had fun. And, eventually, we solved the mystery that had bedevilled us for years.

You see, there's no such thing as a magician.

I'm sure that shocks you, just as much as it shocked us. Tristan wasn't the only one to suffer at the hands of his empowered peers. I too had been hexed mercilessly as I struggled to devise Objects of Protection. Magic was real, right? Well...yes, it was. But it wasn't what we thought it was.

What we discovered was the existence of a magic field, blanketing the entire planet. It was this field that powered magic, just as humans breathed oxygen to live. Magicians had a talent for controlling and directing the magic field, but they didn't have any inherent magic of their own. If they were deprived of contact with the magic field, we theorised, they would be unable to cast spells.

Our Objects of Power actually worked along the same lines. Our inability to touch the magic field allowed us to create Objects of Power that wouldn't be warped and twisted by magic.

Tristan insisted we should keep this discovery to ourselves. Helena sided with him. And I, reluctantly, agreed.

We spent the next six months putting together a prototype Object of Power that would drain the local magic field. Tristan thought it would be useful. I didn't realise, at the time, just what he had in mind. Our original plans were to craft something we could use to safeguard our homes from magic, but Tristan had a far grander plan. He wanted to show his family how it felt to be helpless. He told me that he wanted to deprive his siblings of their magic, just long enough to teach them a lesson.

Helena thought it would be a great joke. And I rather thought, to be honest, that the empire needed the lesson. Our grasp of magic had turned the Eternal City from a tiny city-state on a tiny continent to the undisputed master of much of the known world. We - the Zeroes - had made the city great. And yet, we were treated poorly. Maybe we weren't slaves, but we were expected to work for the empire. I had been taken from my family and brought to the Eternal City because of my nature. I'd never been offered a choice.

Our plan was to show off the new Object of Power during the Summer Festival, a week when the great and good of the empire would assemble to pledge their loyalty, once again, to the emperor. Tristan wanted to use the device in his family home, giving his family a fright before revealing what we'd done. A week before our planned date, I helped him transport the device into his former bedroom, then returned to our mansion. He insisted on remaining behind to talk to his father.

That night, Helena seduced me. We spent the next week in bed together. Tristan told us to have fun, that he would handle everything. I was too busy being grateful for her caresses that it never occurred to me to check what he was doing. I was otherwise occupied as the city filled with the great and the good, with the best and brightest of the empire moving into homes surrounding the palace. Not that anyone moved into our mansion, of course. There was a reason we were on the outside of the city, after all. Zeroes like us upset people. They found us useful, but they detested us.

If I'd known what Tristan was planning, when he'd left us at the mansion and headed into the city, would I have stopped him? I don't know.

Helena and I cuddled on the rooftop at sunset, intending to watch the fireworks exploding above the floating city. Instead...I watched in horror as hundreds of buildings literally fell out of the air, crashing down on the city below. The ground shook violently as thousands upon thousands of spells failed. Hundreds of thousands of people died in that first catastrophic instant. More earthquakes followed as spells intended to keep the city stable abruptly failed, collapsing entire districts into the waves.

Helena laughed. It was a chilling sound. And that, more than anything else, told me what Tristan had done.

The Eternal City was dependent upon magic. Its absence brought the entire city tumbling down. None of the ward spells held, none of the magicians could use their powers to save their lives, let alone the city...the great and good of the empire died before they even realised that they were doomed. I looked at Helena in horror. There was an expression of smug satisfaction on her face. I wondered, grimly, just how long the two of them had been plotting the city's downfall. They both had good reason to want revenge.

"The empire falls today," Helena said, quietly. "A brave new world begins."

She was right.

Of course she was. Every nobleman, every general, every foreign aristocrat eager to claim some of the crumbs from our table...they'd all been in the Eternal City. Everyone who thought they were someone had been there, when the towers fell. Most of them were dead now and the survivors would not live long. And much of their knowledge was gone too. The great universities where magicians had studied advanced magic had collapsed, taking their students and teachers with them. Even the remainder of the Zeroes,

Tristan included, were dead. The flames already licking through the remains of the city would finish the job.

Tristan had had his revenge. It had cost him his life, but he'd had his revenge. The empire was broken.

Helena and I exchanged harsh words as we struggled to flee the collapsing city. The Object of Power had drained the magic over a terrifyingly wide area, leaving me wondering if we'd somehow broken magic itself. We heard strange sounds behind us as we fled, joining thousands of helpless civilians in search of elusive safety. But there was none to be had. By the time we reached the nearest unaffected city, it was clear that the empire was starting to collapse. It had been held in place by magical and military force and now much of that force was gone.

I didn't tell anyone what had happened, afterwards. It would only have gotten us both killed by the survivors, if they believed us. I remembered enough about farming - and basic blacksmithing - to make a living, once we found somewhere to stay. We stayed out of the civil wars, as best as we could. Helena never took well to the simple life, the restrictions placed on common-born women - and, perhaps, the guilt of knowing what she'd helped do. She took poison two years after the Eternal City fell and the wars began. In truth, she wasn't the only one.

That, then, is the truth of what happened to the Eternal City.

People started to forget quickly. The rubble was practically abandoned, strange tales of weird wild magics and dark apparitions scaring away all, but the most determined of fortune hunters. Now, a Zero is a low-level magician, not someone without any link to the magic field. The stories I heard of the city, even a mere five years after the fall, made it sound like a long-lost golden age. And they are right, aren't they? The empire wasn't wonderful, perish the thought. It was still better than the chaos that followed the collapse. The civil wars devastated the continent as surviving officers fought for supremacy. Lacking us, lacking the empire's magical base, their wars eventually stalemated. By then, millions of people had died.

I found this place, ten years after Helena died. A young magician hired me to help outfit his home, laying geas after geas on me to ensure I didn't betray him. I didn't tell him that his spells were useless, not that it mattered. I had no intention of betraying him. All I really wanted was to create this chamber, then ward it. The only person who could find it, once I had completed my work, would be another Zero.

I'm finishing this scroll now, then sealing the chamber. I've done things to the mansion, ensuring that a new Zero - and there will be one, sooner or later - will be steered down here and shown the door. I certainly have no intention of returning...

There's nothing I can do about my role in the fall, not now. Tristan fooled me with Helena's help. If I'd noticed in time, perhaps I would have stopped him. But it is now too late to change anything. I have to live with what I did - and what I failed to do.

I wish I had something to impart, beyond the notes I've hidden here. What use you make of them is up to you. I suggest, however, that you keep the truth a secret. Magicians will not thank you for telling them that they can be deprived of their power in a heartbeat, with the right Object of Power. But that too is up to you.
Good luck.
Tyros of the Eternal City.

CHAPTER
THIRTY-TWO

I sat back in utter shock.

No magicians? No *real* magicians?

It couldn't be right, could it? I'd grown up with magicians. I *knew* that Alana and Bella and my parents - and everyone else - had power. And yet...

"There were duels, once upon a time," Magister Niven had said. His words echoed in my mind. "Twelve magicians to a side, winner takes all. And the more they cast...sometimes, the spells weakened for no reason, sometimes the magicians would find it harder to cast newer spells. Everyone thinks there were just too many spells and the different spellforms were interfering with each other. But is that true?"

I felt cold. It wasn't true. If Tyros was to be believed, there were no true magicians...just a magic field. Perhaps the demand for magic had been so high that the field had dropped, long enough to make it hard for the duellists to cast spells. And yet...I'd thought that magicians were trained to cast stronger and stronger spells. Perhaps, instead, they were being taught to absorb, store and manipulate magic from the magic field.

Magister Niven's question ran through my mind. "Where does the power come from?"

I looked down at the spellcaster in my hand. I knew where the power came from now - the magic field. Objects of Power drew directly on the magic field, rather than channelling power through a magician. The mere contact with a human mind must taint the power, I reasoned slowly, corroding away at the Devices of Power even as they were forged. No *wonder* they didn't last long, I realised slowly. The power couldn't flow through them without being twisted and warped out of all recognition.

And Tyros had built this place...

The glowing orb flickered and went out. Absolute darkness crashed down around me. I jumped, unsure what to do. The chamber had been too dim for me to grasp any of the layout, even before the light had vanished altogether. I clutched the scroll in one hand, shoving it into my bag even as I tried to decide what to do. My friends were frozen, trapped in time, while I was trapped in utter darkness. I couldn't cast a light, not without tools or equipment I didn't have. And for all I knew there was a chasm right next to me.

"Cat," Akin said. "Cat?"

"I'm here," I said, quickly. The magic - the strange magic Tyros had devised - had flickered and died. "Rose?"

"What happened?" Rose asked. A faint light appeared as she cast a light spell. "Cat?"

"Long story," I said, shortly. Neither of them seemed to have realised that they'd been frozen in time. I wasn't sure I wanted to tell them, either. *No one* had even suspected the existence of a magic field, unless Magister Niven had an inkling. If I told them the truth and it got back to our parents...it would, of course. The story would be too good *not* to be shared. "Can you both cast light spells?"

I heard Akin muttering a spell, just loudly enough to be heard. A pearly white light appeared, shimmering unsteadily through the air. Akin was standing next to Rose, his pale skin so white he appeared to have seen a ghost. Rose didn't look much better. I wondered, sourly, just what I *should* tell them. A lie might rebound on me if - when - they discovered the truth.

"I think we stumbled into a trap," I said, as I looked around. The shadows had vanished, revealing a small workroom. I searched it quickly, picking up a handful of the older tools and components for later. Tyros had been a master forger, whatever else he'd been. He'd been thousands of miles ahead of me when he'd died. "But we survived."

I felt a flicker of bitter envy. Tyros…Tyros had been powerless, but he'd known what he was. He'd been useful. And yet…he'd also been exploited. Both Great Aunt Stregheria and Fairuza had sought to exploit me. I wondered, as I worked my way through the drawers, if Dad would try to exploit me in the future. We'd been raised to believe that we had to put the family's interests ahead of our own. I just hadn't been very useful, until now. Dad might expect me to work for him when I grew up.

But I would have done that, wouldn't I? The thought mocked me. *I wanted to be useful.*

"Here," Rose called. "I've found a tunnel!"

I followed her gaze. A dark tunnel, leading into the darkness…I had no way of knowing where it led. But there was no other way out. We must have fallen through a hole in the ceiling - I was sure we'd fallen through a hole - but there was no trace of it. The roof looked smooth, utterly unbroken. I took one last look at the desks and cabinets, then shook my head in amused disbelief. The workroom really wasn't *that* different than any of the workrooms I'd used back home.

The room shook. I heard something crashing to the ground. Rose yelped.

"The building's collapsing," Akin snapped. Another crash drowned out his words. "We have to get out of here!"

"Get down the tunnel," I ordered.

It was the only way out. Tyros wouldn't have wanted to kill anyone who found his lair, but…I had a nasty feeling that the lair's defences had been the only thing keeping the building intact. Tyros…had done something remarkable, I thought. And yet…I touched the scroll in my pocket. He'd also done something very dangerous. *And* he'd been an unwitting accessory to a crime of monstrous proportions.

I tried to grasp the true scale of what he'd done as we stumbled into the tunnel and made our way into the darkness. The population of Shallot was somewhere around 80,000, although that didn't include the people who lived outside the city's walls. If the Eternal City had been five times larger than Shallot, it must have had a population of 400,000, perhaps more. It had been the centre of a world-spanning empire, after all. The population might easily be in the millions.

And Tyros and his friends had torn it all down.

It was unimaginable. I just couldn't make myself *grasp* it. I didn't know every last person in *Shallot*. They were just faceless numbers to me. 400,000 was even worse. I didn't know a single person from the Eternal City. I knew, intellectually, that they'd all had lives of their own, that they'd loved and hated and *lived*, but I couldn't imagine it. Tyros had been party to mass murder on an unimaginable scale and I just couldn't understand what he'd done.

And Tristan was worse, I thought. *He* knew *what was going to happen*.

I was sure of it. He couldn't have been otherwise, not knowing what he did. Draining the magic field would wipe out every spell in the region. The magicians would have some stored power, if I was correct, but nowhere near enough to save the city. Falling buildings and shattering containment spells would have done the rest. And if so many of the great and the good had been in the Eternal City when it died, no wonder the empire had died with them. It had been decapitated.

And yet, there was a part of me that understood. Tristan had been like me: powerless, but born to a powerful family. He would have been mocked and tormented for his lack of power, just as my sisters had tormented me. His family would have known what he was, of course, and sent him to the Zeroes, but that wouldn't make things better. *Alana* had still been able to get the better of *me*, after I'd mastered my talents. Tristan would have had the same problem.

I wouldn't have committed mass murder, I told myself. *I wouldn't...*

But what would I have done, my thoughts asked, if I'd had the ability to strip Alana and Bella of their power? Would I have used it? I *could* use it. I thought I understood how the device must have worked, although forging it would take time. And if I built it, what then? What if someone *else* built it? Fairuza had wanted me to brew a potion that would burn through any wards known to exist. How much worse would it be if she had something that wiped out magic, *all* magic? She could destroy the Great Families in an afternoon.

Akin glanced at me as the ground shook, again. "You're being very quiet."

"I was just thinking about the building," I lied. "It might have come down on their heads."

"Good," Akin said, bluntly. "That will stop them chasing us."

I swallowed, but said nothing as the tunnel began to level out. Akin's light revealed a handful of concealment runes carved into the wall, hiding it from casual inspection. I wondered just what had happened to Tyros after he'd finished the scroll. Perhaps he'd gone in search of his long-lost family or...perhaps he'd just walked into the Eternal City and waited to die. To me, it was the past; to him, it was all too real.

I should destroy the scroll, I thought. I didn't *think* Tyros had done anything to keep a magician from reading it. *What would happen if I did?*

Another faint tremor ran through the ground. No one knew anything about magic fields, not in Shallot. Everyone assumed that magicians had magic and that was all there was to it. They'd be shocked if I told them the truth, then horrified. Someone might just find a way to lower the magic field in a particular area, just to weaken wards before they were smashed. Or...

My blood ran cold. What if the magic never came back?

I clenched my fists as the full horror struck me. The duellist experience *suggested* that the magic field flowed back into place, but...but what if it had limits? What if - one day - the magic field ran out and the magic just...went away? No magicians...no healers, no forgers, no...no magic. And what about the creatures that *depended* on magic? Dragons, unicorns, basilisks, centaurs, werewolves, mermaids...could they even *live* without magic? Would they die with the magic? Or would they slowly fade away?

You don't know that will happen, I told myself, firmly. *You don't know if any of this will happen.*

And yet...I swallowed, hard. Magic hadn't gone away with the empire. Of course not - too much magical knowledge had been spread around for *that*. But magical activity had fallen sharply, in the decades following the empire's collapse. Perhaps...the magic field had weakened too, only no one had noticed. And we'd had to rebuild the principles of magic pretty much from scratch. We might have adapted to the new reality without ever being aware of it.

I couldn't tell anyone. I couldn't even tell my Dad. I couldn't...

It felt like we'd been walking for hours before the tunnel started to slope upwards. I tensed, trying to push my thoughts to the back of my mind. But it didn't work. Where were we? Where had Tyros considered a safe place to hide an exit? Were we outside the city? Maybe not. Tyros clearly hadn't known the…curse…on the Eternal City would spread further, not by where he'd built the villa. I wondered just what the man who'd hired him had been thinking, when he'd issued his orders. Perhaps he'd thought the tainted magic would fade away, allowing him to stake a claim to the remains of the city. Or perhaps Tyros had deliberately misled him. I would never know.

"There's a door up ahead," Akin said. "I'll go first."

"I've got the bracelet," I said. "Let me go first."

I slipped past Akin and pushed the door. It felt like cold stone to my palms, but it opened smoothly. I caught a glimpse of a pair of carved concealment runes as I inched forward, spellcaster at the ready. Tyros had been a *very* skilled forger. I wondered, absently, just what his training had been like as I looked around. We'd come out in a basement, it seemed. The air smelled musty, but there were no hints of wild magic. I crept to the stairwell and listened, carefully. There didn't seem to be anyone above us.

"Be careful," Akin whispered.

"Of course," I said.

I climbed up the stairs carefully, pausing to listen after every step. Dust glimmered in the air as I reached the top, forcing me to cover my mouth. I didn't want to sneeze! But there was no one outside, just darkened corridors. I could see a window, in the distance. The sun was slowly falling behind the distant hills.

"Night time," I said, quietly.

I yawned as we searched the building from top to bottom. It was deserted, save for a colony of mice that squeaked loudly and fled our approach. I took heart from that, even though I disliked the idea of sleeping so close to vermin. We might well be quite some distance from the Eternal City. Tyros certainly wouldn't have wanted his tunnel to come out too close to the warped magic field.

"We should go further," Akin said.

I shook my head and yawned, again. My entire body was starting to ache, reminding me that I'd been awake for over two days. Or at least I thought I had…if it had been night when I'd escaped our captors, I'd been awake for at least forty hours. I'd kept going, somehow, but…but I couldn't go on for much longer.

"I'm tired too," Rose said, practically. "We don't want to push ourselves too far."

Akin didn't argue. I think he was tired as well, just too proud to admit it. He and Rose had burned up a great deal of energy over the last few hours, casting spells…and if their own magic had powered the freeze spell, they'd have been drained of that too. Except it wasn't their magic, was it? They drew on the magic field.

And I have no link to the field, I reminded myself.

I smiled, tiredly, as we made our way back down to the basement. The implications were staggering, assuming I managed to get home. Now I understood, I thought, some of the more complex Objects of Power I'd seen in the books. And I understood *precisely* how a flying machine worked. I could build one now, given time and materials…

"I'll cast a concealment ward on the stairs," Akin said, once we reached the bottom. "Rose, can you block the tunnel entrance?"

"Yeah," Rose said. She sounded laboured. I wondered if she was having problems mustering the magic. Whatever Tyros and his comrades had done, it had permanently warped the magic field near the Eternal City. "Should one of us stay on watch?"

"No point," I said. I appreciated the thought, but it didn't matter. None of us were in any state for a fight. "Let's just get some sleep before morning."

I felt a flicker of amusement as I picked a spot on the floor and lay down. Mum would have a fit if she discovered that I'd shared a room with a boy. She'd never let Alana and Bella have sleepovers where there was an adolescent boy in the house. I'd never understood it, not really. The parents could provide whatever chaperonage was required. And yet…it was the principle of the thing, I supposed. Young girls were not meant to compromise their reputations before they were old enough to make such decisions for themselves.

Not that it matters, I told myself. *We don't want to split up now.*

The floor was cold and hard. I wished for a mattress, a blanket…even a long coat. But I'd just have to endure the discomfort. Rose lay down next to me, looking disgustingly at ease in the semi-darkness. I supposed, unpleasantly, that she was used to sleeping in uncomfortable places. The light snapped out of existence a second later as Akin cancelled the spell. We couldn't risk being found until we were rested.

I reached for the spellcaster and placed it within easy reach, just in case. Akin's wards wouldn't keep out a determined magician, but the noise *should* wake us. I wasn't going to let them take me again, not while I had the scroll on my person. I knew I should destroy it, but…it was history. I didn't dare show it to anyone, yet…I didn't dare destroy it either. Tyros should not be forgotten.

And yet, I'm the only one who remembers him, I reminded myself. *Did anyone read his name in the history books?*

I doubted it. I'd learnt dozens of names from the history books, the men who'd made the Eternal City great, but they'd mostly been emperors or generals. Only a handful of them had been women and only one of them had been a ruler in her own right. The others had shocked what passed for High Society in those days. It puzzled me - women had magic too, magic enough to rule the Great Houses - but I suspected I'd never figure out the truth. Perhaps the women had secretly ruled the empire from behind the scenes. One woman was supposed to have done just that when her husband proved incapable…

"Good night," Akin said. His voice echoed in the darkness. "I'll wake you in the morning."

"Good night," Rose echoed. I could *hear* her smile. "Try not to get up too quickly. It will hurt."

I closed my eyes and tried to sleep. Sleep didn't come easy…

…And when it did, I dreamed of the magic going away.

CHAPTER
THIRTY-THREE

"Cat!"

I jerked awake, my head spinning. For a long moment, I wasn't sure what was real and what wasn't. The nightmares had dragged me into a maelstrom of shadows, where everything I'd known had been wrong and *nothing* I'd done had been able to make things right. I felt sweat dripping down my forehead, even though it was cold. My head felt as if it had overheated. It throbbed, dully, as I fought to steady myself.

"You were having a nightmare," a voice said. I almost hit out before realising that it was Rose. "What were you dreaming about?"

I gasped and opened my eyes as I fought for breath. Rose was kneeling next to me, her face illuminated by a glowing light. Akin was sitting on the other side of the room, watching me nervously. I felt a hot flash of shame, mingled with embarrassment. I'd never had such vivid nightmares in Raven Dorm, and, if I had, the noise-dampening charms would keep me from waking the others.

"Night terrors," I managed. I didn't want to tell her the truth. The scroll felt heavy against my skin. "I think…I think everything just caught up with me at once."

"You've done very well," Akin said, gently. I caught a glimpse of his worried face as he rose and headed for the stairs. "It's nearly morning, I think."

My stomach rumbled, reminding me that I hadn't eaten properly in two days. I sat upright, gritting my teeth. We didn't have much food left, yet if we didn't eat we'd collapse before we made it to safety. We didn't even know where *safety* was! I couldn't go back to the suite, no matter what promises Fairuza made. The scroll would be far too revealing if it fell into her hands. I knew I should destroy it, but…but I couldn't. I couldn't even consider the possibility.

Akin slipped back down the stairs. "It's dawn," he said. "There's no one outside, as far as I can tell."

I nodded. If we were lucky, some of the hunters had been caught when the villa collapsed into rubble. If we were *really* lucky, Fairuza and her comrades would assume we'd been crushed under falling debris and killed. But I knew I didn't dare count on it. Fairuza had every reason to go digging through the wreckage to recover our bodies, just to make sure we actually *were* dead. I looked at the tunnel entrance and shivered. Tyros had done a fantastic job, for someone who'd had to work in secret and alone, but I had no illusions about what would happen if Fairuza started digging through the rubble. She'd uncover the tunnel sooner rather than later.

And our missing bodies will tell her that we made it out, I added, silently.

"We need more food," Akin said, as he opened the bag and passed out the sandwiches. I took one and munched it, savouring every bite. "Perhaps we should go back to their base."

Rose blinked. "Are you mad?"

"They have to be searching the ruins for us," Akin pointed out. "We sneak in, steal what we need, then sneak out again."

It was insane, but I found myself considering it anyway. Fairuza *would* be searching for us, wouldn't she? Of course she would! And she'd need dozens, perhaps hundreds, of people to search a place where tracking spells were unreliable. She'd have to deploy everyone under her command to search for us, leaving only a handful of people at the base. We'd have the spellcasters and the element of surprise. It was tempting…

We can't count on any of this, I reminded myself, sharply. I *wanted* to believe it. That was the danger. *If she thinks the base is the only source of food, she may have it guarded anyway.*

"Or we get caught," I countered, grimly. "What if she's anticipated us sneaking back to the base?"

Another thought struck me and I frowned. "Where *is* the base, anyway?"

Akin and Rose exchanged glances. "Don't you know?"

I shook my head. "It was dark and I was trying to get away," I said. In hindsight, it was clear I'd come far too close to running right into the most dangerous part of the city. "I don't know precisely where I was when I stopped."

"Oh," Akin said.

Rose cleared her throat. "There *is* another possibility," she said. "But... but we'd have to be careful."

I frowned. I'd racked my brains, yet...the only idea I'd had that seemed remotely plausible was walking north, following the ocean, until we crossed the border. The maps made it look easy, but I knew it would take weeks. And we simply didn't have the food to keep going.

"*What* other possibility?"

"There's a farm nearby," Rose said. "We can find it and buy food."

"A farm?" Akin looked disbelieving. His voice was challenging. "How do you *know* there's a farm nearby?"

Rose smirked. "The food they fed us came from a farm," she said, mischievously. "I *told* you it came from a farm. And if there is one farm fairly nearby, there will be others. We find one and trade for food."

I had to giggle. "Good point," I said. And hopefully one Fairuza would miss. Neither I nor Akin had realised where the food had come from. "But what do we have to trade?"

"It depends," Rose said. She nodded to the bag. "That gold chain might be worth something, perhaps. But..."

She paused, just for a second. "You may have to swear to keep their location a secret."

Akin raised his eyebrows. "Why?"

Rose looked reluctant to answer, just for a second. "Because if they're *here*, they're probably trying to keep out of sight," she said. "The last thing they want is someone trying to *tax* them."

I blinked. "I don't understand."

"Farmers are taxed in kind, rather than money." Rose sounded calm, but there was an angry undertone that worried me. "My father has to give a certain amount of crop and livestock to the local nobility, every year. One bad harvest will ruin us. It…it isn't uncommon for farmers to hide their crops or simply flee the land. They just can't keep up with the demands."

"And if they came here, they could live their lives in peace," Akin said. He jabbed a finger at the walls. "They're dangerously close to the Eternal City."

"They may think the city is less dangerous than the taxman," Rose countered. "And they might be right."

I nodded, slowly. It had never occurred to me that anyone would willingly live within a hundred miles of the Eternal City. The entire region was dangerous. And yet, if the danger was limited to the city and suburbs itself…perhaps an entire community could live in the shadow of the ruins, safe from interference. But Fairuza had clearly known about them. I wondered…

It had to be said. "Can we count on them not to betray us?"

"No," Rose said, flatly. "But do you have a better idea?"

I looked at Akin. He looked back and shrugged.

"No," I said. "Shall we go?"

My body ached as I sat up, reminding me that I'd slept on hard stone. My skin didn't show bruises easily, but the aches and pains wouldn't go away. I staggered forward, walking around until my legs started to work properly. I was uneasily aware that I was in no state for running, if Fairuza and her friends caught up with us. Akin was moving gingerly, in a manner that suggested he was aching too. Rose was the only one of us who didn't seem to be suffering any ill effects.

She's probably used to sleeping on hard surfaces, I thought, ungraciously. Mum had insisted that my sisters and I learn to make our own beds before we went to school, but she hadn't made us sleep on the floor. *And if Rose wasn't here, we'd have to find the enemy base and sneak inside.*

I pushed the thought out of my mind as I followed Akin up the stairs and down the corridor, spellcaster at the ready. A faint mist hung in the early morning air, but it felt reassuringly normal…more like the sea mists that drifted over Shallot than something created by wild magic. Sounds echoed through the trees and I lifted the spellcaster, a second before realising that they were birds. Oddly, I found that reassuring. There had been no animals nearer the city itself.

"We might be able to catch a rabbit," Rose said. "I can cook one, if necessary."

I shuddered. I'd watched Dad slaughtering a cow for Solar Day and it had been utterly gruesome. It had taken all of my willpower to eat the beef, after it had been ritually prepared and cooked. I didn't want to *think* about catching a sweet little rabbit and eating it…and yet, I knew I *had* eaten rabbit. I just hadn't made the connection, not emotionally, between the animal and the meat.

My stomach growled. If we didn't find a farm soon, we might have no choice.

We stepped out of the building, watching for anything that wasn't a bird. A cool breeze blew down the street, sending shivers down my spine. I could feel the sun on my back, even though it was lost in the haze. I looked up and down, silently inspecting the rows of buildings. They looked surprisingly intact, given their age, but they were deserted.

"Someone must have built these to house newcomers," Akin said. "And then they were abandoned after the empire fell."

I nodded in agreement. The buildings were sturdy, but they were also identical, as if someone had stamped them out one by one. I'd seen similar buildings in South Shallot, where immigrants to the city rented housing while trying to earn the right to remain. Dad had told me that they either moved upwards within a couple of years or went back home. Either way, no one was investing money in their first homes.

And the builders didn't use magic to put them together, I thought. There was a diagram - a crude drawing of a bull - on the nearest house. *They survived the fall because magic wasn't holding them together.*

"So," Akin said. "Which way?"

I looked down the road. The mist was stronger there, but I could still feel the…*wrongness*…of the Eternal City. "That way," I said, pointing in the other direction. "Let's go."

My legs kept aching as we made our way through the buildings. Akin swore blind we were heading north, but I wasn't so sure. I told myself it didn't matter, anyway. As long as we kept the Eternal City behind us, we were heading away from the danger zone. And yet...the suburbs seemed endless. It felt as if we'd been walking for hours by the time we finally crossed a ruined road and entered the countryside. I wanted to sit down and rest, but...I kept thinking that if I did stop, I'd never be able to move again.

If I make it back home, I promised myself silently, *I'm going to exercise every day.*

"Strange road," Akin commented. "What do you think they were driving on it?"

I shrugged. The road had been astonishingly wide. The King's Roads were in better condition - I'd driven on them when we'd gone to the country estates for summer holidays - but they were thinner, designed for horses and carts rather than anything else. I wondered if I could put together a self-propelled cart, using the Objects of Power I'd seen in the ancient books. It wouldn't be too hard, as long as I was careful. If I built the core Object of Power, Akin or another forger should be able to build the rest.

The thought kept me going as we steadily forced our way through the undergrowth. There were no paths, as far as I could see, although Rose was very good at picking ways through the foliage. Insects buzzed around us, flying through my hair and landing on my skin; I slapped at them when they started to bite, but there were always more. Akin didn't know any insect repelling spells. Rose didn't seem bothered by their attention.

It grew warmer, steadily. The mist had faded out of existence, allowing the sun to beat down on us unrelentingly. We did our best to stay in the shade as much as possible, hiding under the trees. Akin started to redden, despite a handful of protective spells. I silently thanked my parents for the colour of my skin as we walked onwards. At least I wasn't going to burn in a hurry.

Akin coughed. "How far are we from *your* farm?"

"I have no idea." Rose sounded pained. "I couldn't even locate it on a map."

I winced in sympathy. It was hard to remember, at times, just how uneducated Rose truly was. And yet, she had survival skills Akin and I lacked. I wouldn't even know where to begin if I had to catch and slaughter a rabbit. I promised myself that I'd learn that too, even if I had to beg Rose or Sir Griffons for lessons. Fairuza and Rolf might not be the *last* people to try to kidnap me...

Dad won't let me go back to school, I told myself, sourly. A year ago, it would have been a welcome thought. Now...now I knew I'd miss Jude's. *After this, I'll be lucky if he even lets me walk the grounds.*

"It could be close," Akin pressed. "Right?"

"We're well within the borders," Rose told him, crossly. She sounded irked. It dawned on me that she felt tired too, even though she hid it better. "Wherever my farm is, it's a long way from here."

We reached a clearing and paused, catching our breath. A pool sat on the far side, surrounded by churned-up mud. I could see footprints - animal footprints - in the mud, but there were no animals in sight save for the omnipresent insects. Rose tensed, glancing from side to side. I felt a shiver run down my spine at her obvious concern. The clearing looked tranquil, but that didn't make it *safe*.

Something *moved* in the undergrowth. I raised the spellcaster, an instant before a giant...beast...crashed into the clearing. Rose froze, as if she'd been hit by a spell. I couldn't move either as the creature sniffed the air. It looked like a pig, but it was easily three or four times the size of the pigs I'd seen on the estate, with wild eyes and dark fur. A vile smell washed over me as the beast grunted loudly, its hooves pawing the ground. I could barely breathe...

"Stay very still," Rose whispered.

The spellcaster suddenly felt very heavy. It was all I could do to keep it pointed at the beast as it glowered around the clearing with piggy eyes. If it came at us...I was uneasily aware of just what would happen if its massive teeth bit down on my head. I could see muscles rolling and flexing under the fur...slowly, so slowly I was sure the beast was taunting us, it inched towards the pool and started to sup. I gritted my teeth in frustration as it drank its fill, then slowly - very slowly - turned and made its way into the undergrowth.

Rose sagged. "A wild boar," she said. "And a big one too."

Akin smiled. "My Uncle Roderick killed one of them once."

I gave him a sharp look. "Would this be the Uncle Roderick who got eaten by a dragon?"

Akin flushed. "He didn't get *eaten*," he said. "He just got a little barbequed."

Rose glowered at us. "They're *dangerous*," she said, crossly. "Do *not* get in their way."

"A spell would stop it," Akin said.

"It would have to be a strong spell," Rose told him. "I've seen them injure or kill grown men. My father hates them - they get into the fields and start eating everything, even when they're in a good mood. The local squire likes to take his guests hunting for boar, armed with spears and crossbows. It's about the only thing he's ever done for us."

I looked at the muddy tracks. "Can we drink some of the water?"

"Only if you know how to purify it," Rose said. "But we can't stay here for long."

I nodded and followed her as she led us onwards. The sound of wild animals grew louder, crashing their way through the undergrowth. They didn't seem to want to show themselves, although I saw…*things*…in the distance, trying to get away from us. Rose seemed to think that was a good thing. If the animals were scared of humans, she insisted, it meant we were close to a human settlement.

Rose slowed as we reached a path. It looked…odd, as if the users couldn't decide if they wanted to keep it or let it become overgrown and eventually fade back to nothing. A small piece of carved stone sat on the edge, a strange mark clearly visible on the top. It didn't seem magical…

"A boundary marker," Rose told us. "We must be close."

Akin frowned. "A marker?"

"Farmers like to know what is theirs," Rose said. "There are a *lot* of disagreements over who owns what when several families are forced to live and work together."

She shrugged. "I'd better go on alone, while you two wait here," she added. "I don't want them to see you until I've had a chance to talk to whoever's in charge."

I hesitated. "Are you sure? What if you don't speak the language?"

"I'll have to make do," Rose said. "But if they see you two, they may jump to the wrong conclusion. We don't want them thinking we might be dangerous."

"Okay," I said, reluctantly. "Be careful."

CHAPTER
THIRTY-FOUR

I sat down as Rose vanished into the distance, feeling…I wasn't sure *what* I felt. Tired, yes…and…and what? Too much had happened in too short a space of time for me to process it, let alone decide what to do. And I couldn't turn to anyone, even my family, for help. Dad…I had no idea what Dad would want to do, if I told him the truth. Our family *depended* on magic.

Akin sat down next to me, looking as tired as I felt. I somehow mustered the energy to smile, despite everything. His father and mine were enemies and yet…we'd become friends, somehow. We'd gone through too much together for me to think of him as an enemy, but…what would *he* do, if he learnt the truth? What would *Rose* do? What would…I sighed, feeling the scroll in my pocket. It would be better, perhaps, if the truth never came out. I could take it to my grave.

"She might not come back," Akin said. "What do we do then?"

I shot him a sharp look. "She won't abandon us!"

"That's not what I'm worried about," Akin said. A flock of small birds flew through the trees and vanished in the distance. "They might take her prisoner - or kill her."

"She's a farmer," I pointed out.

"She's also a magician," Akin said. "And she's a stranger. And if she's right about these people hiding, they might not want to let her go. Or us."

I frowned. Akin and Rose had magic. And I had my Objects of Power. Magic didn't make someone invincible - I'd humiliated my sisters often enough to make that clear - but we could probably fight our way out if necessary. Unless the farmers had magic of their own. I didn't know why or how they'd made contact with Fairuza, but they might have a magician or two working for them. *That* would make matters much more dangerous.

"We'll wait until nightfall," I said, looking up. It was hard to be sure, but judging by the sun it was early afternoon. "If she doesn't come back, we'll go looking for her then."

Akin nodded. I felt a sudden rush of warm affection. I couldn't imagine Alana or Bella - or *Isabella* - being ready to put their lives on the line for a commoner, magic or no magic. Akin was clearly made from different cloth. Perhaps his father had a point, after all, when he insisted that Akin would succeed him. Isabella would just drive House Rubén into a pointless feud that would eventually unite the entire city against the family.

And yet, our families are enemies, I thought grimly. *What happens if we have to fight in the future?*

I looked down at my hands. There were countless stage shows - I'd watched a couple, although Mum had barred us from going too often - featuring feuding families that were forced to bury the feuds after their heirs fell in love and got married. The ones that ended well were nice stories, I supposed, but…they were unrealistic. Two heirs marrying didn't make the problems just…*go away*. Akin and I might end up facing each other, no matter how much we liked each other. The only way to avoid it, perhaps, was to leave.

"We should swear a blood oath," Akin said, suddenly. "The three of us."

I blinked in surprise - his thoughts had clearly been moving along the same lines as mine - and then nodded slowly. A blood oath would make it impossible for us to fight each other, although…I wasn't sure if it would affect me. There was no magic in my blood, was there? Or…now I knew about the magic field, could I *give* myself magic? It was a tempting thought, despite the dangers. And yet…I just didn't know enough to be sure.

"When we get home, we'll think about it," I said. Blood oaths carried implications. I'd have to make sure *Rose* knew what they were before she swore the oath. We'd be siblings in magic, if not in blood. "What would your father say?"

Akin's eyes darkened. "He wouldn't be pleased," he said. "But if we did it without asking him…"

His voice trailed off, slowly. "We'll discuss it later," he said. He changed the subject. "Who do you think Fairuza is working for?"

I allowed myself a moment of relief. "I don't know," I said. "But they clearly want to cause trouble."

"Or maybe they just want to loot the city," Akin speculated. "They might have wanted the Objects of Power to sift through the wreckage."

It was possible, I supposed. But it didn't seem likely. I didn't *think* that looters would have any use for a wardcracker…not here. The wards were gone, replaced by wild magic…maybe they'd found a tomb they intended to raid. But even that seemed unlikely. Some of the tools I'd made for Fairuza could only really be used to raid a magician's house or break into a city. Or a school.

"The sooner we get home, the better," I said, tersely. Dad had to be warned. "I don't know if they'll have been able to salvage the potion."

Akin frowned. "Why didn't you take it with us?"

I shook my head. "Too dangerous," I said. The potion was terrifyingly volatile. Caitlyn's Boost was far safer and it had nearly killed Rose and I. "I did…a few tricks that *might* spoil it, if they don't catch on in time…"

"I hope you're right," Akin said.

I hoped he was right too. But I was worried. The potion clearly hadn't exploded or Fairuza would have worse problems than hunting for us. Unless it had exploded after she'd led most of her people out to search the ruins. But…I shook my head, again. There was no point in worrying about it now. The potion wouldn't last long, unless they'd invented a completely new way to stabilise it. I didn't think that anyone, even Mum, could do that without triggering an explosion.

"I just don't see who benefits," Akin said, after a moment. "Who wants to get two Great Houses mad at him?"

I shrugged. I'd turned it over and over in my mind, but I hadn't come up with anything beyond wild speculation. Akin's father might want to kidnap or kill me, just to preserve the balance of power, yet he wouldn't want to risk his son. And there weren't many other potential suspects who wanted to pick a fight with *two* Great Houses. Perhaps Rolf hadn't been *meant* to kidnap Akin. He might have exceeded his orders.

But they didn't have to turn Akin into a slave, I thought. *They could have just returned Akin, perhaps making a show of ransoming him, if they'd taken him by accident. It would have made Dad wonder if they'd ransom me too.*

But who else was there? The king? No, he would have just summoned me to Tintagel. A foreign enemy? Maybe more likely, but…they'd be risking war. And surely it would have been safer to kill me, rather than risk using me. I had no doubt that every other kingdom was searching for their own Zeroes, now they knew the secret. It wouldn't be that hard, either.

Unless they get someone who doesn't want to learn how to forge, I thought. *They couldn't guarantee finding someone trained and willing to work.*

I dismissed the thought with a bitter shrug. Fairuza couldn't cast compulsion spells on me, but she'd found other ways to get me to work. Someone else could do the same, if they wished. Regular beatings would suffice, I imagined. A Zero without my skills wouldn't even be able to plan an escape, let alone carry it out.

"Perhaps Lord Rotherham is behind it," Akin mused. "He stands to gain if your house and mine goes to war."

"Perhaps," I agreed. House Rotherham was smaller than either of ours, but…'lets you and him fight' was an old and proud tradition among the Great Houses. "It would still be a serious risk."

I looked up as I heard someone walking down the path. Akin rose, leaning on a tree; I lifted the spellcaster, ready to fight if necessary. Rose stepped into view, followed by a fresh-faced young woman a handful of years older. She wore a very practical set of blue trousers and a loose shirt, her blonde hair falling over her muscular shoulders. Her gaze was sharp, but I saw her eyes go wide as she saw me. I looked a mess.

"This is Valeria," Rose said. "She has agreed to take us in, for the moment."

Akin frowned as he straightened up. "For the moment?"

"For a day or two," Valeria said. Her voice was soft, but oddly accented. I had the distant impression that her family hadn't come from Tintagel. "It depends on how well you can forge."

I felt a flicker of alarm. "How well I can forge?"

"They have old Devices they want fixed," Rose said, hastily. "I said you might be able to fix them."

"I might," I confirmed. I had a handful of tools and supplies with me, but not enough to guarantee anything. "It would depend on the facilities."

Valeria gave me an odd little bow. "If you will come with us, we will find you a place," she said. "Come."

She turned and walked down the path. I glanced at Rose, then at Akin. Rose seemed fine, but...concerned. Akin looked doubtful. And yet, there was nowhere else we could go. I shrugged and followed Valeria as she walked. Her legs moved oddly, as if they'd been injured at some point and never mended. But then, there probably weren't any trained healers within a hundred miles.

The path grew wider as we reached the edge of the forest. I stopped, dead, as I stared at the fields. They were small, far smaller than the fields I'd seen on the estate, yet blooming with life. Pens held sheep, goats and pigs - the latter smaller than the wild boar we'd seen in the forest. A tiny selection of buildings sat at the far end of the clearing, cunningly woven into the trees. My eyes might have passed over them completely if I hadn't known they were there. The inhabitants had concealed their presence as much as possible.

I donned the spectacles, looking around with interest. There didn't seem to be much magic in the fields, save for a single charm lingering on a scarecrow. I puzzled over it for a long moment, then decided it was probably meant to repel birds and insects. It was loose enough that I guessed it needed to be renewed every week. But then, basic cantrips rarely lasted long. I wondered who cast the spell, then decided it didn't matter. Almost *anyone* could cast it with a little practice. I was perhaps the only one on the farm who *couldn't*.

"You'll be housed in the lower bedroom," Valeria informed us. She led the way towards a two-story farmhouse, covered in so many plants that it was practically invisible. "I'm afraid there's very little privacy here."

"Ouch," Akin muttered.

I made a face, but shrugged. There was no point in arguing. Besides, I'd spent the last six months at boarding school, when I hadn't been in the cell. True privacy was rare at the best of times. I just hoped there was water and somewhere to wash. My face felt as if it was caked in mud and dust. Mum would definitely have thrown up her hands in horror.

A handful of people emerged from the far side of the farmhouse and stared at us. I stared back, noting how fit and healthy they looked. The clothes they wore were simple, yet they seemed to be in good spirits. Their eyes lingered on me, long enough to make me feel awkward. I didn't look *that* bad, did I? It couldn't be as bad as the day Alana had pushed me into a muddy puddle, when we'd both been five. We'd been meant to go to a party, but we'd had to go home instead. Mum had been furious.

Because she'd given her word she'd go, I recalled. *And then she had to stay with us instead.*

I heard them talking amongst themselves in low voices as we walked into the farmhouse. I only picked up a handful of words, none of which meant anything to me. I'd thought I knew all of the local languages in this part of the world, but evidently not. Unless the farmers had come from further away than I'd realised...it didn't seem likely. They certainly didn't look *that* different to Rose or Akin.

"You can wash with the lads," Valeria said, addressing Akin. Her voice was utterly uncompromising. "The girls can have the washtub here. I'll bring clean towels and clothes in a minute."

Akin nodded. Valeria led us into the washroom, pointed out a washtub filled with cold water, and then led him out of the room. I glanced around, checking that we weren't being watched. The wooden walls struck me as remarkably flimsy. I could see chinks of light beaming through the walls. And yet...I shook my head as Rose put a finger in the tub, then cast a spell to warm the water. It wasn't my place. I couldn't imagine what it must be like to grow up in such a closed community.

"It has its advantages and disadvantages," Rose said, when I asked. "There are no strangers here. Everyone knows everyone else. There's always someone to watch you when you're a child and your parents have to work. But you can rest assured that any misbehaviour will *also* get back to your parents and you *will* be punished. And anyone who is a little bit different will find it hard to fit in."

"Just like High Society, then," I said.

Rose snorted. "I once had to watch a young man being put in the stocks for theft," she said, dryly. "He sat there for two days, while everyone pointed and laughed. And when he was released, he left the village. We never saw him again."

I smiled. "Definitely like High Society."

The door opened, revealing Valeria. She passed us a set of clothes - shirts and trousers - and a pair of towels. I took them, thanking her with a nod. She eyed me for a long moment, then turned and walked out of the room. I had the distinct impression that she wasn't entirely pleased to see us. We were being hunted. Our enemies wouldn't hesitate to destroy the farmhouses, just to get at us. I couldn't help wondering just how much Valeria actually *knew*.

Rose caught my arm. "One thing to bear in mind," she said, as she started to undress. "They will *not* have much food to go around. Don't eat too much, whatever you do."

My stomach growled. "I'll do my best," I said. My fingers seemed to be having problems undoing my shirt. "You'd better tell Akin that too."

I put the scroll to one side, then undressed hastily, trying to ignore the dust and mud falling to the ground. It felt as though the mud was the only thing holding my tattered clothes together. They certainly didn't *look* as though they could be washed, then worn again. I splashed hot water on my body, washed myself as thoroughly as I could, then dressed hastily. The clothes felt itchy against my bare skin, but they were *clean*. I'd put up with any amount of itching, just to be clean.

"Help me wipe up the mess," Rose said, when we were both dressed. Her voice was very firm. "We don't want to make extra work for Valeria."

I flushed, embarrassed. I'd never thought of that, although I should have. Sandy had forced me to clean the showers, back at Jude's. But then, there was hot running water to help. I had no idea how Valeria had filled the washtub, without magic. Perhaps she'd just used a bucket and walked back and forth until the washtub was filled. Or perhaps someone else had done it for her.

Or perhaps it was meant for someone else, I thought. I felt a sudden pang of guilt. Valeria couldn't have *known* we were coming, yet the washtub had been filled. *Were the others meant to wash?*

We walked outside. The sun was steadily sinking behind the distant hills, casting long shadows over the land. It was cooler, somewhat to my relief. Valeria was waiting outside, chatting to Akin. He'd had etiquette drilled into his head from birth, but he still looked flustered. Valeria was a few years older, pretty, and paying attention to him, a dangerous combination.

I concealed my amusement as Valeria led us past the field and into another large building. A giant table was covered with food, surrounded by farmers and their children. The men were sitting at the table, the younger girls - around my age - pouring drinks or serving food. And yet, they all fell silent and looked at us as we walked into the room. I couldn't shake the feeling they were staring at me.

Valeria introduced us to a handful of older men and women, but the names blurred together as hunger gnawed at me. Rose seemed to hold her own, bowing her head to the men and hugging the women. I found myself totally lost, unsure how to act. All I could do was curtsey to the elders, which they seemed to find amusing. I would have been angry if I wasn't so hungry. And they were all *staring* at me.

"Please, eat," Valeria said, finally. Her voice was warm. "And then you can rest."

"Thank you," I said. It was hard, so hard, to remember Rose's warning. "It looks very good."

"Eat," Valeria said. "Please."

CHAPTER THIRTY-FIVE

"Wake up," Rose said. A cock was crowing outside, loudly. "How are you feeling?"

I started, trying to remember where we were. The farm…we'd found a farm. I would have wondered just how much of the last week had been a dream, if I hadn't been covered in aches and pains. The blankets Valeria had given us were better than a hard stone floor, but not by much. I told myself to stop being ungrateful as I sat upright, rubbing my arms to smooth out the aches. It was better than being left to Fairuza's tender mercies.

"Strange," I said. I hadn't dreamed. I'd been too tired to dream. The scroll remained under the blankets, where I'd left it. "What time is it?"

"Dawn," Rose said. She snickered. "I'm afraid you don't get to sleep late on a farm."

"And to think I thought that *Mum* was bad," I muttered. I stood on wobbly legs and inspected myself. My dark skin was covered with mottled bruises. "If I'm forging, what are *you* going to be doing?"

"Helping with the farm," Rose said. "And probably making sure Akin doesn't make too big a mess of things."

I had to smile. Akin and I were both out of place on the farm. He'd probably start demolishing a flower bed on the grounds it looked as if it was covered in weeds. Alana had done that once, when she'd been grounded for something or other, and the poor gardener had been left in tears. Mum had been *beyond* furious when she'd heard of it.

We dressed slowly, then went to the other farmhouse for breakfast. This time, everyone seemed to be running in, grabbing a bowl of food and heading back out again. Rose took a bowl, filled it with a strange combination of potatoes, eggs, ham and bacon, then passed it to me. I hesitated, then started to eat. It was surprisingly filling.

"Make sure you eat plenty," Valeria ordered, appearing beside us. "You'll need to keep up your strength."

I nodded curtly as I ate. It was bland - I doubted Mum would let Henry serve it for breakfast - but definitely filling. Akin was on the other side of the table, stuffing himself. A middle-aged woman was sitting next to Akin, encouraging him to eat. I glanced at Rose, then decided the women knew what the farmers could and couldn't spare. Potatoes were cheap, anyway. They were a staple food in Shallot.

The children were still staring at me, I noticed, as I finished the bowl. They weren't very subtle about it, either. The older ones looked embarrassed when I caught them staring, but the younger ones just stared back. It made no sense to me. People had stared at me at school, but that had been because they'd known who I was. The farmers didn't, did they? I could be *any* old forger.

"Meet me outside in a moment," Valeria told me. "I'll take you to the forge."

"I'll have to go fetch my bag," I said. I'd left it in our bedroom, along with the scroll. "I'll be there in a moment."

I hurried out the door, half-hoping Rose would follow me. She didn't. Instead, I passed two older farmers, both of whom stared at me. I resisted the urge to bite out a curse as I walked into the farmhouse and scooped up the bag, then the scroll. Leaving it hidden wasn't an option. Rose might not be able to read Old Script - although she had been learning at Jude's - but Akin definitely could. I didn't want to think about what would happen if he learned the truth.

Valeria was waiting for me, impatiently, when I returned. "This way," she said. "The forge has been untouched for two years. I hope it is still usable."

I frowned. "Why was it even here?"

"A travelling forger married my third cousin," Valeria said, curtly. She sounded oddly displeased. "He was interested in studying the cursed city.

Every year, he would go to the city and…and one day, he didn't come back. His wife eventually closed the forge and abandoned it. The tools he forged for us didn't last."

I nodded, slowly. I'd seen the city and heard the stories. I could easily believe that someone had gone there and never come back. It had happened, a thousand times or more. I was surprised his wife had even let him go. And yet, I could understand what the forger had wanted. The man who cracked the secret behind Objects of Power would be renowned…

And he was looking in the wrong direction, I thought. *They were all looking in the wrong direction.*

I took a breath. "Can I ask a question?"

Valeria stopped and turned to look at me. Her blue eyes were sharp. "You may ask," she said. "I may not answer."

"Everyone was staring at me," I said. "Why?"

"It is very unusual to see someone of your skin colour here," Valeria told me. "I will rebuke them for staring."

Just like I'd stare at a Hangchowese man, I though, ruefully. It had never occurred to me that my skin colour would pose a problem. *But if I stick out like a sore thumb, Fairuza won't have any trouble finding me.*

I groaned. Valeria seemed a good person, yet…Dad had insisted, more than once, that everyone had a price. Find a person's price and you could get them to do anything. It might not be money, he'd cautioned, but *everyone* wanted something. I'd been kidnapped because I wanted fame and a patronage network…Rolf had played me and I'd fallen for it, hook, line and sinker. And if Fairuza found out what Valeria wanted, Valeria might hand us over without a second thought.

We can't stay here for long, I told myself. *The longer we stay here, the greater the chance of being discovered.*

Valeria stopped outside a darkened building, hidden in the forest. "This was his territory," she said. "Is it safe to remove the bolt?"

I snapped on my spectacles and examined the wooden barn. There was a hex attached to the upper bolt, so faded that I wasn't sure what - if anything - it would do. I poked it with the dispeller anyway, then helped Valeria pick up and lower the bolt to the ground. She *was* strong, I realised.

I wasn't sure I could have removed the bolt on my own. I definitely didn't want to get into a fight with her.

Valeria pulled open the door, allowing light to spill into the barn. A forge stood in the centre, surrounded by a preservation spell. Another was wrapped around the cupboards, keeping their contents safe. I felt myself smiling as I took a step forward, feeling the musty air tickling my throat. I'd have to open the windows and probably the chimney, but…but I could *work* here.

"No one has disturbed this place since he vanished," Valeria told me. "We don't have any more supplies."

I used the dispeller to release the cupboards, then opened them. Inside, there was a neat collection of wood, metal and potion ingredients. I checked the labels and frowned. The ingredients *should* be safe to use, but…but I had no way to be sure. It was quite possible the preservation spell had contaminated them. I'd have to be very careful what I did, I realised numbly. There was no hope of resupply until we got home.

"It should be fine," I said. I released the forge and inspected it, then the handful of tools. It wasn't *that* well-equipped, compared to my workroom at home, but it would do. "Give me a couple of hours to clean everything, then you can tell me what you want."

Valeria frowned. "Do you want me to ask some of the children to help?"

"No, thank you," I said. Dad had told me, time and time again, that I needed to take care of my tools myself. He wouldn't let me ask the maids to do more than sweep the floor. Even *that* was pushing it. "I need to make sure I know where everything is."

"Then come find me when you're ready," Valeria said. "There are some Devices we need fixed."

I nodded and started to work. The preservation spells had kept the dust from getting into the forge, or the cupboards, but the rest of the barn was *coated* in dust. I opened the windows, found the key to opening the chimney, then started to wipe up the dust as best as I could. It felt clammy against my skin, but…but I'd had worse. I made a mental list of tools and supplies - including some that needed to be replaced soon - as I worked, quietly cataloguing what I could and couldn't do. The forger who'd owned the barn - Valeria had never mentioned his name - had piled a number of metallic devices into the corner. Some of them were strange, but others were recognisable. They'd once been Objects of Power.

They might not be repairable, I thought, as I dusted them. *But I can probably reuse the metal.*

I sighed as I went through the pile. There was a device that looked like a crab skeleton, complete with teeth and claws. I tried to figure it out, then gave up. Maybe it was an animated guard of some kind, although I'd never seen anything like it. Gargoyles and moving statues were far more traditional. Another looked like the wreckage of a flying machine, although far smaller; a third looked like a horseless carriage, with an oddly-familiar device in the front. It took me a moment to realise that it was a scaled-up version of the toy Magister Tallyman had shown me.

Parts of it must have rotted away, I mused. Too many pieces were missing. *Even the Object of Power is useless now.*

And yet...I looked at the wreckage, working out how the Object of Power had provided the energy that made the carriage move. It wasn't that complex, not really. Akin could build the rest of the carriage, if I produced the Object of Power itself. And who knew what we could do then?

I reached for a notebook, then stopped myself. I didn't *have* a notebook, unless I wanted to write on the scroll. Most forgers would have had at least one notebook in their forge, but I couldn't see one. I made a mental note to ask Valeria if she had any paper, then started to put the concept together in my mind. Now I knew about the magic field - now I knew where the power actually came from - I thought I understood precisely how we could get home.

Someone *moved*, behind me. I spun around, raising the spellcaster even though I knew it was already too late. If Fairuza had caught up with us...A small girl stood there, wearing a shapeless garment and a funny expression. I thought she was seven, although it was hard to be sure. She'd have been starting her magic studies if she'd been born to one of the Great Houses. She was staring at my face as if she didn't quite think I was real.

"It's lunch time," she said, spacing the words out carefully. Perhaps it wasn't her native tongue. "Will you come and eat?"

I blinked in surprise. Lunch time? How long had I been working? I glanced at the sun. It was just about midday. I'd worked hard, I knew, but…but it had taken longer than I'd expected. I'd lost track of time. It would have pleased me, I supposed, if I hadn't been worried…

The girl was looking at me, expectantly. "Will you?"

"Coming," I said.

"I always wanted to look in here," the girl said. She reminded me, suddenly, of myself. I'd always asked questions too. "Mummy scolded me when I tried to open the window."

She peered past me. "What is *that*?"

"*That* is a forge," I said. I pushed her out, gently, and closed the door. "It's where metal is heated and then reshaped."

"It sounds like fun," the girl informed me. "Is it a kind of blacksmithing?"

"Just a little," I said wryly, as I brushed myself down. Dust fell everywhere. "But don't say that to anyone else."

I smiled at her confusion, even though it wasn't really funny. I knew forgers who would have cursed her for daring to compare their art to blacksmithing. Blacksmiths don't use magic, not beyond very basic spells. They certainly don't forge magical blades. But then, a broken magical sword would shatter into a thousand pieces if it was smashed into a mundane blade.

We walked back to the farmhouse, where Valeria and the other girls were serving food to the men. Akin looked tired; Rose, beside him, seemed to be having trouble concealing her amusement. The other young men were eying him…I suspected he'd made something of a fool of himself, although it was his first day on the farm. I took a bowl of stew and bread myself, then sat down next to Rose and Akin. Valeria eyed the three of us, but said nothing.

"We're having a good time," Rose said, softly. "But we can't stay for long."

Akin groaned. "Is it always like this?"

"Pretty much," Rose said. "The men work in the fields; the women cook, clean and take care of the animals. As soon as a child is old enough to work, they work; they work every day, even holidays. The work is never ending on the farm."

Her eyes swept the room. I followed her gaze.

"The grown men here are all children of the original farmers," she added, softly. "The young women all married into the extended family. The women born here probably married out as soon as they reached marrying age. Valeria will be married off herself in a couple of years, if she isn't already engaged. I'm surprised she's still here."

"But there are several families here," Akin said, puzzled.

"The elders will keep very close track of the bloodlines," Rose said. "Everyone here will be a cousin, I think. The wider community will hold dances every year for boys and girls to meet partners who aren't too close to them."

I frowned. "How big is the community?"

"I don't know," Rose said. "I'd say there were at least ten similar farming communities in the same general area, but I don't know. Valeria was tight-lipped on the subject."

Akin glanced at her. "This could have been you, couldn't it?"

Rose looked pained. "I always knew I'd be moving away, once someone asked for my hand in marriage," she said. "I just ended up leaving sooner than I'd expected."

I reached out and squeezed her hand. Rose had opportunities that most of her friends and family couldn't even *dream* of, yet they came with a price. By the time she graduated, she would have nothing in common with her former friends…and her family would have effectively disowned her. Even now, she was separate from the rest of the farmers, even though she was one of them. She might never find her place again.

Valeria walked over to us as I finished my plate. "How is the forge?"

"Ready to use," I said. I noticed Akin listening and smiled at him. "What do you want me to forge?"

"I have a list," Valeria said. Her voice was clipped. "Come with me."

I listened as we made our way back to the forge. Some of the Devices of Power she wanted were relatively simple - scythes that never blunted, farming tools that never decayed - while others were surprisingly complex. I understood, suddenly, precisely why the original forger had been welcome in the community. The tools he'd forged for them had made their lives easier.

I could stay here, I thought, suddenly.

It tempted me, just for a second. The scroll could be destroyed, the secret dying with me. *Rose* would be happy in the community…even Akin might come around. But it would mean never seeing my family again, ever. Akin and Rose would miss their families too. I promised myself, silently, that I'd do what I could to thank the farmers, after I made it home. Perhaps Dad could ensure they weren't disturbed by the taxmen…

"Let me know how much of this you can do in a day or two," Valeria said, as we reached the forge. "I don't know how long you can stay here."

"I should be able to do some of it," I assured her. If she needed us, she'd probably try to keep us for longer. A source of Devices of Power would be priceless to the farmers. But…rumours of a dark-skinned girl and an aristocratic brat were probably already spreading through the community. It wouldn't be long before they reached whoever was supplying food to our former captors. "And there's something else I need to make for myself."

"Very good," Valeria said. She looked around the forge, disapproval evident in her cold gaze. "I'll come and find you when it's dinner time."

And don't go wandering around, I finished, silently. I was tempted to ask her why she disliked the forge - or maybe it was me - but I doubted I would get a straight answer. *You want me to stay here.*

I shrugged as she turned and walked out of the forge. Valeria seemed to be in two minds about keeping us here, but as long as we could stay for a day or two it didn't matter. We could leave, once we were rested and fed. And then…

I smiled. I'd had an idea. And if it worked, we could get home *very* quickly indeed.

CHAPTER
THIRTY-SIX

Valeria, I discovered over the next two days, was a harsh mistress. She wasn't as impolite as Fairuza, to be fair. I wasn't her prisoner. But she had a whole list of Objects and Devices of Power that needed to be fixed or rebuilt from scratch. Frictionless tools, ever-sharp blades, water purifiers, heat exchangers...I worked constantly, carefully putting them together while wishing for a better workshop. The abandoned forge simply didn't have an abundance of supplies.

"Valeria hasn't heard of anyone approaching the community," Rose said, at lunch. "We don't know who was selling food to our captors."

Akin scowled, displeased. "How do we know they're not keeping us here so we can be recaptured?"

He rubbed his forearm. There was a nasty bruise, clearly visible against his pale skin. He hadn't been enjoying the farming life at all, although he knew enough magic to make himself useful in other ways. I'd have expected Valeria to put him to work in the forge, but apparently not. Perhaps she just felt that he should be working in the fields.

"They gave us their oath of hospitality," Rose told him. "They won't break it."

"Hah," Akin muttered. "How much is an oath worth?"

Rose shot him an irritated look. "Out here? Quite a bit."

I held up a hand to keep them from arguing. Rose was used to the farming life and I had my forge, but Akin? He simply didn't fit into the farm. And he was right. Word of our presence was spreading, slowly but surely. It wouldn't be long before Fairuza heard of us and came calling, if she hadn't been trapped in the collapsing villa. I didn't think it was too likely. She was strong enough to defend herself against falling debris.

Unless she was caught when I brought the roof down on her head, I thought, as dinner came to an end. *Or she might have destroyed her base and gone into hiding. She might have assumed that we'd made it home already.*

I shook my head. It was wishful thinking and I knew it. Whoever was backing Fairuza would know when we made it home…until then, Fairuza could still redeem herself by recapturing us. She might still be searching the ruins…or she might have reasoned that we would have headed away from the city as fast as possible. I bid farewell to my friends and walked back to the forge, thinking hard. What would I do in her place? I couldn't think of many options beyond searching the surrounding area for a trio of runaways.

Rose changed the subject. "Good food?"

I nodded. The food was bland, yet…there was something about it I liked. Perhaps it was the way the women brought out the natural flavours, rather than smothering the meat in fancy sauce. But we couldn't stay.

Valeria was waiting for me outside the forge when I arrived. "Did you finish the scythes?"

"I did," I said, leading her inside. The scythes sat on the bench, just waiting to be taken out and put to work. I'd carved runes into the metal, then waited for the spellform - the very basic spellform - to take shape. "They'll cut through anything and never lose their sharpness."

"Very good," Valeria said. "And the other projects?"

She cast her eyes over the collection of tools and reworked metal. I wondered, grimly, just how much she actually knew about forging. She hadn't been raised in a magical family, yet…a skilled forger would have realised I'd been working on a number of projects I hadn't told her about. I wasn't sure how she'd react, if she knew the truth. Valeria was unpredictable.

And if she does want to keep us here, I thought sourly, *she won't want to give us any chance to escape.*

It wasn't a pleasant thought, but it had to be faced. Valeria and her people were hiding from the aristocracy. The king might wish to extend our borders towards the Eternal City, if he knew it was possible to survive - and even prosper - so close to the cursed lands. I didn't think he'd want to take the risk, not when it might provoke a war with our neighbours, but I had no way to be sure. Valeria had good reason not to want to either hand us over to our former captors or let us go home.

"They're coming along," I said. I indicated one of the frameworks, hoping she didn't have the knowledge to be aware that I was being economical with the truth. "The thresher is taking shape, slowly. I'm hoping to have it finished in the next couple of days."

Valeria didn't react to my words, something that bothered me. Ice ran down my spine. She didn't expect us to leave, even though our planned departure date had already been pushed back twice. And that meant...I wondered, grimly, if I should expect to have my throat slit in the night. Akin and Rose *might* be able to fit in with the farmers, but me? It was obvious that I hadn't been born anywhere near the community.

But Akin won't want to stay here either, I reminded myself. *And he has enough magic to make it difficult for them to keep him prisoner.*

I scowled, hating myself. The farmers had greeted our arrival with mixed feelings, yet they'd fed us...I shouldn't be so concerned about being betrayed. I hated myself for being careful, but...but I had no choice. Fairuza had made it clear that I was an asset to be exploited, not a person in my own right. Valeria might feel the same way too.

"Very good," Valeria said, again. "And after that...?"

"I don't know," I told her. It was true, more or less. "I'm running out of raw metal and supplies. Getting more will be a problem."

"We can trade with scavengers," Valeria informed me. "It won't be a problem."

She turned and strode out of the barn, leaving me speechless. She *didn't* mean for us to leave, then. I wondered, vaguely, how they planned to keep us prisoner. Akin and Rose had their magic, I had my spellcasters...did Valeria and her family have magic? I'd seen them use a handful of spells, but that didn't prove they were trained magicians. Or were they simply planning to kill all three of us? We were liabilities and they knew it.

I turned back to the Object of Power that was starting to take shape on the bench. It was complex, yet strikingly simple. Understanding the truth behind magic - and how it flowed around and through Objects of Power - made it so much easier to forge. The spellform hadn't snapped into existence yet, but...I picked up the etching tools and resumed carving runes into the metal. It should be ready to be triggered in an hour and then...

We leave after dark, I told myself. Getting out of the farmhouse wouldn't be a problem, not with magic. *And then we go straight home.*

The Object of Power felt warm under my hands as I tested each of the connections, wishing I had access to an apothecary. There was no way to be entirely sure that the metal was pure, not until I triggered the spellform. If it wasn't pure...I'd built redundancies into the design, but I was grimly aware that there were limits. Flashes of raw magic, utterly out of control, would probably reduce the entire design to scrap metal in short order. It certainly wouldn't be able to get us home.

I sighed and walked over to the nearest framework. It had been a carriage of some kind, once upon a time. Or so I thought. All that mattered, now, was that it would provide a convenient host for the Object of Power, as well as giving us somewhere to sit. We'd have to hang on tightly - I had no idea how fast we'd actually move - but it should work.

And it looks like a climbing frame, I thought wryly. *The next one I put together, at home, will be much neater.*

I cleaned the carriage carefully, then attached straps to keep us in place. It *should* suffice...I *hoped* it would suffice. And if it didn't...

We'll cross that bridge when we come to it, I told myself.

I walked back to the Object of Power and - carefully - carved the last runes into place. The Object glowed with a brilliant light, burning so brightly that I feared it was going to set the entire barn on fire. I ducked down, covering my eyes as the light grew brighter, then snapped out of existence. I rose, slowly. The Object of Power sat on the table, waiting for me. It looked...odd, as if my mind couldn't quite grasp the details. And yet...I reached out and touched it, feeling a shimmer of *potential* pass through my mind. The Object of Power was ready to use.

A voice echoed through the air. "Dinnertime!"

I picked up the Object of Power, concealed it near the framework and then hurried out of the barn. The sun was slowly sinking in the distance, although it would be hours yet before it was dark. I silently plotted our next steps as I hurried to the farmhouse. We'd stay awake at night and sneak out when it was completely dark, using magic to conceal our passage. And then we'd go home...

The children waved at me, cheerfully. They weren't staring any longer. I wasn't sure if that was good or bad, although at least they weren't asking any more stupid questions. One of the boys had been smacked on the head by his mother, just for asking if I'd had a forging accident and somehow miscoloured my skin. Now...I was just part of the farm, as far as they were concerned. I wondered, sourly, if Valeria had encouraged them to welcome me.

She could kill my friends and keep me prisoner, I thought. *But she would have to keep a very sharp eye on me if she expects me to be actually useful.*

I pushed the thought to one side as I walked into the farmhouse and joined Rose. Akin was nowhere to be seen. The tables were already covered in food: bread, cheese, cooked meat, eggs...I glanced around, puzzled. Where was Akin?

Rose nudged me. "Some of the boys said they'd show him how to kick a ball around," she said. "I think they're getting him to play with them."

"Oh," I said. Did the boys have *time* to play football? Did the girls play netball or softball or...or chess? I found it hard to believe. And yet...we'd played games at home. Maybe farmers played games too. "Is he having fun?"

"I think it's a pleasant change," Rose said.

We took our food and walked to the table. A handful of older men congratulated me on my work, promising to find more tools for me to repair. I think they intended to hire me out to the community. Perhaps I wouldn't have minded, if things had been different. If I'd never discovered my talents, would I have been happy here? Alana had certainly promised to kick me out of the family when our parents died. Maybe she would have exiled me to a farm and left me there.

She would probably have locked me away in one of the estates, I thought bitterly. I'd heard stories of mad aunts in the attics, children who'd been locked away for being deformed or otherwise embarrassing. Why not a girl with no magic? *And I would have gone mad there.*

Akin came in, looking tired and muddy. There were more bruises on his skin. But he also looked happy.

"It was fun," he said, when I asked. "But it was also rough."

We ate dinner slowly, savouring every bite. I made sure to eat as much as I could, knowing that it might be quite some time before I could eat again. Rose eyed me sharply, then followed my lead. Perhaps she had her doubts too, even though she fitted into the farm better than either of us. I hoped Akin would pick up the cue too. If nothing else, a day of hard work followed by football would give him an appetite...

The ground shook, violently. I started, one hand dropping to my spellcaster as a thunderous roar echoed through the air. People shouted and screamed, the women heading for the rear as the men grabbed makeshift weapons and prepared to fight. I heard a cow mooing in pain as another flash of light flared outside, so bright it turned twilight into day. The farm was under attack!

I jumped to my feet, holding the spellcaster tightly. What should we do? Fight? Or try to run? If we got to the barn...I cursed under my breath. I'd concealed my bag and the scroll in the barn. I didn't dare leave those - and the Object of Power - where our hunters might find them. And yet, how could we get to the barn?

They're not blasting the buildings, I told myself. It was surprisingly reassuring. *They can't be sure of where we are.*

A voice boomed, loud enough to be heard over the racket. "HAND OVER THE FUGITIVES OR YOUR ENTIRE FARM WILL BE DESTROYED!"

There was another flash of blinding light. The sound of chickens squawking in pain suddenly cut off. I pulled my spectacles from my pocket and put them on. There were four sources of magic close by, close enough for their presence to be clearly visible even through the wooden walls. Four magicians? They wouldn't need many more, if the farmers didn't have any magicians on their side. I certainly hadn't seen any protective wards. Even a firstie could conjurer enough fire to burn down the entire village.

Valeria grabbed my shoulder. Her voice was high-pitched, tinged with panic. "I'm sorry, but we can't stop them!"

I jabbed the spellcaster at her. She froze. The room gasped with shock.

"This way," I snapped. I waved the spellcaster around, threateningly. "Come on!"

The men seemed torn between charging at us and fighting the magicians outside. I led Akin and Rose to the rear exit, spellcaster at the ready. A magician outside pointed a finger at me, casting a hex. The bracelet warmed, just for a second, as the hex snapped out of existence. I allowed myself a moment of relief, then jabbed the spellcaster at him repeatedly until he froze in place. The spell wouldn't last for long, but it should keep him in place long enough for us to get away.

Crashes and bangs echoed from behind us as we sneaked around the farmhouse and crept towards the barn. Fairuza's men didn't seem to be trying to burn down the entire farm, much to my relief. I didn't *want* to leave the farm in ashes. But it wouldn't be long before they ran out of patience and started casting stronger spells. There were no wards on the buildings, not even a simple ward to keep out supernatural vermin. Fairuza could just cast a slumber spell and put all the defenders to sleep. It wouldn't have worked against a magical household as such spells were easy to counter…perhaps she wouldn't think of it. I *hoped* she wouldn't think of it.

At least the women and children made it out, I thought. I hoped they'd be safe…I didn't really blame Valeria for wanting to hand us over, even though Fairuza would have put us straight back in the cell. The farmers didn't stand a chance. I felt a pang of guilt, mingled with bitter rage. *We brought this down on them.*

A building exploded in a flash of light, just as we reached the barn. I glanced back, just in time to see the farmhouse catch fire. Fairuza or whoever was in charge had clearly realised we weren't in the building…I wondered, grimly, just how they'd found us. Had someone betrayed us? Or had rumours of a dark-skinned girl reached Fairuza's ears? I hoped it was the latter. I didn't want to think that one of the farmers had betrayed us.

I pushed open the door and ran inside. "Get into the framework," I said. I could hear shouts from behind us. Were they coming? Or were they about to set the barn on fire? Did they know where we were? "Hurry!"

Akin stared at me. "Are you mad?"

"No," I snapped back. I slung the bag over my shoulder, then scooped up the Object of Power. "Grab hold, wrap the straps around yourselves!"

Akin looked as if he didn't believe me. I understood. The framework *did* look like a child's climbing frame, as if we were playing make-believe as all hell broke loose. It definitely looked vaguely silly, to one who hadn't seen me put it together. Even *Rose* looked doubtful, although she took her place without complaint. And yet…

I pulled the Object of Power from cover and slotted it into place. Akin gasped. Beside him, Rose stared in open disbelief. If the Object of Power looked…*strange* to me, what did it look like to them? I rested my hands on top, bracing myself. The power seemed to *thrum* through me, humming with potential…as if something was just waiting to be born. Dad had told me that magic blades merely scratched the surface of what Objects of Power could do. I believed him…

A magnified voice boomed through the air. It was deafeningly loud, but I thought I recognised the sound. Fairuza. It had to be Fairuza.

"COME OUT OR DIE."

"Hang on," I ordered. Power billowed around me as I pushed down on the Object of Power, pressing my fingers into the indentions. "Here we go…"

CHAPTER
THIRTY-SEVEN

For the first time in my life I knew - or thought I knew - what it meant to be a magician.

I was standing - sitting - at the heart of a storm. Power - raw magic - crashed around me, somehow part of me. It buffeted at my mind, making it hard to think; it responded to my thoughts, yet the merest slip risked losing control. I felt the power shimmering through the Object of Power, unsure if I was truly touching the magic itself or something that allowed me to control it. And I had no time to think.

"Hold on," I repeated.

Power billowed out in all directions. The barn exploded outwards, pieces of debris flying in all directions. We lurched backwards, as if we were on a boat that was on the verge of capsizing, then stumbled into the air. It felt weird, as if we were swimming as well as flying…as if we were no longer bound by the law of gravity. I'd been turned into a bird several times, but this was different. The bird-body had known, instinctively, how to fly. Here…I was making it up as I went along.

A flash of light shot past us. I panicked, throwing the framework into the air. A roaring sound echoed past me; I heard someone retch, but I couldn't turn to see who. The ground was suddenly so far below us that my head spun, unable to grasp what I was seeing. We were higher - far higher - than the highest tower in Shallot. And *that* had been bad…

Another hex darted past us. I pushed the framework - the flying machine - away. It veered from side to side, tilting sharply enough to make me panic - again - before it levelled out. I had never felt so helpless, even though I was in control. Something slammed into the framework, hard enough to send us spinning through the air…but what? I hadn't the slightest idea how to control the flying machine.

Keep moving, I told myself.

I peered down, trying to navigate. There was just enough light left for me to pick out the shape of the coastline, a shape I'd seen on countless maps. We could fly directly to Shallot, if we dared cross the Sea of Death. I didn't. There was so much wild magic near the remains of the Eternal City that we might fall out of the sky and plummet to our deaths. I'd have to steer us along the coastline and hope for the best.

We should cross the border soon, I thought. *And then we can land and wait for sunrise before proceeding.*

The flying machine buckled violently as I drove it onwards, as if it was intent on fighting me all the way. I gritted my teeth, wondering if a *real* magician would be able to control the flying machine properly. It felt as if we were being forced back, as if we were trying to move forwards and backwards at the same time. The air was choppy, flickers of light dancing through the looming clouds. I hoped we wouldn't be struck by lightning. The flying machine was unlikely to take it well. *We* certainly wouldn't.

I glanced back. Rose and Akin were both clinging on for dear life, their faces green…I cursed myself, a second later, as the flying machine lurched out of control and plummeted towards the ground. I'd lost control…I fought to recover it as the ground came closer and closer, barely saving us from slamming into the earth at an impossible speed. I wondered if I should fly lower as I resumed my course, but it seemed pointless. If we hit the ground at this speed there wouldn't be enough left of us for our families to bury.

Akin laughed. "Cat, this is magnificent!"

I didn't risk glancing back, not again. "Thanks," I shouted. When we got home, I was going to build Magister Tallyman a flying machine of his very own. If he hadn't shown me the design, I doubted I would have been able to build one in time. "I just need to learn how to fly!"

The framework shook again, heeling over as a gust of wind threatened to blow us in the wrong direction. I concentrated, trying to feel the power as it interacted with the air. Something was wrong, but what? I kicked myself a second later, muttering a word that Mum would have washed my mouth out with soap merely for *thinking*. I'd overlooked the obvious. The power surrounding us wasn't shaped properly, not for flying. We needed an arrow, something that could push through the air. Instead, we had a bubble...

And the wind is kicking us around like a football, I thought, grimly. *And every time we try to recover, we only make matters worse.*

I kicked myself - again - for overlooking the obvious. I'd planned to leave at night. It hadn't occurred to me - and it should have - that navigating in the darkness was pretty much impossible. There was a faint haze to the south, where the remains of the Eternal City lay, but...there were no other lights, not even to the north. I wasn't sure that we were *still* heading north. An angry god slapped the flying machine, sending us into yet another spin. I wasn't even sure that we were high enough to recover before we crashed.

"I may have to land, just to realign the power!" I shouted. I didn't dare try to adjust the power in flight. If the wind blew through the framework, instead of being deflected, we'd be blown off and sent falling to our deaths. Akin and Rose *might* be able to save themselves, with their magic. I couldn't. "Can you see anything down there?"

"No," Akin shouted back. The noise was making it hard to hear anything. "Rose?"

"It's dark down there," Rose said. Her voice was faint, oddly *wrong*. I wondered if she was on the verge of collapse. "We could be over the sea."

We could be, I thought. I didn't know just how far we'd flown, let alone just how badly we'd been blown off course. I risked looking down myself, but saw nothing apart from eternal darkness. *What is down there?*

The flying machine shook, again and again. I saw more flashes of lightning, moving closer and closer. What would happen if we were struck? Surely the ancients had had a solution...*they'd* built flying machines that had spanned the entire empire, crossing whole continents in a matter of hours. My rickety old thing didn't seem to compete, somehow. Perhaps the ancients had known how to configure the power to absorb the lightning or…I mulled it over, then dismissed it. I'd just have to keep going, hoping for the best.

A gust of wind struck us. I screamed as the flying machine heeled over and fell towards the ground. Rose screamed too…I pushed my fingers against the Object of Power until they went numb. We were upside down…up was down and vice versa…I struggled until we were the right way up again, then continued to head away from the Eternal City.

"There are supposed to be mountains to the north," Akin said. I could feel him behind me, peering into the darkness. "What happens if we crash into them?"

I shrugged. There *were* mountains to the north. I'd seen them on the map. They'd blocked the empire's expansion until they'd found passes through the rocky barrier, then spells to reduce some of the smaller mountains to rubble. Now…the roads that had once passed through the mountains were in bad repair. I didn't think anyone used them these days, save for smugglers and renegades. The entire country was supposed to be cursed.

But we found a farming community, I reminded myself. The flying machine steadied, just long enough to lure me into a false sense of security. *Who knows what else might be here?*

Rose cleared her throat. "What happens?"

"We die, I suppose," I said. I'd heard stories about men who'd tried to climb those mountains. Very few of them came back. And a handful who *had* made it to the top had come back mad, raving about strange temples and statues so high above the ground that no one could live there for long. "We may have to land and wait until daylight."

I peered down at the ground, trying to see what was below us. But there was still no way to tell where we were. If we *were* over the ocean…or even a river…we were doomed. Maybe I could lower us slowly enough to give me a chance to reverse thrust, if we discovered we were about to get our feet wet. But I wasn't confident in anything.

"We must have gone quite some distance from the farm," Akin said. He sounded as though he was trying to convince himself. "They couldn't possibly catch up with us, could they?"

"Unless they turn into birds and fly," Rose said, edgily. Her voice was shaking. "It wouldn't be hard for them, would it?"

"They couldn't fly as fast as us," Akin said. "Could they?"

I had no idea. My calculations - insofar as I'd managed to calculate anything in my head - suggested that there was *no* upper speed limit, but it was clear that I'd made a few mistakes along the way. And I hadn't known to take a few factors into account. Air resistance alone slowed us down quite significantly. I'd have to go back to my notes and recalculate, once we got home. The way we were staggering from side to side - and being blown all over the place by gusts of wind - didn't help.

"I think they can't track us," I said. I was fairly sure we'd gone quite some distance from the farm, although it was still tiny compared to the distance we'd have to fly to get home. But now I understood some of the problems, I could modify the Object of Power to allow us to fly faster. "But we might still be close to the city."

I gritted my teeth. Fairuza had been at the farm. She still had a chance to catch us, if she caught up before we reached safety. And yet…if I didn't know where we were going to land, how could *she*?

The wind slapped at us, again. This time, I managed to steer us through the worst of it. The framework shivered under me, uncomfortably. I made a mental note to check it as well, when we landed. It was shielded from the worst of the pounding, but it might still be coming apart. I didn't want it to shatter while we were flying away from the hunters.

"Too close," Akin agreed, thoughtfully. It took me a moment to remember he was talking about the city. "But we should be safe here for a while."

Rose let out a strangled sound. "I…"

"Rose?" Akin sounded concerned. "Are you alright?"

I was torn between glancing back and keeping my concentration on the Object of Power. The wind was picking up again, tapping against the power with steadily growing force. And yet, Rose was in trouble…she sounded as though she was trying to be sick. I could *hear* her trying to retch. I…

The bracelet glowed, suddenly. Heat washed down my arm.

Akin gasped. "Rose, what are you *doing*?"

"I can't..." Rose's voice was different, as if someone else was speaking through her. I wanted to glance at her, but I couldn't take my hands off the Object of Power. "I...help!"

The bracelet heated, again. I heard Akin cast a spell, only to have it deflected into the air. The flying machine lurched violently, falling several metres - perhaps more - in the space of a second. Rose was using magic... Rose was using magic on *me*? What...

I swore out loud. The obvious...I'd overlooked the obvious, once again. Fairuza...the witch had taken a blood sample from Rose, back when we'd been prisoners. Akin and I knew to watch for unexplained cuts on our bodies, but Rose...*she* didn't know to do it, not instinctively. Fairuza had probably tracked us from the moment we'd left the Eternal City. I was surprised she hadn't moved in sooner, before we had a chance to make friends with the farmers. But how could she have expected me to build a flying machine?

"Stop her," I snapped. I heard the sounds of a struggle behind me, but I didn't dare look. We were falling out of the sky, heading down at a terrifying speed...I had no idea how far it was to the ground. "Stop her!"

The flying machine lurched, again. Akin was smart enough not to use magic, but Fairuza - or whoever was trying to control Rose - didn't have any such limitations. If we all died it would solve their problems nicely...I'd made them the wretched potion, after all. I heard Rose gasp as Akin struck her, but she hit him back with greater force. They were both physically, as well as magically, strong.

My bracelet heated, again. I grunted in pain. Rose was slamming spells into my back...I hoped it was a good sign, even though my skin was beginning to blister. I'd had worse, back when I'd been learning to forge, but never when I'd had to concentrate so badly. The Object of Power was losing its grip, the magic starting to flare out of control. Akin was trying to stop Rose...

She might be fighting too, I thought. Blood magics were dangerous, but not unbeatable...not if the victim was strong-willed. *She knows about the bracelet. If she's attacking me, she's wasting magic on me and not attacking him.*

The heat grew stronger, all of a sudden. Perhaps Rose wasn't wasting magic after all. I tried to keep from screaming as I fought for control. I wanted to remove the bracelet, but it was the only thing keeping me from being hexed. And we would all fall to our deaths if the flying machine fell out of the air. It was all I could do to keep the field together. It demanded my full attention...

"I can't hold her," Akin said. "What do we do?"

The struggle behind me was only getting worse. A stab of fire tore through my arm. I was suddenly convinced that I was about to lose it. And if that happened, we were dead...

"Hex her," I ordered. I could see something moving below us. But what? Water? I tried to slow our fall, but it didn't seem to work. The power was disintegrating. Gravity was slowly reasserting itself. "Just...stop her!"

There was a flash of light behind me. The Object of Power flared brightly, then gave up the ghost. I screamed as we plummeted, instinctively drawing up my feet. A second later, we hit the ground so hard that the framework disintegrated. I barely noticed. My arm was hurting so badly that I *had* to remove the bracelet. It took everything I had just to get it down my arm and drop it. And then I froze...

"Hang on," Akin said. I heard the sound of another hex. "Let me..."

The pain faded, just for a second. It came back in force when Akin cast a light spell and removed the hex. I bit my lip, trying not to cry out as I inspected my arm. The skin was blistered badly, so badly that it was going to take weeks to recover without magic. I needed a healer, desperately. If I didn't get treatment in time, I might never be able to forge again. I squeezed my eyes closed, trying not to cry. Everything we'd gone through - everything we'd done - might be for nothing.

"I do know a handful of painkilling spells," Akin said, quietly. His fingers touched my bare skin. I flinched, but held still. He would have seen similar injuries during his training. "Do you want me to use one?"

I opened my eyes. It would be risky - even the simplest painkilling spells were known to have side effects. And yet, I could barely move. I didn't have a choice.

"Please," I said.

Akin cast the spell. My arm went numb. It wouldn't last, I reminded myself. The spell simply wouldn't cling to me for very long. Akin would have to refresh it again and again, risking all sorts of side effects every time he cast the spell. My mind insisted on cataloguing all the things that could go wrong. I might lose the ability to think clearly or, worse, become highly suggestible. Or I might just fall asleep.

Rose was lying on the ground, paralysed. I hoped that Fairuza couldn't force Rose to cast the counterspell while she was frozen. Beyond her, the flying machine was a wreck. The Object of Power was beyond repair. I kicked it several times, just to make sure it was beyond all hope of reverse-forging, then turned to Akin. He was looking around, nervously.

"They'll be able to track Rose," he said. His eyes flickered from side to side, as if he was expecting an attack at any moment. "Even if we keep her frozen and carry her…"

"Or turn her into something lighter," I added. He hadn't suggested abandoning Rose. I silently blessed him for that. My sisters wouldn't have hesitated. "We just have to keep moving."

"And hope for the best," Akin finished. He shrank Rose, then put her in his pocket and nodded northwards. "Let's go."

CHAPTER
THIRTY-EIGHT

"I'm keeping the light on," Akin said, as we found a road and headed north. "There's no point in trying to hide."

I nodded, wordlessly. Fairuza had a sample of Rose's blood. Come to think of it, she *might* have a sample of my blood too. And Akin's...sure, we knew to *look* for unexplained cuts, but what if she'd taken a sample while we were asleep and healed the cuts before we woke? Paranoia gnawed at my mind, making it hard to think clearly. How would I *know* if someone used my blood to attack me? What if Fairuza slowly crept into my mind, instead of trying to take direct control? What if...?

You're being paranoid, I told myself, firmly. *Blood magic might not work on you.*

The thought brought me no comfort. It might not work on *me*, but it would certainly work on Akin! I wondered, absently, what would happen if he wore one of my spare bracelets. It might protect him, but...it would also strip him of the ability to use magic. Rose hadn't worn her own protections in class for the same reason. I wondered if I could give Rose one of the spare bracelets too. It might just restore her to normal.

But we couldn't count on it, I reminded myself. *Blood magics are dangerous.*

I cursed Fairuza, taking refuge in words I hoped Mum didn't know I knew. Fairuza had turned Rose against us, turned my best friend into a weapon that had almost killed us...now, she was a beacon leading Fairuza right *to* us. And yet, what could we *do* about it? Undoing the transfiguration spell might just give her another chance to hex us both, when we were tired…she might not be able to hex me, but she could certainly knock me out. And then she could keep us asleep until Fairuza arrived to collect us.

Akin glanced back at me. "What do we do if we run into another village?"

"We buy our way out," I said. "Unless you think we can just take what we want."

I gritted my teeth as I contemplated the possibilities. Would we find another forge? It didn't seem likely. Perhaps we'd find a sorcerer who could send a message to our parents, although even *that* seemed unlikely. Anyone living so close to the Eternal City would want to keep their head down…I wondered, grimly, just how far we'd actually flown. How long would it take Fairuza to catch up with us? Did they have horses? Or would they turn themselves into birds and fly?

"We might have to," Akin said. He looked as tired as I felt. "We are in no state to haggle."

"We will see," I said.

I felt tiredness seeping into my bones as I walked onwards, steadily putting one leg in front of the other. The road was broken and shattered, covered with potholes; I wondered, as we walked, just how long it had been since anyone had tried to repair it. Tyros had talked of wars, following the collapse. The Sorcerous Wars would have been after him, if my history tutors had been correct. Unless he'd lived longer than I'd thought…

Maybe the wars didn't start immediately, I thought. Everyone assumed that they *had*, but they might be wrong. A month or two might seem a long time to me, yet it would be barely a moment to someone peering back from a thousand years in the future. *Maybe some of them thought the empire could be saved.*

My legs ached as my arm began to throb, again. I rubbed it, hoping - praying - that we found a healer soon. I couldn't forge with only one arm! Perhaps, when the sun rose, we could take the time to search for useful plants. I knew how to put together a healing salve using plants anyone could find in the forest, although the nasty part of my mind insisted on reminding me that they might not be so common here. And they might also be contaminated. I hadn't noticed any problems with forging, not on the farm, but that meant nothing. Potions were far more delicate.

"We need food," Akin said.

"Don't think about it," I told him.

But it was useless. My stomach growled, loudly. I tried to think about something - anything - else, but visions of food ran through my head. Bread and cheese, ham and eggs…I'd even settle for the mess Bella had made, the time Mum had let her work in the kitchen. I don't know what she did, but it took four maids and the cook *hours* to return the kitchen to normal.

Dawn broke, the sun casting long fingers of light over the land. I stared at it, wishing we dared stop for a nap. Surely we could rest for a few hours…and yet, I knew we didn't dare. Fairuza and her friends would know where we were. They would be in hot pursuit. The only good news was that she probably didn't have a blood sample from either of us or she would have used it by now…

Unless that's what she wants you to think, I thought. It was hard not to be paranoid after everything that had happened. *She might be biding her time.*

I eyed Akin's back. He was strong. I'd known that before Fairuza had made him hit me - a forger required considerable physical strength - but now…I knew, deep inside, that he was strong enough to overpower me. And then…I fumbled for the spellcaster, wondering if I should strike first. I could stun him, then…then what? I didn't even *know* he was under her control. What if *I* was being controlled, pushed into striking at him…I gritted my teeth as my head started to pound. I'd be questioning every thought I had for the next few weeks.

It grew warmer, steadily. My arm *hurt*, throbbing with pain. Akin offered more spells, but I turned them down. There was no point in piling on the magic. The spells had done everything they could without knocking me out. I didn't think I'd be able to resist sleep if he cast a few more spells on me.

Akin slowed, then stopped. His face was flushed with exertion. He'd be tanned - or burnt - when we got back home. Shallot got plenty of sun, but it was far hotter here.

"I don't think I can go on for much longer," he said. "Where do we go?"

I shrugged. I felt the same way. My stomach demanded food…my arm hurt, so badly that I knew it wouldn't be long before I collapsed. Perhaps I could put myself to sleep for a few hours…I scowled, knowing it was impossible. And yet…I just couldn't go on.

"I don't know," I said. The sun was growing hotter, as impossible as it seemed. I looked around, but all I could see were trees and the crumbling road. "I think we have to keep going."

We staggered onwards, supporting each other as the heat grew stronger. I stumbled against him more than once as my legs weakened; he leant against me as he fought for breath, trying to keep himself going. I felt a flush of hope as we rounded a corner and approached a roadside village, only to collapse in disappointment when it was clear the village had been abandoned a long time ago. It wasn't even a real village, to be honest. It was more of a hamlet. A handful of houses, a damaged building that had probably been an inn and not much else.

"There's a well over there," Akin said. He pointed at something on the far side of the inn. "If we can get water…"

I followed him, somehow, as he walked over to the well. It was ancient and decayed, but there was water at the bottom. Akin muttered words, his voice too tired to be loud; water floated up, there for the taking. I hesitated - the water might be tainted - then reached for it anyway. I was too desperate to care.

The water tasted funny, but I drank it anyway. Akin summoned more water for himself, then leaned against the well, gasping for breath. I collapsed next to him, feeling worse. It was midday. I'd been awake for nearly two days, again. It had taken a toll.

"We can't stay here," Akin said. It seemed as though we'd been sitting for hours, yet I didn't feel rested at all. "They'll be coming after us."

"I know," I managed. I didn't want to move. My body was so tired that I just wanted to stay where I was. Fairuza could do what she liked, when she caught up with us. I knew that was wrong, I knew that was dangerous, yet…it was hard to care. "Akin…"

Something moved, on the road. I tensed, a second before a hex flew at us. I rolled to one side, forcing my aching body to move. Akin went in the other direction, hurling a spell of his own. The effort tired him. I could hear him gasping for breath as I took cover behind the well.

"Take a spellcaster," I said, pulling one of them from my bag and passing it to him. "Just jab it at the target."

"Got it," Akin said. "And..."

Another hex flashed over our heads and struck a nearby building. There was a flash of light, but no visible effect. A stunner, then. Something to keep us from escaping until we could be recaptured. I held one of the other spellcasters in my hand as I peered around the well, searching for the enemy. Two men appeared, their hands moving in a manner that suggested they were casting a protective ward. I jabbed the spellcaster at them, hitting the ward hard enough to crack it. They jumped back, hastily taking cover before it shattered. Akin stunned one of them before he could escape.

"Take one of the bracelets," I said. I fumbled through my bag with one hand while trying to keep an eye on the enemy. "Just use the spellcaster!"

"No, I need more magic," Akin said. "The spellcaster isn't enough!"

I swallowed a number of angry responses, a second before a hex slammed into the well. The explosion smashed the stonework, sending pieces of debris falling into the water. I rolled away as the ground threatened to collapse, throwing us into the water too. It would make good cover, part of my mind noted, but we'd also be trapped. Whoever had caught us clearly no longer cared if we were dead or alive.

A man in dark armour appeared, running towards us. I jabbed the spellcaster at him and watched the hex explode harmlessly against his wards. He waved his hand in my direction; the bracelet grew warm, just for a second. I jabbed the spellcaster towards the ground in front of his feet and had the pleasure of watching the explosion blasting him into the air. I hit him again before he fell back to the ground, blowing him back to the road. I hoped he hit the ground hard enough to put him out of the fight. But there were more coming...

I searched for Fairuza. But there was no sign of her. Was she on her way? Or had we merely run into a picket? How many people did she *have* anyway? I tried to calculate the answer, but couldn't come up with any solid answer. More than twenty, at least. If nothing else, it was another piece of confirmation that whoever was behind the whole plot had real power. And probably someone from one of the Great Houses...

"This way," Akin said.

I nodded as he cast a spell of his own, then started crawling towards the nearest house. I followed, knowing we had to keep moving. As soon as they caught up with us, we were dead. Or at least on our way back to the cell. I shivered to think what Fairuza would do when we were back in her hands. She needed me, but...there were plenty of ways she could hurt me without doing permanent damage. And she could just kill both of my friends, if she wished.

Dust billowed as Akin's spell went to work, making it harder for them to see us. I hoped it would force them to stay back, but...but there was no way to be sure. Akin might be able to sense magic through the haze; I couldn't, not without the spectacles. And I just didn't have time to put them on. I leaned against the house as we reached it, then followed him around the side. Another man in a dark robe blinked at us, then lifted his hand. Akin stunned him repeatedly with the spellcaster before he could cast a spell.

He laughed. "Cat, these things could be *dangerous*."

I shrugged. I'd never been able to cast spells. Anyone else...they didn't need a spellcaster to be dangerous. A commoner could learn magic, if he or she worked at it. Rose had a talent, but the rest of her family could learn too.

Someone was moving behind us. I jabbed the spellcaster into the dust storm, firing off spells at random. There was no way to know if I'd actually hit anyone, but at least it would force them to keep their distance. Akin hesitated as we rounded the house, then led the way towards the forest. I didn't blame him. Given time, Fairuza could bring the house down on our heads.

Move, I thought.

Spells flashed over our heads as we ran. Two struck me, flickering out of existence. The bracelet heated again and again, burning my other arm. I gritted my teeth, knowing I couldn't take the bracelet off. The risk was just too great. And yet...

I jabbed the spellcaster behind me, again and again. A great rolling series of explosions shook the ground. Someone shouted in pain. Was I overpowering the spells? I wasn't sure...I wasn't funnelling magic into the spellcaster, after all. I couldn't gauge how much power it was using. And yet...it was getting hot, too hot. The ground heaved again, throwing me into the dust. I coughed, trying not to breathe. Akin landed next to me, grunting. His spellcaster fell out of reach.

"Move," I snapped. The dust clogged my throat. I needed water, desperately. I knew I wasn't going to get it. "I..."

A spell struck him. He froze. I felt the bracelet heat up as more spells struck me, the pain rapidly becoming unbearable. I rolled over, waving the spellcaster wildly. If I could just force them to back off long enough for it to cool down...

Another spell slammed into the ground, right next to me. The force picked me up and threw me several metres. I landed hard, dropping the spellcaster. It was blasted apart a second later, pieces flying in all directions. I looked up, watching as Fairuza and two men advanced towards me. One of them held a rope in his hands. They knew I was defenceless.

I tensed. Maybe I could hit Fairuza, perhaps land a blow or two before her friends wrestled me to the ground and removed the bracelet. And then...I gritted my teeth, promising myself that I wouldn't give in. They couldn't use me without giving me tools and then...a moment of carelessness, a single moment of carelessness, would be enough to give me a chance to break free.

"Get up," Fairuza ordered. Her voice was hard. "Now."

"Won't," I said, in a manner that had never failed to annoy my mother. Fairuza would have to force me to stand if she wanted to tie me up. It would give me an opening. I didn't think I could cripple her, but she'd know she'd been punched. "I'm not moving."

"Yes, you are," Fairuza said. She pointed her finger at me, then at Akin. All trace of pleasantness, however forced, was gone. "Get up now or your friend will spend the next hour in screaming agony."

I tensed. If she had been threatening me, I believe I would have stayed where I was. But Akin? He was already exhausted. A torture curse might kill him...

There will be a chance, I promised myself, silently. I started to stand, moving as slowly as I dared. *And she will pay...*

Fairuza's eyes went wide. I froze, staring in confusion...a heartbeat before a man in silver armour landed between me and her. Others followed, crashing out of the forest. The leader was holding a glowing sword...*Sir Griffons*? Fairuza cast a spell, only to see him deflect it with his sword. He backhanded her a second later, sending her dropping to the dust. The other knights advanced through the hamlet as darker hexes and curses lashed out at them. I ducked low as fireballs and killing shadows flashed and flared, tearing at the silver armour. Buildings shattered as other spells struck them, pieces of debris hurled towards enemy magicians. Dad had told me that *real* duels were intense, but...I hadn't believed him. His words were empty compared to the reality.

A hand touched my shoulder. I looked up into a familiar face. "Caitlyn?"

"Sir Griffons," I said. I felt a wave of pure relief. We were *safe*! And yet...how had he found us? "I..."

I swallowed hard. There were too many other things to worry about.

"Take off my bracelet," I managed. The healer wouldn't be able to work if he couldn't use magic on me. There was a roaring sound in my ears. I didn't like it at all. "I...Rose...find Rose..."

The world went dark. I was vaguely aware of him shouting for a healer...

...And then nothing, nothing at all.

CHAPTER
THIRTY-NINE

I awoke, slowly. I was in my own bed.

"Cat," Mum said. She was sitting beside the bed, looking down at me with worried brown eyes. A warm fire crackled in the grate. "How are you feeling?"

I wasn't sure. My body felt...odd. I...I *itched*. And yet...I sat upright and looked at my arm. It was covered in patches of pale skin, slowly fading to black. Someone had mended my arm while I slept, I realised slowly. It would be weeks before the grafted skin was the same colour as the rest of me.

"Oh, Cat," Mum said. She reached out suddenly and hugged me tightly. "I'm so glad you're alive!"

I hugged her back, despite the growing itch. My stomach growled, reminding me that I hadn't eaten for...I wasn't sure how long I'd been asleep. Sir Griffons and the rest of his party had clearly kept me asleep, just to ensure I healed properly. I promised myself to thank him, when I saw him next. And, perhaps, to tell him that he no longer owed me anything.

"Rose," I said, suddenly. "Where is she?"

"In one of the guest rooms," Mum said. "Your friend wasn't quite as seriously injured as yourself."

She let go of me and sat back. "And your *other* friend is with his family. I believe you will see him again soon."

I nodded. "Good."

Mum gave me a sharp look, then rose. "Have a shower, then come down to the dining room," she said. "Your father is waiting for you."

I swung my legs over the side of the bed and stood, tottering over to the bathroom. My legs felt wobbly at first - it was clear that the healers had worked on them too - but steadied as I forced them to work. They'd probably fed me nutrient potions too, I decided. They might impede my ability to forge for a few days, until the magic faded completely. I made a mental note to pick up one of my spare earrings. One of them should dispel the magic in short order.

A thought struck me. "My bag," I said. "Where is it?"

Mum pointed to the desk. My bag stood there, seemingly unopened. I nodded, hoping Sir Griffons hadn't taken the time to search my possessions. The scroll was inside, waiting for me. I groaned as I stepped into the bathroom, realising that I would never know. Unless someone *else* started talking about the magic field...

I showered hastily, then pulled on a dressing gown. Mum said nothing when I came out of the bathroom, even though I wasn't dressed for dinner. She *had* to have been worried, more worried than she cared to admit. I felt a stab of guilt, mingled with bitter helplessness. I was a tool, as far as Fairuza and her ilk were concerned. And controlling me wasn't difficult as long as my captors were careful.

My curse, I thought, mournfully.

I followed Mum down to the dining room. Rose sat in a chair, looking massively out of place; Alana and Bella sat next to her, their faces suggesting they didn't know what to say or do. Dad rose as I entered and gave me a hug, holding me tightly. I held him for a long moment, feeling tears prickle at the corner of my eyes. There had been times, when I'd been a prisoner, when I'd despaired of seeing my parents ever again.

"Welcome back," Dad whispered.

We sat. Lucy entered, carrying a tray of food. I ate quickly, feeling ravenous. Rose looked as though she didn't know which piece of silverware to use first. Bella whispered instructions in her ear, while my parents pointedly ignored her table manners. I'd have to make sure she learned better manners too, I told myself. The next people she dined with might not be so forgiving. Perhaps Akin would help.

"There are a number of points that need to be discussed," Dad said, when we'd satisfied our hunger. "For starters, I need you to tell me everything."

I swallowed. I couldn't tell him about the magic field. I didn't *dare* tell him about the magic field. And yet...he might have searched my bag too. It was against etiquette, but *that* wouldn't stand in Dad's way if he thought there was something in the bag that shouldn't be brought into the house. I'd overheard some of the other girls complaining that their parents regularly searched and warded their rooms. Dad wasn't like that, but...he had good cause to search my room now.

Hope for the best, I told myself.

"I was tricked," I said. It was a bitter pill to swallow, but it had to be faced. "Rolf and his friends lured me off the grounds."

Dad looked grim as I went through the entire story, starting from the moment Rolf had talked me into doing a private commission for him and ending with the rescue. He asked a handful of questions, mainly clarifying points, but didn't seem inclined to push me any harder. I'd faced tougher interrogations when *someone* - Alana, I was sure - had committed some awful crime and tried to blame it on her sisters. I hoped that meant he hadn't seen the scroll. Any magician worth his salt would try to determine if the scroll was actually genuine, if he knew it existed.

"And I assume we were brought home," I finished. I'd been careful not to mention the ancient scroll. He hadn't shown any reaction to its absence. "How did they find us?"

"We'll get to that in a moment," Dad promised. He leaned forward. "A roll call was taken, as soon as it became clear that you were missing. Rolf and his fellow students were found to have vanished too. They haven't been seen since."

"Not unless they were among the people chasing us," I said. The nasty part of my mind hoped they'd been trapped when the building collapsed. "Didn't Sir Griffons manage to capture Fairuza?"

Dad looked pained. "In a manner of speaking," he said. "Fairuza's memories were completely wiped. When she awoke, in a prison cell, she was utterly unable to tell us anything."

Alana snorted. "She's faking."

"You misunderstand," Dad said. "*Everything* was wiped. She doesn't know how to look after herself, let alone how to speak...we have to feed her because she doesn't even know how to put food in her mouth. There's no way she can be interrogated. It's possible that her memories are buried, just awaiting a trigger phrase to bring them back to the surface, but the mind healers are doubtful. Her body may live, Alana. Her soul has gone."

I swallowed, hard. There *were* spells of forgetfulness, charms that could make people forget hours or days of their lives, but…I'd never heard of anything that could wipe out a person's entire life. The *geas* binding Fairuza had to have been *very* strong. I couldn't think of anything I could forge that would help. If her memories had been wiped clean, cancelling the spell would be pointless. The spell would already be gone.

"We are trying some therapy," Mum put in. "But I'm not hopeful."

I looked at Dad. "So who was she working for?"

Dad looked back at me. "We don't know."

He rubbed his forehead. "Carioca Rubén swore a mighty oath that he wasn't responsible for kidnapping the three of you," he added. "Not that I suspected him of kidnapping his own son, of course. Other than that… we don't know. Rolf's family were unaware of his…contact…with Fairuza, while Fairuza herself remains unidentified."

I frowned. "Surely *someone* would remember her if she went through Jude's."

"There have only been five half-Hangchowese girls at Jude's in the past thirty years," Dad said. "All five of them have been accounted for. It's possible she changed her face at some point, yet we found no traces of cosmetic magic on her body. We *are* trying to follow this up with the other kingdoms, on the assumption she attended a different school, but I'm not hopeful. It's far more likely that she was trained privately."

"As if her family were ashamed of her," Alana said.

I looked at her. My sister sounded oddly subdued. It bothered me, more than I cared to admit. The last time I'd seen her, she'd been braying like a mule and probably planning revenge. It wouldn't have been *that* hard for her to deduce who'd spiked her drink.

"It's possible," Dad said. "A child born out of wedlock *might* have been raised by the mother's family, but…neither I nor Carioca were able to dig up any rumours. We simply don't know."

I frowned. "So who was she working for?"

"We don't know," Dad repeated. "And we may never know."

Rose stirred herself. "What about Fairuza's blood relations?"

"We haven't been able to locate them," Dad told her. "Fairuza - I suspect - was disowned at some point. Done properly, the ceremony would have cut the blood tie."

I winced, feeling an odd flicker of sympathy. Alana had threatened to disown me often enough. The ceremony was supposed to be painful, according to the handful of vague descriptions I'd read in Dad's books. Fairuza would have been cut out of her family entirely and thrown onto the streets. It was a miracle she'd survived long enough to be rescued by her unknown patron.

"So whoever did this can do it again," Alana said. "Dad, we *have* to find them!"

"And we will," Dad said. "But it will take time."

Time we may not have, I thought. I'd made too many Objects of Power for Fairuza. *Whoever was backing her is planning something big.*

I looked at Dad. "Did the Kingsmen find anything when they searched our prison?"

"Nothing," Dad said. "The last report stated that they believed the building had been hastily abandoned, after you escaped. Fairuza clearly had an evacuation plan *and* the time to put it into operation. Whatever she couldn't take with her was destroyed. That includes everything you forged for her."

I nodded, slowly. I'd have to make a list, while everything was fresh in my mind. And then…Magus Court was not going to be pleased. If someone finding an Object of Power in some long-forgotten ruin could upset the balance of power between the Great Houses, me making new ones could capsize it. Fairuza's patron could cause a *lot* of damage, simply by selling them to the highest bidder. Or perhaps the patron had something greater in mind.

Dad cleared his throat. "The four of you will return to Jude's tomorrow," he said. He held up a hand before I could start spluttering in disbelief. "Politics, Cat, dictate that you return to school. Akin will be returning too."

"Politics," Mum said. She said the word as if it polluted her mouth. "You know the risks."

"I know," Dad said. They shared a look. "But you know the problem too."

I glanced from Alana to Bella and back again. Our parents rarely argued in front of us. Dad and Mum preferred to present a united front, rather than give us an opportunity to exploit their disagreements. For them to disagree so openly...I swallowed, again. They hadn't had an easy time of it after we'd been kidnapped. Mum and Dad had to have considered the possibility that they would never see me again.

And a year ago, they might even have been relieved, I thought, glumly. *Now...now I'm important.*

"The defences have been improved," Dad said. He looked at me. "The Castellan has already secured the funding to make the school impregnable. I believe you will be assisting with that, Cat. You will find it an interesting job."

I nodded, slowly. Magister Von Rupert *had* been talking about repairing and enhancing the wards, hadn't he? It felt like it had been *years* since we'd chatted, as if it was part of another life. I looked down at my hands, studying the mottled skin. It might be a long time before any of us recovered from our ordeal.

Dad was waiting for an answer. I sighed.

"I hope so," I told him. "But..."

I shook my head slowly. There was nothing to say.

"Magus Court will also want to talk to you at some point, when the inquest gets underway," Dad added. "Before then, do *not* talk to *anyone* about your experience without my permission. Rose, I advise you to do the same. There are already too many rumours flying around the city."

"Ouch," I said. This time, at least, the rumours wouldn't be wholly bad. "What about Akin?"

"I believe his father will give him the same orders, if he hasn't already," Dad said. "In any case, keep your mouth closed."

I nodded. "Yes, Dad."

Dad tapped the table with his fingers. "You've been away for nearly two months," he said, slowly. "There is a possibility that you will have to retake your exams. But we will see."

I blinked. "Two *months*?"

"Two months," Dad confirmed.

I looked at Rose. It hadn't felt *that* long, had it? But then, Fairuza had been careful to ensure we lost track of time. Perhaps she'd dosed us with something too. Two months...I touched my braid, gently. Had it really been that long? Apparently so.

"I will arrange private tuition for you," Dad added, looking at Rose. "You *will* have a chance to enter your second year."

Rose looked down. "Thank you, sir."

Dad cleared his throat. "Are there any more issues?"

"Just one," I said. "How did you find us?"

Dad looked...oddly displeased. "That is a very good question," he said. He looked at Alana, then me. "Perhaps you could explain why a sample of your blood ended up in your sister's possession?"

I stared at Alana, confused. A sample of my blood...?

Understanding clicked. There had been blood - my blood - on the earring she'd stolen. I'd forgotten she'd taken it. And she'd given it to Dad...

"No, I couldn't say," I said.

Dad *looked* at me. I stared back, as evenly as I could. I had no idea what explanation Alana had given Dad, when she'd handed it over to him. I didn't think there were *any* good answers to questions about why she'd have a sample of her sister's blood. Dad certainly wouldn't believe her if she claimed I'd given it to her. Alana would be grounded for so long that her great-grandchildren would be grounded too. And yet...I shook my head, mentally. I wasn't going to tattle on her, not now.

"It was enough to give us a rough idea of your location, once you were away from the Eternal City," Dad said. "The Kingsmen were dispatched at once."

And it took them several days to get into place, I thought. *They arrived in the nick of time.*

"Thank you," I said. I wasn't sure *who* I was thanking. Dad? Or Alana? If she hadn't taken the blood, we would have been recaptured. And yet...I knew she hadn't done it out of the goodness of her heart. "It saved our lives."

"It did," Dad confirmed. "Akin's father *did* try to trace him, but lacking a specific sample it was quite hard to get even a rough location."

I nodded. It wasn't common for parents to keep samples of their children's blood. I wondered, sourly, just how many parents were rethinking that policy. Kidnapping for ransom wasn't entirely unknown, but *we'd* been kidnapped by people who had no intention of returning us. It was every parent's nightmare. And if it had happened to the two most powerful families in the city, it could happen to anyone. The simple fact that the person behind Fairuza had never been identified would chill every parent to the bone.

"Go get some rest," Dad ordered. "You'll be going back to school tomorrow."

"Understood," I said. I felt...I wasn't sure *how* I felt. I didn't want to hide away in the hall, yet...going back to school had its own dangers. Two months ago, everyone had *known* that Jude's was neutral ground. Now... old certainties were falling everywhere. "Come on, Rose. I'll show you my room."

Rose shrank into me as we walked up the stairs. I held her hand, gently. The hall had to seem like a whole other world to her. And yet...

I turned as soon as we were in the room. "Are you alright?"

"My head feels funny," Rose said. She stroked her hair. "But otherwise...I'm alive."

"That's something," I said. "Did you write to your parents?"

"I don't think they know what happened," Rose said. "Did anyone tell them?"

I frowned. I didn't know.

"We'll find out," I promised. If Rose's parents didn't know...should we tell them? Or should we keep it a secret? It would only upset them. "And if they don't know, we can decide what to do."

"Thanks," Rose said. She glanced around. "Is there a bathroom here?"

I pointed. "Over there."

As soon as she was in the bathroom, I walked across the room and opened the bag. The scroll was where I'd left it, buried under a handful of tools. It didn't look as if anyone had read it, although there was no way to be sure. I hadn't been able to rig up any protections for my bag. Dad could have looked at any moment.

It was a priceless scroll. I knew historians who would sell their souls to get a look at it. And yet, I knew I should drop the scroll in the fire. It was too dangerous. Anyone who knew the truth behind magic could use it. I'd taken a hellish risk by not destroying it the moment I finished reading it.

I'm sorry, I thought. *But it has to remain a secret.*

Quite calmly, I dropped the scroll into the fire and watched it burn.

CHAPTER
FORTY

"So you made a flying machine," Magister Tallyman said. "And it flew!"

I bent over the sword, trying to ignore him. It had been an odd couple of days, once we'd returned to school. The tutors had been very gentle with us, the students had either asked questions or made sympathetic remarks…it had made me want to scream. Sandy and everyone else in the dorm had been nice to me, even Isabella. It had been a relief when I'd finally been able to sneak into the workshop and start repairing the sword.

"Akin tells me it flew badly," Magister Tallyman added. "But at least it flew!"

"It did," I confirmed. I'd checked my calculations, when I'd had a chance. I hadn't made any mistakes, as far as I could tell, but I'd failed to take certain factors into account. It would probably take some time to recalibrate everything, after I built the *next* flying machine. And then Dad would have to be talked into letting me fly it. "It got us out of a hole."

I put the next gemstone into place, then checked my work carefully. The sword had been cleaned, thoroughly, and the runes re-etched… I *thought* it would become an Object of Power again, when I inserted the last gemstone. But I wasn't sure. I'd have to devise a whole series of experiments to discover how the magic field actually worked, once I had a chance to sit down and work on them. The surge of energy as the spellform collapsed might just have broken the sword beyond repair.

But at least we'll know if the sword can be repaired or not, I thought, wryly. *And knowing is half the battle.*

I wished Magister Tallyman would go away as I continued my inspection. I liked him - I *did* like him. And yet, I didn't want to *talk* to him. He might figure out that I was keeping *something* to myself, even if he didn't know what. I hadn't dared face Magister Niven either, not now. He'd know I'd solved the mystery and then…and then what?

Better the secret dies with me, I told myself, firmly. *At least until we know if the magic really is going away.*

I sighed. Could the magic run out? Could the magic go away? Or…or what? The field *could* be drained, or weakened, in a limited area. I knew that to be true. But could it go away permanently? What would happen if it did? Could the world survive? Humans could live without magic - I would never have been born if I needed magic to live - but what about the creatures that relied on magic? They might simply vanish when the magic went away.

If the magic goes away, I thought. *The Thousand-Year Empire used magic for over a thousand years. And it still took an Object of Power to wreck the Eternal City.*

"We can start work on a new flying machine," Magister Tallyman said. "Wouldn't it be nice to fly?"

"Perhaps," I said, rolling my eyes. I slotted the last gemstone into place, then stepped backwards. "Let's see…"

The sword blazed with blinding light. I covered my eyes hastily, turning my head to escape the glare. A cracking sound ran through the room, loud enough to make me jump and throw myself to the ground. And then…the light and noise just vanished. I looked at Magister Tallyman - he'd dropped to the floor too - and then stood, turning to look at the blade. It was lying on the table, glowing faintly with light. I hesitated, then reached for it slowly. The hilt felt cold against my hand, but the sword was too heavy to lift. It seemed to be stuck to the table.

"Let me try," Magister Tallyman said. He took the hilt and tried to lift the blade. It refused to budge. "Interesting."

"It's still blood-bound to someone," I said. It would be possible to move the blade, as long as we didn't actually touch it with our bare skin, but there was no way we could use it. Whoever had owned the original blade wasn't related to either of us. "Who owned it originally?"

"Good question," Magister Tallyman said. He shrugged. "We might as well let everyone try to lift the blade."

I shrugged. "If you wish, sir," I said. I was too tired to argue. My parents had warned me that, sooner or later, everything that we'd gone through would *hit* us. And yet, it was hard to care. "Can I get on with my work?"

"Of course," Magister Tallyman said. He waved a hand at the desk. "Just let anyone who wants to try to lift the sword have a go, will you?"

He turned and left. I sighed, wondering precisely who owned the sword now. He'd said I could have it, but the blade was useless to me unless I somehow broke the blood-bond without destroying the sword completely. I didn't think it was possible. And if we did find someone who could lift the blade, they might lodge a claim to it that would supersede our rights. Dad would not be pleased.

One political crisis at a time, I thought. *We still don't know who backed Fairuza.*

The next hour went slowly, very slowly. I would have gotten more done if a couple of dozen students hadn't sauntered into the room, tried to pick up the sword and then flounced out again in a huff. A handful tried to ask me for more commissions, but I turned them down quickly. I just didn't have time to do private work as well as catch up with my classmates, even though I suspected it was a waste of time. There was no way I could pass the practical exams. And without them, I wasn't sure how much my grade would be worth.

Akin peered into the room. "Dinner soon," he said, as he stepped inside. "How are you?"

"I've been better," I said. I studied him for a long moment. "How are you?"

"Coping," Akin said. "My father was not pleased."

He didn't *look* as though he was coping, I thought. His eyes were shadowed, suggesting that he wasn't sleeping very well. I hadn't slept well over the last couple of days either. Rose had had nightmares as well, to the point where she'd had to beg a sleeping draught from the healers. I worried about her, more than I worried about myself. Rose's family *still* didn't know about our little adventure.

"I don't blame him," I said. "Does *he* have any suspects?"

"Plenty, but no proof," Akin said. "And he's not happy at having to work with your father either."

I shrugged. "I thought *we* were meant to be the kids here."

Akin smiled. "We're too young to care about adult stuff," he said. "But even Isabella was glad to see me home."

"I think Alana was glad too," I said. "But she'll never admit it."

"Probably," Akin agreed. He looked at the door. "Did he start nagging you to build another flying machine?"

"Yeah," I said. "And I will, when I have a chance."

"Maybe you should wait a while," Akin said. "Or let someone else fly it."

I grinned. "Not a chance."

Akin smiled back. "I understand," he said. He changed the subject, suddenly. "Will you consider swearing a blood oath with me? Now?"

I blinked in surprise. "Now?"

"Soon," Akin said. He sighed, heavily. "This feud needs to stop."

"I still don't know if I *can* swear a blood oath," I said. "And…and what would your father say?"

"I wasn't planning to tell him," Akin said. "Not until afterwards, at any rate. It would be too late for him to argue."

"He might disown you," I warned. Akin's father had a spare. Isabella would be delighted if she had an unchallengeable claim to succeed her father. "Are you sure you want to take the risk?"

Akin pointed to the workbench. "I can survive on my own," he said. "What about *your* father?"

I shrugged. I didn't think my father would disown me. And if he did…my talents were unique. I could think of a dozen people - starting with Magister Tallyman - who would be happy to employ me. Dad would know it too.

"We'll think about it," I promised. On one hand, he was right; on the other, there was no way to know what would happen if we swore the oath. "And Rose needs to know what she's getting into too."

We sat in companionable silence for a long moment. I thought back to Tyros and his companions, a man and a woman who'd brought down an empire. What could I do, if I put my mind to it? What were the limits of the possible? And what would happen if I built something like his magic-draining device? Part of me wanted to see if I could build one, the rest of me knew it would be dangerous. A world without magic would be a world without civilisation. It would be a nightmare without end.

Do some experiments, I told myself. *And then figure out what you can safely tell others.*

I looked at him. "If I gave you a protective bracelet," I said, "would you wear it?"

Akin frowned. "Why?"

"It might be interesting to see how it felt, for you," I said. It wasn't entirely true. I knew *Rose* couldn't use magic while wearing protective earrings. There was no reason to assume it would be different for Akin. But...what if he tried to forge while wearing one? "I've been doing a lot of research into how Objects of Power interact with magic."

"But you can't feel anything yourself," Akin finished.

"Unless it grows hot," I agreed. It was a shame I needed to keep the amulet - or earring - touching my bare skin. I'd have to make myself a suit of armour, when I had a spare moment. "But I wanted to know how it felt for you."

I smiled as a thought struck me. If I could craft a magic-free bubble, could I cut Akin off from his powers? And if I did, could he forge Objects of Power while he was in the bubble? Or would that block the Object of Power from touching the magic field too?

More research, I told myself, firmly. *And perhaps I should carry it out somewhere a little more private.*

Rose tapped on the door. She looked pale.

"Dinner time," she said. "And then the library?"

I rose. "Definitely. We have a lot of work to do."

Rose looked past me. "Is that the famous sword?"

"Apparently," I agreed. "Try and pick it up."

"I heard Henrietta claiming she would be able to take it," Rose said. She wrapped her fingers around the hilt, but the sword refused to move. "She said her family's insignia was clearly visible on the blade."

Akin stood and inspected the sword. "I can't see it," he said. He looked at me. "Can you?"

"There was nothing beyond the runes," I said. The dinner bell rang. "Do you want to try to pick up the blade before we go?"

"Yeah," Akin said. "Why not?"

His hand curved around the hilt and lifted...

...And the blade glowed brightly as he held it in the air.

End of Book Two

The Story Will Conclude In:
The Zero Equation
Coming Soon

If You Enjoyed *The Zero Curse*, You Might Like...

Instrument of War

Rebecca Hall

The Angels are coming.

Mitch would like to forget the last year ever happened but that doesn't seem likely with Little Red Riding Hood teaching Teratology. The vampire isn't quite as terrifying as he first thought but she's not the only monster at the Academy. The Fallen are spying on them, the new principal is an angel and there's an enchanting new exchange student with Faerie blood.

Angry and afraid, Mitch tries to put the pieces together. He knows that Hayley is the Archangel Gabriel, he knows that she can determine the course of the Eternity War and he knows that the Fallen will do anything to hide her from the Host.

Even allow an innocent girl to be kidnapped.

THE NEW PRINCIPAL

Mitch upended his bag over the bed, tipping everything out and shoving his clothes into drawers at random until they began to overflow. The rest got stuffed in the closet or scattered across the faded carpet. Mum would have tsked if she'd seen him unpacking but she never stuck around that long.

This time she hadn't even bothered to stick around for the entire summer, returning him and Cullum to the Academy three days early so she could get back to her fake pot plants. She wouldn't have done it if Dad had been there, but Dad had never come. At first Mitch had thought that they were finally going to come clean about the divorce but apparently Dad just couldn't be bothered.

He tossed the bag aside, sufficiently unpacked for now, and glared at the open window. It didn't appear to have made an appreciable difference to the temperature of the room and the curtains failed to stir in the non-existent breeze. He hesitated, he hadn't had any formal lessons on cryomancy yet but he'd done plenty of informal experiments over the holidays, well away from Mum's watchful eye of course; enough to cool his tiny room.

He focused, willing the air around him to cool and wondering if he had anything that could serve as a heat-sink. He couldn't keep this up forever. Nothing came to mind. He scowled and released the magic; at least it would take a while for his room to heat up again.

He flopped across the bed, almost banging his head on the wall. It was nice to be home again, he just wished home came with a larger bed and air conditioning. He sighed; it was too quiet. All he could hear was the ticking of his indestructible alarm clock and the buzz of insects outside. It was going to drive him crazy.

He rolled off the bed and went outside, creeping past the level that his brother was living on. He'd just spent two months with Cullum, he didn't want to spend any more time with him. He already missed the days when his brother was on the primary campus.

The heat was just as unrelenting outside, the air still and lifeless. The usually lush Academy grounds were yellowing in the sun and heat haze shimmered over the footpath. Mitch was seriously reconsidering his decision to never set foot in the lake again. It was only a matter of time before some hare-brained lesson took him out on it, he might as well go swimming. Everyone had gone to great pains to assure him that the Taniwha was a herbivore. Of course, no one else had had to listen to its telepathic voice.

He wasn't the only one to think of the lake. He spied another figure by the shore as he approached. He slowed and sharpened his vision, relaxing when he realised that his unanticipated companion was too pale to be his brother. Someone from the northern hemisphere? Sometimes they came back early to recover from the jet lag.

"Hayley?" Mitch said, finally recognising her. Auckland wasn't quite as far north as he'd been imagining.

"Hi Mitch," she waved at him lazily and he sat on the grass beside her.

"Did you spend Christmas under a rock or something?" he asked. They were at the tail end of summer and she looked like a ghost.

"Or something," Hayley replied, sitting up and brushing bits of grass from her wavy black hair.

"You'll burn," he warned. He could feel himself burning already and Lake Moawhango was looking more inviting by the second.

"I've got sunscreen," she replied.

"So where did you go for the holidays?" Mitch asked. She should have been as darkly tanned as he was.

"Away. My parents don't know about magic. Going home was awkward."

Mitch blinked, "so you just ditched them for the other side of the world?" Her adopted family could probably afford the flights but he'd assumed that they weren't as detached as his.

"No," she said, blue eyes paling slightly. Mitch abandoned that line of conversation, it gave him the creeps when her eyes did that. Last time it had left him badly burned and in need of Fae help. He shivered and used a little magic to render himself sun resistant. He hadn't thought to put on sunscreen.

"Do you think the Taniwha still has enough water?" he asked. The lake level was lower than usual, low enough to allow him to sneak out of the Academy without getting his feet wet. Not that he would, last time he'd gone out that way he'd been chased down by a zombie horse.

Hayley shrugged, "It can just return to Faerie if it doesn't."

"So it won't be popping up to demand more water then?" It would probably call him Cursed One again and demand to know why he hadn't delivered its message to the archangels. Maybe he should have asked Azrael to pass it on, but Azrael had been consuming Dr Dalman's soul at the time. He shivered again; there were parts of last year that he would dearly love to forget. It said a lot about the year that a telepathic lake lizard didn't even make the list despite the splitting headache and nose bleed it had given him.

"Probably not. I imagine it can get water from Faerie as well if it really needs to."

"As long as that's all it's getting," Mitch mumbled. He'd met the Fae before: the first had tried to kill him, the second had healed him before threatening to do the same, he didn't want to know what the third would do.

"Why didn't you just tell your parents about the Academy?" Mitch asked. Hayley was a good magician, there was no danger of her being locked up for insanity.

"I got a lengthy lecture on the subject by Mr McCalis," she replied. "And it just seemed easier not to explain that I'm attending a cursed school of magic."

"It's not cursed anymore," Mitch replied. Unless someone had cursed it while he wasn't looking. It wouldn't surprise him. He sneaked a glance at the mountains but even Ruapehu was quiet with no sign of the clouds of ash and smoke that had plagued them the year before. The Eternity War had moved away for the time being.

"I'm sure they'd find that vastly reassuring," Hayley said. Mitch shrugged, he'd never really gotten the hang of talking to Hayley. He usually ended up yelling at her or putting his foot in his mouth and she'd stare at him with those blue eyes that sometimes seemed to pale and...She wasn't even on the list of people he'd prefer to avoid talking to after last year.

"I still have your feather," Mitch said to fill in the growing silence. Wavelets and insects did not count as noise in his opinion and even the birds had given up under the unrelenting heat. "And I don't need it to protect me from the curse anymore..."

"Keep it," Hayley replied, "it's just a feather."

"But..." The archangel feather was the only link she had to her birth parents and archangels didn't just leave them lying around.

"Hayley," Belle yelled, rushing over to them, the sun bringing out red highlights in her dark curls.

"Hi Belle," Hayley said, half rising to hug the younger girl.

"Hey," Mitch said, smiling at her. He liked Belle, but if she was back then her sister probably was too and Mindy was right at the top of the list of people he didn't want to talk to.

"Hey Mitch," Belle said, sitting down between them.

"You're back early," he said. Belle was another person he'd never worked out how to talk to.

Belle grinned, "I told my parents that a snowstorm was going to close the airport so they sent us back early."

"Was it?" Mitch asked. Belle was clairvoyant and what she saw always happened but he didn't think she could control the weather and she could certainly lie. After the zombie horse incident she liked Mindy even less than he did.

"An airport anyway."

Mitch snorted; she probably hadn't specified when either. Maybe she'd seen it closing ten years from now.

"Mindy is in her room."

"I'll avoid the girls' dormitory then," Mitch said. At least he could avoid their resident psychopath until dinner. "See ya later," he said, deciding to leave before he could become any more of a third wheel. He wasn't that desperate for company.

He meandered back to his room, circling around the old buildings and wondering what new tortures their teachers had planned for them this year. Probably dissections, man eating trees and vats of acid.

He paused outside his room, it looked as if one of the other doors was closed. He crossed the corridor, trying to get a clear view and took a couple of steps in its direction. It was closed and it was Nikola's room. He grinned to himself and knocked softly.

The door opened.

"Mitch," Nikola croaked and started to cough.

"Sick already?" Mitch asked as Nikola stepped back and motioned for him to take the desk chair. Nikola returned to the bed, wrapping himself in a large green blanket and reaching for a tissue.

"You know I can't travel," Nikola said after he'd blown his nose. It only made him sound more congested and the bin was already half full.

"I didn't think you'd want to come back early." Cursed or not the Academy was Mitch's home but Nikola hated it.

"My guardian's idea," Nikola explained. "She thought that if I came back early then I'd have plenty of time to recover before classes start."

"Sorry," Mitch said, shaking his head. Sensible people would have left Nikola to be home schooled. Nikola had a lot of contact with the Seelie Court and the Fae's magical knowledge was second to none, but Mitch wasn't sure his guardian counted as a sensible person.

Nikola shrugged, "it's only one more year. Besides, I get to see you a few days early as well."

"Nikola…"

Nikola coughed, groping for his drink bottle until Mitch pressed it into his hand.

"Thanks." He coughed some more, draining his bottle and tossing it aside. Mitch refilled it for him and by the time he got back Nikola had stopped coughing and was leaning against the wall, his grey eyes almost closed and his cheeks flushed. He was still wrapped in his blanket though his room was just as hot as Mitch's had been.

"I should let you rest," Mitch said.

Nikola groaned, "You mean escape before you catch my bugs."

"I mean let you rest," Mitch said. He could heal himself if he got sick, Nikola had to recover the old fashioned way and he was lousy at it.

"That's all I ever seem to do," Nikola said, his expression downcast. "Rest, rest, rest. Rest for what? So I can go to class and get sick again?"

"You must have done something fun over the holidays," Mitch said, "I'm sure that was worth resting for."

"Getting my b–" he sneezed, "brain rewired? When Gawain let me have a day off I was too exhausted to do anything." He sneezed again, looking so utterly miserable that Mitch sat on the bed next to him and put an arm around his shoulders.

"We'll find something fun to do over Easter then," Mitch promised. "No rewiring then right?"

"Just a cold or the flu, or allergies or–"

"We'll find something fun to do," Mitch said, cutting him off and squeezing his shoulder.

"That would be nice," Nikola replied.

"Now get some rest," Mitch smiled at his friend and pretended not to see the answering glare.

＊＊

If he hadn't been so on edge Mitch would have been bored. He wished that they could have held the assembly somewhere else, or, even better, not held it at all. He was missing maths to be tortured by constant replays of Dr Dalman's death and Miss Band's suicide. He liked maths.

Unfortunately they had a new principal to welcome to the Academy. And new teachers. And naturally that had to take place during his favourite class in the auditorium where the old principal had died. He slouched a little lower in his seat. No one else seemed bothered by their location. His best friend, Bates, was having a whispered conversation with Mindy. He'd been cursed when Dr Dalman died and if he could get past his girlfriend's attempted sororicide with undead weapon, then their principal inexplicably turning into goo was unlikely to bother him.

On his other side Nikola seemed just as unfazed but he'd missed that particular assembly and he was still sniffling.

"You should have stayed in bed," Mitch whispered when he sneezed.

"That would have defeated the purpose of coming back early," Nikola replied. A tissue appeared in his hand just in time to smother another sneeze. As far as Mitch knew Nikola's ability to teleport objects was unique, but he'd probably have traded it for Mitch's ability to heal himself.

Mr McCalis's speech came to an end, he'd kept it short at least, and Mitch sat up a little straighter. Now they just had to introduce the new teachers and principal and then he could get out of here and stop listening to the sound of Miss Band's neck snapping as she hanged herself to break the Twisted Curse's influence on the Academy.

The first new teacher was a stick of a man who would only be interesting as the subject of a dissection. Maybe that was why he'd decided to teach Xenobiology. Mitch already disliked him; Xenobiology was his worst subject and he hated dissections. At least with the Twisted Curse gone no one was likely to try dissecting him. Mitch swallowed, he could have done without that mental image, he'd seen enough dead teachers. Nikola patted him on the arm and gave him a reassuring smile.

Next was the new chemistry teacher, Mitch didn't pay much attention to her; he wasn't taking chemistry anymore and with any luck his brother wouldn't try dissolving the teacher's chair again. She was followed by Little Red Riding Hood.

Mitch froze, his eyes widening. He gripped his seat with whitening hands, his bile rising. Little Red Riding Hood, no doubt she had a real name but that was how he knew her. He'd danced with her at the Dance with the Dead and then he'd watch her rip Superman's throat out and…

"Breathe Mitchell," Nikola whispered, one hand on Mitch's shoulder. Mitch gasped, drawing in a deep, shuddery breath, followed by another. Mr McCalis was telling them Red's real name but Mitch couldn't hear it over the screaming in his head. The snap of Miss Band's neck replaced by the carnage of the Feast for the Dead.

"What's up Mitch?" Bates asked.

"She's a vampire," Mitch said staring at the petite figure on stage. She didn't look threatening, he couldn't even see her fangs from back here but he knew that they were there. On Bates' other side Mindy giggled. She was a necromancer, she'd probably worked the vampire thing out already.

"She looks kinda familiar," Bates said, peering up at the stage.

Mitch swallowed, Adnan would not appreciate it if Mitch threw up over him.

"It's ok Mitch," Nikola said, "they won't let one of the teachers eat you."

Mitch nodded. He'd never been able to relate the horrors of the Dance with the Dead to Bates, or the resulting nightmares, but Nikola had heard all about them. No doubt he'd be hearing even more over the next few days. Nikola coughed, withdrawing his hand, and Mitch felt the panic rising once more.

"Hey, didn't you dance with her?" Mindy asked, her voice slightly too loud. Mitch cringed, surely their teachers would hear her. They didn't and Red was still on stage. Mr McCalis must have said her name, but he'd missed it and now she had an excuse to eat him.

Nikola patted his shoulder and whispered reassurances and Mitch tried to remind himself that she hadn't eaten him last time they'd met. Once she'd realised that he was underage she'd told him to leave. He kept telling himself that, the fear and panic giving way to a soothing wave of calm tinged with magic. He blinked.

"You're an empath?" he hissed at Nikola.

"Not really," Nikola replied, "this is the limit of my abilities but it felt like you needed it."

"Thanks," Mitch said. Rational thought was beginning to reassert itself, telling him that, although he'd missed the announcement of what she was teaching, there would be plenty of chances to learn Red's name before his first class with her, and that she would probably be fired if she started snacking on the students.

"Don't mention it," Nikola said. He raised his free hand to his bleeding nose and blinked at the blood.

"Nikola?" Mitch asked, doing his best to ignore Bates and Mindy's whispered conversation about Red and the Dance. He had not asked her to dance because she looked like Hayley; that was like saying he and Nikola looked alike because they both had blond hair and grey eyes. Never mind that Nikola kept his golden curls hanging around his face in a way that would have infuriated Mitch, or that he was built like a stick insect.

Nikola's eyes widened, his grip on Mitch's shoulder tightening as he swayed. He was still using his empathic magic and Mitch could feel something else creeping in along with the calm, a harsh edge that worked its way through his brain and set alarm bells ringing.

Red had slunk off the stage and Mr McCalis was holding a moment of silence for Dr Dalman before introducing the new principal. Bates and Mindy were still having their whispered conversation and everyone else was beginning to fidget. Blood dripped off Nikola's chin, he hadn't used his magic to summon a tissue through Mitch had seen him do so when he was too sick to get out of bed.

"I would like you all to welcome Ms Saris to the Academy," Mr McCalis said. A woman stepped onto the stage, looking as if she'd just come from the boardroom of a fortune 500 company and her proportions were so artificially perfect that Mitch immediately filed her under inhuman. Whatever she was she didn't belong here.

The empathic calm vanished, replaced by an instant of shock that was rapidly overwritten by pain. Mitch gasped, biting back a whimper, and Nikola's hand dropped away, leaving him with only phantom sensations.

"Hey," Mitch said, tentatively patting him on the shoulder and relaxing when the empathic magic failed to materialise. Nikola was doubled over, his head in his hands, blood dripping steadily from his nose. "Nikola?"

He glanced up at the stage, Ms Saris was making a speech. Everyone else was pretending to listen. It didn't sound like she was saying anything other than the usual rubbish and even if she had been Mitch wasn't sure that he cared.

"Come on," he whispered, though he wasn't sure Nikola was listening. "Let's go." He rose, gently pulling a trembling Nikola to his feet and shaking off Bates' attempt to keep him in his seat. He was suddenly glad that Nikola had insisted on sitting at the end of the row.

Nikola swayed, his gaze unfocused and Mitch put an arm around him. They shuffled towards the nearest door, Mitch taking most of Nikola's weight. He wondered what the deal with Ms Saris was. Nikola was hypersensitive to magic and that usually manifested as migraines, nosebleeds and nausea. He'd probably be fine once they got him away from Ms Saris, though Mitch had no intention of stopping before they reached the infirmary. Fortunately it wasn't far; the infirmary had been built close to everything.

Nikola pulled away and threw up and Mitch barely caught him before he could fall. They skirted around the pool of vomit and out of the backdoor, Mitch casting a final look at the stage. Ms Saris was saying all the usual things but her voice sounded curiously empty, as if she was reading off a script. She wasn't demanding to know why two of her students were trying to slip out though, so Mitch ignored her.

Mr McCalis was walking towards them but he'd always been reasonable. Mitch didn't think he'd mind them slipping out. Nikola had admitted to throwing up on him before and he knew how much Nikola's physiology left to be desired.

They shuffled outside and Mitch cursed when he saw the cloud of smoke dominating the sky and the rain of ash settling around them.

"Not the fucking war again," he muttered. The Earth was a big place, surely the Eternity War could be fought on some other corner of it. Nikola coughed and threw up again, adding vomit to the blood already staining his shirt.

"We're almost there," Mitch said, using a little magic to strengthen himself and accelerate their shuffle. The ground shook, almost overbalancing them. On any other day Mitch barely would have paused, it hadn't been much of a quake, but today his eyes were drawn to Mt Ruapehu in time to see a fresh gout of ash and smoke erupt into the air.

Nikola's trembling worsened and Mitch remembered that he'd had seizures before. He'd never said how to recognise one though, or what to do. Mitch settled for hauling Nikola up the steps to the infirmary and pushing open the door. It had only been a small earthquake.

"The usual room," the nurse said, looking up from the desk, "I'll get the doctor." Nikola seemed to relax a little once they reached the private room; he had said that it was warded against outside magic. Mitch managed to get him onto the bed and find a box of tissues and a bowl for him to throw up in and then he had nothing to do but pace.

"I had hoped to wait a little longer before seeing you again," the doctor said, striding into the room. "I suppose I shouldn't be surprised though."

Mitch felt the tingle of magic, a diagnostic spell he guessed, and Nikola threw up.

"I'll do this the old fashioned way then," the doctor said, beginning a more mundane check-up. "How are you feeling Nikola?"

"Lousy," Nikola groaned and curled up, burrowing into the pillow. "It's too bright."

"We'll close the curtains in a moment. Do you want something for the pain?"

Nikola nodded.

"Ok I'm keeping you here for the rest of the day." He glanced at Mitch, "you can stay until second period." He left, returning with a couple of pills and a glass of water which Nikola choked down. "I'll send someone to get you a change of clothes," he said before leaving. Mitch closed the curtains and resumed pacing.

"You'll wear the floor out," Nikola croaked.

"No I won't," Mitch said, sitting on the edge of the bed where Nikola could see him. "Hospital floors are pace resistant."

Nikola managed a tiny smile and a laugh that turned into a cough.

"So much for not missing the first day of class," Mitch said.

"I should have stayed in bed. I'm a mess aren't I?"

Mitch nodded, forcing himself to look at Nikola when his gaze wanted to flick away from the blood covering his face.

"How much longer can you stay?"

"Ten minutes," Mitch said, glancing at his newly repaired watch. He'd been pacing for longer than he thought. "Are you really alright?"

"For now," Nikola sighed. "Give it a few months and all the hormones and neuro-chemicals will mess up my brain again but for now I'll manage."

"Oh good," Mitch said, rather unconvincingly. "Maybe the war will move away by then."

"It won't," Nikola said, running a hand through sweat soaked hair. "Ms Saris is an angel and she wasn't the only one there."

"Fuck." So much for closing the loopholes in the school wards. It would be nice if that actually surprised him.

"Very articulate," Nikola breathed, his eyelashes fluttering. Mitch hopped off the bed and helped him pull the blankets up.

"I'll come visit later."

Nikola mumbled something in reply, his eyes closing, and Mitch left him to sleep.

Angels. An angel was in charge of the Academy. They were all completely screwed.

FIRST DAY

Today clearly wasn't Mitch's day. First he'd missed Maths for the assembly from Hell and now he had Teratology. Last year Teratology had been tolerable right up until the incident with the paper planes, this year it was being taught by a vampire.

Mitch saw her as soon as he walked through the door and made a beeline for the back of the class. He wanted to just turn around and walk out but she'd probably notice and he didn't want to start the year by getting on the vampire's bad side. He didn't even know her name yet and he couldn't ask with her standing at the front of the room.

He pulled out his books and pens, fighting the urge to huddle under the desk and cower in fear. He should have stayed in the infirmary and watched Nikola sleep. Nikola would never try to bite him. At least there were eleven other people in the room with him. If she decided to eat them all he'd have time to escape. Unless she started with him. She probably would.

"I'm Miss Bordeaux," she said, standing at the front of the room and making no attempt to hide her needle like fangs as she talked. Chairs scraped as a few of his classmates inched away. Mindy was actually leaning forward, but she thought zombie horses were fun. "And I'm a vampire." Her gaze flicked to the back of the room and Mitch gulped, drying his hands on his pants. She definitely remembered him.

"As such, it behoves me to tell you the truth before any silly rumours start. If you arrive late, disrupt the class, fail to complete your homework or misbehave in any way I will be putting you in detention. I will not bite you, compel you or throw you into a wall or any of a dozen other things that vampires are always doing in bad movies. You are just as safe in here as you are in any other classroom."

Mitch would have found that a lot more believable if he hadn't seen a teacher killed in this classroom the year before and she hadn't been smiling at them with a mouthful of hypodermic fangs that were perfect for draining the blood of misbehaving students. He suspected that some of his classmates felt the same though a couple were relaxing, lulled into a false sense of security. Mitch carefully stayed where he was, not wanting to attract any kind of attention and resolving to do his Teratology homework first.

Rationally he knew that she couldn't go around eating students. It would probably get her fired. Hell, it was probably in her contract. Mr McCalis wouldn't have hired a vampire if she was going to eat them. She'd even tried to protect him at the Dance, she'd told him to leave. Mindy had made him stay. He glared at the back of her head. If he had to pick between the vampire and the zombie horse wielding psychopath he knew which one he'd choose.

"To answer what I'm sure will be your next question, I was turned in the battle of Neuve Chapelle in 1915."

Mitch supposed that explained her conservative attire. Vampires were photosensitive, not inflammable, but the knee length dress and stockings had to be hot. She didn't look like a terrifying monster, not so long as her mouth was closed anyway, she didn't look like a teacher either. She looked all of sixteen. Perhaps that was how old she'd been when she died, vampires aged very slowly.

"The use of magic in warfare was outlawed shortly afterwards, making me one of the youngest vampires in existence. Are there any questions?"

Mindy's hand shot into the air, everyone else seemed to be trying to avoid eye contact. Mitch had a few questions himself but they weren't the sort you asked out-loud. He silently promised himself that he'd never miss a deadline.

"This can't possibly be good," Mitch said. Sam nodded in agreement.

"First day never is," Hikari said. "It almost reminds me of the time on the lake."

Mitch winced; at least they wouldn't be swimming in the Academy gym. At least he devoutly hoped not. Hikari was right; they'd replaced Rodrigo with Hayley, Rodrigo had left after the Twisted Curse was removed, and there was no Gwen but it was basically the same line up as their insane flag collection test.

"Doesn't look like there are any flags this time," Adnan said, waving at the obstacle course set up before them. It looked suspiciously shiny and metallic to Mitch's eye. Why would they need a wire rope swing?

"No ice either," Hikari added, "unless you want to make some for us Mitch? It's hot in here."

"You could give us a little breeze," Mitch replied. He almost wouldn't have minded another lesson on the lake, as long as it didn't freeze. The gym was almost insufferably hot. "You don't think it's fire do you?" Offhand Mitch couldn't think of anything that would challenge a cryomancer, an aeromancer, a thermomancer, a shape-shifter and whatever Hayley was but his teachers were far more creative.

"Could be," Sam said, inspecting the obstacle course. "None of this will burn, or melt unless they do freakishly high."

"I wouldn't put it past them," Mitch muttered.

"They're not cursed any more Mitchell," Hayley said, "they won't try and kill us or overlook a fatal accident."

"They might." Maybe they weren't cursed but sane people didn't hire vampires and angels. Especially not angels. At least there was nothing out of the ordinary in the obstacle course. Hurdles, climbing walls, rope swings, nets, monkey bars…It all looked completely normal and safe and there was nowhere for a monstrous giant weta or over-sized spider to hide.

"I think it's all steel," Sam said.

"Oh joy." Their teachers could do all sorts of creative things with steel.

"Do you think it's booby trapped?" Hikari asked. Mitch shuddered, it wouldn't surprise him if that rope swing was over a pit of hydrochloric acid. He was convinced that the Academy got a bulk discount on the stuff.

"What do you think?" he asked Hayley. She didn't seem to be as worried about their impending doom as the rest of the class.

She shrugged, "we'll find out soon enough."

Mitch rolled his eyes and turned as the door opened. It wasn't like their teachers to be late and whoever it was, was unlikely to let them continue their speculation. Not all of their magic classes actually involved magic, he'd had to learn Tai Chi last year, but the first one of the term always did.

It wasn't their teacher.

"Sorry I'm la...guess I'm not then," Gwen said, looking around. Mitch scowled, he usually tried to avoid his ex. He had hoped that they wouldn't have any practical magic classes together. Gwen was an illusionist; her skills didn't have a lot of overlap with his.

"So fire then?" Adnan said into the growing silence.

"Can you do fireproof?" Hikari asked.

Adnan nodded, the rest of the class looked resigned, they could all do heat resistant even if outright fireproof was out of the question. The silence returned. Mitch carefully not looking at Gwen, or even in her general direction.

"Excellent use of deductive reasoning," Mr Greeves said as flames crackled to life. They blazed under the monkey bars and rope swings and spat through the air over the nets. There was even what looked like a shifting maze of flame. Mitch gulped.

"I expected better of you Miss Fitzgerald," Mr Greeves continued, "that was a fairly simple illusion. And you'll be serving detention for your tardiness this weekend." Gwen glared at him. "Now who wants to go first?"

Mitch imagined crickets chirping in the background as everyone failed to volunteer. Adnan had started working his magic already. Shape-shifting was a slow process hindered by the conservation of mass and the necessity of maintaining all of the vital bodily functions. He seemed to be giving himself scales of some sort, salamander Mitch thought, dragon was supposed to be too dense for shape-shifters without a lot of extra fat.

"Don't all volunteer at once," Mr Greeves said.

"I'll go," Hayley stepped forward, apparently unfazed by the heat though Mitch was beginning to feel a little dried out.

"Very good Miss Lake, proceed." Hayley scrambled up the ladder and began to crab-walk across the highwire, somehow ignoring the flames that were licking at her feet and probably trying to melt the soles of her shoes.

"Pyromancy sir?" Mitch asked sidling over to Mr Greeves, "you work in a library."

"Books are very flammable," Mr Greeves replied. "It's really not that odd if you think about it. You don't plan on working in cryogenics do you?"

Mitch shuddered; he'd hated biology. He just wanted to study maths in a nice quiet office somewhere without anyone asking him to run though insane obstacle courses or trying to eat him. Hayley was almost finished, apparently without any real difficultly.

"How's she doing it?" Mitch asked. No one had any idea what Hayley's speciality was. Being freakishly good at everything wasn't a speciality.

"Rendering herself fireproof it would appear," Mr Greeves replied, frowning at her as she cleared the last rope swing. "She's not manipulating the flames in any way." Hayley came back around the edge of the course, completely unsinged and unstained by smoke or sweat. She might have just come back from a nice leisurely walk though even outside it was far too hot for anything of the sort.

"I'll go next," Mitch said. If Hayley could do it then so could he. He pretended not to hear Gwen's giggle.

"How is it?" Adnan asked awkwardly, he'd transformed most of his skin into scales and it was making it hard for him to talk.

"It's not that hot," Hayley said, "yet."

Sam raised an eyebrow and Mitch reconsidered volunteering, Sam knew exactly how hot it was, but he couldn't back down now. He climbed the ladder, it least this wasn't his first time high-wiring over a pit of fire and there was unlikely to be a giant weta at the end of this one.

It really wasn't as terrible as it could have been. He'd spent most of the summer experimenting with creating a bubble of cool air around himself and he was doing the same thing now, he just had a lot more heat to compete with. The obstacle course wasn't that bad either. He could have avoided the obstacles entirely if he'd wanted to try his hand at fire walking.

Adnan went after him and came back with his clothes crisp and singed. After that he discarded the t-shirt. Sam followed him; like Hayley she came through unscathed. Hikari shot through the course like a cannon ball, sending the flames billowing in every direction and Gwen came back sweat-soaked but unharmed.

"Miss Lake," Mr Greeves called, motioning for her to begin again. This time the flames were hotter. They all went through it a second time, and then a third. Mitch almost froze himself to the monkey bars on his fourth turn after misjudging how much heat they had absorbed. He corrected himself hastily, hoping no one had noticed. It took a special sort of idiot to freeze himself in place in the middle of an inferno.

Hayley was the only one who didn't struggle with the rising temperature. Gwen came back with her hands blistered and burnt on the fourth run, her illusion that it was just an ordinary obstacle course failing to overcome reality. Mr Greeves sent her to the infirmary after running her hands under cold water. Mitch knew she'd be fine by dinner, the combination of illusion and alchemy would have no problem with some minor burns.

Adnan's pants got more and more singed, his scales shining with sweat when he returned until he pulled out on the fifth run, the temperature too hot for him to handle.

Hikari's vortex became increasingly fierce in its efforts to repel the flames and cool the heat. It was torture for the rest of them, the flames rose to the ceiling and the heat scorched the part of the gym where they stood. Like Adnan she dropped out on the fifth run, coming back to them coughing and soot stained. The flames had consumed all of her oxygen. She didn't look hurt but Mr Greeves sent her to the infirmary for a check-up anyway.

Sam dropped out on the sixth run, her clothing marred with soot and smoke and her curly hair frazzled. She was completely unharmed but exhausted and unlike their classmates she had the sense to quit while she was ahead. That just left Mitch and Hayley.

Mitch watched as Hayley waltzed through the obstacle course with the same ease she'd shown on the first run. He doubted he'd be anywhere near as graceful when his turn came. His bubble of cold air had shrunk on each run and now it was little more than a thin membrane protecting him from the heat. This challenge was doing wonders for his control. He couldn't even fully protect his clothes anymore and they'd been burnt and smouldering after the sixth run.

"Are you sure you're up to this?" Sam asked. "It's getting really hot in there."

"Of course I'm sure," Mitch said, glad that he'd remembered to change into his oldest clothes before class. Not that they were that old, Mitch hadn't had the chance to outgrow his clothing in years.

"It's not a competition Mitch."

"I know that."

"Ah ha," Sam said, rolling her eyes.

"I can do it," Mitch said. "Just watch." Sam still looked unconvinced but she didn't say anything. Hayley returned before they could argue any further and then it was his turn.

He scrambled up the ladder to the high wire, gasping when the hot air struck him. His skin felt dry and tight, his sweat drying before it even had a chance to form and his eyes stinging. He wished the flames were advancing on him, then he wouldn't feel like such an idiot for walking into an inferno.

He kept that thought to himself, he didn't want to give Mr Greeves any ideas. He took a deep breath, or as deep as he could in the superheated air, and set off across the high wire.

At first it wasn't so bad. His membrane of cold had shrunk until it was skin-tight and he could feel his clothes crisping and smouldering, his magic too tightly controlled to protect them anymore. He was forced to kick his shoes off halfway through the course when the soles began to melt and stick to the ground.

He could feel the heat tearing at his magic as he forged ahead. It sucked the moisture from his skin and made every breath hot and painful. It pressed in around him, reminding him that their teachers were much stronger and more experienced. Mitch kept going, determined not to quit though the sensible part of his mind had borrowed Sam's voice and was telling him exactly that. Mitch ignored it and focused on his magic.

That had been his first lesson. Focus was the key. You focused on what you wanted and reality bent to your will. In theory. In practice reality liked to remain the way it was and it was less likely to be distracted than he was. Fortunately with his shoes gone the raging inferno he was making his way through was free of distractions. Nothing else was stupid enough to set foot in it.

He staggered onwards, struggling through flames hot enough to flash roast a whole cow. Maybe he should suggest that when he got out, he wouldn't mind roast beef for dinner. The heat pressed in closer, sensing his focus wavering, and Mitch focused on keeping himself cool and fireproof. He was grimly aware that keeping his magic pressed into his skin was a bad idea. He didn't have a margin of error anymore and as exhaustion set in he was finding it harder and harder to focus.

He blinked, trying to work some moisture into his eyes, and shambled forward, groping for the next obstacle. He had to be almost at the end. If he'd been able to spare the focus and magic he would have given himself the ability to see infrared, the obstacles had to be cooler than their surroundings, but even the idea of doing so was almost enough to shatter his concentration.

I'm not burning, he told himself. *The air passing through my lungs is cool and crisp, not unbearably hot. I'm not burning. I'm cold. I'm cold. I should quit now. I'm cold. I won't catch fire. I'm cold. Everything is cold.*

Now he was grateful for their teachers' insistence that they not use gestures and words. The words would have died in his throat and he couldn't climb a wall while gesturing. There were reasons unrelated to raging infernos for not using such crutches but Mitch couldn't remember what they were with his brain baking inside his skull. He didn't speak biology anyway.

He reached the top of the wall and almost fell into the firepit on the other side before he caught himself. He'd arrived at the final rope swing. He groped for the rope and slid his hands along its length, looking for the loops he knew were there but he could no longer see. He found them and shoved his hands through, holding the rope as tightly as he could and telling himself that he was just imagining the burning in his hands.

I'm cold. I'm not burning. I'm not burning.

Clinging to the rope he launched himself across the pit. Fire, fire, fire, freedom. It was as if he'd passed through a wall and on the other side it was mercifully cool. He'd made it through. He began to slow and then swung back towards the inferno. He could feel it licking at his back, eager to welcome his return and he let go, falling to the ground to land in an ungainly heap just outside the flames.

He'd been taught how to fall. He'd been taught to bend his knees and roll with the impact. Instead he face-planted.

He opened his eyes slowly. He wasn't sure how long he'd had them squeezed shut, but it wasn't long enough. There were wetter deserts. The flames had retreated, the inferno fading away to nothing and leaving behind a perfectly ordinary obstacle course. He was supposed to circle back to the start but moving seemed like too much effort, he'd barely managed to roll onto his back.

"You should have quit," Mr Greeves said, running up to him. Sam and Hayley were behind him. Sam handed him a towel, not quite making eye contact and Mitch realised that his clothes were gone. He remembered kicking off his shoes, he didn't remember losing his clothes. He flushed and covered himself with the towel, struggling to keep everything hidden while he rose to his feet.

He fastened the towel in place and hugged himself, shivering. Without the fire to warm him he was freezing, even if it still felt as if his skin was a couple of sizes too small.

"Come on Mitch," Sam said, guiding him towards the door.

"Where are we going?" he struggled to ask through chattering teeth. "Class isn't finished yet."

"Mr Greeves said to take you to the infirmary," Sam replied. They stepped outside, the breeze pulling at his towel and Mitch was forced to stop hugging himself to hold it in place. He was sure that it had been insufferably hot earlier but after the obstacle course everything felt cool.

They reached the infirmary and Hikari helped Sam wrangle him onto a bed, neither of them meeting his eye.

"Drink this," the doctor ordered, pressing a medicine cup to his lips. He drank and the cold faded a little as they wrapped him in blankets and hot water bottles. A steaming cup was pressed into his hands and a plate of chocolate placed within easy reach. Sam and Hikari disappeared.

The doctor cleared his throat and Mitch looked up at him, feeling trapped beneath layer upon layer of blankets.

"I think we'll have to keep you overnight Mitchell," he said. "You almost gave yourself hypothermia and you've twisted your ankle."

"I can…" he trailed off. He could heal himself but that required magic and he had none.

"We gave you a suppressant, you were still using magic to cool yourself when you came in. It will wear off but you won't be doing any magic for the next twenty-four hours. Do you understand?"

Mitch nodded.

"Good. We had some of your clothes brought down for you," he indicated a neatly folded pile on the chair. "And one of your classmates brought up your bag. Get some rest, dinner will be served shortly."

The doctor left, closing the curtains behind him and Mitch struggled free of the blankets to dress. The clothes made him feel a little better though no warmer so he wormed his way back into his cocoon. He devoured the sweets and thermos of hot chocolate they'd left for him, beginning to feel a little warmth seep through his body though not so much that he wanted to discard the heavy blankets.

He twitched the curtains aside and looked around but the ward was empty. He was the only one stupid enough to get himself trapped here. Everyone else had been treated and discharged. They'd have told everyone how he'd made a fool of himself, by the time he got out.

He returned to the bed but there was nothing to do other than listen to the ticking of the clock. He was still shivering too badly to hold a pen. He got up, still swathed in blankets, and shuffled out of the ward and into Nikola's room. His dinner could find him there.

For a second he thought that Nikola was asleep but then he sat up and smiled at him, scooting across the bed and motioning for Mitch to sit next to him.

"I hear you tried making yourself into a human torch," Nikola said softly. He coughed and cleared his throat.

"I did not," Mitch protested. He was already dreading the birthday presents.

"What did you do then?"

"Something stupid," Mitch said, huddling a little closer to him. Nikola was wonderfully warm and didn't seem to mind him leaching his body heat. "You know I can't do fire."

Nikola coughed again and Mitch forced himself to ease back. Nikola might not miss the body heat but he did need to breathe.

"You can't do anything right now," Nikola said, leaning against him. Mitch shifted uneasily, the last person to sit so close him had been Gwen but he needed the warmth and Nikola was too light to be uncomfortable.

"Beats giving myself hypothermia," Mitch replied. "I know you don't like suppressants but they do have their uses."

"So do needles." Nikola yawned and Mitch's next shiver was more of a shudder.

"I thought you were supposed to spend the day in bed resting," Mitch said. He clearly hadn't spent all day in bed. He'd washed the blood from his face and was wearing clean clothes but he looked completely shattered.

"Hard to rest with so many angels about," Nikola said. "And I've still got this wretched cold…"

"So you thought you'd take advantage of your chance to make me sick as well?" He didn't think he could get sick in the twenty-four hours it would take for the suppressants to wear off but he was going to have to risk it. He almost felt warm again and Nikola was nearly asleep, he'd feel bad for disturbing him.

"Something like that. I take it I didn't miss anything else today? Miss Bordeaux doesn't appear to have eaten you yet."

"She's biding her time," Mitch said. "Just wait…"

"If she does I'll get Gawain to come talk to her." Nikola smiled and rested his head on Mitch's shoulder, "she's not allowed to eat you now any more than she was at the feast."

"I'm not a pillow you know," Mitch muttered, choosing not to think about how that conversation with Gawain might look. In his imagination there was a lot of red.

"I know," Nikola replied, "pillows are softer."

Mitch sighed. He would have just shoved Bates aside but Bates didn't look as delicate as Nikola and Nikola's breathing was slowing as he lapsed into sleep. "Sweet dreams," he whispered instead.

Printed in Great Britain
by Amazon